Also by Anna Harrington

A RELENTLESS RAKE

ANNA HARRINGTON

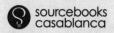

sourcebooks
casablanca

Published by Sourcebooks Casablanca, an imprint of Sourcebooks
P.O. Box 4410, Naperville, Illinois 60567–4410
(630) 961-3900
sourcebooks.com

Printed and bound in Canada.
MBP 10 9 8 7 6 5 4 3 2 1

Dedicated to Beverly Smith, my favorite math teacher,
and to all the math teachers in the world…

$+h\{a_n\}^k \, y\partial \cup$

Prologue

"THANK YOU BOTH FOR JOINING ME." CLAYTON ELLIOT, undersecretary for the Home Office, stood in the center of the Armory's main octagonal room and nodded grimly at the two men with him.

He'd called this predawn meeting here because he wanted to ensure the secrecy of what he intended to reveal to them. No one would be able to eavesdrop through the thick stone walls where iron doors and twin portcullises guarded the only way in and out. He no longer trusted anyone who worked for the Home Office, Bow Street, Whitehall, Parliament…*anyone*.

Well, anyone except for the men of the Armory.

Even the two men standing with him hadn't been told the reason they'd been found and brought here with less than an hour's notice. But these two men would guard themselves. Their dislike of each other would ensure it.

That was why he'd picked them. Alexander Sinclair and Nathaniel Reed, the Earl of St James and a captain in the Horse Guards…the rightful heir and his bastard half brother. The two men would monitor each other closely to make certain the other did his part, and the blood-born rivalry between them would ensure they put forth only their fiercest effort so neither man would be seen as lesser than his half brother.

Just as Clayton was certain that neither man would have shown up if he'd known the other would be here.

"Damned early for a social call, don't you think?" St James bit out, not bothering to hide his irritation. "What's this about?"

Alexander Sinclair hadn't yet been to bed, and his evening clothes still stank of cigar smoke, cheap port, and cheaper women from the King Street gambling hell where he'd been retrieved. He'd been raised to be an earl, with all the privileges that rank and wealth provided, yet he disdained English society and did his best to remain outside it. But Clayton had served with him on the Continent and knew how deeply his patriotism ran, how finely honed his fighting skills. Someone more devoted to crown and country would be hard to find.

Unless it was the man standing beside him.

The hero of the Battle of Toulouse, Nate Reed was currently a captain in the Horse Guards, although Clayton was certain he'd receive many more promotions in the years to come. As tall and broad as his older half brother, Reed possessed a haunted look that had been present as long as Clayton had known him. He was here because he was a good soldier who followed orders.

Reed and St James would work well together. *If* they didn't kill each other first.

"England needs your help," Clayton told them solemnly. "Per special request from the Home Secretary himself."

The two men exchanged puzzled glances. Clayton didn't blame them. Lord Sidmouth, Secretary of the Home Office, had half the government at his disposal to call on for help. He didn't need them.

Until now.

"As you know," Clayton continued, "two days ago, an explosion tore through the Admiralty Club."

Neither man registered a reaction, although both had certainly heard the news about the explosion that killed Viscount Waverly and injured dozens more. All of London had been talking about it.

"The new gas lighting they'd put in." St James offered the gossip that had sped through all the gentleman's clubs and Westminster in the past forty-eight hours. "The lines hadn't been properly bled, fumes had built up. When a footman lit a sconce, he sent the place up."

Clayton leveled a solemn look on the earl. "That's the story that Sidmouth wants everyone to believe."

Nate Reed frowned. "And the truth?"

"The explosion was intentional." Clayton blew out a hard breath at the memory of the carnage. He'd been among the first to arrive at the Admiralty and spent the next three hours digging bodies out of the rubble. Thank God only one man had been killed. "Explosives were set off deliberately in an attempt to assassinate the prime minister."

"Good God," Reed muttered.

"Fortunately, Lord Liverpool had been delayed." Only

by sheer luck. An apple cart had overturned in the Mall and stopped traffic. Liverpool had been stepping down from his carriage in front of the club when the explosives detonated. "We believe another attack will be planned unless we stop it. One that might very well succeed."

St James cursed softly beneath his breath. Liverpool was close friends with the Sinclair family. "Who did this?"

Clayton crossed his arms, leaned back against the arm of a leather sofa, and said gravely, "All evidence points to Scepter."

The criminal organization had pledged itself to over-throwing the monarchy. It had wrapped its tentacles around men at all levels of society and in the government, blackmailing and murdering anyone who stood in its way, including the men of the Armory and their families.

And what better way to start a revolution than by assassinating the prime minister?

During the past six months, Scepter had placed into government positions more than enough of their own men and those they could control through blackmail to easily replace Liverpool with one of their own and with resounding cries of support throughout the empire...enough support to turn even more public opinion against the mad king and his debauched sons, seize power, and end the monarchy. A second Glorious Revolution. Who would be able to stop them? As the recent riots had proven, the regent lacked the strength and spine to put down a rebellion of any substantial size. It was up to the men of the Armory to save him.

A new leading minister who had the backing of the

military, a large portion of the government, and a significant number of reformist Englishmen could far too easily come sweeping into power. For God's sake, Oliver Cromwell had certainly proved the possibility of doing just that. Now, with revolutions that were replacing monarchs with elected governments spreading across the world, the average Englishman would simply think the time for change had come.

But Scepter would never give true voice to the people. They'd seize power just as tyrannically as Napoleon, slide their own corrupt dictator into place, and change the election laws to make certain he remained in power.

Yet in the last year since the Armory's group of former soldiers had pledged to find Scepter's leaders and arrest them, they were still no closer to their goal.

But now, it seemed Scepter had finally made a mistake.

"Sidmouth put me in charge of the investigation," Clayton told Reed and St James. "It led me to an inn where the men responsible for the explosion had been meeting, but they'd already tossed all their documents into the fireplace and fled by the time I arrived." His mouth twisted. "I believe they were warned of my arrival."

"Then you have a mole in the Home Office," St James drawled.

Clayton confirmed that with a curt nod. "Which is why I've called upon you two. This investigation needs to remain secret. Only the three of us and Lord Sidmouth know about it. No one else inside the Home Office, Bow Street, or any of the offices in Whitehall are aware of this meeting." He paused to make certain they understood the importance of their mission. "Not even General Braddock and the other men of the Armory have been told. Nor will they be. Not by me. Not by you."

The two men exchanged assessing looks, but neither was willing to refuse the mission in front of the other, just as Clayton had hoped.

He straightened to his full height and announced, "By authorization of Lord Sidmouth, Secretary of the Home Office, you have been charged with stopping the men responsible for the bombing by any means necessary." He paused before adding, "And with complete legal immunity."

Reed and St James stilled. Both pairs of identical hazel eyes turned somber with understanding. They had just been sanctioned to commit murder if necessary.

"But how do we find them?" Reed asked. "You said that all the evidence had been destroyed."

"Except this." Clayton reached into his jacket's inside breast pocket. "I found this buried in the ashes of the inn's fireplace. No one at the Home Office knows it exists, not even Sidmouth."

He held up a tiny scrap of paper. Its edges had been burned black from the fire, but enough of it remained legible to identify it as a building plan. It was filled with mathematical symbols and calculations along with a single scribbled name—*Everett*.

Clayton handed it to St James. "You start with this."

One

OLIVIA EVERETT STARED AT THE THREE MEN COMING toward her and Mrs. Adams in the dark alley and choked back a useless scream. No one lingered near enough to hear, and even if anyone did, they wouldn't come to her rescue. Not here. Not at this time of night. And certainly not in a part of London where screams were as common as rats.

"Get behind me," she whispered to Mrs. Adams and slid herself between the men and the woman who served as the Everett School's housekeeper. The older woman had insisted on accompanying Olivia when she found her trying to sneak out just after midnight to look for her brother. Olivia had tried to talk her out of it, and now—oh, how she regretted not trying harder!

Their hired hackney waited two streets over. The rig had been unable to navigate the final hundred yards up the dark narrow alley to her brother's last known location before he disappeared two days ago. If they could slip past the men who leered at them with toothless smiles as they came closer, they might have a chance of escape. Olivia inhaled a deep breath for courage. If she could only get Mrs. Adams to safety—

She pulled the kitchen knife from her skirt pocket and shoved Mrs. Adams away. "Run!"

Mrs. Adams shot off down the dark alley.

Olivia remained to fight and give the housekeeper time to flee. She slashed the knife back and forth in front of her in warning.

The three men laughed. Helplessness rose sickeningly like bile into her throat.

"Stay away from her!"

A man dropped into the alley from an overhanging roof and landed on the balls of his feet as gracefully as a panther. Dressed in all black, he'd covered the upper half of his face behind a black silk mask that revealed only the cold gaze of his eyes and a jaw clenched in anger. In his right hand, a blade the size of a bayonet glinted in the dim moonlight.

The three attackers hesitated, as startled at his sudden appearance as Olivia. Then their expressions hardened, and they charged.

The masked man slashed his sword. The blade caught one of the men in the forearm, and the sharp steel sliced through coat sleeve, shirt, and flesh beneath with a sickening slide. Howling in pain, the attacker fell back. Another man clenched his fists and swung.

The masked man ducked. A fist sailed harmlessly over his head.

"Go!" he shouted at Olivia as he lunged forward and thrust his blade.

But Olivia was glued in place from terror, unable to tear her eyes away from the fight. Fear strangled in her throat and sent her heart pounding wildly. With one hand gripping the handle of the knife at her side, she pressed herself against the stone wall and watched as the masked stranger expertly dodged the threatening blows.

His blade flashed as it swung low and struck the second attacker's thigh. The man screamed and fell hard to the cobblestones, then crawled away toward the street and escape. A trail of blood colored the stones in his wake.

The masked stranger stepped back to ready himself for a new charge from the remaining attacker. The brute swung, and a lucky fist landed against the side of his masked face. The hard blow snapped back his head and sent him reeling.

But as the masked man staggered back, he dropped onto his rear foot, spun in a circle, and slashed the short sword in a fierce arc. The tip of the blade sliced through the attacker's jacket and into his waistcoat beneath, but the carefully controlled thrust stopped a hairsbreadth from touching flesh.

The brute froze and paled instantly. His only movement was a jerking, terrified breath and a wet spot that formed at his crotch. He turned and ran.

The masked man's shoulders sagged from the exertion of the fight. His arm dropped to his side, and his broad chest rose and fell beneath his black tunic with each heavy pant as he labored to catch his breath.

When he finally turned to face her, his eyes gleamed like the devil's own.

Olivia's breath strangled in her throat. He'd saved her from the attackers. But who was going to save her from *him*?

Terrified, she ran.

He caught her before she reached the end of the alley. He grabbed her around the waist, swung her off her feet in a circle, and pushed her back against the stone wall. He shifted forward to trap her between his large body and the building as he quickly sheathed his blade in the thin scabbard at his waist.

With a cry, she shoved at him. *Useless!* All her strength wasn't enough to move him back, not even enough to make him sway off-balance.

"I've got a knife," she warned as fiercely as possible despite her shaking knees. "I *will* use it!"

He laughed at her. The deep sound only angered her more.

Olivia raised the knife over her head. The blade was poised ready to slash downward if he reached for her, if he dared to touch her. Closing her eyes, she steeled herself for the sickening puncture of flesh—

He clasped her wrist and pinned her arm to the wall above her head. She gasped. God help her, she couldn't move!

But the blasted devil only grinned, as if he found her threat to stab him simply adorable.

"Never strike with a knife from overhead," he instructed in a rough whisper that Olivia instinctively knew was meant to disguise his voice, just as the mask hid his face. Yet the deep sound trickled through her like a warm summer rain. "You're a petite and slender woman…delicate and fine-boned."

She swallowed. Hard. He certainly didn't mean that as flattery, yet the words fell from his sensuous lips so easily, so smoothly, that a corresponding pull triggered low in her belly. Oh, this man was dangerous! In so many ways…

"You're not strong enough to score more than a glancing

blow, and you'll put yourself off-balance. Always strike low instead. Like this." He lowered her arm and positioned the knife between them until the tip of the blade pointed at his stomach. "Let the attacker use his own force against himself. Let him run into the knife."

Her chest squeezed as his hand covered hers on the handle and kept the knife positioned low between their bodies. He turned her hand slowly back and forth to show her how to work it.

"Do you feel that?" he murmured. "How smooth and steady to stroke the blade?" His mouth was so close to hers that his breath tickled warmly against her lips, even as hers came fast and shallow. "As soon as you feel the tip puncture the skin, twist the blade and slash hard."

His velvety smooth voice contradicted the violence of his instructions, as did the smooth way he continued to work his hand over hers at the handle. The gesture was indecent… and thrillingly irresistible.

"Cause as much damage as possible, and keep causing damage until you're certain the bastard is unable to hurt you." His gaze dropped to her mouth, and she caught her breath, suspecting for a heartbeat that he wanted to kiss her. "Then, when you have him down, kick him."

Her head swam. Was he giving her a lesson on fighting or attempting to seduce her? With the way his hand continued to stroke suggestively over hers on the knife handle, for the life of her she couldn't have said which.

"And if you're going to bother bringing a knife with you"—he wrenched it from her hand and held it up in front of her with a sarcastic twitch of his lips—"make it a real knife. Not something you'd use to carve a roast chicken."

He dropped it. It clanged against the stones at their feet.

"Who are you?" she whispered hoarsely, too unsettled to find her voice to speak properly.

"I should ask the same of you." He straightened away from her yet didn't step back far enough that she could escape, and the amused gleam vanished from his eyes. Apparently, the time for play—and fighting lessons—was over. "And why are you in a dark city alley where you don't belong?"

Her lips pressed tightly together. She had no intention of telling him anything. He might have saved her life tonight, but he was just as dangerous as the men he'd chased away. Worse—the men who'd attacked her hadn't worn masks.

What was he hiding? Was he connected to Henry's disappearance?

"After all, you're a long way from Vine Street in Westminster, Miss Everett."

The ground dropped away beneath her, and she grabbed at the wall behind her to keep from falling away. How did he know…? "*What* did you say?"

"What brought you out of the safety of your bed tonight and led you here?" His gloved fingers stole a caress across her cheek, but his touch wasn't at all flirtatious. It was a subtle warning. "You should have stayed in your schoolroom where you belong."

His first comment had surprised her. *This* one angered her, and she shot back, "Obviously, I wanted to carve a chicken."

His mouth twisted at her impudence. He lowered his face until it was even with hers and placed both palms flat against the wall on either side of her shoulders.

"Where is Henry Everett?" he demanded. "Where has your brother gone?"

An electric jolt slammed through her that stripped away her breath. "How do you— Who *are* you?" A deafening rush of blood pounded in her ears with every terrified heartbeat. *No one* but she and Mrs. Adams knew her brother was missing. Not even the other school employees or the students. "What do you know about Henry?"

The hard set of his face told her he wouldn't answer. "Where is—"

A clamor went up in the darkness. Shouts and the sound of racing hoofbeats striking over the cobblestones reverberated off the stone walls until the noise seemed to come from everywhere at once.

The man turned away from her as a rider on horseback charged into the alley toward them.

Olivia shoved him. She caught him off-balance, and when he staggered back, she darted away, hitched up her skirts, and ran as fast as she could toward the far end of the alley and the safety of the darkness beyond.

"Damnation!" Alec Sinclair ripped his mask off as Nate Reed rode toward him.

Two days of nonstop searching—*ruined*. The name on the

charred slip of building plans had led them to Westminster, to a man named Henry Everett, who was a schoolteacher and mathematician vying for fellowship in the Royal Society. But Everett had gone missing. So the two men had split up. Reed was tracking down Everett's last known movements, and Alec had taken watch over Everett's sister. But for both to collide here—

Fate must have been laughing.

"You have lousy timing," Alec muttered.

"I saved your aristocratic arse," Reed shot back. "Those men had grabbed up clubs and were headed back this way."

Alec grimaced. The last thing he wanted was to be in Reed's debt. "You also chased away the sister."

Alec glanced toward where the alley emptied into the street to the south and where Olivia Everett had fled into the darkness. God only knew where she'd gone in the rabbit warren of streets and alleys that formed this part of the City.

Reed's black horse pranced anxiously in a circle. The beast was as eager as his master to give chase. "I'll go after her."

"No." She was already frightened from being attacked— and from Alec's botched rescue. Even if Reed caught her, she was in no state to offer up the kind of information about her brother they needed to drive their mission forward.

Yet.

But he would gain that information from her, no matter what he had to do.

He crumpled the mask in his fist. "Olivia Everett is mine."

Two

"DRIVE!" OLIVIA SHOUTED AT THE JARVEY AS SHE RAN toward the waiting hackney. Mrs. Adams was already inside and gesturing fiercely through the open door for her to hurry.

She jumped inside and slammed shut the door. Her bottom just barely touched the seat before the driver flicked his whip and sent the horses scrambling forward. He was as anxious as the two women to drive away from the dark backstreets of the City and into a better area of London.

Olivia leaned back and pulled in a deep, jerking lungful of air.

"What happened?" Mrs. Adams's voice pulsed with worry. "I saw that man ride into the alley."

Olivia nodded and squeezed her eyes shut as she tried to slow the relentless pounding of her heart and gain back her breath. "He arrived," she panted out, "just in time."

Mrs. Adams reached across the small compartment to clasp her hand. "Did those men hurt you?"

Olivia shook her head, unable to open her eyes for the roiling of her stomach. Good heavens—she might just cast up her accounts right there on the carriage floor! "Another man fought them off. They didn't harm me."

"Thank goodness!" The housekeeper hugged Olivia

tightly against her bosom. "I thought we were both going to be killed—or worse."

Oh God, she *was* going to be sick!

Olivia pushed the woman away, flung open the window, and stuck her head outside as she gulped in several mouthfuls of cold night air.

Finally, when her stomach had stopped churning and her head had ceased pounding, she eased down against the squabs and pressed the back of her hand against her mouth. Her breath slowly returned to normal with each passing street that brought them closer to home and safety, and her nausea settled into a hard knot in her belly.

He knew her. The masked man who'd questioned her in the alley *knew* who she was, where she lived, and that she was searching for her missing brother.

But how?

Henry had disappeared without word or reason from the old town house that held both the Everett School and their private quarters. Vanishing like that hadn't been like him. Not at all. He was a boring, staid schoolmaster and mathematician whose biggest dream was being admitted to the Royal Society, and he'd never missed two days of instruction before, not even when he'd been sick with fever last winter. Even then, pale and weak, he'd dragged himself into the classroom every morning.

But there had been no note left in his room, and no message had arrived during the two days since he'd disappeared. When her worry finally overtook her this evening, Olivia had broken down and frantically searched his room, but all she'd been able to find for explanation was a note with directions to an alley in the City of London and a time— midnight, three nights ago.

Foolish! She never should have gone out in the middle of the night on this wild goose chase. Her head knew that. But her heart would have made her do it all again if it meant a chance to find Henry. Since their father died five years ago, her older brother was the only family she had left.

"Not the proper way for a young lady to behave," Mrs. Adams muttered beneath her breath. "Disgraceful and scandalous!"

Olivia bit her lip. Now was probably not the time to admit she'd lost the woman's best kitchen knife.

Mrs. Adams had a right to be angry, just as she was correct that tonight Olivia had put at risk not only her safety but also her reputation. And on her reputation rested the school's future.

Her propriety was the backbone of the Everett School's good standing. That was why families sent their daughters to them. She'd promised to teach the girls well while carefully safeguarding their virtue and instilling strong moral values in them. But Olivia also made room for scholarship girls who wouldn't otherwise receive an education at all by carefully managing every penny in the budget—and by throwing in several extra pounds from Henry's salary and hers. That left the school hovering on the knife's edge of economic ruin, always just one unexpected bill away from going into debt, but those scholarship girls would be able to become governesses, companions, or ladies' maids. The cut in her pay was well worth giving them a chance at a good life.

Yet all that would be destroyed if her reputation were ever questioned.

Which would *never* happen. She'd taken great pains to ensure no one ever found out about her past, just as she'd made certain no one would find out about tonight. As far as anyone knew, she was a prim and proper schoolmistress, as sexless as the companions who gathered in corners at society soirees and aging gracefully into spinsterhood at the ripe old age of twenty-five.

That was exactly how she meant to keep things.

"You must never do anything like this again, do you hear?" Mrs. Adams scolded. She was near the same age as Olivia's mother, had Mama lived, and the housekeeper saw it as her duty to not only keep house for the school but also provide maternal influence.

"Yes, Mrs. Adams," Olivia answered dutifully, because it was expected and she always did as expected. *Now.* Tonight's outing was an anomaly.

Mrs. Adams's hand flew to her mouth in horror. "You have blood on your hem!"

Olivia grabbed at her skirt. A dark spot marred the light blue muslin. "It isn't mine," she assured Mrs. Adams quickly. The masked man must have gotten bloodied when he fought off the attackers and rubbed it onto her skirt when he'd pressed her against the wall.

Her shoulders sagged. The dress would have to be thrown away, and she couldn't afford a new one. Tonight was proving to be one disaster after another.

The carriage finally stopped in front of the school. Four

stories tall and three bays wide, the century-old building that stood on the fringes of Westminster had once been home to barristers, physicians, and respectable middle-class merchants until London's fortunes shifted to the west. Now it served as both a school for two dozen girls and home for her, Henry, and the limited staff who kept the place operating smoothly. It barely contained its handful of offices and common rooms on the ground floor, three schoolrooms on the first, two dormitories on the second, and the staff's rooms tucked beneath the eaves wherever they could fit, including hers and Henry's.

At this late hour, though, the normally bustling building sat quiet and dark, with all the girls nestled in their beds and the staff gratefully at rest in theirs. The only light was the lamp that glowed over the front door, and not one sound or movement came from within. Exactly as it should have been.

Olivia paid the driver a precious coin, then escorted Mrs. Adams inside. The housekeeper mumbled a harsh good night and headed upstairs to her room.

Olivia paused in the dark stair hall and pulled in a deep but trembling breath. She shook to her bones, and not just from how close they'd come to being hurt tonight but also by the encounter with the masked stranger.

Did he know Henry? Was that how he knew who she was and why she was in the alley tonight? And if he did, then perhaps—

"Olivia."

She jumped in fright as a dark figure stepped out from

the shadows in the hall. A terrified beat passed before she recognized him.

"Henry!" She ran to him and threw her arms around his neck.

But something was wrong. He was stiff in her arms, tense... She pulled back to search his face for answers, but he set her away from him before she could ask where he'd been or give him the scolding he deeply deserved for worrying her.

"Olivia, where were you tonight?" he demanded, resting his hands on her shoulders.

"Where was I?" Her mouth fell open incredulously. "Where were *you*?"

Ignoring that, he swept his gaze over her, as if he knew she'd been attacked in the alley and was checking for injuries. She shifted to move her bloodied hem out of view.

"Why were you out so late?" Panic edged his voice. "Did something happen to you?"

"Nothing happened." A swift prick of guilt accompanied the lie, but she didn't want to upset him.

His frown deepened. "Olivia, the truth."

Even when they were children, he'd been able to tell when she was lying. So she admitted with an annoyed sigh, "I went looking for you."

He paled. "You shouldn't have done that."

"But you'd disappeared. No one knew where—"

"You should have stayed here!"

The force of that startled her. He seldom raised his voice to her. "I was worried about you," she said as calmly as possible, despite her racing heart. "Where were you?"

His hands tightened on her shoulders. "You were safe, then? No one forced you to go with them?"

"Of course not." *Forced* her? Why on earth would he think... *Good God.* Fear prickled at the backs of her knees. "Henry, where were you?"

He dropped his hands to his sides, then rubbed one at his forehead as he turned away. "I had business to attend to."

"What kind of business would you—"

He cut her off with a wave of his hand. "Personal business."

Oh no. She wouldn't be dismissed that easily, not after everything she'd been through tonight. "For two days?" she challenged. "Why didn't you send word?"

"I couldn't. I wanted to, but I..." His voice drifted away.

A chill snaked down her spine. "If you're in trouble, then—"

"I wasn't in trouble," he bit out. "Damnation, Olivia! You're not the only one who's allowed to keep secrets."

His words hit her like a blow, and she staggered back, gaping at him. He'd *never* used her past as a weapon against her before.

Guilt immediately gripped his face. Apologetically, he reached for her hand, but she pulled it back, keeping well away.

"I *couldn't* tell you," he repeated firmly, as if that should be explanation enough. "It had to do with my work."

"Your work?" she whispered, too wounded to speak more loudly. "This had to do with the Royal Society?"

He hesitated as if weighing whether he could trust her. Then he blurted out in a rush, "You know how much earning a fellowship means to me. So when I had the chance for dinner at one of the fellows' country boxes, I couldn't just pass it by. It was the perfect opportunity to ingratiate myself with them."

"For *two days*?"

"You know how society men are. Dinner turned into a night away, and the next day there was hunting, drinking, cards, followed by another dinner and another night... I only managed to finally make my excuses and sneak away tonight to come straight back home. Don't you see? I couldn't let them think that I had to report to my little sister or to the school. They wouldn't respect me if I did."

"Why didn't you send a message, then?"

His shoulders slumped in self-chastisement. "The servants would have told the host if I'd sent a message. He'd have wanted to know what it was about, and I couldn't say my little sister needed to know my plans. That's why I couldn't contact you."

"And the alley?" She wanted to believe him. After all, he had answers for everything. But so many pieces didn't fit... "I found a note with directions to an alley in the City and a meeting time."

He frowned, deeply puzzled. "An alley?" Then he gave a dismissive laugh. "Oh, that! There's a printer's shop there. I sent my paper to them to have copies made to hand out at the Society."

"At midnight?"

"At *noon*." He ran his hand through his hair and muttered, "I must have written down twelve midnight by mistake, and that's what you saw. I took the paper there right before I left for the country. The copies should arrive tomorrow." He grimaced, his mouth tightening. "That's where you were tonight, wasn't it? The printer's alley. For God's sake, Olivia! You could have been killed." His somber tone told her he wasn't lying when he added quietly, "And all because of me."

Her shoulders slumped, sharing the guilt he felt over her own foolishness. "I was worried about you."

"I'm sorry." He placed a kiss to her forehead. "I never meant to worry you. It was only two days in the country. That's all." He wore the same apologetic look from their childhood that always graced his face whenever he'd broken one of their toys or stolen her share of the pudding. "Forgive me?"

Olivia bit her lip, then slowly nodded.

"I'm home now, safe and sound." He smiled at her and squeezed her hands. "If all goes well, by this time next month, I'll be a fellow of the Royal Society. The school will benefit from the notoriety, and all the worry will have been worth it. You'll see."

She gave another nod.

"We'll talk more tomorrow, I promise. But I'm tired and need to sleep. So do you." He released her hands. "I'll see you at breakfast."

He disappeared up the stairs toward their rooms in the garret.

When the sound of his footsteps faded, she lowered herself to the bottom step and hung her head in her hands.

You're not the only one who's allowed to keep secrets.

Anguish overwhelmed her until she could barely breathe. Henry had always been loyal and loving, but he was also the one person in the world who held the power to devastate her.

He'd just done exactly that.

A soft sound came from the stairs above her. As she raised her head and glanced over her shoulder, she pasted a smile in place even though her heart was breaking. She'd become very good at hiding her true feelings over the years. "Who's there?"

A five-year-old girl stood on the landing in her night rail and bare feet. From her hand dangled the rag doll that Mrs. Adams had made for her last Christmas. Rather, what was left of the well-loved doll, whose threadbare arms and legs would soon need to be replaced.

"It's me," the girl whispered.

"Cora." Olivia held open her arms.

The girl ran down the stairs and into her embrace. Resting her head against Olivia's shoulder, Cora wrapped one arm tightly around her neck while the other protectively held her beloved doll.

Olivia rested her cheek against the girl's head. "You should be in bed."

"I heard voices and got scared."

"That was only Mr. Everett and me talking." She placed a reassuring kiss on the girl's temple and brushed away the stray strands of hair that had come loose from the braid that Olivia had worked when she'd put Cora to bed just after supper. "We were discussing tomorrow's lessons."

Thank goodness Cora was still too young to discern lies.

Of all the children at the school, Cora held a special place in Olivia's heart. Normally, the school didn't accept students this young, not even the scholarship girls. But Cora's mother and father were both dead, and her aunt and uncle already had seven children of their own to care for. So the girl had been left to run wild on the streets without proper clothes or food. Most likely her aunt and uncle had simply been waiting until Cora was old enough to sell her into service of one kind or another.

The moment Olivia spied the neglected girl by the river, she knew she had to help her. She'd cried when she'd seen her stringy and matted hair, filthy face, soiled dress...and the fear in her eyes. Olivia knew the girl's future would have been limited to being a washerwoman if she were lucky or a prostitute if she weren't. Either way, she'd most likely have been dead before she'd reached twenty. Olivia had taken Cora home with her right then.

"Do I have to go back to bed?" Cora asked softly.

"No, sweetling, not yet." Olivia rocked the girl on her lap. "We can just sit here for a while if you'd like."

Cora cradled her doll in her arms the way that Olivia was cradling her. "I'd like that."

"Me too," she whispered and pulled the child closer.

Three

"MY LORD, YOU MUST WAKE."

Alec opened one eye and squinted at Thompson as the valet leaned over him in bed. "No." He snapped his eye shut, rolled over, and turned his back to the man.

His head ached from both lack of sleep and from where one of the men in last night's fight had caught him by surprise. He knew without having to check in the mirror that a nasty bruise had formed there. *Damned chit.* Forcing him to follow her into the City on a wild goose chase, nearly getting herself raped or killed—nearly getting *him* killed when he'd had to jump in to save her—

Thompson threw open the heavy window drapes. Sunlight exploded into the room.

Alec let loose a string of curses as the light blinded him. "Close those curtains and get out!"

"Sir, I wish for nothing more." Yet Thompson moved to the next window and tossed open its drapes.

Alec shielded his eyes from the second blast of sunlight by shoving a pillow over his face.

"But you have a visitor waiting in the drawing room, sir."

A visitor? *Good lord…* "What time is it?"

"Just shy of ten o'clock."

"In the *morning*?" He threw the pillow to the floor and sat up. How dare anyone come calling before noon? And how dare Thompson risk both his position and his life by rousing him so damnably early to tell him?

The valet's eyes slid sideways to the bright day beyond the tall windows, and he answered dryly, "I believe so, yes."

Alec bit back a sleep-deprived snarl. "I have half a mind to fire you for this, Thompson."

"If I were you, sir, I certainly would." The man walked into the dressing room to fetch a set of clothes, unperturbed by the usual barrage of empty threats that occurred whenever he had to rouse Alec from bed before noon.

Thompson was one of the best valets in England, not so much for his dressing skills but for his discretion about his employers. His quick grab of the black mask from the floor without so much as a lift of an eyebrow proved that.

Alec would never fire the man. He would be lost without him, and they both knew it.

But ten o'clock…*God's mercy*. Nothing good ever happened this early in the day. "Tell whoever is waiting that he can shove his calling card up his—"

"Lady St James is in the drawing room, sir."

His mother? His head pounded even harder.

"I told the countess you were…under the weather," Thompson called out from the dressing room, emphasizing the usual euphemism for mornings when Alec was unfit from a night of too much carousing. "But she insisted on seeing you."

Biting down a groan, Alec tossed back the velvet coverlet

and pushed himself out of bed. He still wore the black trousers and tunic he'd donned for last night's watch for Henry Everett at the school, only to end up following his sister halfway across London and back when the silly gel decided to go into the City and get herself attacked.

He ran a hand across his chin to rub at the night's growth of stubbly beard as he crossed to the washbasin. Olivia Everett... What the devil was a respectable schoolmistress doing in a dark alleyway at midnight? And what exactly did she know about her brother's involvement with Scepter?

Alec had no bloody idea. He also had no good reason in the first place why Henry Everett's name would be scrawled on the half-burned slip of paper that connected him to the bombing. And no possible answers.

"Damned hard to question a man about treason when he's vanished," he muttered to himself as he stripped off the tunic and bared his body from the waist up. Then he poured cold water into the basin, took a deep breath to steel himself, and plunged his head into the bowl.

He was tired, sore, and now incredibly frustrated at the lack of leads in their mission. Robert Jenkinson, Earl of Liverpool and current prime minister, was an old family friend. Hell, he'd been more of a father to Alec than Rupert Sinclair had ever been. If Liverpool's life was in danger, Alec would do everything he could to protect him.

But he had to do it soon before another assassination attempt was made. Time was not on his side.

He threw back his head and flung water across the room. Cold rivulets ran down his bare back and chest. He wiped the towel over his face and grimaced as Thompson returned with a suit of clothes draped over his arm.

"Just a shirt," Alec ordered.

The valet looked as stunned as if Alec had just admitted to seducing the queen. "But you won't be properly dressed to receive the countess!"

Alec smoothed back his wet hair. "If my mother has the audacity to come calling this early in the morning"—he winced at the mere thought of it—"then she deserves what she gets."

He pulled on the fresh shirt and let it hang loose around his hips as he headed for the door.

"Sir, at least put on your banyan!"

"I already have one mother waiting in the drawing room, Thompson," he reminded the valet as he strode from the room. "I don't need a second one."

He sauntered down the hall toward the stairs. Around him, St James House was quiet. Like him, it wasn't yet fully awake to face the day, and he preferred it this way. The property was one of the grandest houses in London and his prize jewel. He'd inherited it, the ancestral home at Pelham Park, the title, and what very little was left of the family fortune six years ago when his father died unexpectedly. In bed. In a prostitute's bed. *On top* of the prostitute, to be exact, while the woman lay spread-eagle with her wrists and ankles tied to the bedposts. Alec had been serving in the army on the Continent when word of his father's death reached him.

Thank God the message had arrived too late for him to attend the bastard's funeral.

He'd returned to England to discover that the old earl had secretly wasted the Sinclair fortune. Gambling, whores, bad business ventures—his father had put liens against whatever property he could, sold whatever wasn't entailed, and endangered the estate's ability to maintain itself. To make matters worse, his mother had suddenly withdrawn twelve hundred pounds shortly after the funeral from what little was left in the bank accounts. When Alec questioned her about it, Isabel Sinclair claimed she'd spent it on new mourning clothes for the family.

A lie. There wasn't enough black crepe in England to account for such a large sum, but she refused to tell him the truth. He'd been furious with her for putting their family's future further into jeopardy, on top of the already simmering resentment that she'd not been aware of the full extent of her husband's debaucheries and corruptions. To this day, he still had no idea what she'd done with the money.

So at twenty-four, Alec sold his army commission and dedicated himself to salvaging what was left of the family fortune. He was able to squeeze out enough profits to invest in solid ventures, pay off his father's debts, and make repairs to neglected properties. But even then, once the family's fortunes were returned, he didn't stop. He was driven on to do more. In just six years, he'd doubled the family's fortune and become one of the most powerful men in England.

Just like everything else in his life, he'd done it simply to spite his father.

"Mother." He flung open wide both doors to the drawing room. "How lovely of you to call." He grumbled as he came into the room, "And so early, too."

Isabel Sinclair, Countess of St James, stood by the tall windows overlooking the street and smiled lovingly at him.

As usual, she was dressed impeccably. The pale green day dress with its matching pelisse made her hair appear not just blond but golden, as befitting a countess. So did the pearls around her throat and at her ears. Her skin was still as smooth and pale as porcelain despite her five decades of age, and her complexion still glowed pink from a lingering youth that even marriage to Rupert Sinclair hadn't diminished.

"Alexander." She admonished both his appearance and his greeting in that single word.

He softened her chastisement—but only slightly—by dutifully kissing her cheek. Then he crossed to the tea tray that his butler, Bivvens, had already brought up. He poured himself a cup of tea and silently cursed that it wasn't the strong American coffee he preferred in the mornings. He didn't wait for her to sit before slumping down into a chair.

He couldn't stomach false proprieties at the best of times. This morning, he was simply too exhausted for them.

"To what do I owe this visit?" He grimaced into his cup as he took a long swallow of the hot liquid. Good Lord, how could Englishmen stand this stuff?

Not letting him hurry her into answering, she sank gracefully onto the settee across from him. Her back remained impossibly straight even as she reached to refill her cup of tea. Then she raised it slowly to her lips and studied him over the gold-edged rim.

She narrowed her eyes at the bruise on his cheek. "You've been in a fight."

"It's nothing." He dismissed the painful knot with a shrug. "It'll be gone by evening."

Her lips tightened as she took inventory of the rest of his appearance. "Slept in your clothes, too, I see."

"But I put on a clean shirt just for you."

She gave his flippant comment a scolding lift of her brow. "I didn't expect you to be home yet at all, actually."

Ah…so *that* was why she'd arrived so early. She'd wanted to catch him in the act of stumbling home, foxed to the gills. Thank God he'd cheated her out of the opportunity. He loved his mother, but her interference in his personal life wasn't at all welcome.

He replied with a touch of sarcasm, "It was a slow evening."

She leveled a hard gaze on him and asked bluntly, "Did you spend your night in the stews?"

"I don't visit brothels."

"That's not what the gossips say."

"The gossips are wrong." After all, men like him didn't pay for sex. They didn't need to. Half the wives and widows in Mayfair were panting to be his next conquest just so they could whisper behind their fans to each other that they'd tupped him.

"Then perhaps you've been preoccupied with a mistress," she countered.

He fought back a laugh at her roundabout attempt at interrogation. "You know I don't keep mistresses either."

The exact opposite, in fact. The late earl had secretly kept mistresses, all the while pretending to the world that he was first and foremost a family man. Alec would *never* lie to the world the way his father had.

"You should stop believing the rumors," he suggested.

She flicked at an invisible crumb on her skirt and sniffed. "Rumors seem to be the only way I know what my son has been doing lately."

At that, he could no longer hold back a burst of laughter. Good God, she was a terrible actress! She was no more concerned about his escapades than he was. Whatever brought her here this morning, it wasn't gossip.

Unfortunately, his mother *did* have a history of being blind to what her family was doing, even inside her own home. His father had certainly proven that.

Rupert Sinclair, Earl of St James, had been a monster. Society only ever saw a respectable peer who donated generously to the poor, never missed a church service, preached in Parliament about moral fortitude, and never uttered one word in anger or impropriety. Yet that same man had preyed upon innocent women and children, squandered the greater portion of the family fortune on drunken binges, gambling, bad investments... That is, the part he hadn't wasted on the prostitutes he'd paid to let him preach to them while he beat them in an attempt to drive the wickedness from them. As for the children, those he bought outright from men in dark alleys. God only knew what he'd done to them. After all, if he'd beaten his own son, what would he have done to someone else's child?

It wasn't until after the earl's death when Alec returned from the Continent that he learned the full extent of his father's evil, but his mother had been here the entire time. Had Isabel Sinclair truly been oblivious to her husband's malevolence, or had she simply turned a blind eye, even to the evil carried out in her own home?

Alec had never possessed the courage to ask her.

"Is this the reason for your visit, then?" he baited her. "Are you proposing that I take a mistress?"

"Of course not."

He lifted his cup to take a sip of tea. "What a shame, then, because—"

"I'm proposing you take a wife."

That brought him sputtering to attention. Coughing to clear his throat, he sat up straight and steadied his teacup before he spilled it on the Turkish rug. "I do not want a wife."

"This is not about what you want. This is about what you *need*. And you, Alexander, need a wife." She reached casually to take one of the biscuits from the tray as if they were discussing nothing more contentious than the weather. "I've seldom seen a man more in need of a wife than you."

And *there* was the mother he knew. A lioness disguised in sprigged muslin.

"You're thirty years old now," she continued. "You need to establish a respectable, solid, and secure future for yourself and the earldom, and the only way to do that is for you to stop behaving disreputably."

Christ. She made him sound like a lecherous old man.

"No mother will let a man with a questionable reputation within a mile of her daughter."

Oh, she was wrong there! Marriage-minded mamas

would rush toward him like moths to a flame the moment they discovered he was looking for a wife. They wanted his fortune and his title. His indiscretions be damned.

"You need to establish a proper household for yourself with an appropriate wife who can support you in society and Parliament. Someone who can give you a real home to return to at the end of the day, who can provide companionship and guidance."

He rolled his eyes. "Have you been reading books on courtship again?"

She ignored that. "Besides, I want grandchildren." She paused to drive home her point. "*Lots* of grandchildren."

Thank God he had a sister. "I'm certain Elizabeth will give you dozens to—"

"I also want you to be happy."

The concern behind her words sliced into him. He might disagree with her methods, but he couldn't argue that she didn't want the best for her family. "But I am happy." *Happy enough, anyway.* "I like my life the way it is, with all the freedoms that come with being a bachelor gentleman. And I have no plans to change."

His mother said quietly, "Neither did your father."

His eyes darted up to hers as his heart thudded painfully against his ribs, yet he kept his expression inscrutable. He didn't want her to know how much she'd just wounded him.

He was *nothing* like his father.

For God's sake, he'd spent his entire life making certain of it. When he was younger, he'd thought his father was respectable and pious, and Alec had dedicated himself to being the worst scapegrace and rogue he could, just to spite the man. Years later, when Rupert Sinclair died and he'd discovered the depth of his father's debaucheries, he'd dedicated himself to being the truly respectable man his father had never been.

She set her teacup onto the tray. "Everyone in society is whispering about how you've been gambling, drinking all night, and having assignations with all kinds of widows and wives."

"A man needs hobbies," he replied, deadpan.

She shot him a chastising glare.

"I'm a *reformed* rake, Mother," he explained. "Isn't that the type of man all women claim they love most?"

Her glare deepened.

Well, this conversation wasn't going at all in his favor. Wanting to smooth her ruffled feathers, he admitted, "I don't live like a monk, I'll grant you, but I'm also not the scapegrace I was before I joined the army. Those days are over. Whatever rumors the gossipy old biddies are spreading about me aren't true."

"They don't have to be true," she reminded him. "They only have to be believed."

Damned if he did, damned if he didn't… He shook his head in exasperation. "I have never neglected my duties, neither in Parliament nor to the title nor my family, which you very well know. So does society. And unlike the old earl"—he still couldn't bring himself to call the man *Father*—"I have never hurt anyone in seeking my pleasures."

A pained expression darkened her face. "You're hurting *yourself*, Alexander. Don't you see that? If a man doesn't have his reputation, what does he have?"

He shrugged. "Five estates, two town houses, and one of the largest fortunes in the Bank of England?"

Her mouth tightened. She clearly didn't find that amusing. "How does any of that keep you from being lonely?"

"You'd be surprised how helpful it is for making friends and finding bed partners."

Pity clouded her eyes. "And how does it feel to know that they're making love to your money and couldn't care less about you?"

"Quite wonderful, actually." But his hand shook as he set the tea down onto the tray and shoved himself to his feet.

He crossed to the cabinet in the corner and withdrew a crystal tumbler and decanter of brandy. Despite the early hour, he needed something far stronger than tea.

"Perhaps for now," his mother continued. "But it wears, not knowing who you can trust or who truly cares about you, not knowing when you enter a room and find women gossiping in whispers behind their fans if they're talking about you. A wife would put an end to that."

"Your concern is misplaced." So was her proposed solution. *Marriage?* He nearly laughed. "I am perfectly happy."

"You're lying."

His hand froze as he pulled the crystal stopper from the decanter.

"Do you think your father did what he did because he was *happy*? I've never known a more miserable man in my life." She added quietly, "Except for you."

He curled an icy grin and finished pouring his drink. "Do you really think that leg-shackling myself to some society chit will make me happy?" Nearly every marriage among the *ton*—including hers—said otherwise.

"If she's the right chit, yes. There are many fine young misses out this season who would make good countesses."

"Then let them marry other earls. I'm not interested in wedding anyone." He replaced the stopper and sauntered back to his chair, flopped down, and took a gasping swallow. "I like my life exactly as it is. I harm no one with my activities, and I do no more gambling, drinking, and pursuing women than any other peer." He stretched out his long legs in the most devil-may-care pose he could muster. "If gossipy old prigs are determined to discuss how I spend my time, that's their—"

"You're becoming like your father."

The soft interruption came with the force of a blow. For a moment, he was too stunned to reply.

Finally, he found his voice and answered coldly, "I am *nothing* like him." His hand tightened around the glass. "I have no tolerance for people who hide behind lies and abuse."

Or those who refuse to see them.

It was far too early in the day for this discussion. Hell, *midnight* would have been far too early. Needing to quash his rising anger, he tossed back the rest of the brandy and welcomed the burn down his throat.

His mother remained silent and still for a long moment before answering quietly, "Perhaps not." She dropped her gaze to her hands, folded in her lap. "But life is not as cleanly cut as you'd like it to be. Honorable people make mistakes, while villains are capable of goodness, and both deserve our understanding."

Bitterness covered his tongue like acid. She meant her marriage.

Alec could applaud his mother's devotion to her family and marriage vows. He could empathize with the constant fear of ruination that had hung over her head since Rupert Sinclair died and the family discovered all he'd done—*almost* all he'd done. Alec could even understand why his mother wanted to pry into his personal life, although it bothered the hell out of him.

But for the life of him, he simply couldn't fathom how she could have been so blind to what was happening in her own home.

He bit out, "Rupert Sinclair hurt people." *He hurt his own son.* But he couldn't utter those words. Even now, he had too much pride to admit how weak he'd once been, even when little more than a boy. "He destroyed lives. And you want me to find the goodness in that?"

"I want you to accept that the same man who did all those horrible things also gave me the greatest gifts of my life— you and your sister."

He muttered into his glass, "Perhaps he shouldn't have."

She flinched.

Immediately guilt flooded through him at his thoughtless words. *Damnation.* He apologetically shook his head. "I didn't mean that."

She stared at him silently for so long that he shifted uncomfortably in his chair. Finally, she said, "It must be wonderful to be you, living in a world in which people are so easily categorized, so clearly divided into sinners and saints."

Her voice was quiet and thoughtful, but underneath lurked something worse—*disappointment*. "But in truth, there are all kinds of people living between your two extremes. I wish you could see that because you will never be happy until you do."

His jaw tightened. He needed neither her interference in his life nor her concern. And he certainly didn't want her solution. This conversation was finished.

He set his empty glass onto the tea table. "Will that be all then?"

"Not quite." She rose elegantly to her feet, which brought him to his. She reached into her reticule, withdrew a large white card, and laid it onto the tea table. "An invitation to my ball. You haven't yet confirmed that you'll be attending, so your sister and aunt asked me to raise the subject with you. They both very much want you to be there."

That was a knife to his heart. He would do anything for Elizabeth and Aunt Agnes, and that included attending his mother's balls. She knew it, too.

"*I* also would like you to be there." She didn't look at him, as if afraid of the expression she might see on his face. "Like in the old days before you joined the army."

Before I fled from the earl as far and as fast as I could go. And *that* simply twisted the knife deeper. Because while fleeing meant not killing the bastard, it had also meant leaving behind the Sinclair women whom Alec loved.

"Besides, your absence will be conspicuous." She swept her gaze through the room to indicate the grand house around them before settling it on him. "Since the party is going to be held in your ballroom."

Alec certainly didn't need a reminder of that. His household had been turned upside down during the past fortnight, carrying out preparations for the annual St James ball, just as he'd made plans to disappear into the country until it was all over. But that was before Clayton Elliott ambushed him with the Home Office's mission, before Scepter attempted to assassinate Lord Liverpool.

Damnation. He was going to be stuck here for the blasted thing after all.

As his mother left, she called over her shoulder, "You might just enjoy yourself, you know."

And hell might just freeze over.

Biting back a curse, he moved to the window overlooking the wide street and watched his mother minutes later as she glided from the town house to her waiting carriage. When he was a boy, he'd adored her, and they'd hardly ever fought. Then everything changed. He'd been subjected to constant punishments from his father for not being the perfect son, and nothing had been the same between them since.

Punishments? Good God. That made what Rupert Sinclair had done to him sound normal.

Memories flooded back…fists, belts, sticks…red-hot fireplace pokers laid across the bare backs of his legs… shouts and curses—

He squeezed his eyes shut against the pounding at the base of his skull.

Damn him. Damn him to hell!

A soft knock came at the door.

Sucking in a steadying breath, he opened his eyes and turned away from the window in time to see Bivvens slink into the room to clear the tea things. Alec forced his breathing to remain steady and calm, his back ramrod straight. No signs of weakness were allowed in the son of the Earl of St James. He'd learned that lesson the hard way.

The butler set the used cups and saucers back onto the tray. Then he picked up the invitation. "What should I do with this, my lord?"

"Burn it." Then Alec rolled his eyes at the thought of Elizabeth and Aunt Agnes and at the fresh wave of guilt toward his mother. She'd had no idea what Rupert Sinclair had done to him. He and Bivvens had hidden it well. "No. Put it in my study. I'll tend to it later."

"Yes, sir." Bivvens discretely slipped it into his jacket and carried out the tray with a parting nod.

A clatter of hooves broke the morning's stillness. Alec pulled back the curtain to watch as a horse trotted up the gravel drive to his front door. Clayton Elliott dismounted and tossed the reins to the groom who ran up to meet him.

Alec grimaced. Now was definitely not the time for an update on the mission, especially when irritation still sizzled inside him that Clayton had forced him together with Reed in the first place. If Alec had known that his half brother would be involved, he never would have gone to the Armory for that first meeting. And damn Clayton, because the man had certainly known that, too.

Captain Reed was the unacknowledged product of Rupert Sinclair and an upstairs maid. The man's existence had been unknown to Alec until two years ago when the brothers had come face-to-face in Wellington's drawing room.

Apparently, though, Reed had known about him for years.

The two sons of St James had both fought in the wars but at different times and in different regiments. Alec had been in the infantry, Reed in the cavalry. Alec had already left the army and was headed back to England when Reed purchased his commission. If anyone within the army or War Department bothered to notice how similar the two men stood in appearance and bearing—possessing the same hazel eyes as their father, same coloring, same jaw lines—no one had dared comment. At least not openly. The two men had never crossed paths.

That is until Wellington unknowingly invited them both to the same party to celebrate his return from Paris.

When Alec walked into the drawing room and saw Reed, he could have sworn he was staring at his father's ghost. He knew then exactly who Reed was, and from that moment, he'd done everything he could to avoid his half brother.

He grimaced. Leave it to Clayton to thrust the two of them together.

As soon as this mission was finished, he would most likely never see Reed again. Which was perfectly fine with Alec. The last thing he needed was another reminder of his father's depravity.

He arrived downstairs just as Bivvens was showing Clayton into his study.

"Clayton," he greeted as he strode into the room.

"St James." Clayton nodded, his face held carefully blank as he waved off Bivvens's attempt to take his coat and hat. "I won't be staying."

Bivvens nodded and left the room, securely closing the door in his wake.

Alec circled behind the massive desk in the center of the oak-paneled room. Like every room in this house, he'd had it stripped and completely redecorated when he inherited it from his father. "You have news."

"Henry Everett returned."

His gut tightened. "When?"

"Last night while you were following his sister."

On a wild goose chase... "Where was he?"

"No idea. But he's back now as if he'd never left." Clayton held out a handbill. "He's giving a presentation today at the Royal Society."

Alec took the announcement and scanned it. "About mathematics?"

"You should attend his talk."

He repeated, deadpan, "About mathematics?"

Clayton sensibly refrained from giving that question the answer it deserved.

A Royal Society lecture. *Christ.* Alec would rather have spent the day in the pillory. "I would never question the wisdom of the Home Office's investigators, but are you certain we're on the right scent in this hunt?" He tossed the handbill onto his desk. "Why would a mathematician want to kill the prime minister? A poor schoolmaster isn't at all the kind of man likely to be involved in an assassination plot. Or with Scepter."

"And yet he is. I need you to find out how. He'll point us to their leaders."

Via the hell of a mathematics lecture first. Alec grimaced. "So what will you be doing while I'm sleeping away the afternoon at the Royal Society?"

The gleam in Clayton's eyes shone piercingly. "I'm going mole hunting. I think I've found the Home Office employee who alerted Scepter's men." He sauntered toward the door. "Reed turned up nothing in his search last night for Everett except that handbill. But he did give me a message for you."

Alec frowned. "What's that?"

"Next time, don't let the damned gel get away." With a grin at Alec's expense, Clayton exited into the hall.

Alec sank into his chair and picked up the handbill. An irritated curse passed his lips. They were back at the beginning, with nothing more to show for their work than a piece of charred building plans and the name of a mathematician.

Clayton believed Henry Everett held the key to unlocking the assassination plot, and Alec knew Everett's sister possessed more information than she'd disclosed. But two schoolteachers involved with Scepter? *Unbelievable.*

Yet if they were, Henry Everett would swing at the gallows, along with his sister. No matter how pretty her neck.

A carving knife! The little hellcat brought a *kitchen* knife with her for protection. He'd had half a mind to ask her if she'd confused him for a Christmas goose, but he knew better. A smart man never antagonized a woman with a weapon.

Still, he found her courage admirable, if wholly misplaced.

He tossed the handbill onto the desk, and it landed on his mother's invitation. He laughed at the absurdity of the sight. Prove that a mousey schoolmaster was the mastermind behind an assassination attempt while also keeping his mother from trapping him into marriage?

Might as well unleash the hounds of hell on himself right now.

Still… He picked up the invitation and turned it over thoughtfully in his fingers. Perhaps he could make both work in his favor. "Bivvens!"

The butler appeared in the doorway. "Yes, my lord?"

"Send a footman to Harlow House." He reached for his inkwell and scratched out a message on the back of the invitation. "Tell the countess that I'd be happy to attend her ball." He blotted the ink. "On one condition."

He handed the card to the butler, and Bivvens scanned the message. "An additional invitation, sir?"

Alec smiled. "For Miss Olivia Everett."

Four

Olivia blinked at the card in her hand. An invitation to the Countess of St James's annual ball?

Well, *this* was obviously a mistake. Her name would never have been on the guest list otherwise.

She put it aside. She'd send it back this afternoon. Now, though, she wanted to take advantage of the school's late morning calm to catch up on work, so she reached for the rest of the mail. But she also couldn't resist touching the small wooden box sitting on the corner of her desk. Her father had carved it for her as a birthday gift the year before he died, and now it held a place of honor in her office, the same room where he'd once worked so hard in running the school.

As her fingers lovingly traced over the floral carving on its lid, a melancholy smile pulled at her lips. Oh, how much she missed him! But she knew he'd be proud of what she'd made of his school.

For once, the building was quiet, the students all spending the day in the park. The outing had been carefully planned to give Henry time away from the classroom for his presentation at the Royal Society. To a lesser degree, it also allowed Olivia to be out of her office so she could attend.

The presentation was a notable achievement for them and would—

"For him," she corrected. "A notable achievement for *him*."

This was Henry's moment. Not hers.

He'd been trying so hard to gain the Society's attention, and finally, it had recognized his latest work about architectural stresses. The Society's journal had accepted his article for publication, and he'd been invited to present his findings—honors that would undoubtedly earn him full fellowship.

She was thrilled for him, of course, and for the school. More recognition meant more patrons and donations, which meant that more scholarship girls could be accepted. It also meant that more influential families might consider enrolling their daughters, perhaps even members of the *ton*. And that would mean more profits.

More profits? She laughed as she added two more unpaid invoices to this week's growing stack. Good heavens, *any* profits! And any profit would make a difference.

She did what she could to minimize expenses and find patrons. So far, with a lot of hard work and even more luck, she'd managed to raise enough money to keep the doors open for another year and her father's dream alive.

Of course, it helped that she and Henry resided in the school instead of maintaining a separate household. Just as it helped that she'd resigned herself to the life of an unmarried manageress. No need for fancy dresses or stylish accessories, no need for tickets to the theatre or opera, no need for carriages, maids, dressmakers—no matter how much she longed to have that life. Soon, Henry would catch the eye of a daughter of a vicar or merchant, marry her, and have a house and children of his own.

But Olivia's future belonged solely to the school. She would make that be enough.

Somehow.

A soft knock sounded on her door, and Mrs. Adams entered. "Lady Gantry has called on you, miss."

"Please show her in." Olivia came forward to greet their most generous patron.

Baroness Gantry breezed into Olivia's office. The woman was a force unto herself with all the subtlety of a Viking raid, and Olivia thanked heaven that the woman liked her and the Everett School. God help anyone who crossed her.

"My lady." Olivia bobbed a curtsy before taking both of the baroness's outstretched hands in a familiar greeting. "How wonderful to see you." She glanced past her at the housekeeper. "Mrs. Adams, would you please fetch a tea tray?"

Lady Gantry dismissingly waved her gloved hand. "Not necessary, my dear. I shan't be staying long enough, I'm afraid, although your hospitality is impeccable, as always."

Olivia smiled. Maintaining the appearance of propriety and good manners had become her life's objective. Her reputation *was* the school's reputation, and if the baroness thought she was a good hostess, then so did the rest of the *ton*. "I wasn't expecting you this afternoon. Did I forget we'd made an appointment?"

The baroness often stopped by the school. Usually, though, she made an appointment far enough in advance that their cook could bake those lemon biscuits she loved so much.

Lady Gantry gave a curt headshake. "I've come with an urgent request. I hope you'll be willing to help me."

Olivia blinked. Well, *that* was new. Normally, she was the one asking for help.

"Of course." She gestured at one of the chairs in front of her desk. "Whatever do you need?"

Lady Gantry sank into the chair. "I can, of course, count on your complete discretion?"

"Always." Olivia took the chair opposite her.

The baroness focused her attention on her white kid gloves as she fussed with the pearl buttons at her wrists. "To my great dismay, my sister's youngest daughter, Justine, has placed herself into a scandalous position."

In other words, her niece had allowed herself to be compromised. Olivia's chest constricted with empathy for the poor girl.

"Fortunately," Lady Gantry drawled, "the family was able to keep secret what happened, but my niece can no longer remain at her parents' estate."

"Is she…increasing?" Olivia asked delicately.

"Thank goodness no! The foolish chit would have found herself banished to Ireland if she were." She pursed her thin lips in aggravation. "The young man's family owns the property bordering theirs, you see, and Georgiana is worried that her daughter might very well find herself *just so* if half of England isn't put between the two."

"Marriage isn't possible?"

Lady Gantry looked appalled. "The boy's family are Whigs!"

Olivia cleared her throat to cover her laughter. "Normally, we don't enroll girls over fifteen years old."

At that age, most of the girls who attended the Everett School for the Education of Proper Young Ladies returned home to study how to find the most advantageous marriage match. A proper education in philosophy, science, history, and the classics fell by the wayside in favor of how to create seating plans for grand dinners, paint watercolors, and make floral arrangements. After all, society gentlemen preferred wives who knew the pianoforte over Plato. Olivia was grateful that families were willing to educate their daughters for even this limited amount, as their tuition allowed her to find positions in shops and houses for the scholarship girls.

"However," she continued, "if your niece is willing, we could hire her as a companion for the younger girls, and I could give her private lessons to continue her education until she's ready to return home."

Such an arrangement would end the gossip before it began. If anyone dared spread rumors about Justine's sudden arrival in London, it wouldn't be because she was ruined but rather that Lady Gantry had used her influence to secure a position for a poor relation. Both the Everett School and Lady Gantry would be viewed as generous, and the girl would have a second chance at a respectable life.

"That arrangement would do perfectly," Lady Gantry assured her but then followed it with a sigh of defeat.

"Although I daresay that an education will be wasted on the gel."

Olivia struggled to keep her smile in place against her rising anger. An education was *never* wasted on anyone. Justine had made a mistake, and no matter how impulsive the decision, she still deserved to have her mind developed, especially if she were to be imprisoned as a governess or schoolmistress for the rest of her life. After all, didn't Olivia know well what refuge the intellect could provide when the heart turned traitorous?

Lady Gantry rose and retreated toward the door. "I am very grateful, Miss Everett, for your willingness to assist me with this bothersome problem."

Bothersome problem? The girl had given her innocence to a man she loved and could potentially spend the rest of her life paying for that mistake. It wasn't a bothersome problem. It was utter devastation.

Yet Olivia bit her tongue and forced out, "Of course."

Lady Gantry paused in the doorway to pin her with a look. "I am certain you understand the possibility of scandal over this."

Olivia caught her breath. Did the baroness know about her past? But how—

"Surely you know other schoolmistresses who have accepted fallen girls and attempted to bring them back into respectability, only to have their indiscretions made public."

The air rushed from Olivia's lungs in a pulse of relief so hard that it made her dizzy. Lady Gantry didn't know... *Thank heavens.*

"Your example of spotless propriety will be a good model for Justine." Lady Gantry smiled brightly, certain she was giving Olivia the highest compliment she could, but it tore at Olivia's heart. "I've never met a more respectable woman in my life than you. Good day, Miss Everett."

Olivia stiffly bobbed a curtsy and mumbled, "Good day."

She closed the door and returned to her desk. She sank into her chair and stared at the papers, bills, and messages stacked so tidily on the desktop. So ordered and neat.

So *perfect*.

That was her, she thought miserably, the perfect model of orderliness and propriety. Positioned by society at the edges of rooms where elderly spinsters and ladies' companions dressed in grays and browns did their best to fade unnoticed into the wallpaper. Traditional and mannered. Chaste. Sexless. Destined to simply wither away a little bit more each day until nothing was left but a shriveled, empty husk.

She pressed the back of her hand against her mouth to force down a rising scream of desolation.

Oh, how she wanted so much more! She wanted the happiness that came with having a home of her own, a husband who loved her, and children. Most of all, she wanted the passion and joy that should have been part of living and loving. She'd tasted that once, had believed it could be hers…

But that was so long ago now that it seemed like a dream. No, a nightmare. She'd been only eighteen and swept up in the promise of a future with the man she'd loved, so young and foolish…so lucky to escape without completely ruining herself and her family.

This was her life now, as a paragon of moral propriety. A role model of respectability.

A fraud.

A loud rap sounded at the door, and she startled. She barely had time to wipe her eyes before Henry hurried inside.

His ingratiating smile faded into a puzzled frown as he glanced around the room. "Mrs. Adams said Lady Gantry was here."

"She was but couldn't linger." Olivia reached for her account book and flipped it open to that month's ledger. She kept her gaze lowered to the columns of figures that never seemed to balance so he wouldn't see any trace of emotion on her face. "Her niece is coming to work for us. She's going to serve as a companion for the younger girls."

He scoffed. "You mean Lady Gantry coerced you into creating a position for a poor relative."

She didn't dare raise her eyes. "Exactly."

"If you think it best." He blew out a frustrated sigh. "But I wanted to invite the baroness to my Society presentation."

Olivia looked up, surprised. "Lady Gantry would never attend a lecture at the Royal Society. Too bluestocking for her tastes."

"I know." He approached her desk and, without asking, looked through the papers she'd put there. "But I wanted to invite her anyway. Flatter her so she would tell her friends that she was a special guest."

She arched a brow at that bit of dishonesty. "You mean so the fellows would see her name on the guest list and know that you have connections in society?"

Caught in his lie, Henry answered that with a grin and reached for the stack of mail.

"Looking for something in particular on *my* desk?" she asked, unable to hold back her irritation. Even after five years of successfully managing the school, Henry didn't completely trust her.

"Just checking what's arrived." He held up the white card. "From the Countess of St James?"

"Her annual ball is tomorrow evening." She put out her hand and waited for him to place it on her palm. "That invitation needs to be returned."

Several society ladies were patronesses of the Everett School, so Olivia often received invitations to afternoon teas and book clubs where having a bluestocking in attendance gave the gathering intellectual credibility. If that same bluestocking also happened to manage the school for which the hostess served as patroness, then the woman could also flaunt her charitable works. Two birds, one stone. Despite knowing the real reason behind the invitations, Olivia attended every event she could.

But those weren't balls, and Lady St James wasn't a patroness. This one was a mistake.

"You're attending, of course," Henry said.

She snatched back the invitation. "Of course I am *not*."

"Why not?"

She nearly laughed. "Women like me don't attend soirees like this." The countess's ball would be the event of the season, certain to be a crush, and the kind of see-and-be-seen evening that drew princes and dukes. Perhaps even the regent himself. There wasn't room for a schoolmistress. "I'd be a misfit."

"You should go," he told her. "You might meet someone—"

A bitter knot twisted in her stomach. He didn't mean she would meet a gentleman. She wasn't foolish enough to misunderstand that.

"—who will donate to the school," he finished.

Being right didn't dull the prick to her pride.

"We can't pass up opportunities like this. You know that."

Her shoulders slumped. She *did* know. But knowing something to be true and wanting desperately to believe something else… Well, wasn't that exactly what her life had become?

She muttered the first excuse that popped into her head, "I have nothing to wear."

"Wear your best dress. No one will expect you to attend in furs and jewels." He circled her desk and took her shoulders in his hands. "I also want you to dance, drink too much punch, and have a jolly time."

Her heart bounced. "Truly?"

"Most truly. You deserve it."

When he grinned at her, she saw the old Henry in him, the carefree young man she'd known before Papa died and the Everett School fell on hard times. She loved her brother, despite all the frustrations, and would do anything for him. Including attending the ball.

He turned his attention back to the papers on her desk and cleared his throat. "Have you finished looking over my new article? I wanted to show Banks my progress. He said it could be printed in the next issue of *Philosophical Transactions* if I finished it quickly enough."

"Mostly." She forced down a stab of jealousy and reached into her desk drawer. Henry's pages—and her corrections—testified to the culmination of work that would gain him a Society fellowship. "I still have a few pages to finish." When disappointment flitted across his face, she added quickly, "But I can have them done by tomorrow."

He beamed her a smile. "I knew I could count on you."

As he scanned through the sheets, he nodded in appreciation. Olivia's chest warmed at that small compliment.

A thought struck her. "There was something mixed in with your notes that didn't belong. A page of data points for a different set of parabolas." She reached for the last sheet to show him. "The page marked Waterloo." She teased, "Have you moved from arches to arms?"

With a laugh at the idea, he pulled out the page, folded it, and placed it into his breast pocket. "It's nothing. Just some notes I made for the next project."

"Good, because I've had enough of war for a long while," she said quietly. "I don't think I want to work to make it even more deadly."

His mouth twisted guiltily. "As I said, it's nothing. But this one on arches—*this* is what matters." He tapped his finger to the pages like a proud papa. "This article will make us famous!"

Him, she corrected silently and tried not to let her jealousy show. It would make *him* famous, not her.

But if helping benefited Henry, then it also benefited the school. In the end, that was what mattered.

Or at least that was what she told herself. Perhaps some-day a woman could receive credit for doing a man's work.

"I'm heading out. I'll see you at the lecture, then. I need your support to get me through this."

"You'll be fine without me." She'd gone over his notes again that morning to catch any last mistakes. "But I'll be there just the same."

Grateful relief relaxed his features, and he squeezed her shoulders affectionately. His grin faded. "I'm sorry you can't have balls and parties all the time. I never wanted this life for you."

"I know," she mumbled despite the self-recrimination that tightened her throat.

"But there is no one better to run this school than you, and I could never have wished for a more precious sister." Love and concern—perhaps a tinge of regret—registered on his face. "I would do anything for you. You know that."

She forced a smile.

He handed back the papers, then gestured at the invi-tation as he made his way toward the door. "Be certain to accept that right away. You have no idea what might come of attending."

She smiled wistfully as he closed the door. Henry could be a wonderful brother most of the time. When he wasn't irritating the daylights out of her.

Then her smile blossomed into a full-out grin, and she laughed as an excited thrill shot through her. She was going *to a ball*!

Yet she still had nothing proper to wear. She had two

days to either buy a proper dress or steal a fairy godmother's magic wand.

Her gaze fell onto the account book and its total of available funds. Her shoulders sagged.

Where exactly did one find a fairy godmother?

Five

ALEC STIFLED A YAWN AS THE LECTURE ENTERED ITS second hour. The first had detailed mathematical ratios between points on a Roman arch. He'd hoped the second half would be more interesting, until he discovered that the new topic was the Roman dome. Which was simply a continuous arch.

Good Lord, Henry Everett was boring!

But his sister—Alec's gaze roamed to where she sat at the back of the auditorium, raptly hanging on every word—was most definitely *not*.

Olivia Everett appeared strikingly different from last night. In the alley, she'd possessed bright, flashing eyes even in the dark shadows, and her hair had fallen free of its pins, making her appear even more like a wild creature.

But here, beneath the sunlight that streamed through the tall windows, she was simply…angelic. Nothing about her demure appearance gave even the slightest hint that this same woman had brandished a carving knife at him.

Sweet Lucifer, what an appearance, too. Although her hair was twisted into a conservative chignon, he could finally see its true color—pale gold, the same yellow as the morning sky when the sun first peeks over the horizon. The cornflower blue of her dress matched her eyes and high-lighted the pink in her cheeks, and even from this distance, he could see that her lips were just as full as he remembered. Whenever her brother made a comment she found particu-larly interesting—perhaps the only person in the hall who did—she bit that pouty bottom lip of hers in concentration. That same lip Alec inexplicably wanted to bite himself. If he did that, then she truly would take a knife to him.

A ripple of applause moved through the audience.

Alec dragged his attention back to the brother. Finally, the lecture was over, and Henry Everett was taking his bows. *Thank God.* Alec might not have learned anything about mathematics, but he now knew for certain that the name on the charred fragment belonged to this man.

But why on earth would a schoolmaster attempt to assas-sinate the prime minister?

His gaze darted back to Olivia Everett as she rose grace-fully from her seat to make her way down from the gallery where the women were seated. What was *her* role in this? A fair-skinned, golden-haired, pink-cheeked mystery who didn't even know enough about fighting to bring a better knife with her into a dark alley? Who didn't know enough about the evils men committed to not enter dark alleys in the first place? Who now looked upon her brother with adora-tion even as he ignored her to shake hands with the men who were congratulating him?

Alec had no idea.

But he planned on finding out.

Everett was joyfully led from the hall by a group of

Society fellows, but his sister remained behind at the front of the room long after the audience had all left, unaware that Alec lingered in the shadows near the wall. He half expected her to follow after the men. Instead, with a glance over her shoulder to make certain no one was watching, she stepped up to the blackboard where Everett had written his equations and diagrams.

She hesitated, then picked up a piece of chalk and made a quick correction.

Alec watched her, incredulous. She ran her fingers across the long blackboard as if keeping track of printed lines on a page in a novel, her lips moving as she read the symbols and equations. After every few marks she made, she stepped back to survey her work, then darted to the right toward the two diagrams—one an arch, the other a dome—and erased the marks Everett had made, only to place new ones. Finally, she stepped back to take one long scan of the equations and symbols covering the board. With a nod of satisfaction, she returned the chalk to its tray, gathered up the lecture notes, and moved toward the door.

A cold realization lapped at the back of Alec's knees. Could the Home Office be chasing the wrong Everett?

Impossible. Yet he shoved himself out of his seat and dashed after her just the same.

He caught up with her on the footpath outside the towering front doors. She was leaning into the street in an attempt to wave down a hackney.

"Miss Everett." With a pleasant smile, Alec slid between her and the avenue, trapping her into conversation.

She took a surprised step back. "I'm sorry." Her face was blank with a lack of recognition. "Have we met?"

"Not formally." Fighting back an amused twist of his mouth, he sketched a bow. "Alexander Sinclair."

"A pleasure to meet you, Mr. Sinclair."

Still no recognition of him. *Good.* "I found your brother's presentation today extremely fascinating." And he had. Just not for the reasons she'd assume.

"Ah, so you were in the lecture hall." Her puzzled expression softened, and pride for her brother lit her eyes. They were the same bright blue as the afternoon sky.

For a moment, he lost his train of thought.

"What exactly did you find fascinating?"

You, he almost answered just to see the shocked flush he knew would color her cheeks and part her lips. Yet it would also be the God's truth. After all, she'd corrected her brother's work with so much assurance that it was impossible she should be wrong. He knew as certainly as he knew her hair would smell of lavender if he lowered his head to breathe her in that her calculations were correct.

But he also knew from his stint in the army that sometimes the most successful attack required patience and cunning. A frontal assault was not always the best option.

Unable to stop himself, he raked his gaze down her front. *Pity.*

"Your brother's work was compelling." He watched closely for her reaction. "But it was also wrong. That's why you corrected it, in case the men from the Society returned and gave it closer scrutiny."

She froze like a doe before the hounds, and Alec suspected she might just bolt.

Instead, the brave creature from last night returned. Fearlessly not moving her gaze from his, she tangled her right hand in her skirt to wipe away all evidence of any chalk dust that might still be clinging to her fingertips.

"You're mistaken," she said softly.

"I'm not."

A flash of guilt flitted across her pretty face, not at correcting the equations but at getting caught. It was the same expression his sister Elizabeth used to make whenever he'd found her sneaking biscuits from Cook and later stealing kisses from suitors.

"I don't know what you mean," she challenged. "I didn't make any corrections." Despite the trembling in her voice at that blatant lie, her blue eyes flared in defiance, and this time, it was Alec who caught his breath. Sweet Lucifer, she was enthralling. "My brother is a brilliant mathematician."

"Perhaps." He leaned closer and lowered his voice. "But I have a feeling his sister is even better."

Her lips parted in speechless surprise.

He doffed his hat and sauntered away, grinning to himself. Clayton's mission had just become very interesting.

Six

In her dreams, Olivia searched the narrow alleys of the City, but they weren't the barren, dark places she remembered. They had transformed into a masquerade ball with a crush of couples in fine clothes and jewels, old-fashioned wigs and masks, all laughing and dancing wildly over the cobblestones to eerie music played by unseen musicians in the darkness. Her heart pounded harder with every step she took, her breathing fast and shallow, and while the others danced to normal timing, Olivia moved in frustratingly slow motion. She was searching—no, hunting—for the masked man. But every masked face was wrong, every masculine set of eyes not bright enough, not devilish enough to be—

She awoke with a silent gasp. As her sleep-fuzzed mind cleared, her heart skipped.

Someone was in her room.

She sat up in bed and clutched the coverlet to her chest. Around her, her attic bedroom was flooded with darkness except for the faint glow of the banked fire, which lit the room just enough to reveal a large figure dressed all in black standing in front of her dresser. Silently, he opened each drawer and searched methodically through its contents. She glanced across the room. The doors of her armoire hung half-open. Proof he'd already searched it.

His broad back faced her, but she knew without having to see—

Her masked man.

She should have been terrified, but she wasn't. He could have hurt her in the alley if he'd wanted, but instead, he'd saved her life. He could have harmed her here, too, while she'd been sleeping, but he hadn't.

What she was, though, was immensely curious.

She took a deep breath and blurted out before she lost her courage, "Are you finding what you're looking for?"

His head snapped up, his hand frozen in midreach into the drawer. Then he returned his attention to the dresser and continued his search.

"No, I'm not," he answered in the same low, raspy whisper she remembered from the alley. He closed the drawer and opened the next.

Olivia studied him through the shadows. Who *was* this man? The mask disguised his face and the rasp hid his voice, but he possessed the bearing and speech of a gentleman. Yet from his muscular build and the way he moved so fluidly, she suspected that last night wasn't the first time he'd been in a fight. He was a walking, talking, masked contradiction.

"You won't find anything in there but stockings and garters," she put in helpfully, "and I don't think I have any in your size."

When he shot her an irritated look over his shoulder, she pointed at the bottom drawer.

"I should warn you that I keep my shifts and stays in there. I wouldn't want you to be unduly embarrassed when you see them."

He slid the drawer closed, turned to face her, and crossed his arms as he leaned back against the dresser. His stance was as casual as if breaking into a woman's bedroom in the middle of the night was an everyday occurrence for him. But then, for all she knew, it might very well be.

"Trust me." His full lips curled in amusement beneath the dark silk of the mask covering the upper half of his face. "I've seen enough stays and shifts with women still in them that yours won't cause a second glance."

If he'd meant to shock her, he wasn't even close. She drew her knees to her chest beneath the coverlet and waved her hand nonchalantly. "Then by all means, continue with your search, but I own nothing worth stealing."

"I'm not a thief," he bit out, as if offended by the notion. Even through the dark shadows, she felt the heat of his stare as his eyes narrowed on her. "You're not frightened?"

"Should I be?"

"A proper lady like yourself, an unmarried innocent…" His eyes gleamed. "I'd have thought you'd have screamed to find a man in your bedroom."

"In a mask," she added helpfully. "Don't forget that."

He drawled with chagrin, "How could I?"

"If you're not a thief, then why do you wear it?" *What are you hiding?*

"For protection."

"From me?" She laughed. As if a tall and broad man with

such hard muscles should need protecting! And from someone like her, no less. "Then it's a good thing I left all the
knives in the kitchen."

When he smiled rakishly, her foolish heart skittered, and
not from fear.

"Protection from the men your brother is working for,"
he clarified.

That was a turn of conversation she hadn't expected and
one she couldn't follow. She frowned. "My brother works
here, helping me run the school. His room is just down the
hall. Should I call for him and introduce you?"

Her question was a subtle warning that if he tried to harm
her, a single cry for help would have everyone in the building
running to her rescue. She wasn't afraid of him...but trusting him was a completely different matter.

"He's not the Everett I'm interested in knowing better."

Her breath hitched at that blatant flirtation, and her suddenly blank mind couldn't latch on to the cutting reply he
deserved. Not when her traitorous body wanted to let him
do just that.

"Tell me, Miss Everett," he murmured. "Do you often let
your brother take credit for your work?"

So...not a flirtation after all.

Ignoring an inexplicable pang of disappointment, she
arched a brow and challenged, "And do *you* often break into
ladies' bedrooms in the middle of the night?"

A slow grin crossed his face. The charm of it was disarm-
ing. "You'd be surprised."

All kinds of wanton images filled her head, and beneath

the coverlet, her body tingled shamefully. If she knew what was good for her, she *would* scream and end this encounter. But she couldn't bring herself to do it. "Then you've entered the wrong—"

"It's all you, isn't it?" he asked.

She blinked, confused. "I have no idea what you mean."

"His mathematical work, the lectures, the articles…" His eyes gleamed in the light of the banked coals like the devil's own, tempting her into revealing the truth and selling her soul. "Henry Everett didn't do those. You did."

His husky whisper twined down her spine, and she shivered. She would never admit that. Doing so would end Henry's fellowship with the Society before it had begun.

"I have no idea what you mean," she repeated.

"It's admirable, really, the brilliant gift you must have for it," he mused, the compliment warming her more than his flirtations, "to be able to outshine your brother, who is no doubt a fine mind in his own right. What I don't understand is why you let him take all the credit."

Because that's what a younger, foolish sister does for a brother who risked his own career to save her reputation. "We're collaborators."

"Oh? On what do you collaborate?"

From the way he asked that, as if he couldn't have cared less what the answer was—oh, he very much wanted to know! But why? "Architectural mathematics, mostly."

"Is there truly such a thing?"

She crossed her arms and blew out an aggravated sigh. Now her work was being disparaged by a masked intruder.

Wonderful. "It's a vital connection, I'll have you know, that allows for—"

She broke off as an idea struck her. A devilishly preposterous idea…but could anyone blame her? She tilted her head as she studied him. Fairy godmothers came in all shapes and sizes, she supposed.

"Would you like to know more?" She dangled the question in front of him the way a little girl dangles a string of yarn in front of a kitten. Although as a cat, he was really more of a panther. "I *could* tell you…"

His jaw tightened. The panther knew he was being toyed with. By the mouse. "If you care to enlighten me."

Tracing her fingertip idly over the coverlet, she coerced, "I would be happy to, but…I need a dress."

"A *dress*?" he repeated as if he couldn't possibly have heard her correctly.

"A gown, actually. You see, I've been invited to a ball tomorrow evening, and I don't have an appropriate dress to wear."

His eyes narrowed. "What does any of this have to do with mathematics?"

"Oh, a great deal." Her fingers plucked at the coverlet, no more concerned with his dark glare than if he'd invited her for an afternoon picnic. "*I* need a dress, *you* want answers…" She shrugged.

He pushed away from the dresser and drew himself up to his full height. "Blackmail, Miss Everett?"

"I prefer to think of it as an exchange of favors." She pinned him beneath her gaze, all feigned interest in the coverlet now gone. "I'll tell you about my brother's work, and you'll have a gown delivered to me tomorrow." And then she would find a way to repay him the cost of it…somehow. One ha'penny at a time.

"And what makes you think I know anything about ball gowns?"

"You speak in a whisper to hide your voice, but your tone and cadence are clearly that of a gentleman," she said matter-of-factly. "And one educated enough to know about my brother's work. You're knowledgeable enough about Westminster to know of the Everett School, which means you're either wealthy enough to afford to live on the west side of London or you're a servant for someone who does." She slid an assessing look over him. "But you're no man's servant. From what I can see, you're not someone who takes orders. You're someone who's used to giving them."

"And what," he bit out each word, "does that have to do with dresses?"

"A man who moves in your social circles would surely have access to fashionable ladies and know where to find a ball gown on such short notice." She taunted him with another glance through lowered lashes, another look of mock innocence. "Certainly a man who knows so much about shifts and stays and the women still inside them."

He cursed beneath his breath, then snarled, "Stand up."

Her heart skipped at the brusque order, and she squeaked out, "Why?"

"If I'm going to find you a dress, then I need to know if it will fit." He gestured for her to crawl out of bed and approach the faint glow of the banked fire. "Unless you'd prefer I take one of your stays with me for measurements?"

She shot him a glare as she slid out of bed. She grabbed her dressing robe from the chair and scrambled into it, then cinched the belt tightly around her waist.

With a crook of his finger, he called her closer. "Come."

She approached slowly on bare feet, her heart pounding harder with each step.

He rotated his finger in the air. "Circle."

She hesitated. This man was certainly no fairy god-mother, and stealing a magic wand would surely have been easier than coercing him. Yet she pulled in a deep breath and did as he ordered, turning in a circle so he could have a complete look. His gaze felt as palpable as if he were touching her with his hands…down her front and across her hips, down her legs to her bare toes.

Then his eyes slowly retraced their path, this time lingering in places that made her flush and stirred a low ache between her thighs. As if she weren't wearing her dressing gown. As if she were wearing nothing at all.

"Your turn," he prompted, suddenly hoarse. "Your brother's work?"

She cleared her throat to remove the knot his gaze had put there. "Roman arches establish an equilibrium of tensions and compressions with downward weight equalizing outward pressures, inward stresses matching outer strains, and a prime focal—"

He put up a hand and interrupted her. "Roman arches?"

"You said you wanted to know about my brother's work."

Their work, she corrected herself, even though most of the calculations were hers. The masked man had been right about that, although she hated to admit it. "His work focuses on compression and stress ratios."

"What does that have to do with architecture?"

"Everything." She placed her hands on her hips and leveled at him the same no-nonsense look that quelled even the most rowdy of schoolgirls. "Have you ever crossed a bridge in London or stepped foot into St Paul's Cathedral or Westminster Abbey without it crashing down around you? Then thank an ancient Roman."

His mouth twisted at that chastisement, but wisely, he said nothing.

"It was the Roman arch," she continued, a schoolmistress taking advantage of a teaching moment, "that the Gothic architects exploited to build Europe's great cathedrals and last century's engineers to stretch bridges over—"

"The Royal Society is forward thinking and concerned with building the current empire, not with resurrecting dead ones," he interrupted, his patience clearly thinning. "What's so innovative about your brother's work that would earn him the respect of the Royal Society?"

She gave a soft shake of her head, aware for the first time that her hair was completely undone and shamelessly loose around her shoulders. "I'll also need shoes for my ball gown."

"Then lift your skirts."

"*Pardon?*" Instead of the squeak she'd anticipated, her voice emerged as a throaty breath.

Amusement pulled at his lips, as if this devil knew the

unsettling effect he had on her. Especially his dark eyes. The darkness hid their true color and had her wondering if they were brown or green, blue or hazel… Yet even in the shadows, they possessed an intensity that shivered through her.

"Have to see what kind of slippers to give you." He repeated in a deep murmur, "Lift your skirts for me, my lady."

The low command tickled at her inner thighs and stirred a heated ache between them. He hadn't meant that as a flirtation. She was blackmailing him, for heaven's sake! But no man had spoken to her in such a voice in years, had looked at her the way he was staring at her now… Not as a respectable lady but as a woman.

He stood so close that she could smell his heady scent of leather and cigars, bergamot and lemons. Sweet heavens, the man smelled of *lemons*! She couldn't resist breathing him in.

Nor could she resist clutching the skirts of her robe and night rail and slowly raising them.

He trailed his gaze down her body to her bare calves as she lifted the hems to just above her knees. She froze, except for the rise and fall of her bosom with her rapid, shallow breaths. What she was doing was scandalous, utterly ruinous. Yet she had the inexplicable urge to lift her skirts even higher just to see his reaction, to dare him to flirt with her. Or do even more.

"Satin," he rasped.

Her breath hitched. "What?"

He gave a shake of his head to dismiss her question…or was it to chase away whatever wicked thoughts were spinning through his mind? God knew enough of them were certainly whirling through hers. "You'll need satin slippers, I think."

She let her skirts slip through her fingers and fall back into place. She would have sworn an expression of disappointment darkened what little of his face she could see.

"Arches," he murmured. "You were telling me about arches."

"Oh…yes. Arches." She cleared her suddenly dry throat. "Tension is everything."

A rakish grin teased at his lips. "I've always thought so."

Drat the devil! Apparently, he was the only man in history who was aroused by Roman arches.

"Tension—that is, downward forces—" *That* wasn't any better. She was digging herself to China, so she dragged in a deep breath and started over. "The Romans created arches by placing a capstone on the top of the curve, and the downward force—the compression"—she somehow managed not to blush—"kept the arch in place even without mortar. But build too high, and the downward stresses become outward strains that will bring down the arch. That's why Gothic cathedrals have buttresses, to keep their high walls from collapsing outward. My brother's work focuses on finding exact mathematical equations to make buttresses unnecessary at great heights and spans never before considered by engineers and architects."

She was certain her eyes sparkled now with excitement for her work—*their* work. She simply couldn't help herself.

"Just imagine the possibilities. If builders can harness downward and outward pressures, if they can figure out the proper ratios, then they can build higher, longer, and wider than ever before." Excitement sparked inside her. "Buildings and bridges without limits."

She waited, hoping he found the work as thrilling as she did. The wonder of it, the marvel, the ingenuity...all fresh and exhilarating! That excitement had drawn her into mathematics in the first place, and it was faith in new discoveries that kept her going. If Henry took public credit for her calculations, well, that was a small price to pay for helping to advance architecture and engineering.

Yet it wasn't excitement she saw in her masked man. It was aggravation.

His jaw tightened. "But how would any of your brother's theories translate into real building plans?"

"Because architecture is mathematics at heart. All good architects are good mathematicians." She smiled a bit smugly. "Or they know where to hire one."

"So your brother consults with architects on building plans?"

Unease prickled across her skin at that question. He wanted to know far more about Henry and their work than she felt comfortable divulging. Even for a ball gown. "Sometimes."

He took a single step toward her to close the distance between them. She pressed her hand against his shoulder to keep him back, but she might have been nothing more than a bothersome gnat for all it did. She swallowed. Or a mouse stalked by a panther.

"Who are you?" she breathed as the heat of his body seeped through his clothes and into her fingertips.

"No one important."

"I very much doubt that," she drawled.

His eyes shone wickedly.

She scowled. "What do you want? Why are you here?" But the harsh demand she'd aimed for emerged as a breathless whisper.

"Your brother disappeared a few days ago." His dark gaze lowered to her neck as if he were contemplating kissing her there. "Where was he?"

"I don't know." A lie, and she didn't care. She didn't mind discussing their work, but their personal lives were off-limits. "Who are you? Surely, you have a name."

Ignoring her question, he raised his hand to her shoulder and slid his palm across the thin material of the robe to her neck. Goose bumps formed on her skin in the wake of his touch. "You're not playing by the rules."

His fingers trailed down her throat to the hollow at her collarbone, where she feared he could feel her racing pulse. When he smiled down at her, she *knew* he felt it, which only made it race harder. She rasped out, "What rules?"

"Surely you want sparkling jewels to wear around this pretty neck of yours with that ball gown and slippers." He gently brushed his fingertip against her earlobe, and electricity jolted through her. "And earbobs. It would be a shame if you appeared at your ball half-dressed." His seductive voice wrapped around her like a velvet ribbon. "I would hate to put you into a state of dishabille if I wasn't allowed to witness it."

An ache throbbed wantonly between her thighs. Their conversation had taken an intimate turn, although she couldn't have said through the foggy confusion muddling her mind whether he was flirting with her or warning her away.

"If you want a full costume for your ball, then you need to offer up more information." His dark eyes fell hungrily to her mouth. "And I don't mean about arches."

Beneath his stare, she couldn't help but dart out the tip of her tongue to wet her suddenly dry lips.

A faint groan sounded in the back of his throat, and her eyes dropped to his neck. It should have been covered by a cloth, yet it was rakishly bare. Inexplicably, she longed to put her mouth there, to feel the warmth of his skin beneath her lips and taste the salty flavor of him.

"Where was your brother?" He touched her chin and lifted her face to keep her attention on him, although she couldn't have looked away if she tried. "Who was he with?"

"He was at some silly country party," she whispered, unable to speak any louder. "With the men from the Royal Society."

"That's what he told you?"

"Not until he returned." His mouth lingered close to hers, so close that surely they breathed the same air. Disappointment panged in her chest that he wasn't kissing her, that his lips weren't on hers and flaming the ache between her legs into a wildfire. All he had to do to kiss her was simply lower his head. All she had to do was rise up on tiptoes...

"That's why you were looking for him last night," he murmured. "You had no idea where he'd gone."

"Yes." She frowned. "But I found you instead."

He smiled faintly at that, and his thumb slipped across her chin to trace over her bottom lip. She trembled. If she touched the tip of her tongue to his thumb, what would he do? Would he pull back in surprise, or would he let her taste him?

"Why didn't he tell you before he left?" he prompted gently. "Was it because he wanted to hide from his sister that he was drinking, gambling, and enjoying women?"

"Henry doesn't do those sorts of things." She would have laughed at the idea if her insides weren't churning with confusion and desire.

His thumb looped up to trace along the heart-shaped curve of her upper lip and teased lightly at its center dip. "He doesn't enjoy gentlemanly amusements?"

"He's not that kind of gentleman." Her lips tickled against his thumb with each word.

"And you?" he purred wickedly. He hooked his thumb over her bottom lip and gently tugged to open her mouth so he could slip his thumb inside and caress across her smooth inner lip. "Are you that kind of woman?"

She fought back a moan, far too tempted to close her lips around his thumb and suck—

Yes, she wanted to admit. *Yes, I am.* Even now, her body traitorously remembered the solid feel of a man on top of her and his body moving inside hers, and her heart remembered the exquisite warmth of being with the man she loved. God help her, but she wanted to capture those sensations again and pull them deep inside until she burst from the fullness of them all. Until she shattered with need and release—

"No," he answered his own question with a sigh of disappointment. "Of course you're not." He dropped his hand away and muttered, "You're too prim and proper...every inch respectable."

Apparently, he also thought she was every inch a bore. Oh, if only he knew the truth! But she couldn't tell him. No one could *ever* know.

Just as she knew she could never tell anyone about this evening. No one would believe her masked man wasn't a dream. She could barely believe it herself.

She cleared her throat to dislodge the knot there, but she could do nothing about the throbbing ache at her core. "Is that all, then?" She stepped back. There was safety in distance. "Did you find the information you came seeking tonight?"

"Did you get the dress you wanted for the ball?" he countered.

She managed a self-pleased smile. "Is it too much to request that the gown be blue?"

"Yes," he growled.

Without warning, he swept her into his arms, carried her to the bed, and deposited her on the mattress before she could think to cry out. Then he surprised her again by pulling the coverlet over her body and up to her chin to tuck her into bed.

"Good night." He placed an impossibly chaste kiss on her forehead and moved toward the door to escape back through the dark school to the street below. "And the next time you find a strange man in your bedroom," he warned as he cast a longing look back at her, "scream."

Then he was gone.

Seven

ALEC RAISED THE GLASS OF MADEIRA TO HIS LIPS AND glanced across the crush of bodies in the ballroom of St James House. Olivia Everett was late to the ball.

Last night's visit had been interesting, to say the least. He couldn't think of another time when he'd experienced such an exhilarating exchange in a woman's bedroom that didn't involve removing clothing. For that matter, he couldn't think of any time when he'd been in a woman's bedroom and *not* removed his clothing, although she had no idea how close he'd come to removing hers.

She was nothing like the other women he knew...those world-weary society wives and widows whom little could shock, those virginal debutantes who were shocked by everything. Olivia Everett was singularly different, right down to her bare toes.

Brilliant and beautiful, challenging and fearless, alluring yet innocent... He'd found himself wanting to do more last night than simply tuck her into bed. He'd wanted to crawl right in on top of her, strip off that dowdy robe and night rail, and run his hands and mouth over her beautiful body until she begged to be taken. He'd been semihard from the moment she naïvely tugged up her skirts. All it would have taken was a whisper of surrender from her.

A virgin schoolmistress... *Good God*. That alone should have had him fleeing as fast as he could run because he would never seduce an innocent. But paradoxically, it also had him longing to teach her about arousal and satisfaction, bodies and the pleasures they could give. Half of his gut wanted to turn her into a debauched creature; the other half wanted to keep her pure. But *all* of him had wanted her.

He chuckled to himself. The little hellcat had the audacity to blackmail him! And not for money or position but for a dress, of all things.

His amusement faded into a frown. Unfortunately, he'd gotten even less than she had from last night's exchange. He'd uncovered just enough to confirm that both she and her brother were capable of working the equations on the fragment of building plans Clayton had found at the warehouse. But there wasn't enough information on the charred slip to prove any connection to the bombing, and there was no reason why Scepter needed either Everett sibling to provide mathematical equations or how any building plans fit into their assassination attempt.

That was why he'd searched the school. He'd hoped to find a full copy of the building plans that matched the charred fragment, plans that would surely provide more answers. But his search had turned up empty, and questioning Olivia Everett directly had gotten him nothing except a lecture on architecture.

So he now intended to take a different approach. Tonight, he would charm information from her, and he very much planned on enjoying himself in the process.

"Ah, beauty," he murmured against the rim of his glass as she appeared in the doorway. "There you are at last."

She handed her invitation to the master of ceremonies and was announced to a roomful of people who couldn't have cared less that she'd arrived. Except for one. And *his* lips pulled into a slow smile.

She wore her blackmailed gown. One of his sister Elizabeth's from last season, he'd had it delivered that morning by a porter whom he'd threatened to within an inch of his life to not reveal the identity of her mysterious benefactor. Alec had hoped that she'd look attractive in the dress. He was wrong.

She was simply stunning.

In a shade of light blue that matched her eyes, the satin gown shimmered in the light of the chandeliers as she glided into the ballroom. She blended well with the society ladies in that dress with its high waist and skirt that cascaded straight down to her slippered feet and a tight bodice that revealed just enough of her breasts to tantalize. Thin straps of ribbons over her creamy shoulders made his fingers itch to untie them and let the bodice fall away. Surely it was a sin to imagine undressing an innocent when she appeared so angelic. But he couldn't help himself. The bluestocking school manageress he'd met had been transformed like Cinderella, and the difference was breathtaking.

She stopped to sweep her bright gaze around the room, most likely searching for anyone she knew in the crowd. Yet her beautiful face didn't register even the slightest recognition of him as her gaze passed by.

Pricked at the unwitting cut, he tossed back the rest of his wine.

Why *would* she have noticed him, though? She'd seen him without his mask for only a few seconds on a busy footpath two days ago and most likely didn't remember him at all. It was the masked man whom she'd sparred with in the alley and in her bedroom, whom she'd teased and taunted. Not him.

He placed his empty glass onto the tray of a passing footman and snatched up a full one. He needed plenty of drink to get through this evening.

"I'm so glad you're here, Alec." Elizabeth Sinclair sidled gracefully up to him and wrapped her arm through his. She gave him an affectionate squeeze. "It would have been absolutely dreadful without you."

At twenty-three, his sister was in the middle of her fifth London season. And her last. She'd settled on marrying Arthur Mullins, a young bureaucrat currently serving in the Treasury. He was from a good family of landed gentry in Kent and possessed an income large enough to see them settled in comfort, a position that garnered respect, and a promising career ahead of him. What mattered, though, was that Mullins doted on Beth and loved her. Alec expected the man to ask for her hand any day now.

He was happy for her. She'd found the love match he'd long ago given up for himself.

"You would have suffered through the evening just fine without me." He kissed the top of her head as he'd done since she was in braids, then turned his attention back to Miss Everett.

With a bright smile, Olivia curtsied to the Duke and Duchess of Strathmore and to the Duke of Dartmoor who stood with them. Dartmoor, that blackguard, gave her a flirtatious look that made Alec grit his teeth.

Beth followed his gaze. "So who *is* that woman who's wearing my dress?"

Alec grimaced, although she had the right to be curious. After all, she'd helped him in her dressing room at six o'clock that morning, still half-asleep and blurry-eyed, while he'd looked through her clothes to find the perfect dress. One deserving of blackmail. He hadn't shared any details with her, and Beth loved him enough—or had been simply too sleepy—to demand answers.

Until now.

"She's Miss Olivia Everett." When she glanced at him blankly, not recognizing the name, he added, "Manageress of the Everett School in Westminster."

"She's the one you had Mama invite!" Incredulousness rang in her voice as she made the connection, and her mouth fell open. "A *schoolmistress*?"

He slanted an irritated glance at her. "You thought I'd ask Mother to invite a courtesan?"

"Well, no…not exactly." From the tone of her voice, though, that was exactly what his family had expected. At least Beth had the decency to look chagrinned. "But you have to admit"—she gestured at Miss Everett as the woman moved through the room toward the refreshment tables—"a schoolmistress isn't exactly the sort of woman to snag your attention."

"She hasn't, not in the way you're implying." He dismissed that notion by lifting his glass to his lips. "I'm not interested in repressed spinsters."

"Perhaps you should be. It's the repressed ones who go wild when given the chance."

Alec choked on his Madeira. He forced out between coughs, "*Where* did you hear that?"

The little imp had the nerve to look offended. "I'm no longer in the schoolroom, you know. I'm twenty-three, and I know that half the misses at Almack's shouldn't be wearing white."

His eyes narrowed. "Has Mullins ever tried—"

"Goodness, no!" She squeezed his arm again. "I have one of the deadliest dueling shots in all of England for my brother. Arthur is a bit unconventional, but he's not a bedlamite." Her eyes drifted back to Miss Everett as Lady Gantry pulled her into a group of guests. "So why did my rake of a bachelor brother invite to our ball a chaste schoolmistress whom none of us have ever met, and why is she wearing my gown?"

Good God, Beth was worse than a tenacious hound after a fox. "She's wearing your dress, imp," he answered irritably, "because she doesn't own a ball gown and otherwise wouldn't have been able to attend tonight, special invitation or no. And she was sent that invitation because her brother is an expert at mathematics who recently lectured before the Royal Society."

A brother who was being followed by Reed at that very moment in hopes the man would lead them to Scepter tonight while his sister was here. Alec's job was to keep

Olivia Everett out of trouble and learn whatever more he could from her.

"Her brother?" Beth blinked with confusion, his vague explanation not nearly enough to satisfy her. "What does that—"

"She's also a very dedicated, hard-working woman who deserves to spend an evening enjoying herself at a ball. An opportunity she wouldn't otherwise have."

For some reason Alec couldn't name, it rankled him that he and Miss Everett occupied two very different social circles. There was no better reminder of that than the scene in front of him. A wave of his hand took in the ballroom and the sea of sparkling jewels, silk dresses, superfine jackets—hell, the diamond cravat pin worn by the Duke of Dartmoor was worth more than a schoolmistress would earn in ten years.

"You take all this for granted, Beth." When she opened her mouth to protest, he cut her off. "Which is how it should be for the daughter of an earl. But what is a dreadful bore and obligation for you is a fairy tale for her. Why is it so wrong to want to give her this experience?"

"It isn't, I suppose." Her dubious gaze followed Miss Everett as Lady Gantry introduced her to the group. Then they swung sideways to Alec and narrowed suspiciously. "Just very unusual for *you*."

Unusual? He nearly laughed. His sister had no idea just how strange his life had become, with Olivia Everett only one part of it.

He set his glass onto a table behind him. "If you'll excuse me, I have a dance to request."

He slipped away before she could trap him in a new barrage of questions.

As he moved through the ballroom, he nodded to acknowledge the women who smiled at him or called out to get his attention, yet he otherwise ignored them and kept walking. There were dukes and marquesses at the party who outranked him and gentlemen with estates and fortunes that outweighed the Sinclair wealth. But he was the only man present to possess rank, wealth, *and* bachelor status. He was certain Isabel Sinclair had carefully planned her guest list just so to make him even more appealing to the unmarried ladies and their mamas. She could have spared herself the waste of time. He had no intention of considering any of them.

Tonight, his attention rested fully on a spinster schoolmistress.

When he reached Lady Gantry's group, he bowed politely to the women and nodded to the men. He fought down his annoyance that everyone's eyes lit up at his presence.

"St James." Lady Gantry sank into a low curtsy that would have done the regent honors but only served to irritate him with its ingratiating demeanor. "What a pleasure to see you this evening!"

"And you, my lady." Despite himself, he knew his duty, and he accepted her hand to bow over it. "You've been well, I hope."

"Certainly." She sent him a beaming smile and gestured her fan at her husband. "Gantry was just wondering if you'd be present tonight or if you'd escaped to the hells of Covent Garden instead."

"Well, the night is still early." Alec kept his forced smile in place and shot a sideways glance at Lord Gantry. "But duty brings me here." The baron had blocked many of the bills Alec had proposed in the Lords during the last session, done to serve the man's own financial interests rather than for the good of England. "You understand duty, don't you, Gantry?"

"I meant no offense, St James." The man reddened, immediately flustered, but for the wrong reason. "Everyone knows you go out of your way to avoid these events."

Alec smiled lazily in private amusement. "You'd be surprised to learn my true interests."

He didn't dare glance at Miss Everett, although he was aware of her incredulous gaze on him. So…she recognized him now. But who did she think he was—an attendee at the Royal Society or a masked intruder?

"You can't fault Gantry," Charles Langley, Marquess of Hawking, drawled. "I can't remember the last time you attended one of your mother's soirees."

As always, Hawking was impeccably dressed and possessed a dignity befitting his influential position as lord chancellor, second only to the prime minister in parliamentary rank and power. It was a position he'd worked hard to achieve. If the man's bearing weren't so severe and cold, Alec was certain the marriage-minded mamas would have been thrusting their daughters at him tonight. Despite being well into his fourth decade, Hawking was one of England's best catches and even more so since his younger brother had been killed three years ago in the latest war with the Americans. The widowed marquess now had no heir and needed to find a new wife who could give him one to save the title. But few of the young misses seemed eager to dance attendance on him.

From the way Hawking sent lingering glances at Baroness Rowland beside him, perhaps they sensed that the man had already decided on his future wife.

"I'm here to support my sister," Alec explained. "To keep the wolves of English society at bay."

That brought knowing chuckles from the group. Except for Miss Everett, whose gaping surprise had changed into barely concealed irritation.

"St James," Sir George Pittens interrupted impatiently. The portly man belonged to the House of Commons and was always peddling some bill or other of questionable importance. "I'd like to discuss with you the imports bill that was—"

"Let's leave politics in Westminster for the evening, shall we?" Alec smiled to soften his comment, but the last thing he wanted tonight was to be dragged into a political argument.

He turned toward the woman standing beside Hawking. Baroness Rowland held out her hand to him in turn and gave him a pleasant smile that made him believe she was sincere when she said, "It is good to see you again, St James."

"Lady Rowland." He bowed with a flirtatious smile for her and noted Hawking's jealousy from the corner of his eye. "As always, a pleasure."

Finally, he turned fully toward Miss Everett, and his heart stuttered. She was a fresh summer breeze amid the usual boring attendees at his mother's ball. She shouldn't be here, tucked into a corner with matrons and widows, wasting her beauty and brilliance. She should have been with Elizabeth's younger set, letting the men flock around her like sheep going willingly to slaughter for the favor of one of her smiles.

He murmured, "I don't believe we've been introduced."

"Not formally, no," she replied with a bit of bristle.

He couldn't help the grin that teased at his lips. Since she hadn't yet slapped him or screamed, she hadn't recognized him as the masked man. *Good.* But that sharp mind of hers surely realized he'd been responsible for her invitation.

"Oh, how rude of me!" Lady Gantry fanned herself apologetically for not providing a proper introduction. "Your lordship, Earl of St James, may I introduce to you Miss Everett, manageress of the Everett School?"

"Miss Everett." He bowed. "A pleasure."

"Your *lordship*." Enough venom filled that word to match a viper pit. Yet even this little hellcat couldn't cut him at his mother's ball, so she sank begrudgingly into a stiff curtsy. Her lips pressed tightly together, and he was certain she was holding back a scolding litany that would have turned the archbishop blue.

Behind them, the master of ceremonies announced the first waltz of the evening. *Perfect timing.*

He held out his hand. "May I have this dance, Miss Everett?"

Her blue eyes widened. "I don't—I can't..." She shot a desperate look at the others, but none of them came to her rescue. They wouldn't, he knew. Despite his rumored reputation and her spotless one, they wouldn't dare dissuade him, given his rank and wealth. Occasionally, that damned title had its benefits. "I mean—shouldn't you dance the first waltz with your mother, my lord?"

"My mother always grants the first waltz to the Duke of Wembley." Without letting her protest further, he placed her hand on his sleeve and led her toward the dance floor. "And trust me, Miss Everett. My giving the waltz to you will please her far more than my dancing with her."

Consternation hardened her face, but having no choice, she allowed him to lead her onward. He brought her into position as the orchestra sent up its first flourishes.

She stiffened in his arms.

A new concern struck him. If she didn't have a gown to wear, then perhaps… "You *do* know how to waltz?"

"Yes, of course. But I—"

He twirled her into the dance.

She certainly did know how, and she waltzed well as he circled her around the room. She moved with natural grace and elegance as she effortlessly glided across the floor and responded easily to every shift of his body as he led her through the steps. In that satin gown, with her long white gloves and golden hair held up by silver and sapphire combs, she appeared as if she belonged here. Anyone looking at her would never be able to tell that she wasn't a member of the *ton*. Polished. Proper. Controlled.

But what he wouldn't have given for a glimpse of the wild creature who lurked beneath.

"Thank you for the dance, my lord," she said politely,

certainly more to fill the silence between them than from gratitude.

"My pleasure." And it was. He couldn't remember the last time he'd danced with such a graceful partner, one who moved in his arms as if she were made to be there. "Are you enjoying yourself this evening?"

"It's been very…interesting."

He chuckled. She'd meant *him*. "Then I hope the rest of your evening is just as memorable."

She silently studied his profile during their promenade.

His chest tightened. Had she figured out that he was the masked man? The moment she did, everything would change—

"Are you really here because of your sister?" she asked bluntly.

Relief pulsed through him. "Yes." Not a lie. He *was* here because Elizabeth had asked him to attend. *Partially.* "She's the unmarried sister of an earl and possesses a large dowry, and every fortune hunter in London knows it. She finds it comforting to have me here."

"And you're unable to deny her anything."

Not a question, he noted. He nodded as his gaze drifted across the floor to find his sister dancing with his friend Merritt Rivers.

Her eyes followed his. "She's beautiful."

He twirled her through a tight circle. "You remind me of her." He needed to charm Miss Everett into trusting him if he had any chance of gaining any more information. Yet flattering her came easily. And honestly. Beneath the glow of the chandeliers, she was simply… "Beautiful."

"You're wrong, my lord." Her voice emerged surprisingly husky. "We don't look anything alike."

"I do believe, Miss Everett, that you and she are the exact same size." How he was able to keep a straight face, he would never know. "And share the same taste in gowns."

She frowned, obviously noticing that Beth's pink dress looked nothing like her blue one. Yet she let that pass and commented instead, "Your devotion to your sister is admirable."

"So is yours to your brother."

She looked away over his shoulder. "I wondered if you remembered our meeting at the Royal Society."

"How could I have forgotten?" He stared at her mouth as she bit her bottom lip. For a mad moment, he wanted to swoop down and capture that lip between his own teeth, right there in the middle of the dance floor, and suck at it until it softened. "A brilliant and beautiful woman like you—never."

Her cheeks pinked deliciously. "Your lordship—"

"Alec," he insisted, far too informally. "My name is Alec."

Her pouty little mouth tightened with irritation, yet that only made him want to kiss her even more. "I could never be so familiar with you, my lord."

"A shame." His deep voice lowered an octave into a simmering purr as he pulled her closer in his arms. "Because I certainly want to be far more familiar with you."

Her eyes flared. "The impropriety of what you're—"

"Oh, most likely." He laughed at her consternation and pulled away from her, back to the proper distance. "I've made a habit of avoiding propriety. Just ask my family."

Her eyes darted to his mother as she danced with the Duke of Wembley, an old family friend and widower. A man, Alec had to admit, for whom the countess truly held affection, and he for her. Yet after six years, they were still no closer to matrimony than an occasional waltz. If Alec needed proof that there was no room for love within the peerage, he only had to look at them.

"I don't have to ask them," she replied stiffly. "I've heard of your reputation."

"Baseless rumors." He turned her gracefully in a circle. "Did your brother accompany you this evening?" he asked and changed the conversation into an unwitting interrogation. That was why they were both here, after all. "I'd welcome the opportunity to discuss his work with him."

Her eyes flitted back to his. Their sharp blueness jolted through him, straight down to the tip of his cock. "No, he's at home."

"Some other time, then." He nodded toward the other side of the room. "How do you know Lord and Lady Gantry and the others?"

"They're patrons of the school."

"Ah, yes. Lady Gantry said you were a manageress...of what school, again?" He feigned ignorance. The masked man knew about the school, but the Earl of St James didn't. Maintaining a double identity was damnably confusing, especially when holding her in his arms made it difficult to think straight.

"The Everett School for the Education of Proper Young Ladies. My brother and I run it."

"Perhaps I should consider making a donation." A thoughtful pause—"The mathematics theories your brother presented…are they related to his work with the school?"

"No, they're not." She looked over his shoulder and grumbled, "Why is everyone suddenly so interested in Henry's work?"

He asked carefully, "Are they?"

"Well, yes—Lord Hawking, you, and that…" She flushed. "That other man."

"What other man?"

"No one important." She unwittingly repeated back to him the masked man's words from last night.

He fought down a chuckle at the irony. "What did you tell them?"

"That my brother's work does not interest me beyond sisterly love and admiration."

A lie. A grand one. But she told it with such conviction that he wondered what other dark secrets she might be capable of keeping that he—

"Why did you ask me to dance, my lord?"

The blunt question surprised him, and he forced a flirtatious smile. "Alec," he corrected, despite knowing her frown would only deepen. Which it did. "Because the waltz was beginning, I needed a dance partner, and you look lovely."

"Please don't dissemble with me." Every inch of her now showed the no-nonsense school manageress she was by day. But he longed for the alluring woman he'd glimpsed at night.

"All right, then. Because I wanted an excuse to leave the group…the waltz was beginning, I needed a dance partner, and you look lovely," he cheekily repeated. "How's that for the truth?"

But the irritated expression on her pretty face announced she still wasn't pleased. "I have no idea how I was placed on tonight's guest list, but you obviously remembered who I was from our meeting at the Royal Society and know that I don't typically attend events like this."

He was tempted to tell her exactly how she was placed on that list and how she came to be wearing that dress, too, just to see her stunned reaction. But he knew better. Tonight was about the Home Office's mission, and he wouldn't betray Reed or Clayton because of a face. Not even one this beautiful.

"You also know I'm not the sort of woman who dances with earls."

He stiffened, all amusement vanishing. Her self-deprecation grated. "What sort would that be?"

"A schoolmistress," she answered, and in her irritation with him, he felt her fingers unconsciously tighten in his. "A woman without position or fortune, with no social standing of any kind except for what people like Lord and Lady Gantry grant me." Her lips pressed together grimly. "You might as well have asked the footman to dance with you."

He shook his head. "Thomas would have wanted to lead, and he doesn't look at all becoming in satin." When she opened her mouth for an angry retort, he interrupted, "But you are simply stunning in yours."

A heated blush darkened her cheeks and made her eyes grow even bluer, her hair even more golden. The flush continued down her front and beneath her bodice toward her breasts. He very much wanted to follow it, to see how far down her lovely body it strayed.

"You are the most beautiful woman at this ball," he murmured. Did that blush extend all the way to her nipples? Were those sweet tips just as rosy as her cheeks? "A man would have to be a fool to pass up the opportunity to hold you in his arms."

"And *I* would have to be a fool to fall for such flattery." She stopped dancing as the music ended, then dropped into a stiff curtsy. "I won't be toyed with, my lord, even by an earl."

"Never fear, Miss Everett." He bowed over her hand. "I have no intention of toying with you."

No. He wanted to devour her whole.

He placed her hand lightly on his sleeve and led her back toward Lady Gantry. Beside him, she walked with her spine straight as a ramrod. She wanted to look prudish and aloof, he knew, but unwittingly only succeeded in looking regal and even more fit to grace the arm of an earl. Whispers scattered among the crowd as they passed through the room, and she earned herself another curious glance from the Duke of Dartmoor.

Alec scowled. The damnable rake needed to find himself a wife.

"I didn't recognize your name when we met on the street, but I've heard of you," she said in a low voice so no one could overhear. "You have a certain reputation, my lord."

"Alec," he insisted, matching her same low, measured tone. "And what reputation would that be, Olivia?"

"A disreputable one." She frowned. "And please do not call me by my Christian name."

"Ah, but that's what we disreputable gentlemen do, I'm afraid." Out of the corner of his eye, he saw his mother's curious stare at the woman on his arm. "We become far too familiar with beautiful ladies. We flatter. We flirt—"

"You seduce."

She said that with such disdain, such boldness, even for a private conversation, that he bit back a laugh. She had no idea of the truth about him!

"Is that what you want, Olivia?" he murmured, unable to help himself. "For me to seduce you?"

"I'd rather be thrown to the wolves."

He murmured wickedly, "Same thing."

The pink in her cheeks blossomed into scarlet. Amazing…he never knew that a woman could turn so red so quickly. Her reaction intrigued him. If she blushed so deeply from only a casual innuendo, what would she do beneath a determined touch?

She yanked her hand away as if he'd burned her and turned to leave.

"Wait." He took her elbow from behind and stopped her, then lowered his head over her shoulder to bring his mouth as close to her ear as he dared and said, "Give me another chance." The husky tone of his voice softened the order into a request. "Dance with me again tonight."

"No."

The bluntness of that brought him up short. "Afraid people will gossip if we share a second dance?"

"Look around you." Her slender shoulders slumped. "They're already gossiping."

He stiffened. Was that a flicker of pain in her eyes? But before he could discern for certain, she curtsied deeply to him. An unequivocal signal that their conversation was over.

So was any chance he had to learn more about her brother and the building plans.

"My apologies," he offered sincerely. "I didn't mean to—"

"Thank you for the honor of the waltz, my lord." The mask of propriety once again veiled her face, and she walked away.

Biting back a curse, he stalked across the room toward the refreshments table. He needed a drink, but his mother served nothing stronger than Madeira tonight, sorely tempting him to bribe a footman to smuggle out brandy from his study.

Christ. His plan to charm her wasn't working. He'd had better luck getting information from her while she'd been blackmailing him.

He glanced across the room at Lord Liverpool. The prime minister was always a welcome visitor at St James House. Tonight, he was also a stark reminder of how little Alec had learned about Scepter's plot and how far he was from stopping them from attempting to kill the man again.

A faint commotion near the entrance caught Alec's attention. Captain Reed. Not bothering to be introduced—and not invited in the first place—Reed waved away the master of ceremonies and ignored the whispers that went up around him as he approached Alec through the crowd, which parted almost magically to let him pass.

Reed reached him and nodded curtly. "Sinclair."

"Captain." It wasn't lost on Alec that Reed had purposefully used his family name and not his title. Or that his half brother's unexpected presence at his mother's ball set far more tongues wagging than Alec's waltz with a schoolmistress.

But when Alec nodded toward him in greeting—and didn't either call the footmen to toss out Rupert Sinclair's bastard son or attempt to do it himself—the guests lost interest, and their whispers died away.

"Good God," Reed muttered with a scowl at the crush of bodies, noise, and heat of the ball. "How can you stand these affairs?"

"I usually don't. But tonight, I have good reason to tolerate it." Alec snatched up a glass of wine from the table and surreptitiously gestured across the room with it. "Our mission."

Reed followed the movement to Olivia. "Have you learned anything more from her?"

"The night's still early," he dodged and lifted the glass to his lips. The last thing he wanted to do was admit to his half brother that he was failing his part of the mission, that he still had no idea why either of the Everetts would provide mathematical equations and building plans to Scepter or what the group planned to do with them. "You have news?"

Grimly, Reed shook his head. "Everett went out, just as we'd expected. But I lost him in the City when he ducked into an abandoned building. I went in after him and found a hidden passageway in the cellar that he used to get away."

Damnation.

"We did learn something, though." Reed ignored a pair of ladies who sent him flirtatious looks as they strolled past. Judging from the blank expression on his face, the two misses hadn't tempted him in the least, although as the handsome hero of the Battle of Toulouse, he could have had his pick of women. "When Clayton and I were watching the school, a lad of about thirteen delivered a message to Everett. Clayton decided we should question him."

"Question?" Alec raised a brow.

"We threw a sack over his head, stuffed him into a carriage to frighten the daylights out of him, then asked him what he knew about Everett."

"A typical Home Office interrogation, then," Alec drawled dryly and took a sip of wine.

Reed ignored that except for a slight clenching of his jaw. "The boy was a runaway apprentice who was given a coin for memorizing and delivering the message. He'd never before seen the man who hired him, and he wasn't given a name."

"And what was the message?"

"One word—'Midnight.'"

Alec stared into his glass as he swirled the wine. If Everett already knew the location of the meeting, all he would need to be summoned was the time. And that meant— "Everett isn't one of the leaders."

"No. He's only a foot soldier."

His eyes narrowed on Olivia as he muttered, "Whose orders is he following, then?"

Reed shook his head. "The lad claimed he knew other

boys who'd been hired to deliver similar messages. I'm going to track some of them down tonight. Maybe I can put together enough of a description to identify him."

Alec wasn't certain Reed would learn anything. Whoever was leading Scepter clearly trusted no one, not even men like Everett who were working for them. Yet Alec said nothing to contradict Reed's plan. After all, it was the only one they had.

"I'll leave you to your quadrilles, then." Reed cast a disdainful glance around the room. "Places like this aren't for me."

Alec eyed the man. Young and handsome, a dashing army officer, the hero of Toulouse who had single-handedly saved two dozen women and children... "You're still in the Guards. Aren't you required to attend functions like this to stir up good relations with the War Department?"

"I'm not part of this world."

And don't want to be. The words hung between them as clearly as if Reed had spoken them.

His gaze darted back to Alec—hazel eyes that eerily matched his own. "I'll check in with Clayton to see if he's made any progress on uncovering the Home Office mole."

Alec nodded grimly, hoping Clayton had. Their mission was at a crucial point and not going well. If Henry Everett knew he was being followed, he might never surface again except as a dead body in the Thames.

Alec's own plans to charm information from Olivia had also come to nothing. After that waltz, she'd never again allow herself to be alone with him so he could question her privately. Unless...

An idea struck him.

"I'll join you and Clayton later tonight to look for Everett," Alec assured Reed. "But there's something I need your help with first."

"What?"

Alec nodded across the room at Olivia. "Her."

He explained his plan, and Reed gaped at him as if he were mad. Perhaps he was, but it was also his best chance for gaining more information from her tonight. His *only* chance.

Yet Reed nodded his agreement to the scheme and sauntered over to the punch table.

As he walked away, Isabel Sinclair approached through the crowd. She took Alec's elbow tightly, with her gaze fixed on Reed. "Isn't that…Captain Reed?"

"Yes." Alec frowned. Few things in this world rattled his mother, especially when she was in her element like tonight. Yet Reed's unexpected appearance seemed to have done just that, right down to her shaking fingers on his arm and her sudden pallor. But then she didn't cross paths with her late husband's bastard son every day.

"Why is he here?"

"He had some information for me." Not technically a lie, he supposed, but it was safer to keep his family as far away from the mission as possible. "Don't worry. He won't cause a scene." Although his mere presence here was enough to do that by itself. Even now, whispers and curious stares sped like a wave through the house.

"No, of course not." She watched Reed select a glass of punch.

Alec placed his hand over hers on his sleeve. "I know it's unnerving for you to encounter him like this." At her own ball, no less. "But we've all known for nearly two years that he was assigned to London." For God's sake, Aunt Agnes had chastised Wellington himself just last month for not giving Reed the field promotion he deserved at Toulouse, and Elizabeth kept asking Alec about their half brother and if she would ever be able to meet him. "He wants nothing from our family except to be left alone. I'm certain tonight will be his one and only visit here."

"It's just that... I've been thinking..."

"Yes?"

She shook her head. "Nothing." She waved away whatever it was she was about to say with a nervous flick of her wrist. "It's nothing." She forced a smile and released his arm. "I just didn't realize that you and he knew each other."

"Only recently."

"And you're...on friendly terms?"

"We're civil."

That small admission brought color back to her face and faded the odd mix of worry and guilt lingering there. "Enjoy your evening, then. We're all so very glad you're here, Alexander."

She placed a kiss to his cheek. He didn't move away to avoid her touch, but the old pain resurfaced. How had she not known what Rupert Sinclair had done to him?

"Remember to dance with your aunt," she called out as she retreated into the crush. "None of the other gentlemen are brave enough to reel with her."

That was the God's truth, although Alec didn't blame them.

Instead of looking for his aunt, though, he set down his unwanted glass and slipped quickly through the room to find Beth.

His sister stood surrounded by a group of young gentlemen and ladies, the brightest star of the bunch. She laughed and smiled at all of them, but her hand rested lovingly on Arthur Mullins's sleeve.

Alec sidled up to Beth and lowered his lips close to her ear. "I sincerely apologize."

She frowned, puzzled. "Whatever for?"

"I am about to ruin your dress."

She blinked in confusion. "Pardon?"

On the other side of the ballroom, Reed threw his glass of punch at Olivia.

Eight

RUINED! ALL OF IT…JUST *RUINED*.

Olivia stared at her reflection in the full-length mirror in the retiring room as hot tears of humiliation stung at her eyes. Having removed her gloves before she could stain those, too, she dabbed futilely with a cloth at the large red spot that covered her front.

The dress was completely ruined. Most likely so was any remaining chance she had of finding new patrons for the school. She certainly couldn't go back into the party looking like this! Her night at the ball had come to an end—a splashing, punchy end.

Her shoulders sagged. She'd been enjoying herself tonight, too. Even that waltz hadn't dampened her excitement of being at such a grand ball…until everyone had seen her humiliation over the spill, including that blasted Earl of St James. From the way he'd seemed to delight in her ill luck when that man flung his punch at her, it was as if the scoundrel had found a way to *cause* it.

Oh, the gall of that man! Obsequious with his compliments, oozing charm, flashing his smile—that routine might work with less unyielding women, but *she* refused to fall for a rogue like St James. Not again. The first time had nearly destroyed her life and all she'd loved. A second time... Well, she wouldn't survive it.

"At least I'll never have to encounter him again," she whispered reassuringly to herself. After all, earls didn't frequent girls' schools or any of the places she normally visited, and after her humiliation tonight, she doubted anyone would ever again make the mistake of accidentally putting her name on their guest list.

The door opened. Olivia glanced up to see Lady Rowland slip into the room with a concerned expression.

The young widow was beautiful, Olivia couldn't deny it. Her sable hair had been pulled into a bounty of loose curls on her crown, and her eyes, which matched her forest-green dress, dazzled almost as much as the gold locket at her throat. *She* was the sort of woman with whom the Earl of St James should have been spending his time.

Olivia glanced back at her punch-stained reflection. *Not me.*

The baroness asked sympathetically, "Can I offer any assistance?"

"I'm afraid it's beyond salvaging." Olivia pulled at the bodice where the red punch had turned the blue satin purple, then gave a disappointed sigh. "And so is my evening."

Lady Rowland squeezed her arm.

"It was an accident," Olivia whispered, unable to speak any louder for fear of sobbing openly. "That man didn't mean to spill his drink on me." Although, at the time, Olivia was certain he'd been aiming straight for her. Her heart broke as she choked out, "But it was such a beautiful dress."

"Maybe it can still be saved," the baroness suggested helpfully. "My maid uses soda ash to treat stains. I can ask one of the footmen to bring some from the kitchen."

Tears of gratitude blurred her vision, even though Olivia doubted it would work. "Thank you."

"Why don't you take off your dress to make it easier to clean?" Lady Rowland gestured toward a screen in the corner of the room before dashing toward the door. "I'll be right back. Wait here."

Olivia glanced into the mirror, and the stain glared angrily back. *Wait here?* Where had the baroness expected her to go looking like this? She bit her quavering lip. She didn't even have a cape to cover herself for the ride home, having brought with her tonight only a small shawl that barely covered her shoulders.

With no choice but to do as Lady Rowland asked, she stepped behind the screen. She managed to unfasten the buttons down her back after a series of twisting contortions, and then she kicked off her slippers, stepped out of the dress, and tossed it over the top of the screen. The satin material was thick enough that her shift and corset were undamaged, and relief swept through her that they'd escaped the punch. She'd lied to the masked man when he'd been searching her dresser. She *didn't* have a drawer full of shifts and stays; in truth, she owned less than a handful, and these two old things were her best.

She heard the door open.

"That was quick," she called out, then stepped out from behind the screen. "I would have thought—" She looked up and gasped.

The Earl of St James leaned casually back against the closed door.

"You." She angrily slapped her hands on her hips in the same pose she took with misbehaving girls at the school.

He lazily trailed his gaze over her front, which was hidden only by the thin layer of undergarments that scooped down low across her breasts and barely reached her knees. He arched an appreciative brow. "And...*you*."

With a shocked cry of embarrassment, she dove back behind the screen, only for her cry to transform into a low curse at his deeply amused chuckle. *Just wonderful.* Could she be any more humiliated tonight?

"Leave!" she ordered through clenched teeth. "Go back to the party where you belong."

"But it's so much more entertaining in here."

She reached for the dress so she could scramble back into it and salvage whatever trace amounts of her dignity remained. But the satin slipped through her fingertips as he pulled it away from the other side of the screen.

She made a desperate grab but missed. "Give that back!"

"Sweet Lucifer, that's a big stain," he murmured, as if surprised himself at the damage one glass of punch could do.

"Please, go! If anyone finds us together—"

"No one will find us."

"You can't guarantee—"

"I locked the door."

"You locked..." She darted around the side of the screen and pointed a stern finger at the door. "Well, *unlock* it!"

He clucked his tongue. "And risk someone coming inside to find you undressed? I think not."

His hazel eyes traveled slowly over her again, and this time, she refused to cower. Mustering as much decorum as she could scrape together, she lifted her chin and bravely stood her ground, even when his gaze lingered at her breasts, thrust up by her corset. The dress's bodice had been just a little too small, so she'd had to lace up far tighter than normal. But no one except Mrs. Adams should have seen—

Oh, fate was surely laughing at her!

"Undressed with *you*, my lord," she warned, an idea striking her. "Surely, you wouldn't risk a situation that might force you in front of a priest."

"Not if the door's locked." He smiled confidently, as if he locked himself into rooms with half-dressed women all the time. For all Olivia knew, he probably did just that. "At my mother's balls, half the rooms are locked by the first waltz by couples seeking their own privacy. No one trying this room would think anything amiss."

"But Lady Rowland is due back any moment and knows I'm inside." *And undressed.*

"The baroness is a friend who won't mind leaving if I ask."

Drat him! She clenched her hands at her sides. "Someone could have seen you enter."

"The hallway was empty. Besides, it's my house." He took a step toward her, the ruined dress dangling from his hand. "No one would give me a second glance wherever I roamed."

"Convenient," she muttered. Dear heavens, she was trapped with him! Yet she wasn't afraid. She was furious.

"I don't make the rules." A half grin crooked his mouth. "I just enjoy them."

"*Why* are you bothering me?" She scowled in aggravation and crossed her arms.

Instantly, she knew that was a mistake because the posture only worked to thrust up her breasts even higher. His half grin blossomed into a full-out smile. Infuriating man!

She pointed at her face to lift his attention from her breasts. "Eye contact, if you please."

"Pity." He sighed with exaggerated disappointment. He met her gaze as she'd requested, but his eyes gleamed with wickedness.

She let out a frustrated groan and dropped her hands to her sides. "You are the most exasperating man I've ever—"

"Yes." He gave another sigh with even more exaggerated disappointment than before. "Yes, I am."

She wanted to grab him and shake him hard! "Please give back my dress."

He looked aghast at the idea. "I can't let you put this ruined thing back on."

"You're an earl," she reminded him as her shoulders sagged in defeat. "At least be a gentleman and give me your jacket to cover myself."

Something dark flickered in his eyes. "I *am* an earl." His voice lowered. "But don't confuse that with being a gentleman."

His warning twisted down her spine and spawned a shiver in its wake, one that left her stunned and breathless. Yet he shed his black kerseymere jacket and handed it to her.

When she slipped it on, she could still feel the heat of his body clinging to the material, just as she could smell the masculine scent of him, of cigars and port, bergamot, and… and something else she couldn't quite place but breathed in deeply. The jacket engulfed her small shoulders, and when she pulled it closed across her front, the long cut of the tails covered her down to midthigh. *Thank heavens.*

Now that she was covered, his gaze returned to her face. Rather, to her chagrin, it focused on her mouth.

"What do you want with me, my lord?" she demanded and did her best to ignore the heat blossoming at her lips beneath his stare.

He rakishly arched a brow.

She caught her breath at her mistake. "I-I didn't mean—" Oh, the devil take him! "I did *not* mean it that way."

"What way?" He feigned innocence.

She gritted her teeth and clenched his lapels so tightly in her hands that she feared she might rip them from his jacket. She had no intention of answering *that*.

He chuckled, although she couldn't have said whether at her or himself. "My intentions are pure, I assure you." Then the mocking left his voice. "You fled the ballroom. I wanted to make certain you were unharmed. That's all."

Ha! *That* was a lie if ever she heard one. He could have sent his sister to check on her, or Lady Gantry, or one of the dozen other women who were falling all over themselves to catch his attention this evening. Yet he'd come after her himself.

But why? He knew well enough already that she wouldn't

be swayed by the charms of a rake. Even such an attractive one.

She arched a brow. "Am I truly supposed to believe that you're a gentleman and not the blackguard your reputation claims?"

"My reputation is exaggerated."

Olivia didn't believe that for a second. "So you haven't done all the things they're gossiping about in the ballroom?"

"Oh, I've done them. So have all the other gentlemen in attendance tonight." He reached past her to toss the dress over the screen. Instead of stepping back, he placed his palm flat against the screen at her shoulder and lowered his head until his face was level with hers. "The difference, Miss Everett, is that I've done nothing to hide my activities."

She pushed at his shoulder to make him step back, but the frustrating man didn't move. "You're proud of being a rake?"

"I'm proud of living my life honestly, and recently that includes living it respectably, despite what the gossips believe. That also includes managing my fortune, maintaining my estates, taking care of my family..." A mischievous gleam sparked in the depths of his eyes. "And occasionally asking beautiful women to dance."

Her stomach pinched. He was standing over her the same way the masked man had in the alley, and she couldn't help but make comparisons. The two men were alike in build, with the same muscular shoulders and broad chests. But that was where all similarities ended.

She much preferred her masked man to *him*.

"Why me?" She was exasperated and wanted nothing more than for him to leave. And to leave her alone. "I'm not an heiress or a fashionable widow. I'm not even supposed to be here tonight. My invitation was a mistake."

"It wasn't."

She froze, just long enough to feel her heartbeat hammer against her ribs. "Then why?"

"You intrigue me."

"*I* intrigue *you*?" A strangled laugh of disbelief tore from her before she could stop it.

"You're a contradiction, Miss Everett. A puzzle. You've put yourself on the shelf in dedication to your school, yet you're alluring enough to find a suitable husband. You let your brother take credit for your work—"

She shook her head. "My brother's work is—"

"Of no interest to you, I know," he finished, repeating her earlier lie back to her. "Yet you lingered in the lecture hall just to correct his equations." He added huskily, "As I said… an intriguing contradiction."

He reached down to take her hand and brushed his fingertips over hers, as if expecting to find chalk dust there.

She slipped her hand away. But he held tightly enough that his fingertips caressed across her palm as he released her, and a shiver sparked up her arm.

She didn't like him. She did *not* like him— Damn those goose bumps on her arm!

He touched one of the tendrils of her hair that had fallen free of her combs and curled it around his finger. "Every other innocent miss would have fainted the moment she realized I'd seen her in her shift," he murmured. "But not you."

"I would never faint in front of a scoundrel." She meant the words to chastise, but they emerged as a throaty hum. She scowled at herself. She did *not* like him!

"I'm not nearly the scoundrel you think." He released her curl, but instead of dropping his hand away, he brushed his fingers down her neck. "But your contradictions make you the most interesting lady at tonight's ball." He traced his fingers over the hollow at the base of her throat, where her pulse raced uncontrollably. "So which contradiction will win, Olivia—do you want me to think of you as an untouchable schoolmistress, or do you want to be kissed?"

He was so close that the warmth of his body heated down her front, and she could smell the spicy, masculine scent of him, of port and cigars, leather and... "Lemons?"

He tilted his head. "Pardon?"

She frowned. The fragrant memory was fuzzy, remaining just beyond her grasp as his nearness fogged her mind. "You smell like lemons."

"Do I?" His mouth lingered so close to hers that his warm breath tickled her lips. "Would you like to find out if I taste like lemons, too?"

She should cry out, scream, slap him—

Yet she couldn't find the will to do any of that. A traitorous part of her *did* want to know how those sensuous lips tasted, how they would feel against hers.

Why this man should raise her curiosity in such a primal way she had no idea. He'd done nothing but threaten the peaceful existence she'd worked so hard to create for herself, the proper reputation she guarded like a treasure. He saw her as nothing more than a toy to be played with, a mouse to be batted around by a—

Oh.

Dear.

God.

Her breath ripped from her stunned lungs. He couldn't be—he simply *could not* be! It was impossible. But her mind replayed every word, every move and gesture, every grin and laugh... *She knew*.

And she felt like a fool.

She ducked beneath his arm and slipped behind the screen. She grabbed the dress before he could snatch it away again, ripped off his jacket, and yanked the gown over her head and into place. The reeking punch sickened her nearly as much as realizing his true identity, and she swallowed in great gulps of air to calm herself. Heavens, she couldn't reach the buttons at her back! Fabric ripped as she twisted to fasten up as many of them as possible, but the tears couldn't be helped. She needed to leave, to flee from him—*now*.

"If I've offended you, I apologize," he called out quietly to her, suddenly and surprisingly contrite. "I only wanted to know you better."

He knew her *more* than well enough. He'd looked through her intimates drawer, for heaven's sake! And now she could just picture his tall, solid body leaning against the wall beside the screen, with muscular arms folded over his broad chest, ankles crossed casually, a lock of chestnut hair falling boyishly over his forehead that the mask had covered before... *Damn him!*

When she stepped from behind the screen, he snapped up straight at the fury that seethed unchecked from her.

"Never." Blinking hard and desperate to cling to whatever shreds of dignity she had left, she jabbed her chin into the air. "I will *never* let that happen."

"Olivia," he whispered, stunned by the change in her. "What's the—"

She fled before he could stop her.

Nine

ALEC KEPT TO THE SHADOWS AS HE RAN DOWN THE dark alley behind the row of terrace houses. He could have ridden his horse, he supposed. Hell, he could have had his grooms hitch up the St James carriage and driven right through Westminster for the lack of attention such a sight would have brought. But tonight, he felt caged and restless. He wanted to be part of the night, so he'd struck out on foot. He also needed to burn off the frustration of not seeing any trace of Henry Everett tonight. And of seeing too much of Olivia.

With a quiet curse, he jumped a puddle and hurried on.

Olivia Everett was an absolute conundrum. She was brilliant enough to have worked the equations on the building plans herself, and Alec couldn't shake the fact that the name on the charred slip of paper could just as easily have been hers as her brother's.

But she hadn't been with the assassins in the warehouse, he knew that in his gut. Her never-break-the-rules propriety wouldn't have stood for it. After all, assassination simply wasn't proper.

Yet she'd frustrated him at every turn, and not just with the mission. She'd not softened at all beneath his flattery and

flirtations tonight. He'd never before met a woman as aggravating, challenging, maddening...*alluring*.

It was time to stop playing games.

So once more, he'd donned his black clothes and
satin mask to sneak through the back alleys at the edge of
Westminster. This time when he entered her room, there
would be no blackmail, no flirtations. He planned on thor-
oughly interrogating her to secure all the information he
needed. Then he would never have to be bothered with her
again.

He stopped, glanced up and down the alley to make certain no one was there to see him, and easily scrambled over
a stone wall into the school's service yard. Crouching low
in the shadows, he crossed to the back of the house where
he silently pried open the lock on the rear door and slipped
inside.

He made his way through the dark and quiet school to
Olivia's room in the attic garret. Her door was unlocked.
With a smile, he entered—

"Good evening," a soft voice called out.

He froze. Olivia sat in a chair in front of the fire, her legs
tucked under her until all that showed were the tips of her
bare toes. She was wide awake.

And waiting for him.

He closed the door and leaned back against it. Then he
glanced around the room for the trap he suspected she'd set
for him.

He forced a smile. "You're home from the ball already?"
He knew she'd left—rather, *Alec* knew, but the masked

man didn't. Good Lord, his life was becoming damnably confusing.

"The evening ended early for me." She gestured toward the gown she'd hung on the armoire door. The red punch stain glared like a purple bruise. "I've ruined the dress."

She ruined it? No, Reed and he had, and a twinge of guilt at spoiling her ball pricked him.

"I'll find a way to repay you for it," she offered. Then bit her bottom lip. "Somehow."

"No need." The twinge of guilt turned into a piercing stab. "I'm certain it was an accident."

"Are you? Because I'm not." She glanced regretfully toward the dress. "Still, I'd planned on returning it to you. But now…"

"The dress is yours. You blackmailed me for it fair and square."

Her lips curled wryly, but something warned him that she wasn't amused. As she sat there in her white dressing gown, her blond hair cascading loose around her shoulders and her blue eyes bright, she looked like an angel.

An angel he didn't trust one whit.

He asked cautiously, "How did you know I'd return tonight?"

"I didn't know," she answered, "but I suspected. Something tells me you haven't gotten everything you want from me yet."

Everything he wanted… His cock jumped. What he wanted from this most proper woman was hours and hours of completely *im*proper distraction. Hell, he'd even let the chit lecture him on arches and bridges if she wanted to. As long as she was naked.

He cleared his throat and dragged his focus back to his mission. "Not yet."

"Well, it must be something very important or you wouldn't be bothering with me."

She had no idea how important. "Perhaps I simply find you interesting."

She gave a gentle laugh of disbelief.

He resisted the urge to cross the room to her, knowing that would only lead to trouble. "The punch stain aside," he asked, "did you enjoy yourself at the ball?"

"No," she said bluntly. "Thanks to the Earl of St James."

He feigned ignorance. "Who?"

"Alexander Sinclair, Earl of St James." She picked at an invisible speck on her dressing gown. "Oh, I'm certain you know him. He's a perfectly horrid man who forced me to waltz with him."

Shame squeezed his chest.

"That's unfair of me." She shook her head. "He isn't horrid so much as difficult…shameless, vexing, arrogant, self-important…" She shrugged, but her hard gaze never left him. "A cad."

"I'm sorry to hear that." *Very sorry.* "Was he inappropriate with you? Did he touch you?" Good Lord, he sounded jealous of himself. "You said he forced you to dance with him."

She smiled as if he'd said something amusing. "A lady can't refuse an earl, no matter how much she wants to."

That stung. "And you wanted to refuse him?"

"Yes."

He shifted awkwardly. This conversation was making him damnably uncomfortable. "He's a bore?"

"Not at all."

"Hideously scarred and missing a leg, then."

He thought he saw her eyes sparkle, but it could have been a trick of the firelight. "He's quite handsome, actually."

Handsome. *That* was better. "Well, then—"

"But he's also disreputable," she interrupted. "Rumors follow him everywhere he goes, and the gossipy old hens cackle constantly about all the women he's seduced, the bets he's wagered, the drunken orgies—"

"Orgies?" *Christ.* His reputation was worse than he'd thought.

"For someone like him to choose me for the first waltz…" She shrugged a slender shoulder. "Well, everyone was thinking it."

"Thinking what?" he prompted despite himself. The picture she was painting of him wasn't at all one he could be proud of, even if most of it was wrong. Yet he couldn't deny any of it without giving himself away.

"That the Earl of St James would give the first waltz to someone like me only because he planned on bedding me." Her voice lowered with embarrassment. "Or already had."

Every soft word stabbed into him as if she'd gone after him with her carving knife after all.

"My reputation is all I have, and he placed it in jeopardy tonight. It was a shame, really," she added remorsefully, "because I did like his intelligence and wit, and I really did enjoy dancing with him. Had he been anyone else—like you—I might have had a perfectly marvelous time."

With that, the knife stabbed straight into his heart.

She rose from the chair and picked up the iron poker to stir the fire. The small flames bit into the last pieces of coal. "But I don't think you're here to hear about the ball or my opinion of St James."

As she returned the poker and faced him, she pulled back her shoulders and rubbed her hands down her robe. That was battle preparation if ever he'd seen it. Then she slowly approached him.

Alec pulled himself up straight. She was behaving oddly, suddenly confident and bold. She'd never been afraid of him, not even in the alleyway when he'd saved her from those toughs, but always before, she'd hesitated to approach him. Now, he couldn't see a trace of trepidation in her anywhere.

He stood still as a statue when she lifted her hand to touch his mask. Oh, she was behaving *very* oddly, yet when she trailed her fingers along the side of his face, he didn't have the resolve to stop her.

She caressed the black satin. "Why do you wear this?"

"It's romantic," he replied sardonically. Then he swallowed. Hard. The heat of her fingertips seeped through the satin and into his skin, and he fought down the tremble that threatened to rise at her touch.

"That's not it."

His eyes held hers, and their blue depths shimmered in the firelight. "It's erotic, then."

"That's not it either." This time, her voice held a throaty edge.

"Because it's necessary." That was the God's truth. "People in masks can do all kinds of things that people can't otherwise do. They can break laws, learn secrets, and take part in wicked pleasures, and no one will ever know."

"That's deceitful."

He couldn't deny that. He'd pledged to live his life out in the open, warts and all, refusing to hide beneath a blanket of lies and secrecy the way his father had. Until she'd come along. For the first time, doubts pricked at him, although he couldn't have said with certainty why. She made it hard to think straight.

Straight? When she brushed her fingers through the hair at his temple, he lost all thought completely.

She arched a brow, seemingly unaware of the effect she had on him, of the tightening of his gut and the tingling at his crotch. "And here I thought it was to hide your identity, *my lord.*"

Alec froze. *Oh damn…*

"After all, it wouldn't do to let London society know that the Earl of St James accosts unmarried misses in dark alleyways."

Damn, damn, damn! He ground out, "I didn't accost you. I saved you." He pushed her hand away and yanked off the mask. His jaw clenched. "How did you figure it out?"

"Lemons."

"*Lemons?*" Of all the stuff and nonsense—

"You smell like lemons, my lord. I'd only met you without a mask once before tonight, for a short time outside the Royal Society. Every other time, you'd worn that mask, and it was in the dark. You even disguised your voice. But you couldn't hide your scent, my lord."

Alec gritted his teeth. Damn all of her *my lords*! And damn his valet. The blasted man squeezed lemon juice into his bath because he said it cut the smell of horse, cigar smoke, and cheap perfume that followed him home. Leave it to Olivia to notice.

"So why don't we start again, shall we?" She took a step back and folded her arms across her chest in challenge. "That is, now that I know who you are."

"Disappointed?" he drawled.

She haughtily sniffed. "In which man?"

He bit back the devilish urge to ask her which man she'd wanted more to appear in her bedroom tonight, the masked man or him—

Good God, he *was* jealous of himself!

"No," she admitted with a shake of her head, her posture softening but not yielding. "I'm not disappointed."

He took more satisfaction from that than he had a right to.

"Not completely."

His mouth twisted. "Glad to hear."

"But *why*? Why did you go to such lengths to hide your identity? Why did you follow me into that alley, then sneak into my room and search my things?" She pulled in a deep breath and repeated the question she'd pressed upon him at the ball—"What do you want with me?"

This time, he found the question not at all amusing. He studied her closely. Could he trust her with the truth? She wasn't a traitor; he'd bet his right arm on that. But how far would she go to protect her brother, who very likely was?

If he lost her trust, though, the mission would be over. With Everett leading them on a wild goose chase every time he left the school, the challenging woman standing so defiantly in front of him was their only way forward.

He blew out a harsh breath. "Because you wouldn't have believed the truth."

"Try me."

"All right." He fixed his gaze on hers. "I've been working to prevent a group of revolutionaries from overthrowing the government."

She laughed. "Oh, that's funny!"

When he didn't join in the laughter, the sound choked in her throat. Even in the dim firelight, he saw her pale.

"A group of..." Her eyes widened. "You're *mad*!"

He swept a slow look over her and felt the frustration coil in his gut. "Quite possibly." More so with every aching moment he spent in her company. "And yet I've agreed to find those men and stop them. The same men who've recruited your brother's help."

Her mouth fell open. From the way she stared, she might scream yet. "Henry would *never* work with traitors!"

"Perhaps not freely. Perhaps not even knowingly." He was willing to grant her this hopeful bit of solace until the mission proved otherwise. "But I've seen the evidence myself. There's no mistake. Your brother's connected to those men." The question was how. What did a mathematician have to do with the bombing?

"That's why you were in the alley, at the lecture, at the ball..." she whispered. "You've been following me."

"I was assigned to you," he admitted somberly. There was no point lying to her. "Your brother had disappeared, and I'd followed you into the City, hoping you'd lead me to him. When I saw you were in trouble, I intervened." He grimaced. "You were never supposed to have known I was watching you. That's why I wore the mask."

"Then why are you still wearing it? Did you plan to continue to deceive me to get the information you wanted?"

"No," he said firmly, as much to convince himself as her. "I planned on telling you tonight."

She gave him an icy glare. "Before or after you saw me in my undergarments?"

Jesus, when she put it like that... "*That* wasn't planned."

Her eyes flickered with disbelief and anger. "It must have been difficult for you to keep a straight face when you were introduced to me tonight." There was no bitterness in her voice, only a steady disappointment that troubled him even more than if she'd screamed. "Or rather, when you came to my room tonight and asked if I'd enjoyed my evening."

"I had to learn about your brother's work. There was no other way."

She gestured toward her brother's room. "Then go ask him yourself."

"I would," he countered grimly, "but he's not home, is he?" He'd suspected that when he hadn't seen Clayton or Reed outside, watching over the house. The blood that drained from her face proved it. "Where do you think he went tonight without telling you, when you were at the ball so you wouldn't notice he was gone again?"

"He's only a schoolmaster," she protested, her voice hoarse. "He's not a radical or an anarchist. He isn't political at all."

Ignoring her protests, he pressed gently, "What work has he done recently?"

"You attended his lecture. You saw for yourself. Next month, his paper will be published in their journal, and he has enough data for a second article." She raised her chin victoriously. "If he wanted to cause a revolution, he has an odd way of keeping it secret."

"*If* he's even aware that he's part of it." He took a step toward her to keep her off-balance and took a different tack. "What building plans has he been working on?"

"None." Blinking with confusion at the sudden change in conversation, she moved away. "I don't understand what that has to do with—"

"Are you certain?"

"I'd have seen them."

He circled her around the room in a very slow chase to keep her concentration scattered enough to unwittingly reveal information. "Perhaps he's hiding them from you."

"Henry has never hidden his work from me, and he wouldn't start now."

"Because you always do it for him?"

She halted in anger, placed her hand on his chest, and stopped him. He looked down at her hand. Could she feel his heart pounding beneath her fingertips?

"Because we've always *collaborated*," she answered. "I would know if he's taken a commission. He hasn't."

"Does he receive a lot of visitors?" What would it feel like if she clenched her fingers into his chest?

"Only those connected to the school."

This hellcat had claws, and he wanted to feel them scratch across his skin. "Does he receive a lot of messages and correspondence?"

"He's a schoolmaster. What correspondence could he possibly have?"

By the time this conversation was finished, though, he'd be lucky if she didn't slap him. "He's also a famous mathematician."

"He's lauded in certain circles." Fresh irritation—tinged by jealousy—colored her voice. "He receives some correspondence related to that, I suppose. Why does it matter?"

"He has friends."

"Of course."

"Who?"

"Men from the Society, friends from university, people he knows from—"

"Does he spend a lot of time with them?"

"I don't know if he—"

"Have you noticed any new friends lately?"

"I don't know!" She tossed up her hands, overwhelmed by his questioning. "I don't know who all he spends time with or writes to. How would I know that?" Her aggravation had reached its boiling point, and she pressed an angry finger against his chest. "*Why* are you asking me this?"

He slowly reached up to cover her hand with his to hold it against his chest. So she couldn't slap him. "Because if you don't know who he spends his time with, then how can you be certain that he's not doing work behind your back?" he said quietly. "He disappeared for two days and didn't tell you he was leaving. Don't you wonder what else he's keeping from you?"

She parted her lips in stunned silence.

"Trust me. I know all about how people keep secrets." Her fingers trembled, and he couldn't stop himself from tightening his hold reassuringly around them. "Tell me, Olivia. What would revolutionaries want with your brother's work?"

With a strangled laugh, she nodded toward the stained gown. "I can't even attend a ball without making a spectacle of myself. You think I'm cagey enough to know anything about sedition?"

"I think you're brilliant." He squeezed her hand and felt her sharp intake of breath in response. "And I think you've probably noticed a lot more than you realize." When she opened her mouth to refute that, he lifted her hand to his lips and placed a kiss to the backs of her fingers. He pressed again, "Has your brother worked on any architectural plans recently?"

"No, not for almost two years." She blinked, confused. "What on earth do building plans have to do with a revolution?"

I wish I knew. "Does he keep copies of his work?"

"Usually." She frowned. "Why does that matter?"

"Because if I can see the copies, then I might be able to discover what part he's playing in this."

And who he's working with. Alec needed the copy of the building plans that matched the charred fragment. Something on those plans would lead them to Scepter and prevent the next assassination attempt, he was certain. Yet time was not on his side.

Right then, neither was Olivia. She crossed her arms and glared at him. "So you can have him arrested?"

"So I can use the copies to prove him innocent." *Or make certain he hangs if he isn't.* "If I don't have them and your brother's arrested, I won't be able to save him."

She bit her bottom lip, and he could practically see her mind whirling to determine if she could believe him. "Why are you telling me this? Aren't you worried I'll tell Henry?"

"Because I trust you." He added somberly, "And because part of you already doubts your brother, too, or you would have screamed by now and alerted the entire school that I was here."

Her silence proved him right.

"Where are the copies of his work, Olivia?"

A betrayed look clouded her face. "That's what you were looking for that first night when I found you going through my dresser, wasn't it?"

"Yes." There was no point now in pretending otherwise. "But I didn't find them."

"Because he hasn't done any work recently except for his presentation and article for the Society." Then she capitulated to what he was telling her and whispered so softly that her words were barely louder than a breath, "If he's done any other work, I would know. He needs me to check his calculations."

He believed her. Fate had just slammed the door on his best chance at finding Scepter.

He blew out a harsh breath. "You'll inform me if you come across anything?"

Another nod, but he knew he'd get no more information from her. The stubborn woman would only entrench herself deeper in defending her brother.

But he needed to leave her with this— "You can't tell anyone about me or what we've discussed tonight." He fixed his gaze on hers. He wanted no misunderstanding about this. "Not even your brother."

When she began to protest, he placed his fingers against her lips to silence her.

"These men are dangerous. If they discover that you know about them—if they even *suspect*—they'll kill you both."

"You're exaggerating," she whispered.

"I'm not. You're caught in the middle between men who want to overthrow the government and those who want to stop them. The *only* thing that can save you for certain is your silence."

She looked down at the mask that dangled from his hand. "And I'm supposed to simply trust you?"

He placed his forefinger beneath her chin and lifted her face until she had no choice but to look straight into his eyes. "Right now, I'm the only person you *can* trust."

Ten

OLIVIA STOOD IN FRONT OF THE TWO SCHOOLGIRLS IN her most studied governess pose, with her hands on her hips and a disappointed expression on her face. Yet she fought to keep her lips from twitching with laughter at their latest antics.

At fifteen, Mary and Daphne were a handful. Enrolled at the school since they were both twelve and as close as if they were real sisters, one did nothing without the other. Including, it seemed, getting into trouble.

"You left school without notifying anyone and without taking a chaperone." Olivia announced their offense like a magistrate at the Courts, injecting a gravity into her voice she certainly didn't feel.

What they'd done was relatively harmless. They'd heard that palace and Whitehall officials were rehearsing a grand spectacle to mark the official opening of the new Waterloo Bridge and the second anniversary of the battle, so they'd sneaked out when the students had their midafternoon pause for tea and biscuits, waved down a hackney, and sped toward the embankment. They would have gotten away with it, too, if Mrs. Adams hadn't noticed the open sitting room window, then promptly closed and locked it. Upon their return, the two girls had no choice but to enter through the front door and face their punishment.

Olivia didn't blame them for wanting to witness all the royal pomp and grandeur. But she also couldn't allow any infraction of the rules to go unpunished, or next time, God forbid, they might decide to do something that would endanger their reputations. Or their lives.

"We weren't planning on being gone long," Mary began.

"Just to the end of break, honest," Daphne added with an earnest and rapid nodding.

"And then we came right back—"

"We didn't get into any trouble—"

"Or do anything you would have objected to."

"We just stood and watched, honest."

"And oh, Miss! T'were so grand! The gold carriages—"

"All the horses!"

"And the guards in their red uniforms were so handsome!"

"Oh! They had a band, too, with drums and fifes—"

"And the royal barge with all its gold—"

Olivia put up her hand and swiftly silenced them. Her head had started to pound from the back-and-forth. *Good heavens.* It was like watching a tennis match. "You know the rules, girls, and you know they must be followed for your own safety."

Daphne lowered her eyes. "Will we be punished, Miss?"

"I'm afraid so. Tomorrow, instead of spending the afternoon in the park with the other girls, you'll remain here and help Mrs. Adams clean the kitchen."

A stricken look flashed over Mary's face. "Miss the park? But Papa sent money for ices!"

Once again, Olivia fought back a smile. Oh, to be so young and innocent again that happiness revolved around something as simple as purchasing ices. "That will have to wait until the next outing. Perhaps you'll spend that time thinking about what you did and why you shouldn't have done it."

"Yes, Miss." Both girls looked glumly at their shoes.

"Please return to your lessons, and we'll never mention this again."

They turned toward the door.

"And, girls," Olivia called after them, "if you behave yourselves, I might be persuaded to let Miss Smith chaperone you to the official bridge opening to see the parade."

"Really?" Daphne squeaked hopefully.

"Truly?" Mary seconded.

"Really and truly." Olivia settled into her chair and sighed at the daunting chore of having to work through the endless stack of bills and correspondence waiting for her. "Now, back to your lessons." She gestured toward the older girl who stood quietly by the door. "Miss Smith? A moment please."

Lady Gantry's young niece Justine remained after the two girls chattered their way toward the classrooms on the first floor. When Justine closed the door, Olivia let go of the laughter she'd been holding back.

Justine pressed her hand against her mouth as her own giggles came.

Olivia let out a long sigh. "They can be troublesome, but pressing against the rules is all part of growing up, isn't it?" Then she felt obligated to warn, "As long as one doesn't go too far, of course."

"Yes, Miss Everett."

Olivia smiled warmly at the girl. Slender, tall, and pretty, it was little wonder she'd caught the attention of the neighboring gentleman at her family's country house. When she finally made her debut, she was going to take society by storm. She had the beauty to be considered an Incomparable, and with her social standing as the daughter of a wealthy landowner and the niece of a baron, the right future husband would be understanding—if not completely uncaring—about her past indiscretions.

Olivia had already decided to discuss Justine with Lady Gantry. She hoped to persuade the baroness to sponsor the girl next season. True, Justine had made a mistake, but should a young woman be punished for the rest of her life for daring to follow her heart?

"Keep a close watch on those two, will you? They're well behaved when they're apart." Olivia rolled her eyes and muttered, "Together, they are an absolute trial!"

Justine smiled, and her entire face shone. Oh, yes. She was definitely pretty enough to find a good husband.

Settling in to work, Olivia reached for the first letter in her stack and asked casually, "Is Mr. Everett in the school?"

"I think he went to the coffeehouse to meet his friends," Justine answered. "He was gone before I came down for breakfast."

No. Olivia knew the truth, although she hadn't wanted to face it—he hadn't come home at all last night.

Justine turned toward the door, then paused. "Miss Everett?"

"Yes?" Olivia looked up from the letter.

"Thank you for all you've done for me. I mean, for letting me stay here with you and keeping silent about…well, you know."

Olivia knew well. More than Justine would ever have suspected. "Everyone makes mistakes. What matters is how we choose to deal with them."

"Perhaps." Then Justine said almost to herself, "But some of us make bigger mistakes than others."

That soft confession reverberated inside Olivia's chest, and her fingers tightened on the paper. "Are you in love with the young man?"

Justine's face darkened with guilt. "I suppose I shouldn't be. He couldn't possibly love me back, could he? Or he wouldn't have asked me to…" Her soft voice trailed off.

"Or maybe he loved you too much not to ask," Olivia whispered gently. "And maybe he loves you so much that he knows it's better for you to marry someone else."

A lie. The seduction of innocents rarely had anything to do with love. But Olivia knew what this girl was going through and wanted to do anything she could to ease the heaviness inside her and the doubts that kept her awake at night. That included lying to her if necessary. Accepting the harsh reality of her situation would only cause more pain.

"I hope you're right, Miss."

Olivia forced a smile. "I know so."

The girl's slim shoulders relaxed with relief. "When my aunt told me that I would be coming here, I didn't know

what to expect. But you're nothing at all like I imagined."
She beamed at Olivia. "If I can be half as proper as you, Miss
Everett, then I know everything will be just fine."

Justine slipped out the door.

Olivia stared after her. Half as proper? If the girl only
knew…which she *never* could. As far as Lady Gantry and the
rest of society were concerned, Olivia was a paragon of propriety. They could never suspect that she'd once reached for
a bright future she'd believed was hers for the taking, only for
it to all come crashing down around her.

Olivia swiped her hand at her eyes, but she couldn't
stop the tears from coming, just as she couldn't stop those
anguished thoughts of what her life could have been…a safe
and secure future, a home and children, marriage, a man
steadfast enough to return her love—

A knock sounded at the door. Olivia grabbed for her
handkerchief and quickly dried her eyes, then reached for
her quill to pretend that she'd been busily working. "Yes?"

Mrs. Adams stuck her head inside. "A young woman is
here to see you, Miss."

Her chest tightened. *Please don't let it be another girl seeking a scholarship position!* They barely had the money to
house the ones they had now. "Who is it?"

"Lady Elizabeth Sinclair."

Her mouth fell open. *Alec's sister?* What on earth…?

Last night had not gone well. Olivia nearly laughed at
herself. *Not well?* That was a grand understatement! Between
her humiliation at the ball and Alec's betrayal over his identity, she'd been furious and far more hurt than she wanted to

admit. Then, his accusations of Henry being a revolutionary...*simply ludicrous.*

She never wanted to see that devil again. And now to have
his sister appear unexpectedly on her doorstep—

Good Lord, the Sinclair family was beginning to make
her head spin!

But she couldn't snub the sister of an earl. After all, it
wasn't Lady Elizabeth's fault that her brother was a villain.

Gathering herself with a deep breath, she stood. "Please,
show her in."

Elizabeth Sinclair bounced into the office with a bright
smile. Removing her bonnet, she revealed chestnut hair
the same color as Alec's swept gently back into a simple
knot and bright hazel eyes. Cream-colored lace edged the
modest neckline of her pale yellow dress, giving the frock
an air of high-fashioned style with old-fashioned modesty.
All of it conspired to create a warm, friendly presence that
Olivia never would have suspected from someone of Lady
Elizabeth's rank. Or relation to St James.

"Miss Everett." Elizabeth hurried forward to take Olivia's
hands in hers and prevent her from dropping into a curtsy.

"Lady Elizabeth," Olivia said with surprise. "What an
unexpected pleasure."

Elizabeth squeezed Olivia's hands, and her eager excitement only increased Olivia's wariness. "I apologize for calling on you without notice. I hope you don't mind."

"Of course not. You're welcome to visit the school any-
time, my lady." She nodded toward the two chairs in front of
her desk. "Shall I call for refreshments?"

Elizabeth shook her head with a sweet smile. "I would love that, truly, but I'm afraid I can't linger. I'm needed back at Harlow House to help with Mama's garden party." She released Olivia's hands. "I only came by to return your wrap. You left it at the ball." She gestured a gloved hand toward the hallway. "I gave it to your housekeeper."

"I'm grateful." Olivia truly was. In her desperation to flee last night, she'd forgotten all about it. "But you needn't have come all the way here just to return it."

Certainly not when Lady Elizabeth had a house full of footmen and maids she could have sent instead. Olivia suspected some other motive…a tall, dark, and impossibly devilish one.

Had Alec sent his sister to pry about Henry?

Elizabeth's face fell. "I felt terrible about what happened to you last night. I wanted to see for myself if you were all right."

Her voice turned so soft that it was as if she were speaking of scandal instead of stain. Heaven only knew how she would react if she discovered Olivia had been locked undressed in the retiring room with her brother.

"I'm fine." Olivia dismissed her concerns with a smile. "No need to worry."

"But your lovely dress was ruined."

Something about the way Lady Elizabeth said that…did her lips twitch? "It was only an accident," Olivia reassured her. "What I regret is that the evening ended so early."

"Do you?" Elizabeth pressed. "You were truly having an enjoyable time?"

"I was." Her answer seemed to matter a great deal, so Olivia didn't have the heart to tell her that the only part she hadn't enjoyed was waltzing with her brother, even if he *was* the best dance partner she'd ever had.

Elizabeth impulsively hugged her. "Oh, I'm so glad!" She fixed Olivia with a determined gaze. "Then you *must* attend tea tomorrow afternoon at Harlow House. Mama wants to show off her flowers to the garden club, and it will give us the chance to make up for what happened to you at the ball." When Olivia hesitated to accept, Elizabeth laughed. "I simply refuse to let you refuse!"

Olivia bit her lip. Unless she wanted to offend one of the most influential families in England and hurt Lady Elizabeth's feelings, she had no choice but to accept.

Yet to bring herself so close to Alec again made her feel as if she were playing with fire.

Still, an afternoon tea surrounded by society ladies seemed harmless enough. Perhaps she might meet potential patrons among the countess's friends, since she wasn't able to discuss the school with anyone at the ball. And, she tried to convince herself, it was highly unlikely that Alec would attend a ladies' garden party.

"I would be honored," Olivia agreed. "Thank you for thinking of me."

The young woman flashed her the brightest smile yet and drew one from Olivia in return. She genuinely liked Lady Elizabeth, although she had no idea how Elizabeth and Alec could be siblings. They might look alike, but they were as different in personality and presence as night and day.

"Wonderful!" Bubbling with excitement, Elizabeth withdrew the invitation from her reticule and handed it to Olivia. "I'm so thrilled you'll be there. You've rescued me." When Olivia frowned, puzzled, Elizabeth lowered her voice and leaned closer as if sharing a secret. "I didn't want to say anything before, but without you, tea with all those old matrons and widows would have been absolutely tedious!"

Olivia gave her a conspiratorial smile. "Then I'll be happy to rescue you." The conversation was drawing to an end, but Olivia was enjoying spending time with her. "Are you certain you can't stay for a tour of the school? I'd be honored to show it to you."

The girls would be thrilled to meet the sister of an earl. Except for the scholarship students, the girls weren't poor, but their families also weren't part of the *ton*. They—and most of their mothers—were dazzled by fashionable ladies like Elizabeth and longed to be part of that world.

"Perhaps some other time?" Genuine regret played across Elizabeth's face. "Alec told me about the work you do here. I think it's wonderful."

Olivia lost her breath. "His lordship told you about me?"

Elizabeth's eyes gleamed. "You're practically all he's talked about during the past few days. Well, and the school, of course."

"Of course." She frowned, convinced that Lady Elizabeth had just lied to her. "Will your brother also be attending the tea?"

"I certainly hope not! Alec's an utter bore at these events." Elizabeth rolled her eyes. "Nothing exciting ever happens when he's around."

With a parting wave of her hand, Elizabeth hurried from the room, as if afraid Olivia might change her mind and refuse to attend after all.

Olivia stared after her, flabbergasted. Nothing exciting ever happened around her brother? If only Elizabeth knew the truth! The Alec Sinclair whom Olivia had encountered was far from an utter bore.

If anything more exciting happened between the two of them, she might not survive it.

Eleven

"I'm very happy you're here, Alexander." Isabel Sinclair patted Alec's arm as he escorted her onto the rear terrace of Harlow House. "Two events in three days is unprecedented for you."

"I know how important this is to Elizabeth."

His mother glanced across the garden into the afternoon sun and blinked against its brightness. "It's also important to me." She paused. "Someday, I hope we can be close again, as we were before you joined the army."

He stiffened. He wasn't daft enough to pretend that he didn't know what she meant, that she hadn't felt the tension between them since his return.

But he also wasn't ready to confront her about exactly how much she knew about her husband's evils, how she could have turned such a blind eye to what happened within her own home. Scars still lurked where she couldn't see them, and most likely always would. He wasn't ready yet to expose them to the light.

He glanced across the terrace at the gathered guests and quietly admitted, "I hope for that, too." *Someday.*

But it wasn't going to come from sipping tea among society matrons.

Truly, he had no idea why Elizabeth had issued the invitation to this afternoon's garden party in the first place, knowing how he felt about matrons' teas and knowing how *she* felt about them herself. Yet she'd insisted, so he'd come. He'd always done everything he could to protect Beth and make her happy. Now that his little sister was on the verge of becoming another man's responsibility, he found himself doting on her even more.

But a society tea? *Good Lord.* This was unusual even for Beth, and testimony to how much he loved her. Not only because being here subjected him to the company of two dozen matrons, all of whom would invariably have a female relative in need of a husband, but also because he regretted not being out on the hunt for any trace of the men Henry Everett had been meeting with. So far, tracking them had come to nothing. Despite watching his every move, Everett had led them nowhere, and Reed hadn't been able to identify the man who'd paid the boy to deliver the last message. As for Alec's part in the mission, Olivia had provided only frustration.

Was this mission nothing more than a wild goose chase? Had Clayton gotten the evidence wrong, and that charred piece of building plans had nothing to do with the bombing?

No. He couldn't start down that forking path. If Clayton was wrong, then they had no way of stopping another attempt on the prime minister's life, and next time Scepter would succeed. He had to forget about whatever information he'd hoped Olivia Everett would provide and focus on finding another way forward.

"Lady Rowland!" Isabel waved her fingers at Sydney Rowland as the baroness approached. "So nice of you to attend. Of course, you know my son?"

"Lady Rowland and I have long been acquaintances." Alec bowed more formally than necessary in a pitiful attempt to ward off what he knew was another effort at matchmaking by his mother. "In fact, her late husband and I worked together in Parliament."

"Rowland spoke fondly of you," Lady Rowland assured him, but her voice had gone noticeably cold at the mention of her late husband. The baron had been dead nearly two years. Was she still grieving?

"Don't believe a word." Alec lowered his voice with mock secrecy and teased her. "I bribed him for every compliment."

Just as he'd hoped, she relaxed and returned his smile.

Well, he had to give his mother credit. Sydney Rowland would have made a good match for an earl. A wealthy heiress in her own right, she was pretty and elegant, cultured and well-schooled, although unpopular among the *ton*, who regarded her as nothing more than an upstart cit. She'd make a good society wife, perhaps even more so to a man who wanted a true partner in marriage.

But Alec would not be that man.

Based on the complete lack of interest she showed in him as anything but a friend, she agreed. *Thank heavens.*

His mother conveniently released his arm. "Why don't you escort Lady Rowland to one of the tables and join her for the tea? The footmen are bringing out the services now."

"My apologies, Countess," Lady Rowland interjected.

"But I've already promised Mrs. Jennings that I'd join her and her friends." She looked at Alec, and private amusement danced in her eyes. She knew as well as he did exactly what his mother was attempting. "Perhaps another time."

Relief swelled through him. "I look forward to it."

The baroness excused herself. His mother went with her, ostensibly to help her find her place but clearly so she could plant more seeds of interest about Alec in the woman's ear.

Alec frowned. The last thing he needed was a matchmaker.

"You're here!" Elizabeth swept up from behind and latched on to his arm. "I was afraid you'd changed your mind."

"Perhaps I should have," he muttered. "Why is this tea so important?"

She ignored the commanding tone in his voice just as she'd done her entire life and affectionately squeezed his arm. He could frighten grown men with a single look, but irritatingly, this little imp feared nothing about him. "Without you here, dear brother, it would have been an utter bore among all these old matrons and widows."

"Then you should have invited Mr. Mullins."

"I did, but Arthur wanted to attend the auctions at Tattersall's." Her brow furrowed quizzically. "Do you think it says something about his feelings for me that he'd rather spend the day dodging horse leavings than attend Mama's garden party?"

"I think it says more about his intelligence," he answered. "He's smart enough to dodge society matrons and their leavings."

Her mouth and eyes grew wide at that wholly improper

statement before slamming shut and narrowing. She swatted his shoulder. "Just because *you* think afternoon teas are—" A smile burst across her face as she glanced toward the open terrace doors. "She's arrived. How wonderful!"

"Who?" He followed her gaze. And froze.

Olivia.

She'd dressed perfectly for a garden party, reminding him of a bouquet of spring flowers. Her soft blue dress and matching pelisse, both the color of bluebells, brought out the pink in her cheeks and lips. A pink and white flower-strewn bonnet framed her oval face, but Alec knew exactly what her hair would look like in the sunlight if she removed the hat— warm gold, like the sunshine itself.

She swept in like a breath of fresh air, only to pause just inside the terrace doors to glance uncertainly around the garden before her. Her gaze landed on his mother and Aunt Agnes as they stood at the edge of the terrace, and she stilled. For a moment, Alec thought she might just flee.

Aunt Agnes must have thought so, too, because she waved her yellow handkerchief wildly at her, as if attempting to flag down the mail coach on its run to Dover.

"Miss Everett!" Agnes called out, loud enough to be heard all the way to Covent Garden. "How delightful that you could attend our little tea!"

Despite the widening of Olivia's eyes, Agnes hurried across the terrace to grab her arm before she could bolt, and barely in time, too, based on the look of longing Olivia threw over her shoulder at the doors. Yet Agnes latched on to her as if she were a prodigal daughter. Chattering nonstop, Agnes led her through the cluster of little tables on the terrace to introduce her to the other guests.

Alec slid a narrowed glance at Elizabeth. "What wicked little scheme have you planned, imp?"

"Why, none at all." But her forced innocence only confirmed his suspicions. Olivia was here because of Beth. "I'm doing a good deed."

He arched a brow.

"Her evening at the ball was ruined—you know, that whole horrible punch incident."

Oh, he certainly knew, all right, and still felt guilty about it. "And?"

"And I wanted to make it up to her by inviting her to the tea. That's all."

"Why don't I believe you?"

She gave a small *hmph* of irritation and scowled. "Would I play matchmaker for you?"

"Why not? Mother and Aunt Agnes do every chance they get."

"All right, then." She gestured toward Olivia as if the answer were obvious. "Would I play matchmaker with someone who is so clearly *wrong* for you?"

His eyes snapped back to Beth. "What's wrong with her?"

"She's not the kind of woman you usually pursue."

"What do you mean by that?" His hackles were rising, despite himself.

"Oh please," she muttered with a long sigh. "You're exact opposites, for one. She's a schoolmistress with an impeccable reputation, and you're a gentleman who—"

"She's lovely," he interrupted, unwilling to subject himself to a critique of his faults. Or Olivia's.

"Indeed."

"Hard-working, brilliant, and caring to a fault, unable to deny her brother or those girls at her school anything they ask of her."

"Certainly."

"There is nothing wrong with her."

Beth flashed an overly bright, knowing smile. "And *that*, dear brother," she assured him as she patted his arm again and slipped away, "is why I'm keeping her away from *you*!"

She strolled across the terrace and held out her hands to Olivia in welcome. The two women greeted each other like old friends, all smiles and easy laughter.

Alec blew out a harsh breath. *Hell.* He was in tea hell. The afternoon was shaping up to be his miserable penance for the ball.

"St James!"

Mrs. Peterson rushed up to him and curtsied so deeply that the rotund woman nearly fell over. Alec grabbed her arm to steady her.

The woman panted out excited breaths. "Your mother said…I should find you immediately…and tell you all about my niece…Iphigenia Dunwoody… I thought perhaps you might be interested…"

Bloody hell.

From the corner of her eye, Olivia saw Alec reach to steady the chatty woman who had swooped down upon him like a hawk.

Oh Lord, he was *here*, even though Elizabeth had assured her he wouldn't be. The Earl of St James...her masked menace.

From the way his dark gaze darted over the woman's head to land on Olivia for a long moment before he grimaced and looked away, he was no happier to see her than she was to see him.

Good. Maybe he would keep his distance.

"Don't worry about Alec," Elizabeth assured her as she followed Olivia's gaze to her brother. She led her toward a tea table at the side of the terrace where night-blooming jasmine mixed with morning glories across a brick wall. "He's only here today because Mama asked him to help welcome the guests. I'm certain he'll leave as soon as possible."

Very good.

His sister smiled with amusement at Alec's expense. "He'll be too busy dodging requests to call on their unmarried female relations to bother us."

Olivia frowned. Perhaps *not* so good after all. It wasn't relief that gnawed at her then but jealousy.

"We're all so delighted that you could attend the tea, my dear." Lady Agnes patted her hand as she sank into the chair next to Olivia's. "Young things like you always brighten up a gathering."

So did Agnes, apparently. In an orange dress and yellow turban, the older woman was nearly as bright as the sun herself, and with strings of jewels dripping from around her neck and rings covering her fingers, she was also every bit as eccentric as rumors had led Olivia to believe. Lady Agnes Sinclair was uncommonly lively for a pillar of society, with an energy and vivaciousness that simply burst from her.

From her place as hostess on the other side of the terrace, Isabel Sinclair sent Olivia a welcoming smile that lit up her beautiful face. Then the countess turned her attention back to making certain that all her guests were seated and gave a silent nod to the butler to begin the service.

Clearly, Lady Elizabeth had inherited the best of her family's traits—the beauty of her mother and the exuberance of her aunt. But thankfully none of the dark brooding of her brother.

Olivia sat back as a footman placed a plate covered with tiny cakes and sandwiches in front of her. Another footman placed a teacup and saucer beside the plate. The butler followed behind with a teapot, pouring out each cup. The men moved through the forest of small tables like a well-trained army in synchronized battle maneuvers.

She turned her attention back to the table to find Lady Agnes studying her closely. From the other side of her, so was Lady Elizabeth. Good heavens! She felt like an animal on display at the Tower menagerie.

Olivia cleared her throat. "Thank you both for inviting me."

"It was the least we could do after your evening at the ball was ruined," Elizabeth answered.

"Oh, yes! The punch. Strange incident, that." Agnes frowned. "I've been watching Captain Reed quite closely since he returned from the wars. Usually, the man is much more graceful."

Captain Reed. So that was the name of her punch perpetrator. But Olivia couldn't blame him for ruining her evening when it was another man who'd truly done that. She placed her napkin on her lap and assured them, "It was an accident."

"Well, yes." Agnes reached for a cucumber sandwich. "But Elizabeth's dress was completely ruined."

"Oh?" Olivia lifted the teacup to her lips and turned toward Elizabeth. "Did something happen to you at the ball as well?"

"Not at all." Elizabeth smiled and nibbled at a lemon biscuit.

Olivia turned back toward Agnes again for clarification. "What did—"

Her gaze accidentally landed on Alec, who stared boldly at her from his chair. His heated gaze melted into a frown.

She glanced away but not before a flush rose in her cheeks.

Agnes leaned toward her, shoulder to shoulder. "I would warn you about my nephew," she said in a low voice, "but you've nothing to fear. He's not at all the rake that society portrays him to be."

"That's good to—"

"But he used to be absolutely terrible! Could have given the Prince of Wales a run for his money when it came to women, drink, and gambling." Lady Agnes swept an assessing look over her. "Besides, you're not at all his sort."

Olivia caught her breath on an unexpected pang of disappointment. "Oh?"

"Intelligent and proper." Agnes sighed wearily. "Unfortunately, he prefers women who are frivolous, sadly lacking in intellect, and far too simpering."

"I see." Olivia dropped her attention to her tea.

Agnes was right, of course. Alec had flirted with her only for information about her brother. She should have been grateful that she wouldn't have to fend off the devil's attentions again, and certainly not since he'd learned she could provide no more information. That had surely deflated whatever interest he'd taken in her.

Yet she felt oddly out of sorts at being confronted by it like this.

"They pose no challenge to him, you see," Agnes continued, sharing much more about Alec than she should have. "And so they're no threat." The older woman paused and watched closely as Olivia took a sip from her cup. "Unlike you."

Olivia choked on her tea, and only partially from the woman's unexpected comment. Coughing to clear her throat, she stared into her cup. Good Lord, was that *whiskey*?

She looked up at Lady Agnes, and a mischievous gleam lit the older woman's eyes. She patted Olivia's arm. "Just stay fixed to your nature, my dear, and you'll have no worries about my nephew."

When Lady Agnes turned away to call for a footman to bring an extra plate of cakes to the table, Elizabeth slyly exchanged teacups with Olivia.

"Auntie's as mad as a hatter," Elizabeth confided. "But she's our hatter, and we love her dearly. Best to watch your tea around her, though, or you'll find yourself foxed to the gills." Elizabeth slowly pushed away the teacup and gestured for the footman to bring her a new one. "She's right about Alec, however. You're not at all his sort."

Olivia was glad to hear it, yet his sister's far-too-happy smile corkscrewed unease through her, right down to her toes. "Your brother's an earl. I would never dare to presume something like that."

Elizabeth looked away and mumbled, "That's a pity."

She blinked. "Pardon?"

"I said you *needn't worry*," Elizabeth said more loudly, then shifted back so the footman could set down the fresh cup of tea and its saucer. "Alec is actually a very good man."

Olivia bit her bottom lip. She wasn't at all convinced of *that*.

Twelve

To Olivia's chagrin, Alec didn't leave.

Not when the footmen finished serving tea and Mrs. Peterson competed with Lady Gantry for his attention. Nor did he leave when the footmen cleared away the tea carts and a woman began to pluck at a harp on the corner of the terrace. Not even when Lady St James finally stood and invited everyone to stroll at their leisure through her beautiful gardens and enjoy the flowers.

No, Alec remained through it all, looking grim and uncomfortable, especially whenever Olivia caught him avoiding eye contact with Mrs. Peterson and Lady Gantry... and looking at her.

"Would you like to see Aunt Agnes's roses?" Elizabeth linked her arm with Olivia's and led her down the terrace steps into the garden. "They were a gift from the Duke of Wellington for her support during the war."

They strolled along the path and away from the other guests until the harp music faded on the air. Olivia asked, "How exactly did your aunt support Wellington?"

"No one really knows, and Auntie refuses to discuss it. But gossip says it had to do with the dragoons and either leather or bayonets." Her nose scrunched up as she leaned over and sniffed a pink blossom. "Possibly both. Wellington did send an awful lot of roses. All red." She paused thoughtfully as she reached to touch the blossom. "Leather and bayonets... You know, I'm beginning to think there might very well be a hidden meaning behind that gossip."

Olivia glanced away and pressed her hand to her lips.

Chatting on about the gardens, Lady Elizabeth led her farther down the path until they reached the brick wall at the far end of the property where a massive bower supported the weight of more climbing roses than Olivia had ever seen in her life. Framed by two weeping willows on either end and supported by wooden arches underneath, the roses entwined so thickly that they touched the ground and created a hidden space beneath, their fragrant and wild blossoms framing the narrow entrance. Inside, where the sunlight couldn't quite reach, dappled shadows cooled a small stone bench.

"My," Olivia murmured, stunned at the sight. "There must have been a lot of bayonets."

Elizabeth frowned. "And undoubtedly lots of leather."

Olivia bit the inside of her cheek and silently nodded.

"This way." Elizabeth led her beneath the bower.

As Olivia slipped under the towering bushes, she felt as if she were entering a fairyland. She half expected at any moment to see gnomes and pixies playing among the rose petals.

"Lady Elizabeth?" a footman called from the path outside the bower.

She cocked her head. "Yes?"

"You're wanted at the house, Miss."

"Coming!" Elizabeth gestured toward the bench and instructed Olivia, "Wait here and enjoy the flowers. I'll be back as soon as I can."

Before Olivia could protest that she didn't mind returning to the house, Elizabeth darted out from beneath the bower and disappeared into the garden.

Olivia swept her gaze around the bower's draping canopy of roses. Well, if she had to wait, then she couldn't imagine a more beautiful place to do it.

She sank onto the stone bench. In the dappled sunlight, the garden was silent and private, so unlike the small service yard behind the school that was barely big enough for the tiny kitchen garden Mrs. Adams had squeezed into it. Here, there was space and fresh air, full blooms tilting toward the sun and tiny flowers carpeting the ground, lush bushes and trees…*freedom*.

With a soft laugh, she pulled loose the ribbon tied beneath her chin, removed her bonnet, and set it on the bench beside her. What would the girls at the school say if they saw this bower, this cathedral of flowers and vines around her? She could almost hear the squeals of delight that—

"Elizabeth? What did you—"

Startled, she caught her breath.

Then caught it a second time for a completely different reason.

Alec stood in the bower's entrance, his large body filling the narrow gap. In the sunlight that filtered through the bower and fell softly on his chestnut hair and broad shoulders, he reminded her of one of those paintings of Greek heroes and gods that lined the walls of Somerset House. He should have been out of place here—a tall and muscular man in a lady's elegant walled garden. Yet inexplicably, he seemed to belong among the vines and bushes. Like a lion in the jungle.

"Not Elizabeth." His eyes gleamed with surprise as they swept over her, and he murmured in a deep voice, "Olivia."

"*You*." Her irritation hid the flush in her cheeks. Thank God he couldn't see the way her body tingled. "What kind of game are you playing now?"

"None, but I'm always up for—" He broke off and quirked a half grin, the gentleman in him obviously thinking twice about what wicked suggestion the rake was about to make. "The footman said Beth was in the bower and wanted to see me."

Ha! Olivia didn't believe that for a second. "A footman just called Lady Elizabeth away to see the countess." She crossed her arms. "How convenient for you to find me here. Alone."

"I didn't plan this." When she opened her mouth to retort, he cut her off with a lift of his brow. "If I wanted to be alone with you, Olivia, I wouldn't have to arrange a surprise meeting at a ladies' garden party."

"True," she admitted in an exasperated grumble. "*You'd* climb through my window at midnight."

A slow grin pulled at his sensuous lips. "Is that an invitation?"

She narrowed her eyes. There was no way in the world she'd answer that! Yet instead of the scolding tone she'd hoped for, her voice emerged as a throaty whisper, "What are you doing here? The *real* reason."

. He leaned casually against the post framing the entryway. The frustrating devil was clearly in no hurry to leave. "Apparently, my sister is playing matchmaker."

"Between us?" Another throaty whisper, one impossibly huskier than the last. *Good Lord.* She needed to take a vow of silence when she was around this man. "An earl and a schoolmistress? But that's—that's—"

"Impossible?"

Exactly. Yet an inexplicable pang of disappointment thumped in her chest. "Surely, she realizes that."

"Beth has a romantic heart." His gaze drifted from the bonnet at her side to her hair. Then he stared at her for so long that she self-consciously reached a hand to her chignon to make certain it hadn't come undone. "She's in love." His eyes moved down to capture hers. "So she believes the rest of the world should be, too, no matter how improbable."

For a moment, she could do nothing but return his stare. And swallow. Hard. She knew now that he was the masked man who'd rescued her in the alley, who'd sneaked into her room and arranged for a ball gown for her. But seeing him here in the sunlight was so very different from those shadow-filled nights. During those encounters, he'd reminded her of a panther. Now…well, he still reminded her of a giant cat stalking its way along, to be honest. Yet the man in front of her was somehow more dangerous than when he'd been behind a mask.

She forced her attention onto the roses around them and

lowered her hand to her lap. "You should return to the house, my lord. The guests are surely missing you."

"Then I should stay right here. After all, you're also a guest."

"But *I* do not miss you."

He laughed, a low and velvety chuckle that filled the bower.

Instead of leaving, he stepped into the vine-dappled shadows with her. He put her bonnet aside and sat uninvited next to her on the bench. *Close* beside her.

Her mouth fell open at his audacity. "What are you doing?"

"It's my duty to make certain that every guest enjoys herself." He leaned toward her. "Are you enjoying the tea, Olivia? After all, attending today was very brave of you."

"Brave?" she scoffed, not trusting the compliment.

"Quite brave," he explained with mocking solemnity. "After that punch incident at the ball, I never thought you'd attend an event based solely on the service of liquids."

Blast the devil! Gritting her teeth, she made a futile grab for her bonnet, but he moved it just out of her reach. She groaned in frustration. "Why won't you leave me alone?"

"Because you're a beautiful and intriguing woman."

She blurted out a laugh. As if he expected her to fall for that!

"And because you know about your brother's work."

The laughter died on her lips. *That* excuse she believed.

He asked quietly, picking up their last conversation where it had left off, "Have you found any evidence or copies of recent building plans?"

"I told you. He hasn't done any commissions in almost two years."

He stilled for a long moment, his hazel eyes narrowing on her as if trying to decide whether he could trust her. More—as if he were attempting to uncover all her secrets and learn the truth of who she truly was. She called on every bit of courage she possessed not to look away.

Thankfully, he let the moment pass and plucked one of the rosebuds near her shoulder. "Did Beth tell you the story about this bower?"

"A gift from Wellington in gratitude for your aunt's support during the wars." Embarrassment made her voice catch as she added, "Dragoons, bayonets, and…leather."

"Knowing Auntie, more like ponies and chickens, and she most likely delivered them to the regiment on the Peninsula herself to make certain they arrived." When her eyes widened in surprise, he explained, "We Sinclairs are a formidable lot."

Undoubtedly. And yet… "Chickens?"

"Can't fight the enemy on an empty stomach."

"Oh." She watched his fingers tease at the rosebud in his hands, and a shameful longing melted her insides. He couldn't be trusted, she knew that. Yet what would it feel like to have those hands on her, those fingers teasing at her body the same way they were playing with the rosebud? "And the ponies?"

"In case they ran out of chickens."

"Oh!" Her hand flew to her mouth in disgust.

He chuckled at her reaction, the sound soft and deep

in the stillness of the bower around them. It contrasted in masculine depths against the light, delicate flowers and the distant notes of the harp wafting through the garden. When his lips curled into a half smile, the longing inside her turned molten.

The man might be a devil, yet he was a temptingly attractive one.

"Compared to that explanation," she murmured through her fingers, "I think I prefer bayonets and leather."

"Me, too," he drawled rakishly.

A flush raced up from the back of her neck and into her cheeks. "That is *not* what I meant—"

"I know." He blew out a regretful breath. "There's not a wicked bone in your body, is there?"

Olivia pressed her lips together, irritation instantly replacing the longing inside her. His last visit to her room had not ended well, and this meeting was faring no better. It was best to simply leave.

"I have no intention of remaining here to be insulted." She grabbed for her bonnet. "Good afternoon, my—"

His hand folded gently around her wrist and stopped her.

She stilled beneath his soft touch, except for the tattoo of her thudding pulse. Could he feel its pounding beneath his fingertips?

"Apparently, I'm no good at speaking with you unless I'm behind a mask." Genuine contrition laced his voice. "My apologies."

Olivia sank back down onto the bench, stunned. The Earl of St James...*apologized*?

She simply couldn't fathom this man. Who *was* he at heart? The gentleman who sent her a gown so she could attend a ball, or the rogue who took advantage of the punch spill to manipulate her into being alone with him? The masked man who chased after her through the dark London streets, or the soldier who gave her a lesson on fighting? The brother and son who would do anything for his family, or the blackguard whose rumored reputation left women trembling?

He'd accused her of being a contradiction, yet here he was—six feet of muscular, masculine contradiction of his own, and all of him looked so attractive that her fingers itched to touch him.

There was so much about him she found intriguing and good. She might even be able to like the man if he ever stopped being so...*himself.*

But right now, he simply confounded the daylights out of her.

"What do you want?" she blurted out, her voice breathless.

He smiled faintly as if he recognized the war raging inside her, then unexpectedly brushed the rose across her cheek. "I thought it was obvious," he murmured and traced the contours of her cheekbone with the soft bud.

Her heart stuttered. There was no mask between them now, no waltz as an excuse to place her into his arms...nothing to blame for his flirtation and her delight in it except themselves. Unless she stood and fled, she would be culpable in whatever happened next.

Yet fleeing was the last thing she wanted to do.

When the rosebud touched her lips, she forced out, "I don't believe you."

"Why not?" He trailed the rose down her throat and touched the hollow at its base. Her pulse raced against its delicate petals. "You don't like me?"

"It isn't—"

"Or do you like me too much?" He dipped the rose into the valley between her breasts. She gasped but couldn't bring herself to make him stop. The feeling he stirred inside her was simply too delicious.

"I like…that," she admitted in a breathless whisper.

"I like it, too." His husky murmur curled heat through her and melted her insides.

Craving his touch, she clenched her hands into fists to keep from reaching for him. She knew the dangers of succumbing to desire. An innocent kiss or caress could lead to so much more, and once begun, it was so hard to stop. She couldn't let that happen, certainly not with him. No matter how much she wanted to.

He traced the rosebud against the inside swells of her breasts. Each featherlight caress pulsed heat between her thighs. A soft moan rose on her lips, and she closed her eyes against the urge to ask for more.

He circled the flower over her bodice. Despite the layers of clothes, her nipples tightened as if he'd touched her bare flesh. Her breath came fast and shallow, then faster and shallower still when he trailed the bud down the front of her body and across her abdomen.

As he drew languid circles over her tightening stomach, her body throbbed just inches below his hand. She bit her lip in confusion, fearing he would caress lower...fearing he wouldn't...

The rose slipped from his fingers and fell into her lap. Her eyes fluttered open, and she looked down at it, recognizing it for what it was.

An invitation to surrender.

Trembling from the arousal throbbing inside her, she was afraid to touch it, as if it alone possessed the power to make her fall. Again.

"Alec," she protested in a whisper, unable to speak any louder. She needed all her strength to simply keep breathing. "You're an earl who—"

"Who very much wants to kiss you," he murmured.

A jolt of disappointment pierced the fog of desire engulfing her. Her chest squeezed around her foolish heart as she admitted the frustrating truth behind his attempted seduction. "Only because you want to know secrets about Henry."

He dropped his gaze to her mouth and caressed his thumb over her bottom lip. "Those secrets aren't the only ones I want to uncover."

She shivered at the temptation he dangled before her. He wasn't being honest with her; she didn't dare believe him. She knew the lies and charms that men like Alec wielded, just as she knew the consequences. The repercussions she'd suffered before with Samuel would be nothing compared to the way her life could be shattered from only a moment's weakness with Alec. Society noticed every move he made, every waltz he requested…every stolen kiss beneath a rose bower. If they were found out, his reputation would simply be confirmed, while hers would be destroyed forever. And the school's right along with it.

Worse—she found herself drawn to him, more than she wanted to admit. Even if they weren't discovered, how would she survive a second shattering of her heart when he left her?

"Let me kiss you," he cajoled. His warm breath tickled across her lips with each word.

Her hand rose to his chest, but instead of pushing him away, the traitorous thing fisted his lapel and pulled him closer. "I don't think that's a good idea."

"I think it's a grand one." The dark gleam in his eyes shone like the devil's own. "Besides, it's only a kiss."

It wasn't. What he offered—what she wanted to claim in return—was so much more.

But when he lowered his head, she released her doubts and welcomed the kiss.

The touch of his lips was so gentle and tender that she barely felt them moving against hers, yet she sensed every inch of him like an electric shock. Its tingling fingers curled around her spine as it shimmered through her. Her body yearned to be beneath his and let the pleasure engulf her like a storm. But her heart—oh, her silly heart! It knew what anguish would follow…and simply didn't care.

When he whispered her name against her lips, she sagged against him with a yielding sigh.

Even with his arms around her, her body seemed to float toward the sky as he deepened the kiss with a gentle but insistent sweep of his tongue against her lips. She wanted this stronger taste of him and parted her lips, and a low groan of appreciation tore from his throat. His tongue delved inside her mouth to explore and claim all that he could. He cupped the back of her head and held her still as his tongue plunged between her lips in a primal rhythm that flamed a throbbing ache between her legs.

She tore her mouth away from his to pant back her breath, but she couldn't find the will to push herself from his arms. As if he knew what thoughts warred within her, he brushed his lips against her temple in a soothing caress, yet he gave no quarter and swept his hand up to her breast. The heat of his palm seeped through the layers of her clothes as if they weren't there at all, and when he began to gently massage her, the whimper of need that rose on her lips was smothered beneath his mouth as it once more captured hers.

Oh, how good it felt to kiss a man like this! How delicious the sculpted muscles beneath her fingers and the firm lips tasting hers. She forgot her anger toward him until all she knew was the wonderful sensation of having her soft body molded against his hard one.

He swept his mouth away from hers, down her neck, and across her chest above her bodice. He placed delicate kisses along her neckline, each one lingering slightly longer than the one before, until his mouth remained on her, giving her hot kisses that made her shiver.

"A brilliant mind coupled with such beauty..." he murmured against her flesh and continued to caress her with his lips. "You have no idea how tempting you are, do you?"

"I'm not…tempting to you…" But her protest emerged as a panting purr and completely undercut the soft chastisement she'd been aiming for. So did the way her hands slipped up from his chest to his neck and buried her trembling fingers in his soft chestnut hair.

He chuckled, and the low rumble flared heat into her bosom. "You have no idea how much… Shall I show you?"

Knowing what she craved, he slipped his fingers beneath her bodice and gently freed her right breast from the layers of clothing until her nipple was exposed above the lace of her neckline. He lazily circled it with his fingertip and smiled wickedly at the way it drew up into a hard pink point. Then he leaned down and captured it between his lips.

Her sharp inhalation faded into a soft sigh as he began to tease at her with the tip of his tongue in slow, wet licks. Surrendering to the throbbing desire he stirred low in her belly, she arched herself into him and pulled his head down tighter against her. The sensation of his mouth on her bare breast was too delicious to stop, and she bit back a moan of pleasure that rose on her lips.

She felt him smile against her flesh at her reaction. Following the path he'd traced over her earlier with the rosebud, his hand trailed down her ribs and belly toward where the flower still rested in her lap—

"Lord St James!" Mrs. Peterson's shrill voice pierced the quiet of the garden. "My lord, wherever have you disappeared to?"

Startled, Olivia pushed him away and scrambled to her feet. Tucking her breast back inside her bodice and straightening her neckline, she backed to the far side of the bower as panic replaced the passion inside her. She swiped the back of one hand across her lips and frantically smoothed at her dress with the other.

Alec remained calmly seated.

"She's looking for you," Olivia whispered through her fingers. Her stomach knotted into a nauseating burn. "I'll hide here, but you have to go—"

In aggravation, he arched a brow, then pointedly dropped his gaze to his lap.

Her eyes followed to the tented line of his trousers. *Heavens*, he was in no condition to go anywhere! An aching heat blossomed low in her belly, and she stared shamelessly at his crotch, causing his brow to arch even higher.

Mrs. Peterson called out again, this time much closer.

With a gasp, Olivia grabbed her bonnet and placed it on his lap, then stepped back to size up her work.

Well, *that* only called more attention to his distress.

They needed another plan. And quickly.

"Stay here," she ordered. Her hands trembled as she reached for her bonnet, her fingers moving close to his… to his…*uncomfortably* close for both of them. With a deep breath of resolve, she snatched up the bonnet. "I'll distract her."

Before he could stop her, she ducked through the bower entrance and out into the bright sunshine of the garden. She finished tying her bonnet ribbons beneath her chin just as the smiling woman came around the curve in the path and spotted her.

"Mrs. Peterson!" Olivia huffed out as she hurried toward the portly woman, suddenly out of breath. "Isn't this just the most beautiful garden? Oh, you really must see the fountain!"

Olivia firmly took the woman's arm and turned her back toward the house.

"But I—I was looking for St James…" Mrs. Peterson gazed back over her shoulder and dragged her feet, but Olivia kept a firm hold and determinedly moved her forward. She'd haul the woman to Newcastle if she had to.

"He's at the house," Olivia assured her. "I saw him go that way at least ten minutes ago."

"No, I was just there." She pointed toward the rear of the garden in the direction of the bower. "A footman said he'd been walking this way."

"I'm certain he went back to the house to find Lady Elizabeth. Oh, look—foxglove!" She tugged the matron quickly up the path. "Aren't they just lovely?"

The woman blinked. "Aren't they poisonous?"

"Well, no one's perfect."

Mrs. Peterson halted in her tracks and narrowed her matronly eyes on Olivia. "My dear, are you unwell? You look rather flushed."

"Do I?" Olivia raised her hands innocently to her cheeks, but she knew darn well that the blasted blush was there. Just as she knew exactly what—and *who*—had put it there. "It's all the fresh air, the exercise of walking in the garden, the flowers…" And *one* rosebud in particular.

"I suppose you're right." Mrs. Peterson glanced over her

shoulder again. Not finding Alec, she frowned and cast her gaze around the rest of the garden. "Whatever could have happened to St James? I wanted to tell him more about my niece."

"Your niece?" Olivia took her arm again, and this time she nudged the rotund woman more gently toward the terrace at the rear of the house and the group of ladies gathered there.

"Iphigenia Dunwoody. Have you met her? Such a lovely girl! Good family, robust figure, well-mannered..." Mrs. Peterson lowered her voice conspiratorially. "And as the daughter of a viscount, a good match for St James, don't you think?"

"Yes." Olivia forced a smile despite an inexplicable burst of jealousy. "Just perfect."

Thirteen

OLIVIA LEANED HER ELBOWS AGAINST THE RAILING OF the supper box and swept her gaze over the crowd. Despite the revelry unfolding around her, she was out of sorts and had been since she kissed Alec that afternoon.

Normally, she would have leapt at the chance to spend the evening at Vauxhall Gardens, and in such a grand box at the ground center of the main avenue, no less. But tonight the musicians sounded flat to her distracted ears, and the acrobats, dancers, and jugglers failed to hold her attention. So did the usual parade of ladies and gentlemen strolling along the avenue. Not even the hot-air balloon tempted her with its exciting ride high into the night sky or the promise of fireworks at the end of the evening.

She was too distracted to enjoy any of it.

Behind her in the box, Henry and a half dozen of his friends laughed and caroused loudly, drinking port and smoking cheroots despite her presence. That is, when they weren't telling bawdy stories. They'd had a fine supper in the box of seven courses served by uniformed footmen, and now that the entertainments had begun, the men had pulled their chairs away from the table and up to the railing to gawk at the sights and call out obnoxious insults to the performers. They were behaving like a bunch of scapegrace lads on holiday from university rather than respected members of the community.

She glanced across the box at her brother, and her eyes narrowed. How had Henry managed to gain access to a private box? Where did he find the money to purchase the dinner, cigars, and port? Was he dipping into school funds to afford this, or was Alec right—had Henry been taking architectural commissions behind her back?

She didn't want to suspect so, but when she'd pressed Henry for answers tonight, he'd dismissed her questions with a wave of his hand and a quick switch of topics.

His elusiveness only added to her unease. So had Alec's warnings about the men he claimed Henry was working with. Had her brother truly taken up with revolutionaries? Doubtful…

Beside her, two of Henry's cronies both let out loud belches and then laughed.

She rolled her eyes. *Very* much doubtful.

Henry *had* been behaving strangely lately; there was no doubt of that. But he was also under pressure to make himself appealing to the Royal Society, which meant participating in all kinds of activities he wouldn't normally have done. Including tonight's visit to Vauxhall.

Henry had met her at the front door when she'd returned from Harlow House with an invitation to join him tonight for supper. She'd begged off, wanting only space and quiet to think about that moment of temporary madness in the garden when she'd let Alec kiss her. No, when she'd allowed him to do far more than simply kiss her.

Yet Henry wouldn't let her refuse and insisted she come. She was certain, though, that it had less with wanting his sister with him and more about her newfound popularity among the *ton*—well, with the Sinclairs and Lady Gantry, anyway. Henry was nothing if not ambitious.

Now, she sat troubled with thoughts of her brother—and unbidden ones of Alec—and waited impatiently for the fireworks that would signal the end of the evening. Then she could go home to find the peace and quiet to sort through her thoughts, figure out if she could trust either man, and plan out what to do next. She'd work through her current situation the way she worked through mathematical proofs—one piece of information at a time.

Henry came up behind her and leaned close to be heard above the noise. "You're not having a good time."

He reeked of port and cigar smoke, and she fought back the urge to crinkle her nose at the pungent stench. She deflected by asking, "Are *you* enjoying yourself?"

He grinned as his friends burst into laughter over a joke about a prostitute and a vicar. "Having a deucedly good time."

She frowned. This wasn't like him. He might drink and laugh with friends, but not publicly and never to excess. This was unusual for—

No.

She wouldn't let her doubts blossom into suspicions. Henry was her brother, for heaven's sake! He wasn't perfect, she knew that better than anyone. But he certainly wasn't a revolutionary and wouldn't knowingly be involved with anyone who was.

"Try to have fun tonight." He teasingly nudged her shoulder. "Or at least look like you are."

She forced a smile for him.

"That's better." He kissed her cheek. "Would you like me to call a footman to fetch you a lemon ice?"

A lemon ice to make her happy…as if she were a child who could easily be manipulated with a simple treat. Somehow she managed to keep her smile fixed. "No, thank you."

"The fireworks will start soon. Those will be grand."

"Yes, they will." Only because it meant the evening had finally come to an end.

Henry moved away from her to rejoin his friends, and relief lightened her chest. Yet inexplicably, she was left feeling even more confused than before.

Alec or Henry…which man could she trust?

A tightrope walker balanced overhead on a wire strung between the buildings, but Olivia turned her attention away to watch the crowd. Most were finely dressed couples who were strolling through the gardens to see and be seen. Others were middle-class families out for an evening's inexpensive entertainment. Footpads and pickpockets lingered unseen among the lot of them, looking for easy prey of the guests who'd overindulged on punch and whiskey.

The narrower alleys stretched beyond the avenue of supper boxes. They were crowded with people and illuminated with lanterns hung among the trees to guide guests toward the refreshment stands around the pavilion at the center of the park.

Beyond the pavilion, the gardens grew darker and

overgrown with bushes and trees. The paths there were narrow and winding, and the lamps gave way to darkness. These close walks formed a shadowy labyrinth where amorous couples in masks and fancy dress could disappear into the darkness for private amusements. It was that far end of the property that had earned Vauxhall its somewhat sordid reputation. After all, they weren't called *pleasure gardens* for nothing. Here, men could buy wanton favors from high-priced prostitutes of both sexes, bored ladies could play at being prostitutes themselves, and husbands and wives could share all kinds of intimacies...with other people's husbands and wives. All their secrets would be safely hidden among the dark trees and shadows.

That was English society, she mused. So staid and proper on the surface with all its rules and manners that had to be followed perfectly for fear of ruination, while in the shadows lurked a soiled world of debauchery. No wonder Vauxhall was the favorite summer entertainment of the *ton*. And no wonder several masquerade masks, cloaks, and capes still lay in the corner of the supper box where its last occupants had left them.

A uniformed attendant walked past the front of the box, and Olivia called out to him. She gestured him over as if asking for an ice. But when he reached the railing, she leaned over and asked instead quietly, "Whose box this is?"

"Lord Hawking's, ma'am." He shot her a look as if she were daft not to know that and hurried on.

Olivia frowned. Why would the Marquess of Hawking loan his box to Henry for the evening? Was he involved with the Royal Society?

Unease pricked at the backs of her knees. She desperately wanted answers. Her hands itched to grab Henry's shoulders and shake him until the truth came out.

But she also didn't want to start a scene that would put her at the center of an unplanned Vauxhall entertainment for anyone who might be watching, including the men Alec had warned her about.

She didn't dare press Henry for information now. But she *would* as soon as they were home. She already lived her life keeping secrets. She couldn't bear adding another one to the list.

A small commotion stirred in the avenue. Speaking of unplanned entertainments… She craned her neck to see.

A small boy, most likely no more than eleven or twelve, made his way down the row of boxes. He stopped every now and then to call over one of the men within, who either laughed or shouted angrily at whatever he had to say before shooing him away.

"What's this?" Henry laughed as the boy finally stepped up to their box. He leaned far over the railing toward the lad, who cupped his hand at his mouth to speak into Henry's ear.

Henry gave a sharp nod, followed by a loud laugh, and reached to box the boy's ears.

The lad ducked and darted away into the thick of the alley crowd until he'd vanished from sight.

"What was that about?" One of Henry's friends pointed the end of his cigar after the boy.

Henry reached for the bottle of port to top off his friends' glasses. "The little urchin was attempting to sell his sister for the evening."

Olivia gaped at him. *A lie.* Oh, she was certain there were any number of men among the crowd tonight who wanted to trade their sisters, daughters, or wives for coin. But the way Henry had reacted—that flash of hardness on his face, his exaggerated laughter, how he'd swung his palm only in afterthought…

Whatever the boy had said, it wasn't an offer of his sister.

"Damnation, Everett!" another of the friends exclaimed, teetering as he tried to rise to his feet. "Why did you send him away? We could have used some female companionship tonight."

Olivia turned away in disgust. Of all the horrible things to say to—

She froze. A flash in the crowd, a fleeting glimpse of dark hair and a masked face… Alec?

Impossible. If rumors could be believed, the Earl of St James sought more adventurous entertainments than those offered here.

Her shoulders slumped. Her mind was playing tricks, that was all. Between the pressures of the school's mounting debts, Henry's peculiar behavior, and her suspicions of what he was hiding from her, she'd been on edge for weeks. None of it was helped by her confusion between the masked man, who teased and taunted her, and Alec, whose play was far more serious.

How could someone so devoted and loving to his family be the same rascal whom society claimed irredeemable? Was it possible that someone so charming and witty could also be a heartless rogue?

And God help her, how could she desire a man who threatened to arrest her brother?

Madness! The man was a scoundrel and a menace. He was irritating and aggravating with no sense of social propriety, or at least no sense of being willing to follow it whenever he was around her.

Yet knowing that didn't stop her from fantasizing about where the encounters might have led if she hadn't discovered his true identity.

Henry slowly rose from his chair and made his way toward the door at the rear of the box.

"Where are you going, Everett?" one of his friends called out.

Olivia watched her brother curiously.

He flashed them a slightly foxed grin. "To fetch us ices. What would an evening at Vauxhall be without treats?"

He ignored the teasing insults from the group and left.

A moment later, Olivia snatched up a discarded mask from the corner of the box and slipped out after him.

She moved carefully to keep Henry in sight yet also remain far enough behind not to be seen. He was up to something…but what?

Ices? Ha! Henry never would have volunteered to fetch treats. No, he would have made a grand show of calling over one of the attendants and ordering the man to bring them. Besides, Henry hated ices. As if to prove her right, he strolled in the opposite direction from the refreshments stands, away from the boxes and crowds, and toward the dark labyrinth of close walks at the rear of the gardens.

Olivia tied her mask in place and followed after.

She swallowed her fear as he made his way deeper into the dark gardens, yet she went on, heedless of her own safety. He led her down a winding path, farther and farther from the distant cacophony of the crowds and entertainments at the front of the park by the grand avenues with their supper boxes and bandstands. Illuminated by only a scattering of lanterns hanging from trees, the gardens turned into a strange fairyland around her. Men and women in fancy dress and masks slipped off into the bushes together, and from the darkness rose soft sounds of deep laughter and light giggles, moans and squeals of delight. Olivia did her best to ignore all of it and focused on not losing Henry amid the shifting shadows.

When he reached the end of the path, he stepped into a small clearing surrounded by thick bushes and trees. All the lamps had been extinguished in this far corner of the gardens, where crumbling walls of strategically placed follies resembled ancient Roman ruins, and the noise of the music and crowds was nothing more than a distant hum.

Silently, she slipped behind a yew hedge edging the clearing and peered through the tangled branches to watch. A movement caught her eye. A dark form slid out from behind the Roman temple wall and glided toward Henry.

Olivia breathed a silent sigh of relief. *A woman.* She nearly laughed. Henry had gone for nothing more than a tryst, after all.

As the woman approached, she lowered her mask. A tree branch stirred in the evening breeze just enough to part the leaves overhead, and a slant of moonlight revealed her face.

Baroness Rowland.

Olivia blinked. Impossible... *Wasn't it?* How did Henry even know Lady Rowland, let alone have the opportunity to carry on an affair with her?

A terrible suspicion clenched Olivia's chest. Was that where Henry had been during those nights when he'd gone missing—with the baroness?

As she watched the pair, their private conversation quickly turned into a heated argument. Henry grew agitated and gestured emphatically toward the main part of the gardens, while Lady Rowland stiffened and clenched her hands at her sides.

Olivia couldn't hear what they were saying, too far away to discern their hushed voices. Silently, she stepped closer to the edge of the bushes.

A hand shot out of the darkness and covered her mouth. A strong arm wrapped around her waist and pulled her back against a hard body. She took a deep breath to scream—

"Hush," a familiar voice warned.

She froze, except for the sudden lurch of her heart into her throat.

Alec.

Fourteen

OLIVIA'S SKIN TINGLED EVERYWHERE HER BODY touched his. Alec held her pressed against his hard front, his palm over her lips and his mouth at her ear. The steady rise and fall of his chest rubbed against her back with each deep breath he took.

"The woman." His lips grazed her earlobe and curled a heated shiver along her spine. He slid his hand down to rest on her shoulder, his fingers spread across her throat. Could he feel her racing pulse beneath his fingertips? "Who is she?"

Through the tangled branches, they both watched as her brother gestured angrily at the baroness, who in turn had become just as upset as Henry. Olivia whispered, "Lady Rowland."

Alec stiffened.

Olivia couldn't prevent a prick of jealousy. Of course Alec personally knew the baroness, given the social circles they both moved within. She was also a wealthy widow, beautiful, intelligent…the perfect companion for an earl. But did Alec know her intimately as well as socially?

Olivia gathered her courage. "Have you and she—"

"Shh." His fingers returned to her mouth. But this time, instead of silencing her, he brushed over her lips in a delicate caress. "Can you hear what they're saying?"

She shook her head. "We can move closer—"

"No." His arm tightened around her. "I won't risk your life."

Risk her life? Her brother was having a lovers' spat. That was all this was…

Wasn't it? Her suspicious attention fixed on Henry as he said something to Lady Rowland that made the baroness shake her head and start away from him. But he grabbed her arm and angrily pulled her back—

A commotion rose from the path.

Henry's head snapped up. He growled some last word to the baroness, then pushed her away.

Henry stormed away and quickly vanished into the darkness.

Lady Rowland remained behind for a moment, breathing deeply to settle herself. Then she squared her slender shoulders and walked toward the path, back toward the light and noise of the party grounds.

Olivia stepped forward to follow—

Alec stopped her. In the privacy of the shadows, he turned her in his arms and guided her backward against a large chestnut tree. He captured her between the tree and his body, but she had no intention of fleeing. She'd never truly feared him, not even when he'd worn a mask, and now, in this strange wonderland of the pleasure gardens, the magnetic pull of him was undeniable.

She dropped her hands to her sides to keep from untying the mask and revealing his face to her. "Shouldn't you follow him?"

"No." Even in the shadows, his eyes flickered brightly. "My job is to follow you."

A tingle blossomed inside her. "Why?"

"Usually, to stay close to your brother." He reached to caress a stray curl that had come loose when she'd darted into the bushes. "But tonight, it's to protect you."

"I don't need protecting." Whatever determination she'd hoped to convey was undercut by a tremor in her voice.

"You walked alone into the dark gardens. It's just as dangerous here as it is in the City." He raised a brow over the top edge of his mask. "Unless you brought your carving knife with you."

Her lips twisted ruefully. "It didn't help against you."

"Because I'm special," he said, deadpan.

She bit back a soft laugh. *Yes, you are*…although she was reluctant to admit to herself just how special he'd become to her. He'd saved her life, had given her a ball gown—well, all right, *that* was only so he could get her alone and ask about her brother's work. But she couldn't deny that he was dedicated to his family, to crown and country, and that perhaps the rumors she'd heard about his scandalous behavior had been greatly exaggerated.

If he had been anyone else but the Earl of St James, she might have even said that she was falling for him.

But he *was* the earl. Anything more enduring than fleeting kisses was impossible.

Still, she couldn't resist the temptation he presented. Surrendering to the urge itching at her fingertips, she reached up and caressed his firm jaw.

"I put on a mask when I left the box." She was mesmerized by the warmth of his skin and his evening beard that scraped provocatively against her fingertips. What would it feel like to brush her mouth across his jaw and feel that same scratch across her lips…or against her inner thigh? "How did you know it was me?"

"I would know you anywhere." He turned his head and placed a light kiss to her palm.

A swirling heat pulled through her, from the throbbing ache between her legs out to the ends of her hair.

"You were never supposed to know I was here tonight," he confessed with chagrin.

"I would know you anywhere," she repeated his words in a breathless whisper.

He smiled, and she outlined his lips with her finger. They were firm but soft, so warm…so inviting…

Until they frowned. "Did you know your brother was meeting with Lady Rowland tonight?"

"Of course not." The question startled her, and she dropped her hand to his chest. Which was a mistake, because she couldn't help but curl her fingers into his waistcoat. Her traitorous body didn't want to let go of him.

"Did they exchange anything—messages, papers, money?"

"Nothing. But I've told you before that my brother isn't—" She realized what he was implying, and her mouth dropped open. "You think Lady Rowland is involved with a group of revolutionaries?" When his expression remained unchanged, she whispered incredulously, "It's one thing to accuse Henry, but *her*… Heavens, she's a baroness!"

"Cromwell was an MP, Napoleon a general, and Lafayette a marquis. Titles make no difference to revolutionaries." His cold warning chilled her through to the bone. "This plot involves officials at the highest levels in the Court of St James's and Whitehall. No one's above suspicion."

"Including me?"

When he didn't immediately reply, a pang of betrayal pierced her, and she glanced away, back toward the path and the route home.

He took her chin and turned her face to meet his gaze. "Not you, Olivia. You intrigue me for completely different reasons." He admitted with a heavy sigh, "*You* frighten me."

Her chest tightened at that unexpected confession. "Because you think that I'm involved with those men, too."

"Because you make it hard for me to keep you safe."

She lifted a brow. "And who keeps me safe from you?"

"Exactly," he answered soberly. Then he lowered his head and kissed her.

The sigh that left her lips at first contact turned into a soft moan as the kiss lingered on. His mouth possessed hers in a way she'd never been kissed before, both rough and sweet at the same time, both savoring and demanding. He ran his hands up and down her body in comforting caresses until she melted against him, boneless.

Then his touches changed. No longer soothing but seductive, he now took bold strokes over her shoulders, breasts, and hips. She slid her mouth away from his as she struggled to regain the air he'd just stripped from her.

She should have been running back to the safety of the

box, fleeing as fast as she could from the temptation he posed. Yet she remained rooted within his embrace, deliciously engulfed by the heat and strength of his body.

He nuzzled her ear. "You like it when I kiss you." He sucked at her earlobe, and the pull of his lips sparked out to the tips of her fingers and toes. "Admit it."

With what little breath she could regain, she forced out, "No, I don't."

"Liar." His deep chuckle reverberated into her chest and made her breasts grow heavy.

It *was* a lie. Yet she was torn over him, pulled between the need to satisfy the arousal quickening in her belly and the need to protect her heart by shoving him away.

"You like my kisses," he murmured, doing just that to her earlobe. "And I sure as hell enjoying kissing you."

"Of course you do," she panted out as his mouth slid down to her neck. "You're a rake."

"I'm not a rake. I'm the exact opposite, in fact." Before she could process that statement, he licked at her pulse as it throbbed wildly at the base of her throat, and her thoughts scattered like leaves in a storm. "But you like rakes."

She shivered as liquid heat cascaded over her like a hot summer rain. "No, I don't. I'm a respectable schoolmistress who—"

"Who likes rakes."

Oh, the frustrating man! And even more frustrating with the way his hands roamed deliciously over her.

"Admit it. You like me." He nuzzled the small stretch of

bare shoulder between her neck and the sleeve cap of her dress. "You like me *because* you think I'm a rake."

"You're disreputable, the subject of gossip and rumors and—"

He nipped her flesh in punishment. She sucked in a sharp breath as pleasure-pain shot through her.

"I'm a man who lives his life openly and makes no excuses for it," he corrected with a soothing lick to her shoulder. "There are lines I won't cross, but I also take pleasure from anyone willing to freely give it and accept it in return. If that makes me a rake in society's eyes—or those of a beautiful woman—then so be it."

To prove his point, his hand at her back toyed with the tiny buttons holding up her bodice, but he didn't unfasten them. Not yet. She knew he was giving her the chance to stop him, would release her from his arms with only a single whisper from her lips. But she didn't want him to stop. *Willing to freely give pleasure and accept it in return*... Never had she been more tempted in her life to do just that.

When he tantalizingly slipped free a single button, a heated shiver raced straight down her spine and landed with a fierce throb between her legs.

"Wouldn't you like to do the same?" he murmured. "Wouldn't you like to accept pleasure rather than deny yourself?"

She didn't stop him when he hooked his thumb beneath the sleeve cap of her dress, *couldn't* find the will to stop him when he pulled it down to bare her shoulder to the moonlight and his sensuous lips. Heat prickled across her skin, and she felt herself sliding toward surrender.

"Do you want to be like me, Olivia?" With each button he freed, her bodice loosened a little more. "Uninhibited, daring…"

The last button slipped open, and her dress fell down to her elbows.

"You can be exactly that tonight."

He nudged down her stays and chemise to bare her breasts to the cool air. Her nipples appeared just above the tight fabric, but far enough for him to flutter his fingertips over them.

"Tonight," he purred, his eyes gleaming in the darkness at the sight of her, "you can claim whatever pleasures you'd like."

He dipped his head to capture her nipple in his mouth, and she was lost.

With a soft cry, she dug her fingernails into his shoulders, and the sinews of his muscles flexed beneath her grasping hands. Each suck of his lips pulled a delicious heat up from the ache between her legs to her breasts, to flame right there beneath his mouth.

He moved his attentions to her other breast and laved at her greedily. The dark shadows and gardens cocooned them, and all she heard was the mutual panting of their breaths and the soft, wet sounds of his mouth adoring her. The most erotic sounds she'd ever heard in her life.

Her senses were fully awake now, all of her longing to surrender and let herself be taken. Alec could give her that. Here, in the darkness and shadows of this strange wonderland, he could give her the pleasure and release she craved.

No one would ever know. Not Lady Gantry or the other patrons, not Mrs. Adams, not even Henry—

"Tell me what you want," he cajoled against her breast.

The deep whisper tickled down to her toes in a spark of arousal and need that terrified her with its intensity. If she surrendered to him tonight, the physical joining would be wonderful—how could it be otherwise? But sex was all it would be. All it could ever be. He was incapable of giving her the future she wanted.

Yet to give up the only opportunity she might ever have to be in his arms, to feel his body moving inside hers, to be close to the only man her heart had cared about since Samuel…

"Olivia," he whispered, half pleading for her to capitulate.

She pulled in a deep breath. "I want…"

"Yes, sweet?"

"I want…" Her face flushed hot. She felt like a goose! Yet she wanted… "To taste you."

His lips quirked upward in a devilish smile. "Then taste me."

Emboldened, she pulled loose his cravat and collar. She placed her mouth against his bare neck and fought back a groan as she brushed her lips over his skin. *Delicious.* Unable to resist, she licked at his flesh and captured on her tongue a wonderful mix of spices, salt, man—she smiled—and *lemons.*

"What else do you want?" he rasped out. Beneath her lips, she felt his pulse race.

"Touch me," she commanded, daring to give this powerful man orders. "Down…there."

"Are you certain?"

She gave a jerking nod of permission. Taking his hand, she laced her fingers through his, then lifted her skirt high enough to slip his hand beneath.

He caressed his palm up and down her thighs above her garters in slow strokes that were both comforting and exciting at the same time. Nervousness stirred inside her even as her knees shook in anticipation of a more intimate touch, but he hadn't yet given her what her body craved.

Need blazed low in her belly, and she panted out, "Alec... please..."

With a low groan, he slipped his hand between her thighs. The whimper on her lips turned into a low moan as he gently parted her folds and teased his fingers tantalizingly against her core. She melted against the tree behind her for support. Only her hands on his shoulders kept her from falling into a puddle on the ground.

"Is this what you want?" he whispered as his fingers explored deeper. "To be touched like this?"

In answer, she shifted her hips to widen her stance and give him more room to pleasure her. She wanted this touch— wanted *him*—too much to stop. Soon he would be inside her, filling her with his strength and warmth, but for now she gloried in the long, deep strokes that left her shaking.

"Or do you prefer this?" He pressed against the hard little nub nestled in her folds.

Her hips bucked. "Alec!"

"I know," he murmured as his lips kissed tenderly at her temple. "You want this."

He slipped his finger deep inside her tight warmth.

She shuddered with pleasure and clung to him. The sensation was wonderful, so wonderful that her folds began to quiver around him as if attempting to draw him deeper through their own volition. But when he slipped a second finger inside, stretching her wider and filling her even more—

Oh, that was simply divine!

"Harder," she choked out as the pressure building inside her demanded release. "Oh, please…"

He did as she asked, stroking into her hard and fast. Liquid fire nipped at her toes, licked at her thighs and breasts, and threatened to consume her.

Still, it wasn't enough. She craved more of him.

She arched into him to beg with her body what she couldn't find the words to utter. In answer, he shifted his weight into her. A solid wall of male hardness pressed against her, all focused right there at the pulsing nub beneath his thumb—

A spasm of release cascaded through her, and she buried her face in his shoulder to muffle the noise as she cried out. Her body electrified, losing all awareness of everything around her, everything but him.

A muffled growl of pain tore from him. "Damnation, woman!"

Her hand flew to her mouth, and she pulled back, appalled at herself. "Oh no—I bit you!"

He laughed wickedly, the sound a low warning. "Revenge is sweet," he said hoarsely, then brought himself to his knees in front of her and pushed her skirts out of his way. "My turn to bite."

He lowered his head and claimed her with his mouth.

She tensed for a fleeting moment at the shock of what they were doing, outdoors and hidden only by shadows. But the delicious sensations he spiraled through her chased away all reservations until she was lost in the moment. With Alec.

If only she could strip away all the clothes between them and bring warm skin against skin, have his sculpted shoulders bare to her fingers and eyes as his head lingered between her legs. Yet even fully clothed, he brought her such pleasures that she could barely keep her breath in her lungs and a scream from escaping her throat.

Raw need coursed through her. She arched her back and rocked her pelvis against him.

He groaned, and his hands clasped tighter at her buttocks, his tongue driving deeper inside her. He wasn't giving her pleasure now; she was demanding it from him, and he eagerly complied.

Release flooded over her, and she shuddered with a cry as she convulsed against his mouth.

Every inch of her tingled with pleasure. It took all her strength to capture back the breath that had been ripped from her, while the man who had stolen it continued to worship between her legs, but now with tender kisses and soothing licks.

Yet all too soon, he climbed to his feet and gathered her into his arms. As he held her, his hard erection jutted into her soft belly, and fresh desire pulsed through her.

He placed a soft kiss to her temple. "We have to stop now."

She pulled back to look up at him, confused by the need that fogged her mind. "Why?"

"Because I want you too much."

"I want you, too," she admitted, her voice no more than a breathless whisper. "All of you." *Too much…*

With an aching groan, he rested his forehead against hers. "That's exactly why." He squeezed his eyes shut as if pained. "If we don't stop right now…"

"Then we don't stop." She'd made her decision. She couldn't deny herself the chance to be with him tonight, and damn the dawn to come.

He grimaced and straightened. When he took a single step away, the cool air chilled through her. She wanted nothing more than to be buried in his arms again, engulfed by his heat and strength. She reached for him—

He took her hand and enfolded it in both of his. "We can't. No matter how much I want to."

She dropped her gaze to his chest and blinked hard to keep back the stinging tears at his rejection. "Because you're an earl," she whispered. The brutal truth ripped a hole through her chest. "And I'm only a schoolmistress."

When she tried to slip her hand away, he tightened his hold. He touched her chin and tilted her face up to look into her eyes. "Because you're an innocent, and I am *not* a rake."

"But that's not—" She choked off as her heart lurched into her throat with relief. A smile broke across her face. "It's all right. You can make love to me."

"No." He dropped his hand away as if touching her even

this harmlessly was too much temptation. "I told you. There are lines I won't cross." He groaned with desire. "No matter how tempting you are."

No! This night couldn't end like this, not after the desires he'd awakened inside her. She couldn't have borne not being with him. The long-hidden truth emerged from her as little more than a breath. "But I'm not."

His mouth twisted with chagrin. "Trust me. You are incredibly tempting."

"No, I mean—I'm not...innocent." She swallowed hard, then confessed in a rush, "I was going to be married. We eloped but didn't—"

He stilled. "You eloped?"

"No one knows but Henry." She forced a smile to break the sudden tension between them. "It's the only secret he knows, believe me."

"Is it?" he drawled, his voice suddenly cold.

"Yes." She held her breath, desperately wanting him to take her back into his arms, sweep her off her feet, and carry her away. "So we don't have to—"

Overhead, fireworks screamed into the night. They exploded and rained blue and red sparks across the sky. She jumped at the echoing booms, startled, and whirled around as her hand flew to her throat at the fright.

Only fireworks. She let out a deep breath. What a goose she was! With a quiet laugh at herself, she turned back—

He was gone.

Fifteen

ALEC PACED THE LENGTH OF HIS DARK STUDY, NOT having bothered to light any lamps. Dawn was only a few hours away, yet he couldn't quash the icy anger inside him to find enough peace to sleep.

He could barely fathom it. Olivia Everett had run away with a man, surrendered her innocence, and then lied to the world about it, letting everyone believe she was still a respectable, virtuous miss. She'd been lying to *him*. All those times when he'd mentioned how innocent she was, how unspoiled and proper…all those times when she didn't correct him. He felt like a fool.

Damn her! Damn her secrets and her lies. Damn her façade of respectability—

No, damn *himself* for letting her into his head and under his skin.

He halted in front of his desk to rake his fingers through his hair. He'd lost his mind tonight when he'd followed her into the dark shadows. Apparently, he'd lost control of his cock as well, because he'd certainly been thinking with it instead of his brain or he never would have kissed her like that, never would have bared her breasts to his greedy eyes and lips, never would have dropped to his knees. But he'd been too intoxicated by the taste and feel of her to deny himself.

Or to realize that she was living a lie. Just as his father had.

He'd thought he'd known exactly who she was—a woman so unlike the others he'd ever known that she'd seemed to sweep into his life like a fresh breeze. Not someone world-weary or jaded, not someone looking for a liaison to fend off an evening's boredom, but a woman who shared his view of the world by living her life honestly about who she was and the actions she took.

A woman who was opening her heart and body for the first time. To him.

It was nothing but lies.

He took a gasping swallow of whiskey. Its burn seared down his throat and straight into his chest. *Good.* He wanted it to cauterize his heart to her and put her back where she should have been from the beginning, as nothing more than a mission asset.

But even now, the memory of her made his blood boil, his body ache—

Christ! He hurled his tumbler into the fireplace. It exploded in a shower of glass and flames.

"What did that glass ever do to you?" a soft voice chided from the doorway.

He spun around. *Olivia.*

She leaned against the doorframe in the flickering fire-light as the flames drank up the whiskey and slowly dimin-ished, but her blue eyes remained bright even in the shadows. Beneath her cloak, she wore the same dress he'd nearly stripped off her tonight, and her hair still showed signs of being mussed from their embrace. His gut twisted, and it wasn't from anger or blame. Despite her deception, he still ached to finish what they'd started in the gardens, remove that dress completely, and lose himself in her.

He bit back a curse. "How did you get in here?"

"The rear door was unlocked." She gave a small shrug. "But I can leave and come back in through the window if you'd prefer."

Despite her teasing words and her calm demeanor, he could sense both frustration and pain boiling inside her the way old sailors sensed changes in the weather. Tonight, one hell of a storm was brewing.

"And you'd like an explanation for what happened in the gardens," he drawled.

Her blue eyes boldly met his. A quick pain pierced him when he saw their puffiness. She'd been crying.

His shoulders sagged. She'd deceived him, but she didn't deserve to be wounded. Life with his father's brutality had taught him that much compassion at least.

She crossed her arms in feeble protection as she stepped into the room. "A very thorough one, I should think."

He hadn't given her one earlier. At that moment in the gardens, she'd reminded him too much of his father's secret life and lies to remain, so he'd left while fireworks still boomed overhead. He'd desperately needed to put as much distance between them as possible while he struggled to understand what she'd confessed to him and the ramifications of it.

But he didn't have to explain himself to anyone, nor did he plan on starting with a woman who made her way through the world behind a false façade.

"My lord! I heard glass break." Bivvens rushed into the room and drew up short in surprise at finding Olivia. His face reddened. "My apologies, sir. I didn't realize—that is, I didn't know that you had…an appointment this evening."

Alec grimaced. *An appointment.* As if he had so many women coming to his home in the middle of the night that he had to write them into his social calendar.

From the way Olivia silently arched a brow, she certainly thought so.

"Shall I clean up this mess, sir?"

Alec waved him away. There weren't enough kitchen towels and brooms in England to clean up the mess he'd found himself in.

The butler's puzzled gaze shifted to Olivia, and Alec pushed down an aggravated sigh. He could only imagine what Bivvens must be thinking. How wrong the man was, too, because Alec would never sin the way his father had. In the six years since he'd returned from the continent and learned what his father had done, Alec had never once brought a woman into his home.

Yet of all the women to first grace his doorstep after midnight…*her*. The irony was biting.

"Leave it for the morning and retire," Alec ordered quietly. His gaze returned to Olivia. "And please close the door when you leave."

"Yes, sir."

Bivvens hurried from the room. Only a parting glance at Olivia as he drew shut the door registered his disappointment that the son might be falling into the same kinds of perversions as the father.

Alec glanced at the shards of glass and blew out a hard breath. Bivvens, of all people, deserved to know the truth. There would be more than one mess in this house to explain in the morning.

He gestured toward the chairs positioned in front of his desk. "Please have a seat."

"I prefer to stand." She punctuated that by placing her hands on her hips in what he assumed was her best scolding schoolmistress posture.

But the effect was lost on him. He'd faced down both his father's rage and the French artillery. She couldn't wound him. Not that way, at least.

"As you wish." He crossed to the side table by the window and reached for a crystal decanter of cognac. "I approached you in the gardens because I was trailing your brother. I followed him to the clearing and found you there." He yanked out the stopper and splashed a generous pour into a tumbler. "Then I kissed you. Simple as that."

When he didn't continue, she said softly, "You did a lot more than kiss me."

His hand jerked and spilled a trickle of cognac onto the tabletop. *Damnation.* He shoved the stopper back into place. "So we did. And both enjoyed it."

His lips twisted when she gave no challenge to that.

A glance over his shoulder confirmed that she remained

in the same battle stance as before. *Fine.* If she wanted a fight, he'd give her one.

He set down the decanter with a soft thud and faced her. "Then I left."

"Yes, you did." She lifted her chin.

His gaze dropped to the long column of her throat. He knew the feel of having his mouth there, remembered the warmth of her skin and the sweet taste of her...*honey.*

"Why leave?" she pressed. "I thought you wanted..."

Me. The word hung between them as loudly as if she'd actually uttered it.

"I did." He raised the glass for a soothing swallow. "I very much did."

"Did you? Or were you simply attempting to seduce information from me?"

He froze, the glass at his lips.

"When you realized I could share nothing more about my brother, you left." She folded her arms over her chest, although Alec couldn't have said whether in self-protection or to keep from throttling him. "Was it because there was no point in continuing if I couldn't provide information?"

"Oh, sweet," he purred. "There's *always* a point in continuing a seduction."

Her lips pressed into a hard line. He wanted to kiss her mouth until it softened, until her lips parted with a sigh and let him inside.

But could he ever kiss away her deception? He suffered no one who pretended to be something they weren't.

"I kissed you tonight—I did *all* those things to you," he

added pointedly before she could correct him and remind him again of how delicious their encounter had been, "because I wanted to bring us both pleasure. No other reason."

"I don't believe you."

He didn't give a damn what she believed about him. Not anymore.

Except for this. "I didn't attempt to seduce secrets from you tonight, Olivia, because I would never use you like that." He dropped his gaze to his glass. "And I certainly didn't have to. All the Home Office had to do was follow your brother, knowing that sooner or later he would lead us to the men he's working with. Tonight he led us to Lady Rowland, and now we follow her. It's simply a matter of trailing behind in their wake and picking up the pieces until we can spring the trap."

If they didn't run out of time. Every day that passed was another opportunity for Scepter to assassinate the prime minister.

"What pieces?" she asked, frustration and anger edging her voice.

He circled behind his desk. There was no point any longer in keeping his mission from her. "You heard about the bombing at the Admiralty Club?"

She frowned at the strange turn of conversation. "Fumes built up in the new gas system, and there was an accident when the lamps were lit. People were hurt, killed so terribly..."

"It wasn't the gas lamps that exploded, and it wasn't an accident." He pulled open his desk drawer and reached inside for the charred slip of paper Clayton had given him. "It was an attempt to assassinate Lord Liverpool."

Even from across the room, he heard her shocked gasp. Slowly, he slid the fragment across the desk toward her.

"What is that?" she asked warily, remaining where she was by the door.

"The reason I don't have to seduce you for information," he admitted solemnly. *And the reason I can't leave you alone, even now.*

She slowly approached his desk. He nodded for her to pick up the fragment. Her frown deepened as she reached for it, only for it to vanish beneath a sudden pallor as she saw the equations worked across the faint lines of building plans and the name Everett scrawled across the bottom.

"A government operative traced a lead to a nearby inn where the men responsible for the bombing had been meeting," he explained. "The Home Office believes those men were following orders from others higher up in their organization." Alec put his drink aside. He no longer had any taste for the stuff. "They attempted to destroy any evidence linking them to the attack, but that slip of paper was discovered in the fireplace ashes. It's our only clue to the identity of the men who set the explosives. If we find those men, then we can find the leaders who gave the orders and stop them from trying again."

He could almost see her sharp mind whirling to put together what he was telling her. "But you—you said revolutionaries, not assassins…"

"No difference," he said quietly, knowing that to be the

God's truth. After all, he'd fought against the French and knew exactly how much death and destruction their revolution had wrought.

She stared at the paper as if she held a snake in her hands. "This is why you've been asking about Henry's work, following him—following *me*."

"His name is the only one we have." *Had*. Until tonight. But try as hard as he might, Alec simply couldn't believe that Lady Rowland was working for Scepter. He nodded at the paper. He placed his palms flat on the desktop and leaned toward her, his eyes fixed on her face. "You recognize them, don't you?"

"Not the equations." Her face paled. "But the plans beneath."

"What are they for?"

She didn't look up as she whispered, "Renovation plans for the Admiralty Club."

His chest squeezed as he asked carefully, "Your brother worked on the renovations?"

A stiff nod. "The club's manager commissioned Henry to double-check the architect's work." Followed by a shake of her head. "But…"

"But?" he prompted, holding his breath.

"These equations are wrong." Her eyes darted up to his. Confusion swirled in their blue depths. "These aren't the ones for the renovations."

"How do you know?"

"Because I…" She swallowed so hard that he could hear it, then admitted little louder than a breath, "Because I reworked those equations to make certain they were correct."

His heart stuttered. "You worked on plans for the Admiralty Club? When?"

"Over two years ago." She placed the paper on the desk and stepped back, as if certain that the snake would bite. "But I've never seen these equations before. They're not any kind an architect would use."

"What kind are they?"

"It looks as if...as if they're the same type of equations Henry uses in his work with stresses and counter stresses." She added in a whisper, "Not building but...demolition."

At that, Alec's heart stopped completely. "Are you sure?"

She parted her lips as if to answer, then decisively shook her head. "No—there aren't enough equations here for me to be certain."

But Alec was. He knew Henry Everett had reworked the building plans for the Admiralty Club, and he'd done so with the intention of causing as much death and destruction as possible. It was the definitive link he and Reed had been searching for between Everett and Scepter. The question now...who was Everett working for? The answer would lead them to Scepter.

"Where's the rest of the sheet?" Her expression darkened as the realization settled over her. "That's why you asked about copies of building plans, why you searched the school... You don't have it."

There was no point in dissembling. "No, I don't." He straightened to his full height. "But I'd hoped the copy would tell me who hired your brother."

"You're out of luck, then." She placed a single finger on

the charred slip and pushed it across the desktop toward him. "*This* is the copy. The equations penciled onto the original renovations have been erased and these new ones worked on top of them. You can see the rubbing, just there in the middle."

His gaze dropped to the paper to confirm it for himself and stifled a curse. He'd been too busy hunting the copy to notice that he'd had it all along. And in all honesty, he'd been too distracted by her.

She shook her head. "Why go to all that trouble? Why not just question Henry directly?" Fear and frustration warred in her voice. "If you show him this, he'll have no choice but to tell you what he knows."

"He can't."

"If he's in trouble, he'll cooperate and—"

"He *can't*," Alec repeated firmly. "Either the leader of the group has told him nothing, so in case he's caught he'll be unable to give up any information, or he'll be killed before he has the chance to." Trying to ignore the way her face paled even whiter, he returned the charred paper to the desk drawer, then picked up his glass. "For his sake, I'm doing everything I can to keep it from coming to that." There wasn't enough liquor left in the tumbler to do any good, yet he tossed down a last blistering gulp to claim whatever relief he could. "Those plans were our best path to the identity of the men he's working with."

But his explanation did nothing to ease her visible distrust of him. "So you bothered with me only because of Henry…the visits to my room, the ball, the garden tea…"

Raw pain rasped her voice. "And that's why you left tonight, isn't it? Because now that you have Lady Rowland to follow, you no longer have any need of me."

He stifled a laugh. She couldn't begin to fathom the need he still possessed for her. "That wasn't it at all."

"Then why?"

Damnation! "Because you're not who I thought you were."

"A revolutionary?"

"Honest." He punctuated that with the thud of the crystal glass to the desktop. Then he leaned toward her on his palms and brought his face level with hers. "Indiscretions and wanton intimacies I can understand. Hell, I'm part of English society. They're practically a requirement in my world." His eyes locked with hers. "But I won't tolerate deception. Not from myself, not from friends or family, not from—" He broke off. *Not from the women I care about.* "Not from you."

Confusion danced across her face. "I never lied to—"

"You've lied to the whole world." He gestured a frustrated hand to indicate the city around them. "You're pretending to be something you're not, and you're making your living on that lie."

She stilled, except for her lips, which parted slightly. To her credit, she didn't insult either of them by asking what he meant.

"You talk of deception..." Her voice was so soft that he could barely hear it, but her distress was unmistakable. "When I met you, you were hiding your identity behind a mask. I don't even know which man you truly are."

"Both." And all of him still wanted her.

He flopped down onto his desk chair and kicked his long legs out in front of him, then crossed them at the ankles in a casual pose that belied the feelings of betrayal simmering inside him. Never had he felt this kind of emotional churning about a woman before. But then, never had a woman gotten under his skin the way Olivia had.

Yet it was more than just physical craving for her that tore so desperately at him. If that was all, he'd have hunted down a widow or bored society wife who would have welcomed him into her bed, exhausted himself in her, and purged Olivia from his life.

No, what had him so frustrated, so furious at himself was that he wanted *all* of her, not just her body. He wanted to experience the brilliance of her mind, that intriguing smile and quick wit. Her selfless kindness. The wild fearlessness that led her into the dark alley and into his life in the first place. That same wild fearlessness that led her into his arms tonight.

But how much of her was real, how much only pretense?

He reached for his glass to focus his attention anywhere but on her face. "You came here to accuse me of attempting to seduce you to get what I wanted." He traced his fingertips around its rim, then lost the battle and lifted his gaze to hers. "How do I know you weren't attempting to do the same?"

Her eyes flared, their storm-tossed depths churning a brilliant blue. At that moment, they were fierce and dark yet more lovely than he'd ever seen them. "I would never give myself to a man who could be so easily manipulated."

He tightened his jaw, having no idea what to believe about

her. "Then what did you hope to gain from this evening? Money? Favors?" Unable to resist any longer the wounded animal howling inside him, he lifted the glass and drawled, "Another attempt at marriage?"

"Exactly what I received," she answered so low he almost couldn't hear. "To be close to you, and nothing more."

He immediately regretted his accusing words. "Olivia, I never—"

"You're a hypocrite." Her hands clenched into tiny fists at her sides, but her eyes never left his as she challenged in a hoarse breath, "You've made a reputation for yourself by drinking, gambling, and bedding women, yet you judge me."

"I did do those things," he admitted. "For years, I did nothing but work to create the most notorious, scandalous name possible for myself."

"Why?"

"Because I never wanted to be anything like my father." He lifted the empty glass in a mocking toast to the bastard. "Pious, respectable… After all, if he was going to accuse me of being a bad son, shouldn't I actually have been doing the things he accused me of?"

Wisely, she didn't answer.

"Nothing was off-limits in those days. Drinking anything put in front of me and in the greatest quantities I could get. Gambling at every hell that would offer me credit on my family name. Starting all kinds of fights for no reason and bribing my way out of gaol whenever the watch or local constable was brave enough to arrest me. Bedding every woman who was willing to lift her skirts, both widows and wives, and sometimes both at the same time." Stunned surprise registered in her eyes, but he couldn't stop the confession now that it was spilling freely. "I was sixteen, not even old enough for university, yet I could start the most wicked rumors imaginable simply by walking down the street."

She swallowed hard at that information, and her throat undulated. Even now, he wanted to place his mouth against her neck to feel that soft movement against his lips.

"But I never once tried to hide what I was doing or lie about it. Just as I haven't lied about trying to change my ways since my father died and to become a truly respectable man." Because once more, he found himself never wanting to be anything like his father. The irony would have been laughable if it wasn't so terrible. "Ask anyone who knows me, and they will tell you exactly who I am. Not some pretense of who I want the world to think I am, but the man I *truly* am."

But all kinds of ghosts still haunted him despite every attempt to be the complete opposite of his father.

He raised his gaze to Olivia. Perhaps they always would.

"You have every right, just as I have, to give yourself to whomever you choose. But you've pretended to be something you're not. You've lied to everyone." He paused to keep the anger and pain from this voice. "And you've lied to me." The brutal truth tore from him as he admitted, "I have no idea what to believe about you. And I have no idea if I can trust you."

"You can," she said with as much determination as her trembling voice allowed. But the fight in her had been replaced by anguish, and the blazing blue of her eyes had dulled to a watery gray. "My past isn't important."

More than she knew. He stared down into his glass, unwilling to meet her gaze. "How many people have you misled? How many people have you hurt because of it?"

He'd wanted her to be the woman she portrayed to the world. He'd wanted her to be a saint to his sinner, to redeem him of his transgressions and free him from the ghosts that still haunted him.

That hope had proven to be nothing but ashes.

"Tell me." He traced his finger around the glass's rim. "Did you know who you wanted to give yourself to tonight, the true person beneath the surface?"

She whispered, "Of course I knew."

"And that's the problem." He raised the empty glass to his lips and murmured quietly against the rim, "Because I didn't."

Sixteen

Olivia stepped out of the hackney she'd taken from St James house and rushed inside the school. Her eyes were so filled with burning tears that she could barely see the floor in front of her as she raced up the stairs.

Henry's door was closed. She pounded her fist fiercely against it.

"Henry!" She knocked again and swallowed down the roiling in her stomach. "Henry, I need to speak with you."

He'd left Vauxhall with her after she'd returned to the supper box and pleaded a desperate headache. He hadn't been at all happy to leave his friends, but he'd taken her home, where she'd paced for over an hour before sneaking out to find Alec. She'd assumed Henry had gone to bed.

But the silence confirmed he'd gone out again.

"Not this time," she whispered, turning the anger that Alec had unleashed inside her on her brother. "You don't get to hide again."

She took out her master key that unlocked every room in the school and opened his door. Just as she'd suspected, he wasn't there. Tonight, though, that wasn't going to stop her from gaining answers.

She snatched a candle from the bedside table and lit it

on the banked coals in the small fireplace. The circle of dim light revealed his room just as it normally was...spartan and clean, with everything in its place and nothing left out to make it untidy, right down to the pairs of shoes and boots all in a row beneath the window.

But looks could be deceiving. Wasn't that the crux of her confrontation tonight with Alec, the one that had shattered her heart?

Tamping down her anguish and latching on to her resolve, she set the candle on top of his desk and began to search the drawers. She couldn't help herself. She needed to know what Henry had done, if he was innocent or—

What was she thinking? Of course he was innocent! He would never have done what Alec had accused him of doing, what deeds those equations on the burnt paper had led her to suspect. Surely, there had been some kind of mistake.

But the desk held nothing but papers related to his teaching...lectures of all kinds, lists of students, grade books from years ago— Good Lord, didn't the man throw anything away?

When she'd finished with the desk, she rushed to the armoire, flung open the drawers, and searched it. Nothing. She dropped to her knees to look under the bed.

Her breath strangled. Throw things away? Apparently not.

A small wooden box lay tucked beneath the mattress ropes. She pulled it out into the room and opened the lid. Rolls of papers had been carefully arranged inside the box and tied with pieces of string, along with folded sheets and letters with their broken wax seals still in place.

She selected one of the rolls, pulled off the tie, and spread it open on the floor. Her hands shook as she smoothed out the sheets of papers. Building plans...and not ones she recognized.

She grabbed several more from the box and unrolled all of them, scanning each for the date and any clue of who had commissioned them. Evidence of other commissions, too, lay inside the box. Receipts for actuarial work for several of the insurance groups that had recently formed across London, amortization tables for loans...even recipes in varying amounts copied out for apothecaries to use in making all sizes of medicinal batches. Olivia stared at them, stunned. She wasn't familiar with any of these documents.

She sat back on her heels in defeat. Henry had been taking commissions on his own and keeping them secret. Based upon the dates, he'd been doing it for years.

She sucked in a pained breath between clenched teeth. Could she trust *any* of the men in her life?

Anguish overwhelmed her, and a tear of humiliation slid down her cheek. She squeezed her eyes shut and pressed her hand to her bosom. Her foolish heart still beat there, yet she felt as if a hole had been ripped into her chest. Would she ever be whole again?

"Olivia!"

She scrambled to her feet, still clasping one of the rolled plans in her hand.

Henry stood in the doorway, gaping at her. His gaze darted between her and the box of papers piled at her feet. Then it narrowed on the one in her hand.

"What on God's earth are you doing?" With a quick look

over his shoulder into the dark hall to make certain none of the girls or Mrs. Adams was there, he closed the door and tried to snatch the paper from her hand. But she yanked it out of his reach.

"No," she corrected and brandished it at him like a sword. "What have *you* done?"

He stiffened and glanced down at the papers. Faced by the evidence piled on the floor, he let his shoulders sag, caught. "I've been taking commissions and not telling you," he admitted quietly. This time, when he reached gently to take the paper from her hand, she grudgingly surrendered it. "We needed the money."

"You never shared any proceeds from these with the school," she challenged. "I would have known."

"For God's sake, Olivia! I'm a grown man, not a child with an allowance." He shot her an angry look and bent down to put the papers back into the box. He flipped the lid over, but the mess of papers and rolls stopped it from closing. Heedlessly, he shoved it all under his bed. "I'm allowed to earn my own income."

Anger churned inside her so strongly that it sickened her. Any money she'd ever earned had been given back to the school, to keep the doors open and the scholarship girls with a roof over their heads and food in their bellies. It had been two years since she'd bought a new dress or owned a pair of gloves or hat that wasn't secondhand. She hadn't spoiled herself with any kind of outing to art shows or the theatres, no treats like chocolates or perfumes...*nothing*. And all the while, he'd been out wasting every penny he'd earned.

All behind her back.

"Not if it puts the school at risk," she shot back, refusing to let him cow her.

"I haven't done anything—"

"I *know* what you've been doing." She dug deep to find enough courage inside her to challenge him, but even then, it emerged as little more than a whisper, "I know about the Admiralty Club."

He paled instantly. Then he forced a stiff laugh. "Of course you know. *That* commission I told you about. You helped me with it."

He turned his back to her and crossed to the armoire, shrugging out of his jacket as he went.

No. She wouldn't allow him to ignore her or treat her like a simpleton. Not any longer. "Not the renovations from two years ago." She squared her shoulders in preparation for her second fight of the night. "The recent plans for the club."

He froze, his hand stilling on his cuffs as he unbuttoned them.

"The ones you reworked on a copy of the old renovation plans, most likely from that box beneath your bed." Her voice was so full of pain and betrayal that it was barely more than a rasp. "The ones you filled with equations on exactly where the walls were at their weakest."

He slowly turned toward her and asked carefully, "How do you know about those?"

As she stared at him, the truth washed over her like ice water and froze the blood in her veins. *Dear God…* He'd just confirmed her darkest suspicions, and the fresh stab of betrayal was heartrending.

"What you did," she whispered, horrified, "those plans... the explosion...people *died*!"

He closed the distance between them and grabbed her upper arms. Panic darkened his face. "Don't you say a word—don't you *dare* say one word," he warned. "I did what I had to do."

"You helped murder those people!" She tried to pull away, but his grip was too strong.

"No!" His face twisted like a monster's. "I never planted the bombs. I had nothing to do with that."

She winced as his hands tightened around her arms. "You gave them information they used to—"

"I didn't know what they were planning," he insisted. "I thought they were going to buy the place and renovate it or tear it down. All they asked of me was to work some equations, to calculate the weakest points in the club's structure. That's what I did. Numbers. I gave them *numbers*. That's all."

She was going to be sick! He'd taken mathematics, something beautiful and elegant, something nearly sublime in its mix of creativity and practicality, and he'd weaponized it. Creation had become destruction at his hands.

"Who?" she pressed. "Tell me their names and—"

He shook her hard to silence her. "You are *never* to ask me about them, understand?"

She cried out. The sharp sound cut through his panic and startled him into loosening his hold.

Regret flashed over his face, but it didn't replace his fear.

She wasn't seeing her brother—she was staring at a trapped animal.

"Why, Henry?" she choked out. "Why would you do something like that?"

"Money," he admitted, stepping back and raking his fingers through his hair. "To save the school, to give us a livable allowance, to stop the creditors from beating down the front door and casting us into the street. We're in debt, Olivia. The kind that will put both of us into debtors' prison." He bit back a curse. "The school can't afford to remain open much longer."

Lies. *All lies!* She knew it in her bones… But so many lies and deceptions swirled around her now that she couldn't fight her way through their tangled net to the truth.

"That can't be," she corrected. "I've seen the accounts, met with the bankers—"

"Allowed in child after child who couldn't pay tuition but whom we have to feed and clothe. Purchased blankets for the dormitories, desks for the classrooms, rugs for the common rooms…" With each item he listed, his voice grew harsher, more frustrated. *Desperate.* "And what new monies have come in since you caused us to lose our best patroness and Father to work himself to death?"

His words hit her like a slap. Yet she managed to fling back in her own defense, "I never forced you into *this*." The blood drained from her face. She was staring at a complete stranger. She repeated fiercely, "*What* have you done?"

"Exactly what I had to." He paced the room, so agitated that he shook. "It will all be over soon, and then we'll never have to worry about money. Until then, do *not* mention this again, not to me nor to anyone, or it will be more than the school that's destroyed. They'll come for me—for *us*. God only knows who'll be hurt."

His threats didn't intimidate her. "Does that include Lady Rowland?"

He halted in midpace, and his hand that had been clawing at his neckcloth froze. "What do you know about her?"

"I saw you with her tonight. Are you lovers?" She hoped beyond hope that the baroness had played no other role than that.

He scoffed at the idea and continued to pace. "Of course not."

She pressed a hand to her roiling stomach. "Then what is she to you?"

"Someone who can help us with the school."

"How?"

He shook his head. "You just have to trust me."

She nearly laughed. *Never again.* "If it concerns the school, then it—"

He wheeled on her. "Leave it be, Olivia!"

He charged toward her and pushed her out of the room and into the hall. The door slammed shut, and the lock clicked into place.

She retreated until her back hit the wall. Then she crumpled, sliding down to land in a heap on the floor. She wrapped her arms around her knees and rocked back and forth the same way little Cora did whenever the girl had a nightmare. A nightmare—if only that was what this was!

Because that would mean she would eventually wake up and escape it.

She pressed her hand against her mouth and choked back the roiling in her stomach. Alec had been right about Henry from the very beginning. He knew, even that first night in the alley when he'd demanded to know where her brother had gone, when he'd questioned her about his work. All those poor men hurt…some of them killed…and the prime minister—

Alec had known. But she'd refused to believe him.

She stared at the closed door, and the pain of her ripping heart outweighed the sickness balling in her belly. Alec, Henry…who was left for her to trust?

———

Alec stood in the shadows of the school's service yard and let out a short whistle. He cocked his head and listened.

An answering whistle came a few heartbeats later.

He moved forward toward the sound. Reed's dark figure was hidden by the stone wall, and the man remained where he was, not moving out of the shadows to greet Alec as he approached. But his hand was certainly on his knife, Alec knew, just as he knew Reed would be here. He'd lingered long enough after following Olivia safely home to see Everett arrive and knew Reed would be fast on the man's heels.

Reed sheathed his knife but made no gesture of extending his hand. They might have been partners on this mission, but that certainly didn't mean the ill blood between them had been cleansed. "What are you doing here?"

"Following the sister home," Alec replied, grateful that the darkness hid any stray emotions regarding Olivia that might have been on his face. "Where's Clayton?"

"Trying to track down the man who hired the messenger boy at Vauxhall." Reed slid him a look. "You have information?"

Alec gave a tight nod and turned toward the house. "I know why Scepter recruited Everett. Two years ago, he worked on renovation plans for the Admiralty Club. Scepter couldn't approach the club manager for copies of the building plans without raising suspicions, but Henry Everett had kept a copy. They knew that. That's what they worked from, where our slip of charred paper came from."

Reed frowned. "What would Scepter want with building plans?"

"If they knew exactly where the structure was weakest, they could maximize destruction with minimal explosives." Alec dropped his hands to his sides. The weight of the world hung on his shoulders tonight. Or perhaps just the weight of his heart. "All they needed were the building plans and a willing mathematician." He muttered almost to himself, "To take out a massive arch, you only have to remove one small stone…"

"Christ," Reed breathed out. "But why would Everett agree to work with them? What did they hold over his head?"

"I have no idea." Yet Alec was more determined than ever to find out. "But I think I know someone who does."

"Who?"

"Lady Rowland." He flipped up the collar of his greatcoat

even though he welcomed the biting cold of the night air. "I'm pursuing her as our new lead."

"What about the sister?"

He couldn't make eye contact with Reed. "She's exhausted as a mission asset. She doesn't know anything else." He looked down to tug at his gloves. "Tell Clayton I'm switching my focus to Lady Rowland. I have hopes she can lead us to Scepter."

And hopes he never had to see Olivia Everett again.

He turned on his heel and stalked away.

Seventeen

STANDING IN THE MIDDLE OF LADY GANTRY'S MUSICALE, Alec nodded as he tried to concentrate on what Sir George Pittens was saying about the new canal bill that was expected to come up in Parliament. He'd been cornered by Sir George as soon as he'd arrived, and now he found himself trying to maintain a political discussion about a bill whose merits he couldn't have listed and whose outcome he cared even less about, no matter how emphatic the gentleman's argument. Tonight, his attention belonged to a woman.

Unfortunately, she was the wrong woman.

Olivia Everett stood on the far side of the room, flanked by two of her charges from the school. The two girls were both overly excited by their first official social outing, yet she kept them firmly in place at her sides as if they were battle shields.

Perhaps they were. After all, she knew he was here, despite the determined way she ignored him. Her ramrod-straight back, the square set of her shoulders, the way her eyes swept through the room every few minutes and noticed everyone but him… Oh, she was keenly aware of his presence just as much as he was of hers. Of every move she made, in fact, right down to the way her fingers trembled as she tucked a stray strand of golden hair behind her ear because she knew he was watching her.

He should have been watching Lady Rowland instead.

"Don't you agree, St James?"

"Pardon?" He glanced at Sir George, who stared at him with an expectant look. He was clearly awaiting an answer, and Alec had no idea what the question was.

"The canals, man," Sir George exclaimed. "What do you think of the canals?"

He didn't. His attention was too focused on the woman he was supposed to be following and the woman he couldn't seem to forget. So he dodged, "I haven't made up my mind."

That non-answer seemed to appease Sir George well enough that the man prattled on anew about the benefits of waterways and lockkeepers in hopes that he could yet win Alec over to his side. Whatever side that was.

Alec couldn't have cared less, and his attention drifted once more to Olivia.

Even in her plain muslin dress, she was the loveliest woman in the room. The elegant stretch of her neck, that pert little nose that turned up just slightly at the tip, those expressive blue eyes, her lilting laugh— Whenever she laughed at something Lord Gantry said, the sound floated across the room to him, as musical as tonight's performance, and pierced into Alec's chest like a blade.

Yet Olivia's presence was no concern of his. Tonight, his focus belonged to Lady Rowland.

Or it should have.

He forced his gaze across the room to the baroness. He'd

been following her for the past two days, since she met with Everett at Vauxhall. That meeting linked her to Scepter...but in what role? She wasn't high-ranking or powerful enough to be part of the group's leadership, and for all their claims for radical revolt, he was certain they weren't progressive enough to place a woman into their upper ranks. So what did she want with Everett?

So far, though, Alec had gained no new answers, while Reed was still tracking Everett, and Clayton was still hunting down the Home Office's mole. But at least Alec's part of the mission was easier now. After all, Sydney Rowland and he were invited to the same society events, so he didn't have to depend upon his mother or sister to arrange for invitations to be near her. And he no longer required a mask to hide his identity.

His gaze strayed back to Olivia. He missed those heated flirtatious exchanges with her when he was anonymous and not the Earl of St James. He'd never been more himself than when he'd been behind that mask. He missed her softness yet admired her courage, missed her capitulating kisses yet craved the hellcat in her, missed her sharp mind—

Christ, he missed *her*.

But he also couldn't trust her.

Pale blue eyes caught him staring and held him powerless for a heartbeat before flicking away. Her nose rose into the air in a silent cut.

Damnation. He tossed back the last of his wine. He owed her no explanations, no apologies. She was simply another woman who'd snared his desires, that was all. He would replace her in his thoughts and in his arms soon enough. In fact, he was tempted to approach the opera singer Lady Gantry had hired for the evening and arrange to spend the night with her. A beautiful and curvaceous Italian just to his taste, she'd been casting interested glances at him all evening. It would take little to get himself invited to her rooms beyond a flirtatious smile and a pretty bauble of some kind.

Yes, that was exactly what he should do. It was what he *would* have done just a few weeks ago. But now—

Lies. All of it. Because now he only wanted Olivia. The woman who had deceived him.

"St James?" Irritation edged Sir George's voice.

Alec's attention snapped back to the conversation. "What is it?"

"The canals, sir! Have you no care for what's best for England?"

Alec pulled in a deep breath to keep from slamming his fist into Sir George's face. He muttered as he placed his empty glass on the tray of a passing footman and snatched up a fresh one, "You have no idea what lengths I'm willing to go to for England."

He turned on his heel and stalked away, leaving Sir George gaping openmouthed after him.

Elizabeth stood beside Arthur Mullins with a group of their friends, all of them chatting and laughing and having a grand time. Jealousy panged in Alec's gut as Beth rested her hand lovingly on Mullins's arm. The only time Alec had ever experienced such casual affection had been with Olivia.

"Elizabeth." He stopped at the edge of the group and gestured toward the side of the room. "May I have a word?"

Her smile dulled with sudden concern, and he bit back a curse. Leave it to Beth to notice how on edge he was tonight. She quickly gave her apologies to her friends and allowed him to lead her away so they could speak privately.

"Is something wrong?" she asked. "You're looking a bit—"

"You knew she was going to be here and didn't tell me." *Not* a question.

"Whomever do you mean?" She feigned ignorance, but her expression came a beat too late to be believable.

For the first time in ten years, he was tempted to toss her over his knee and spank her. "Don't dissemble with me. You know who." He ground out her name, the very sound of it stinging, "Miss Everett."

"Of course she's here." She smiled with smug satisfaction. "She was invited to chaperone Lady Gantry's niece. As a relative, the girl was obligated to attend, so we thought Miss Everett would—"

"*We?*" He should have known that Beth was behind this not-so-chance meeting.

Yet his sister wasn't embarrassed at all to have been caught meddling. Again. "Lady Gantry asked Mama whom she thought should serve as Miss Smith's chaperone for the evening, and Miss Everett was the perfect choice. Surely, you realized she'd be here, given her position."

"No," he half snarled, "I didn't realize that."

"How fortunate, then, that you have the chance to see her again." Her knowing gaze pinned him with a sideways look.

"And make a better impression upon her. After all, you two seemed to have a rocky start to your acquaintanceship at the ball."

"It was a pleasant enough meeting," he corrected and took a healthy swallow of wine. Good Lord, he needed fortification. "We even waltzed."

"You had Captain Reed douse her with punch," Beth corrected bluntly. When Alec shot her a surprised look, she scolded lightly, "Don't think I've forgotten about that. *And* you've not yet explained why you would do such a thing."

Nor would he ever. He directed the conversation back to the disaster at hand. "You knew she would be attending tonight and didn't tell me." He shot her a look that made grown men quake in their boots but that only seemed to amuse her. "Stop meddling in my personal life."

The stubborn imp had the nerve to look offended. "Why, I would *nev*—"

"She is a schoolmistress, and I'm an earl." He reminded himself of that as much as her. "You know I can't marry her."

"Not *marry*, for goodness' sake!" she corrected defensively, her eyes widening in surprise. "Who said anything about marriage?"

No one. Apparently, all those thoughts of Olivia and elopement had sneaked into his head.

"Just spend time in her company, that's all," she explained. When he began to give that scheme the opinion it deserved, she cut him off. "It's for your own good! You have a terrible reputation."

He rolled his eyes. *Not this again.* "I'm reformed."

"You have a better chance at convincing society that unicorns exist." She shook her head. "Mama, Auntie, and I know you're not the wicked person those gossipy old harpies make you out to be, but no one else knows that."

Wicked? Exactly what rumors were circulating about him now?

"But Miss Everett has a sterling reputation," Beth rushed on. "If you spend more time in her company, everyone might think you truly have turned a new leaf and left your old pre-army days behind."

So that was it. Because Olivia had a sterling reputation. But he knew the truth. She had a *false* one. "You're wrong."

"For heaven's sake, Alec! If you're going to spend time in women's company, then why not spend it with proper ones? Especially a woman like Miss Everett. She's attractive, intelligent, funny, witty…" She counted off each item on her fingers, and with each tick off her list, his ire grew. He certainly didn't need her to point out how special Olivia was. "Charitable and kind with a spotless reputation that—"

His patience snapped, and he bit out without thinking, "She's living a lie."

Beth froze, then tilted her head as if she hadn't heard him correctly. "Pardon?"

He pulled in a deep breath and muttered against the rim of his glass, "Miss Everett may be a lot of things, but she's not the spotless schoolmistress she presents to the world."

She frowned, puzzled. "How do you…" Then she gasped. "*What* did you do to her?"

He choked on his wine and sputtered, "Why do you blame me?"

Her eyes narrowed. "Because I know you."

He blew out a harsh breath and glanced away—straight at Olivia. Her gaze pierced him as painfully as if she'd managed to stab him with that carving knife after all.

"I've done nothing to harm her or her reputation." He felt the loss of Olivia's gaze as harshly as if he'd lost a limb when she turned her attention back to Gantry's niece. "I never would."

"Then what happened that you're both keeping the length of the room and two pianofortes between you?"

As if he'd answer that! "I'm not having this conversation with—"

"Oh yes, you are, dear brother." She linked her arm through his to keep him from walking away and smiled sharply enough to cut glass. "I'm certain I'm not the only one noting the tension between you two. So explain yourself." She tapped his arm playfully with her fan, although he was certain she wanted to break it over his head. "And for goodness' sake, smile."

While he would always do his best to give Beth whatever she asked, he couldn't do that. Instead, he admitted grimly, "She's pretending to be something she's not."

"I see." Elizabeth's eyes flicked between him and Olivia. "So you're upset because a woman lied to you? I'm certain it's not the first time…or the one-thousandth, given the sort of woman you normally associate with."

He wisely ignored that baiting. "What she's done is worse than a mere lie. She's hiding the truth about herself."

Beth frowned. "And because of that, she was cruel to you?"

"No." Olivia had never been cruel, not intentionally. Not even when he deserved it.

"So…she's a beautiful, intelligent woman who is dedicated to her students and has never been cruel to you." She feigned shock. "Good God, the woman deserves to be hanged!"

He clenched his jaw at her blatant sarcasm. "She's living a lie, Beth."

"Lots of women do."

"She's been pretending to be virtuous."

"Lots of women do," she repeated just as dryly.

For Christ's sake! He ran a shaking hand through his hair, not caring about the mess he made of it. "She's built a reputation on something she's not. She's been lying to the world, to her students, to their parents." *She's been lying to me.* "Hiding behind a façade, pretending to be—"

"She's not our father, Alec."

He froze, his heart stopping as Beth's quiet words struck him like a blow.

He turned toward her and searched her face for answers. How could she have known what Rupert Sinclair had done? Beth had been only a child when their father died, still in braids in the schoolroom. She'd never been exposed to the old earl's brutality, had never been told about the other lives he'd ruined, and Alec had done everything possible to shield her from all of it.

But the knowledge glistened solemnly in her eyes.

He choked out, "How—how do you know…?"

"I know," she said quietly. "I know what a horrible person he was, all the terrible things he did."

No. Not all of them. She didn't know what that bastard had done to Alec, or she wouldn't be looking at him in shared grief. Instead, she'd be looking at him with pity, the same way Bivvens had every time he'd taken care of Alec after the beatings his father had unleashed. Even now, the old scars on the backs of his legs began to ache as if the wounds were still fresh. But he'd go to his grave before she ever learned about those.

"There's no forgiving the sins he committed." She reassuringly squeezed his arm, as if she truly knew and understood…yet she didn't. Neither did his mother or aunt. They simply couldn't. "But I also know that some people have perfectly good reasons for creating new lives for themselves and burying their pasts. Pasts that *should* be buried."

He forced out around the knot in his throat, "And how many people are allowed to be deceived in the process? How many lies allowed to be told?" *How much pain forced on others to endure?*

"Oh, Alec." Her face darkened with grief. For him. "The world isn't nearly as simple as you want it to be."

He almost laughed. "I know that."

"Then why aren't you more forgiving?" The concern on her face undid him. "You forgive strangers all the time for their weaknesses, but when it comes to the people you care about, you hold them to an impossibly higher standard. When you love them, you don't—"

She cut herself off, and her fingers dug hard into his arm as her mouth fell open wide. Her eyes flicked across the room to Olivia, then back to search his face, then back to Olivia…

"Oh my goodness," she whispered.

Aggravation surged inside him. "What's the matter?"

"*Oh. My. Goodness.*" Her hand shot up to her mouth, and she blurted out between her fingers— "You're in love with Olivia Everett!"

His head snapped back as if she'd slapped him. "I am not—" They were drawing attention, especially Olivia's. He took her arm to pull her closer and lowered his voice. "I am not in love with that woman."

Yet even as he said the words, he couldn't keep from watching Olivia as she slipped away with her two charges toward the terrace to take a break from the stifling heat of the crowded room. Even from this far away, he could feel her presence like the intensity of a summer storm.

"That explains everything."

His eyes darted back to Beth, and he scowled. From the way she continued to gape at him, she hadn't believed a word he'd said. "It explains nothing because it damned well isn't true." How could he be in love with a woman when he didn't even know who she truly was?

"Yes, everything—why you danced with her only once at the ball, why you ignored her at the tea, why you're so angry with her again tonight…"

He forced a laugh. "That's evidence of *dislike*, imp. Not love."

She shook her head. "You care about her. That's why

you're pushing her away." Her shoulders sagged, and with that came the look of pity he'd been dreading. "Oh, Alec…"

"I do *not* love Olivia Everett." He tolerated her to find leads for his mission, he followed her to stay close to her brother, he lusted after her, both her mind and body—hell, he would even admit that he'd missed that haughty schoolmistress demeanor of hers.

But *love*? Ludicrous.

"That's a very good thing, then." Beth flitted her fan to hide the surprise—and that damnable pity—showing on her face. "Because if you did, you would have to admit that no one is perfect and that we all have secrets worth hiding. And if you did that, you might just have to start forgiving people." She paused meaningfully, and her eyes found his over her fan. "Beginning with yourself."

With an impetuous kiss to his cheek, she left him to rejoin her group of friends.

Alec swallowed down a curse and turned on his heel to stalk away.

Beth had no idea of the true sins their father had committed or how Alec had been culpable in hiding them. *Had to.* If Rupert Sinclair's deeds were ever revealed, it would mean the end of the earldom, the destruction of the family's reputation, the Sinclair ladies cut off completely from society and forced to live as outcasts.

Hiding what his father had done had nearly been Alec's undoing, a guilt from which he never thought he'd recover. Yet he had, clawing his way through the darkness to survive, not for his own sake but for that of his family.

And now he was supposed to simply ignore all the pain that those lies and deceit had caused and *forgive*?

From the time Alec had left home for the army, he'd been so sure about the world. He'd judged everyone and either accepted or condemned based upon the lessons his father had taught him. Brutal, harsh lessons…but then, hadn't the world proven itself to be nothing but brutality and harshness? All the death and destruction he'd witnessed on the Continent had simply confirmed his suspicions.

Until he'd met Olivia. When his well-ordered existence turned upside down.

Knowing what he knew now, was he still so certain that the world could be divided into black and white, into sinners and saints? Especially now that he had no idea anymore into which group he himself belonged?

It was damned well time he found out.

Pulling in a determined breath, he tossed back the last of his wine and marched toward the terrace.

Eighteen

"OH, MISS EVERETT!" DAPHNE DRAMATICALLY COVERED her heart with her hands. "Wasn't Signorina Poggioli just divine?"

Mary nearly swooned in agreement. "Just *divine*!"

Olivia suppressed a smile. The two girls had overheard Mrs. Cavendish make the same comment about the opera singer who had performed that evening's entertainment, in the same overly dramatic fashion as if she were the diva instead of Signorina Poggioli, and now they were parroting it back. Just as they had done earlier when they'd held their coffee cups so affectedly that Olivia was afraid one of them would put someone's eye out from the way their elbows jutted into the air.

But they were having a good time on their first society outing, and Olivia was relieved to have them here. Oh, it was cowardly of her, but if she surrounded herself with the girls—whose exuberant excitement was enough to keep everyone away—then she wouldn't have to speak to anyone. She could hide in corners and on terraces until it was time for tonight's command performance to be over. Then she could collect Justine from her aunt and go home, where she could slink away to her room, pull the covers up over her head, and cry in peace.

So far, her plan was working. Most of the guests stayed as far away from the chatty girls as possible. Including Alec. Although after what he'd said to her in his study, she was certain he was doing everything in his power to remain as far away from *her* as possible.

He shouldn't have been here. She should have been safe from him. After all, the Earl of St James didn't attend such tame society events as this. Yet there he was, his very tall, broad-shouldered, and undeniably handsome presence constantly reminding her of the horrible mistake she'd made of being in his arms.

She would have to be more careful in the future. For tonight, though, the best course of action was simply to avoid him and somehow find a way to…a way to…

The girls weren't talking. *That* was never a good sign.

Olivia felt the tiny hairs on her arms stand on end as she gazed at the two girls, who both gaped speechless at something, or *someone*, behind her. She knew from the sinking in the pit of her stomach—

"Good evening, ladies." Alec's deep voice rumbled down her spine and sent a cascade of hot shivers prickling across her skin. "I trust you're having an enjoyable time."

Daphne and Mary nodded dumbly in unison, their eyes wide as tea saucers. They made a frantic grab for each other's hands, as if to assure themselves that the moment was real and they were truly being addressed by the Earl of St James.

"Good to hear it," he murmured, sarcasm lightly touching his voice.

Olivia could sense his strong body just behind hers. She

knew without having to look that he was smiling at Daphne and Mary with that charming grin of his, the same one that found its way unbidden into her dreams every night.

"I know what will make this evening even better for you."

Olivia held her breath and waited suspiciously.

"You should ask Lady Gantry to introduce you to Signorina Poggioli."

For a moment, neither girl moved. They just stared past her, entranced, as if he were a living god come down from Olympus.

Olivia rolled her eyes.

"Tell her that St James insisted you be introduced," he prompted.

They squealed with delight at having an earl's introduction, then jumped up and down before rushing back into the music room to descend upon Lady Gantry and the unsuspecting opera singer like a very small plague of locusts.

"You really shouldn't have done that," Olivia scolded in a low voice and turned to face him. Despite all the reasons why she needed to stay away, her body panged with sudden arousal at his nearness, and her heart tugged her toward him.

Inhaling a sharp breath, she stepped back.

He frowned at her reaction, but together, they watched the two girls gush out compliments to the singer. "I wanted to speak with you alone."

"And so trapped that poor woman." Yet Olivia couldn't help the pulse of satisfaction that Signorina Poggioli was now being bombarded by a hundred questions at once, since that same very alluring, very buxom woman had sent flirtatious looks in Alec's direction all evening. "Go on, then," she urged curtly. "We're as alone now as we're ever going to be again."

He visibly stiffened at the cutting edge to her words.

She immediately regretted them, and her shoulders slumped as she softened. "What do you want to say to me?"

"That night at Vauxhall, what happened…"

She caught her breath to steel herself for what was coming. He'd cut right to the crux, as if he were afraid the signorina would remember she was a diva and send the girls away at any moment and back to the terrace to interrupt them.

"You surprised me."

"So I gathered." Her heart plunged to the ground. He didn't offer an apology. She was so naïve to expect one! A man like Alec Sinclair would never apologize to a woman, certainly not for having her in his arms.

"I believed you were as scrupulous and forthright as you portray to society. A virtuous schoolmistress with a spotless reputation."

She winced at that description of herself, but he wasn't wrong. That was exactly what the matrons and gossips said about her. It was the same persona she courted in order to give enough respectability to the school that parents felt secure in sending their daughters to her.

"I felt deceived."

Her eyes snapped to him. "Because I chose to keep private what was none of your business?" She choked out, "That is, until I thought I could trust you enough to… I was the one who was deceived."

"Olivia—"

"*No.*" Something deep inside her snapped, and the pain was blinding. He had no idea of the hell she'd suffered through during the past seven years, the pain she'd put her family through—or the fresh agony he was causing her now. What sliver of pride remained in her refused to let him see how much he'd wounded her, but her voice was hoarse with emotion. "You have no right to judge me, about that or anything I've done." Blinking hard, she stepped forward to leave. "Excuse me. I need to rescue Signorina Poggioli."

His fingers lightly gripped her elbow, stopping her. "Please, let me explain."

She wanted to scream! Yet somehow she was able to keep her voice low as she admitted, "You were right about my brother."

She would give Alec this gift of information, then put him out of her life forever.

"He did work for the men who bombed the Admiralty Club, but he had no idea what they wanted the plans for. He thought the club was going to be torn down, and he had been hired to check the stresses, that's all. We've often worked with builders on projects to do just that." It wasn't the explanation he wanted, but it was the only concession she'd give. "Henry is a good man who was simply caught up in a plot beyond his knowledge and control."

With that, she was done with this conversation. Done with *him*.

"There's nothing more I can share with you. Find your answers from Lady Rowland now. But you should know that Henry denied that he and she are lovers, and I believe him."

"What makes you so certain?" he asked.

"Because I know what it's like when lovers look at each other." She glanced sideways at him then, boldly meeting those hazel eyes that stared at her so intensely and proved her point. "And they didn't look at each other that way."

She turned her tear-blurred gaze back to the two girls and the opera singer. The woman was now doing her best to slide away from them, only to end up with Daphne and Mary chasing her slowly around the room as they advanced with each retreat she made.

"He's not a revolutionary," she insisted. "He's innocent."

His voice came softly, "Has he really fooled you that much, Olivia?"

The quiet question cut through her, yet she forced her expression to remain inscrutable. "Apparently, I've been fooled by many men."

She walked away. This time, he let her go.

Instead of rescuing the signorina, Olivia headed in the other direction, toward the door leading to the hallway and the retiring room. There, she could find some peace for a few minutes and collect herself, then somehow find the strength to continue with the evening as if nothing was wrong.

A laugh echoed from her left, solid and masculine. She stopped to look.

Lord Hawking was engaged in a conversation with Sir George Pittens, the two men leaning toward each other over their cups of weak coffee and apparently up to their necks in political intrigue. She'd never spent much time talking with the marquess, but she knew Hawking was powerful in the

House of Lords, his family almost as rich as the Sinclairs and his title nearly as old. Exactly the kind of person the Everett School needed for a patron. Someone who could give enough money to keep them solvent and, unlike St James, with a solid reputation that would increase the school's respectability. She had no idea of the nature of the storm that was coming because of Henry, but she knew she needed allies.

Throwing all propriety aside, she walked up to the two men and flashed the most adoring smile she could muster.

Lord Hawking abruptly stopped the conversation and straightened his spine at her approach. "Miss Everett, what a pleasant surprise."

"Lord Hawking." She gave a deep curtsy that would have done Prinny proud, then a second. "Sir George." She turned back to the marquess. "I wanted to thank you for Saturday evening."

Hawking frowned. "Saturday evening?"

"For letting my brother Henry have your box at Vauxhall."

"Oh, that. Yes, of course." He rocked back on his heels and smiled. "My way of saying congratulations on his lecture at the Royal Society. Besides, I was glad the box could be of use. I hardly ever go there anymore, but I can't bring myself to let it go." Something behind his smile hardened for just an instant, then was gone, and he confessed, "My late brother Jonas enjoyed the gardens a great deal, so giving up the box feels like giving up a bit of his memory."

"I understand." His younger brother and heir had died only a few years ago in the most recent war with the

Americans, and sorrow for him tightened her chest. "It was the same for me when Papa died…wanting to carry on just the same. I continued to set out his pipe every evening for a year after he passed because I couldn't bring myself to face that he was gone."

His expression softened. "Your father would be very proud of all that you and your brother have accomplished with his school."

"Thank you." The compliment landed with heartfelt gratitude and emboldened her further. "But that's the problem, you see. Lord and Lady Gantry have been very generous with their patronage, but there are so many more girls who desperately need an education, one their families cannot afford and—"

He smiled at her boldness, the forced expression cutting her off midsentence. Oh heavens, she'd overstepped! And all because of Alec. She never would have been this forward in seeking donations if that devil hadn't shaken her so badly.

"I'm being terribly impertinent, I'm afraid," she apologized as heat gathered in her cheeks, and all the courage she'd found only moments before now died beneath his amused expression. "And wholly improper to raise such a topic tonight. My sincere apologies."

"There's no need to apologize, Miss Everett. Your devotion to your school is admirable." He leaned toward her, and his eyes sparkled knowingly. "If I might venture a guess, you'd like to invite me to become a patron?"

Her heart thumped. She wanted exactly that. If Lord Hawking became their patron, then the school would have more than enough money, and Henry would never again have to risk their lives as he was doing now. "Yes," she answered breathlessly, "I would."

"Done."

Relief poured through her. "Oh, thank you! You have no idea how much this means to me."

"Come now, Miss Everett." He chuckled. "I help many charities and even sit on the board of an orphanage in Southwark. If I can help them, I can certainly find the resources to help a few school girls."

Oh, how she wanted to throw her arms around his neck and hug him! Instead, she simply beamed, although the brightness of her smile was surely tempered by a hint of embarrassment. "I cannot thank you enough. Now Henry doesn't have to take any more commissions."

Not knowing how else to show her gratitude, she lowered into another curtsy.

"It's the least I can do." He nodded toward George Pittens. "Now, if you don't mind, Sir George and I were in the middle of a conversation about shipping routes."

"An argument, you mean," Sir George corrected peevishly.

Hawking gave a long-suffering sigh. "The business of Parliament never ends. We'd invite you to stay and join us, but I'm afraid you'd be bored stiff."

Even that backhanded dismissal didn't deflate her spirits. No, she wanted to fly! "Of course. Have a good evening, my lord." A nod to Pittens. "Sir George."

With her chest feeling lighter than it had in a fortnight, she walked away from the men and completely forgot that she'd been on her way to the retiring room. Her eyes deliberately avoided Alec's dark gaze from across the room as she collected Mary and Daphne from the besieged singer and Justine from her aunt, then herded all three girls from the town house.

The worst was finally over.

Nineteen

ALEC PLACED HIS HAND OVER OLIVIA'S MOUTH AS SHE stepped into her room. "Hush."

His other arm encircled her waist and held her pressed against him as he closed the door with a push of his foot, then reached behind to flip the lock.

When he was certain she wasn't going to cry out and rouse the school, he lowered his hand from her mouth to rest it on her shoulder. She trembled beneath his palm, whether in anger or surprise was anyone's guess.

"I should scream," she threatened, then caught her breath as his finger traced along the side of her neck. "A masked man once told me to scream if I ever found anyone in my room."

Her pulse pounded beneath his fingertips, and he smiled lazily. There was hope in that racing heartbeat. "He didn't mean me."

"*Especially* you."

Swatting his hand away, she stepped out of his reach. Her blue eyes flared in the dark shadows. He'd only just beaten her here from the musicale, making better time on foot than she had in the hired hackney. She hadn't even been able to remove her cloak yet, and his fingers itched to untie it and slip it slowly from her body.

As if reading his mind, she scowled, tore off her cloak, and hung it on its hook beside the door. Her hands went to her hips. "What are you doing here?"

A very good question, and one he wished he could answer. But all he knew was that he couldn't stay away, no matter how upset he was with her. Or with himself. He felt that same undeniable need to be with her that he'd experienced since the moment he first laid eyes on her.

"Waiting for you," he dodged.

Her brow arched sharply. She was clearly in no mood for any dissembling tonight and demanded, "Why are you here, Alec?"

"I was worried about you."

"Liar. You saw with your own eyes at the musicale that I was fine."

"I don't trust your brother to keep you safe." That was the God's honest truth, if not the reason he was here.

She smiled tightly. "Then you can guard me from outside."

He stilled. Did she know that Reed and Clayton had been watching the school? But now the building was unguarded, the two men positioned at Lady Rowland's house instead. Alec should have been with them—hell, he should have still been at Lord and Lady Gantry's town house with the baroness. But he'd felt compelled to come after Olivia in a way he'd never chased after a woman before in his life.

"We need to talk, and I can't talk to you from the outside." He casually gestured at the window. "Unless you want me to shout up from the service yard and let the neighbors eavesdrop."

Her smile vanished. "Then you might as well leave because I know nothing more about the Admiralty Club, and we've said everything we've needed to say to each other about everything else."

Not by a long shot. "I'm not here because of your brother. And I'm not leaving until we've settled what's between us."

She crossed her arms, being just as obstinate as he was. "Then you're going to be here a very long time."

"That's all right." He reached beneath his greatcoat and withdrew the bottle of whiskey he'd snagged from Gantry's study. "I've brought fortification."

She made a show of leaning forward to examine the bottle. "Rot gut."

"Only the finest," he countered dryly. Then he pulled out the loosened cork with his teeth and spat it onto the floor.

"I don't drink." She rocked back on her heels with a disdainful sniff.

"Who said it was for you?" He took a swallow, then relented by holding it out to her like a peace offering.

She stared at it for a long while, and he could almost see the workings of her sharp mind spinning as she considered whether she should take it and which action would be the most defiant. Blowing out a loud breath, she accepted it from him and took a small sip.

Immediately, she began to cough.

"That's disgusting!" she forced out between coughs and shoved the bottle back at him.

He fought down a smile. "Yes, but it gets the job done."

"And what job is that?" she asked, falling for his ploy.

"Dulling your reaction so you're more likely to miss when you come after me with your carving knife."

Her eyes narrowed to slits. "If you insist upon—"

"Tell me about your past." Her breath caught at his unexpected but soft order, made even softer by the lowering of his voice. "I'm not leaving until I learn who you really are."

"Olivia Maria Everett. Schoolmistress." But the sharp tone she'd undoubtedly hoped for was lost beneath the unexpected huskiness in her voice. "There. Now you know who I am."

Impertinent chit. "I promise not to tell your secrets to anyone." He set the bottle on the fireplace mantel, snatched the cork from the floor, and tossed it into the banked coals. "But you're living behind a false façade, and I've seen more than enough people suffer from living a lie. I only want to understand why you're doing it."

She hesitated. "Why does it matter to you?"

"Because I want to help you."

"I don't need your help."

More than she realized. "Perhaps not. But I need your trust."

"You need to leave."

He needed *her*. Frustration pulsed through him that even now she refused to reveal herself. But he hadn't lied; he wasn't going anywhere until he discovered the real woman behind the beautiful façade, the one who'd given him only a glimpse of her true spirit and wild soul. The same one who'd gotten under his skin and into his heart.

"I wanted to make love to you that night at Vauxhall," he confessed in a murmur.

"I know." But the haughty sniff accompanying that was undercut by the tremor in her voice.

"What stopped me was that I thought you were innocent." His shoulders dropped. "Then everything I thought I knew about you suddenly wasn't true."

"You know all the important things about me," she whispered, hoarse with emotion. "The rest doesn't matter."

If only he could believe that. But he knew firsthand the suffering that deception could bring. "Tell me about your past," he pressed gently. "About the man you ran away with... and why he's not here with you."

She bit her bottom lip, as if considering answering, but didn't.

Her lack of trust gnawed at him. "I know I don't deserve your confidence, that I certainly haven't earned it." The truth of that stung. "But I need to know."

"Why?" The curious word lingered in the shadows between them.

For the first time tonight, she'd not spoken to him in anger or suspicion, and he took hope in that.

"Because I've made past mistakes myself and know the burden of living with secrets." He paused, then admitted, "Because I am truly sorry that I have caused you any pain."

Her expression softened, and she bit her bottom lip.

"Because I care about you," he added quietly. He'd never uttered truer words in his life. "And I don't want you to be hurt."

A sad smile ruefully twisted her lips. "You're seven years too late."

When she turned away, he resisted the urge to grab her into his arms and kiss away the pain he'd seen on her face and the grief in her eyes. But if he did, the fragile trust they were slowly building would be destroyed.

He had to be patient and wait for her to come to him. Even if it killed him.

Putting the distance of the room between them, she began to pace. Restless, embarrassed, ashamed, uncertain… He could read every emotion flash across her face even in the shadows cast by the faint glow of the coals in the banked fire.

"There has only been one man, once—I was eighteen," she began quietly, "and I loved him."

He'd expected that, yet the stab of pain at her admission hurt so deeply that he lost his breath. "And he loved you."

Her look of shame nearly undid him. "Not enough in the end."

"Then he was a fool," he murmured.

She spun to face him midpace and raised her chin. "Yes, he was." But her show of resilience deflated like a balloon as her shoulders sank. "And so was I for eloping with him."

She stepped past him to the fireplace, reached a shaking hand to grab the iron poker, and then bent down on her heels. With a stir of the coals, the small flames came back to life. She didn't rise. Instead, she remained crouched into a small ball and let the poker fall to the floor in front of her. The firelight lit up her bleak expression as she stared into the flames, saying nothing.

Alec pulled in a deep breath. He was afraid of the answer even as he asked it, but he had to know— "Are you still in love with him?"

"No," she answered into the fire. A bitter smile tightened her lips. "It's amazing how well ruination and abandonment on her wedding day can purge love from a woman's heart."

"I should think so," he murmured. *Good God…* "Tell me about him."

"No." The word was little more than a breath.

"Why not? As you said, it was seven years ago."

She didn't look at him. "Because I'm certain you know him."

His heart froze, and in that moment's stillness, he offered a silent prayer that it wasn't one of the men of the Armory. "Who?"

She didn't answer. Instead, she wordlessly picked up the poker and stirred listlessly once more at the fire. A jagged valley through the black coals glowed hellishly red.

He allowed himself a single step toward her. "You're an amazing woman, Olivia," he whispered. "So strong and fierce, so brilliant. But you're keeping yourself from me, your *true* self, and it's killing me."

She looked at him over her shoulder, and the glistening of tears in her eyes undid him.

But he couldn't stop pressing her for the truth. Because once he knew, then he could begin to forgive, and she could learn to trust.

"I want to know the real you," he cajoled as he slowly approached her. "Not the façade you present to the world."

"You do know me."

"No, I don't." He knelt beside her and took the poker from her hand, then laced his fingers through hers. "Let me see into your heart."

"If I do that," she said so softly that he could barely hear her, "then my life could be destroyed."

"I'll protect you." He placed a kiss to her temple and felt her shudder beneath his lips. "I'll save you from the darkness."

She slowly rose to her feet and slid her hand from his. She didn't come into his arms. Instead, she crossed the room and leaned back against the door, putting as much distance between them as possible. If she could have flung open the door and stepped into the hallway to be even farther away, he suspected she would have done just that.

"It was Samuel Deering," she confessed. "Viscount Deering's youngest son."

The man's face flashed before Alec's eyes. Lazy and pompous, thinking he could make his way in the world on his charms and his father's wealth...

Yes, Alec knew him. And couldn't stand the man.

He said as normally as possible past the bitterness on his tongue, "I never knew you and he..." He couldn't finish.

"No one knew. His family made certain of it, and then... so did mine."

To hide the anger inside him, Alec removed his hat and gloves, then shrugged out of his greatcoat and tossed the lot over a nearby chair. He reached for the bottle of whiskey and took a large swallow that burned all the way down his throat into his chest.

"What happened?" He offered her the bottle.

She waved it away with a humiliated shake of her head. "I was foolish and in love. I believed him when he told me that he wanted to marry me, that he wanted a future together." She rolled her shoulders in a disheartened shrug. "Perhaps he did… But he's the youngest son, you see, and so he couldn't disobey his parents."

An icy chill slithered down his spine. "Disobey how?"

"We couldn't court openly because his family would never have approved, not of their son with a poor school-teacher's daughter. But his family supported the school— they were our most important patrons then—and so it was easy to find excuses to spend time together. When he asked me to marry him, I said yes." Her voice grew impossibly softer. "And we eloped."

Her quiet words punched him in the gut. He turned away with the excuse of removing his jacket before she could see his jealousy and anger. He tossed it over the chair with his greatcoat and fussed with his cuffs and shirtsleeves. "Obviously, you didn't marry him."

"We didn't have the chance." Her gaze remained firmly fixed on the floor. "When we arrived in Gretna Green, it was past midnight, too late to take our vows, and we were exhausted from traveling. So we took a room at the inn." She pulled in a deep breath, and he heard her voice tremble. "Samuel said there was no point in waiting since we were going to be married in the morning, so we…"

So we made love. She didn't have to say it. Still, he felt the unspoken words like a blow to his gut.

"But in the morning, right at dawn, his family arrived at the inn." She shoved herself away from the door and began to pace again, this time wringing her hands. "They'd discovered that we'd eloped, and his father and brothers had chased after us on horseback. They found us in the room, roused us from bed—" Her face flushed red with shame. "Lord Deering told Samuel that he would cut off his allowance and disinherit him if we went through with our vows, that he'd be cast out of the family."

Alec stifled a stunned curse. "But he'd ruined you."

"When a peer or one of his family seduces a girl from the lower classes, no one cares if her life is destroyed by it. You know that." She waved her hand at the school around her. "What could I have done to force a viscount's son to marry me? It was my word against a gentleman's, and no one would have believed me."

Alec knew every word she said was true. A gentleman could be forced to wed a society daughter for being caught simply kissing her. But the same man could rape the upstairs maid and never face punishment. His own father had exemplified that.

He rolled up his sleeves, needing to keep his hands busy to stop himself from reaching for her. Or slamming his fist through the wall. "What happened then?"

With a shrug, she began to pace again. "They rented a horse for Samuel and rode back to London."

He stared at her, aghast. "They *left* you in Scotland?"

"Of course they did. They had no intention of treating me with any respect, not even then." She cut him a sideways glance and never paused in her pacing. "It took every penny I had to buy a seat on top of the mail coach for London. But I suppose it was for the best after all." She began to chew on her thumbnail. "The long days and nights of traveling home gave me time to figure out how to break the news to Papa and Henry."

He watched her pace, stunned by her resilience. Dear God, the humiliation she must have felt, the worry of not knowing if she were with child, the rejection—

But since she was still here in the school, her reputation still intact... "You went on as if none of it had happened."

"I had no choice. Even if my father and brother had tried to save my honor, any public declaration of what Samuel and I had done would only result in destroying the reputation of my family and the school. Who would send their children to a schoolmaster who couldn't even protect the virtue of his own daughter? The school would have closed, and we'd have been kicked penniless into the streets." She paused at the fireplace, and with a scowl at herself, she bent to pick up the poker. "We were already struggling financially, and when Lord and Lady Deering withdrew their support, the school nearly went bankrupt."

"They pulled out their support after what their son had done to you?"

"You shouldn't be surprised." She gave the coals a hard, punishing stir before placing the poker back into the rack. "After all, there was no way to hold them accountable for that either."

She held her hands up to the small fire as if to warm herself against the night. And against the memories.

"But it was such a blow to Papa," she whispered into the fire. "He never recovered from it." She dropped her hands and straightened her spine. "He was dead less than two years later."

His throat constricted in grief for her. The shame and guilt that must have consumed her... *That* was why she'd shut herself away behind a façade of propriety and false virtue, why she always did whatever Henry Everett asked of her, including letting him claim her mathematical work as his own. Because of that, she would never again break the rules or defy anyone in her family, not even her traitorous brother.

"That wasn't your fault," he insisted hoarsely.

"Wasn't it?" She turned to confront him. Her hands clenched into tiny, frustrated fists at her sides as her pain transformed into self-recrimination. "My deception hurts people. Isn't that what you said?"

His parting words to her at St James House... *How many people have you misled? How many people have you hurt?* Christ.

Apologetically, he closed the distance between them. "Olivia—"

She retreated a step to keep away from him, and the small movement stabbed him.

"You were right," she admitted. "I did harm my family, threatened the school...all because I was selfish."

"Because you were in love," he corrected forcefully, as if he could make her believe that from sheer will alone. He cursed himself for every harsh word he'd said to her that night at St James House. "That wasn't your fault either."

Dismissing that with a headshake, she crossed to the

window. She looked out at the blackness, but he was certain she could see nothing but her own faint reflection in the glass.

"I stayed here, took over the management of the school, and did my best to keep it running," she whispered into the darkness. "I let the world believe that I was still a proper young lady who hadn't eloped and let herself be ruined, who could still be trusted to educate their daughters." She lifted her hand to the window and rested it against the cold glass. "So yes, I've lied to the world, but for the exact opposite reason you thought." She drew her fingertip over the pane in a slow circle, as if drawing the nighttime shadows. "I did it to keep from causing any more harm to the people I love."

Every soft word of her story cut into him, and self-recrimination weighed on his chest like a lead ball.

Always, he'd believed that anyone who deceived the world about their true nature deserved his disdain, deserved to be punished for their lies…until now. Olivia had upended his world. His father had hidden his evil behind a façade of propriety; behind hers, Olivia had only hidden her shame and pain.

"There. I've told you everything." She turned to face him and defiantly put her hands on her hips despite the wounds she carried. It was a battle stance if ever he'd seen one, and a warning not to hurt her again. "Do you trust me now?"

"Yes." He sat on her bed and leaned forward, his hands folded between his knees and his expression grave. "I was wrong about you, and I am deeply sorry for it. I do trust you." He sucked in a deep breath and asked the most important question of his life. "But do *you* trust me?"

Her hands fell away to her sides in surprise, yet a storm churned intensely in her eyes. The shadows between them crackled with electricity, and he felt every breath she took, every tremble that shivered through her, even from ten feet away.

"Yes," she breathed, no sound on her lips. "I trust you."

Relief burned through him, and his head slumped between his shoulders. Her soft words came as a benediction, one that purged him of the old pain he'd carried with him since he was a boy and filled him with new hope, new acceptance and forgiveness.

Trust. He'd never realized how gaping the void of it had been in his life until Olivia was here, filling it.

He'd promised to save her. He'd start by setting her free.

Silently, he held out his hand.

Twenty

OLIVIA STARED AT ALEC'S OUTSTRETCHED HAND, YET SHE didn't take it.

She knew what he wanted from her, knew how surrendering to the yearning to be in his arms would change everything between them. The joining of bodies, the melding of desires...a woman was never more vulnerable than when she lay beneath a man and allowed him inside her, his strength and weight pressing her down, his arms entrapping her. He was asking her for the ultimate expression of trust.

Could she give it?

Aware of each beat of her pounding heart and every slow breath, she stepped toward him with so much trepidation that she trembled. How would she survive another wounding by a man she loved?

But wasn't that what trusting meant—taking a leap of faith?

Yet she couldn't jump. She had to start with small steps, and each one she took brought her slowly across the room to him. She stopped just out of his reach.

He lowered his arm, seeming to intuit that each move she made was a test of the fragile trust between them.

With her eyes fixed on his, she reached behind to the

row of buttons on her back. She paused to inhale a steadying breath between each button, yet she slowly slipped each one free until her bodice sagged loose and her capped sleeves slipped from her shoulders. The choice remained hers to stop whenever she wanted, every heartbeat's hesitation a chance for her to change her mind. But she had no intention of stopping.

The dress slid through her fingers and landed in a puddle at her feet.

Alec sat perfectly still as he watched her, except to swallow so hard that she heard it from four feet away.

Her fingers shook as they untied her petticoat, then tangled in the front tie of her short corset. With each layer of clothing she removed, the need to be able to trust him intensified. Yet her heart urged her on, and she pulled loose the tie until she could shrug out of her stays and let them fall away to join the dress on the floor. Leaving her shoes behind, she stepped out of the pile of clothes encircling her feet.

She reached beneath the hem of her shift to roll off her stockings. When a low groan emerged from the back of his throat, her fingers hesitated. Yet she paused only a moment before letting the stockings slip to the floor.

Finally, she stood in front of him in only her shift. If she were going to stop, it would have to be now. To reveal any more of herself...

With a ragged breath of courage, she lifted the hem of her shift over her head and off, baring herself completely.

For a long while, she didn't move. She remained statue-still as she silently returned his heated stare, daring him to notice that she was more than simply naked—she'd revealed everything to him, body and soul. She kept no more secrets from him.

She removed the pins from her hair and tossed them onto her dressing table, then ran her hands through her curls and shook them loose.

His eyes flared, and he shifted awkwardly on the bed. When she finally stepped forward between his knees and into his embrace, he sucked in a hard breath through clenched teeth that left him shuddering.

She silently wrapped her arms around his shoulders and pressed herself against him, the cool silk of his waistcoat caressing against her bare breasts.

"I'm so sorry, Olivia," he murmured against her bare shoulder.

Her heart knew that he didn't mean her failed elopement, and she clung even more tightly to him, never wanting to let go.

"Forgive me." He placed a tender kiss to her neck and rasped out, "Please forgive me."

"Yes." She shifted back only far enough to cup his face between her hands and lift his head toward hers. She whispered his name against his lips in sweet absolution. "Yes."

He arched up to meet her lips, and the kisses that plundered her mouth gave promise of what more would come between them tonight if she'd let it. In silent permission, she climbed onto his lap and straddled him. His hands smoothed over her back and across her bottom.

But when he stroked up her inner thighs and his thumbs

grazed the folds between her legs, she took his hands and stopped him.

He instantly stilled. Only the sounds of their breaths broke the silence, until he murmured, "Trust me, Olivia." He entwined his fingers with hers. "I would never intentionally hurt you. I only want to make you happy."

Her eyes stung. If those words had come from any other man, she would have laughed. But this was Alec, and the sincerity in his gaze overwhelmed her.

With a jerking nod, she released his hands and lowered her mouth to his in a consenting kiss.

Once more, his hands moved up her thighs, and once more, his thumbs caressed her core. This time, she didn't stop him. The sensation was little more than a light tickle against her intimate folds, and her body softened against his.

"You're beautiful," he whispered against her mouth. When she smiled at the compliment, he outlined her lips with the tip of his tongue and flamed the growing heat in her belly. "So soft and warm." He gave a long caress of his thumbs into the valley between her legs and groaned. "So silky smooth."

Then his caresses changed. They grew bolder, harder, deeper. His fingers slipped inside her tight warmth—

"Alec!"

He stroked her in tantalizing plunges and retreats, and her body clenched shamelessly around him. With a whimper of desire, she arched herself against him to bring him deeper, and he rewarded her with a flick of his fingertip across the little nub buried in her folds.

Her hips pulsed against his hand as pleasure sparked through her, and she clung to him as if he were her anchor in a storm-tossed sea.

He rubbed her again. A soft cry broke from her lips, and his mouth covered hers to drink up the sound.

Oh, his touch was wonderful! No…it was wicked. So wickedly good. She moaned as a hot shiver rained through her and made her shudder with need. When she kissed him, she boldly mimicked with her tongue between his lips what his hand was doing between her legs.

This was what came with trust, she knew. Happiness, daring…*freedom.*

With a light push to his shoulder, she lowered him onto his back, still straddling him. His heart pounded beneath her fingers as they rested on his chest, but only for the length of a lingering kiss before she unknotted his cravat. A gentle tug freed it from around his neck.

"You won't be needing this." She held it out and opened her hand to let it spill to the floor.

Her pulse spiked when the corners of his mouth curled into a grin. She'd never done anything so bold to a man in her life. And she liked it. A great deal.

His hazel eyes gleamed with equal parts anticipation and amusement. "You'll have to let me up to remove the rest."

She smiled sinfully in answer to his challenge. "No, I won't."

She undid the buttons of his waistcoat and spread it open wide, then yanked down his shirt and lowered her lips to his bared neck. He tasted delicious, and she couldn't stop herself from taking long, greedy licks across all the soft skin that her seeking mouth could reach.

When she sighed with pleasure, a low laugh rumbled through him that emboldened her to test their newly established trust even further. She slid off beside him to the mattress and reached for his waist.

"Olivia," he warned quietly, but that didn't stop her from pulling his shirt out from his waistband. "You don't…" Or unbuttoning the fall of his trousers. "…have to…" Or gently pulling his manhood free and placing a delicate if slightly nervous kiss to his tip. An incoherent groan fell from his lips. "Ahh…"

He was large and heavy in her hand, steely hard beneath smooth flesh, and he flexed against her lips when she took a tentative lick. She knew women did this—how could she have run a school for young ladies for so many years without hearing their whispers of rumors and curiosities about men? But she had never done anything like it before. Yet this was Alec, and if they were going to place their trust completely in each other, then she couldn't imagine any act that required more trust and exposed more vulnerability than this.

So she closed her lips around him and sucked.

"Olivia…" He dug his trembling hand into her hair.

Encouraged, she deliberately took him deeper into her mouth before slowly pulling back in a long, slow glide. A shudder of pleasure raced through him, so she did it again… and again. A bold and wanton idea gripped her, and during one of the steady but slow plunges and retreats, she swirled her tongue around him as she would a dollop of sweet cream from a spoon.

"Olivia!"

His hips bucked beneath her, and she reflexively tightened her lips around him. Shivers and shudders gripped him, and his nails scraped her scalp from the intensity of the pleasures she brought him.

Feelings of empowerment and joy pulsed through her. She'd never felt its like before! But then, she'd never been so emboldened before, so wanton. So *free*. She knew that he would allow her to do whatever she wanted to him tonight. The panther had been tamed by the mouse. A laugh of happiness bubbled up inside her at the irony and surely vibrated down his length because he flexed in her mouth, and she tasted the first salty drop of his essence on her tongue.

She moaned as desire throbbed through her and landed in that space between her legs that he'd teased to a burning ache. She ached now for a completely different reason—*need*…the need to have him inside her, to be filled with his strength, to join together bodies and souls. A need to be completed.

She lifted her head and let him slip away from between her lips. Keeping her eyes firmly locked with his, she climbed up his body to straddle him again. But this time, she rose onto her knees, then slowly lowered over him to bring him inside her.

She stilled and perched unmoving on top of him for several heartbeats as her body adjusted to his. A faint discomfort at having him inside her vanished as a delicious tingle shivered out from her core. She placed her hands flat on his chest and began to move.

"Do you like this?" she whispered as she rose and fell over him in slow, controlled movements, doing with her body what he'd seemed to enjoy so much from her mouth.

"Yes," he panted out. His hands clasped her hips and urged her to move harder and faster against him. "Sweet Lucifer, yes…"

With each rise and fall, tension coiled tighter inside her, and her body clenched around him as she stroked him as deeply inside her as possible. Flames licked at her toes, and her fingers dug into his chest muscles as she strained toward release.

"You're so beautiful…so brilliant," he murmured. He leaned up to capture her mouth with his in a hot, open-mouthed kiss that tasted of possession and a yearning so fierce that it stunned her. "My sweet angel."

Pleasure shot through her, and she bit her lip to stifle a cry as her breath ripped away. Her body arched above him, and she welcomed the sweet bliss that overcame her.

Alec pulled her down onto his chest and slipped himself free of her tight warmth. His hand dove between them and positioned his still-hard erection between their bellies. Breathless and boneless, Olivia had the strength to do nothing more than lie on his chest as he wrapped his arms around her, gave a shuddering growl, and jerked against her belly. A wet warmth spurted between them, and he relaxed beneath her with a groaning sigh, all of his body suddenly limp and satiated.

Olivia lost all notion of how long they lay there together like that, with his arms around her, with her head on his shoulder and his heartbeat pounding into hers. But she knew she never wanted to move, never wanted the clock to start ticking and move the night toward dawn. She wanted nothing more than this man at this moment for the rest of her life.

Twenty-One

OLIVIA LAY ON HER SIDE WITH HER ARM TUCKED beneath her head and stared at Alec in the shadows as he faced her, staring back. Around them, the school was still and silent, the room cast into shadows as the last of the coals in the grate faded into darkness.

Heavens, she'd never realized before how small her bed was until he was in it, his muscular form large and absurdly masculine against the lace-edged pillows and pastel bedding. The effect only served to make him look even more handsome, even more rakish and dangerous.

She caressed his cheek with her hand and smiled at the rough scratch of midnight beard against her fingertips.

He turned his head to place a tender kiss to her palm, and a long sigh fell from her.

"Are you all right?" Concern laced his deep voice.

She smiled. "I'm fine."

But she didn't trust herself to say what she really felt for fear she'd make an utter fool of herself by begging him to do the impossible and find a way for them to be together. She could smell him on her skin, that sweet intoxication of whiskey, leather, and lemons, now mixing with the musky scent of sex. He'd imprinted himself upon her, and she doubted she'd ever be able to free herself.

She loved him. There was no denying it any longer.

And absolutely nothing could come of it. She'd known that from the beginning. He was a gentleman with fortune and title, obligated to marry a lady befitting his rank, and she was only a schoolmistress with nothing to give as her dowry but an indebted school.

But she also refused to let that ruin this moment. With a smile that felt inexplicably shy, she brushed her hand over his shoulder and rested it on his chest. His heart beat steady and strong beneath her palm. Could she make it race again as she'd done before? And all the other things she'd done...

Her eyes trailed down toward his waist and stopped. His shirt was wet and stained. Embarrassment heated her cheeks. "We ruined your shirt."

"Hmm." He tucked his chin to glance down at himself. "So we have."

With a quick kiss to her lips, he crawled out of bed and shed his waistcoat. His lips twisted at the longing expression on her face as he pulled his braces down over his shoulders to let them dangle around his hips. With her eyes glued to him, he stripped his shirt off over his head and tossed it onto the floor.

She sat up in the bed, and her eyes landed on his chest—on that hard, bare, deliciously sculpted chest with its light dusting of dark hair that trailed down his abdomen and beneath his waistband to where his... *Oh my*. His undone trousers did nothing to hide his manhood, which still hung free from its confines. He lay limp now, but heavens, he was still large, still tempting, and still sending throbs of pleasure through her at just the memory of having him inside her.

He grinned down at her like a cat that had gotten into the cream. Or, more exactly, like the rake who'd gotten into a woman's bed.

"Like what you see?" he drawled in a seductive voice that had her longing to touch everywhere her eyes strayed.

Embarrassment heated her cheeks, and longing heated... somewhere else. She wisely kept silent.

He tucked himself back inside his trousers and fastened up his fall, then pulled his braces into place. When he buttoned up his waistcoat over his bare torso, the silk just barely covered his abdomen. She sighed. A man shouldn't look so delicious as he *put on* his clothes, as if the act of modesty were as erotic as stripping out of them.

But this was Alec. Nothing about him was as expected.

"I should go."

Including that announcement.

Surprised, she glanced at the window. The night outside was black. "Dawn is still hours away." Besides, she wasn't ready to part from him and end this magical evening before she had to.

He turned toward the chair where he'd tossed the rest of his clothes earlier, and his grin faded. "We can't risk that I'm found here."

She watched as he picked up his discarded gloves and shoved them into his greatcoat pocket. A natural movement, not at all awkward, as if he did it all the time. Most likely, he was collecting his things unconsciously, the well-trained rake in him not wanting to leave anything behind. As if he were in any other lady's bedroom and she were simply another conquest.

Olivia pulled the coverlet up to her bosom to cover herself. She suddenly felt cold.

"What are you afraid of?" she asked softly as she watched him wrap his cravat around his neck. She would have said he looked ridiculous as he peered into the little mirror over her dressing table to tie the cloth, with bare arms emerging from the silk waistcoat. But the hard muscles of his biceps bulged with every small movement he made, and the sight of him took her breath away. "That being caught here will call attention to your pursuit of the men my brother is working with?" She paused to take a deep breath. "Or that the Sinclair ladies will force you to marry me?"

He froze, his hazel eyes pinning hers in the mirror's reflection. "That isn't it, and you know it." He looked back at his reflection and finished tying the cravat in a tangled knot, but at least it covered his lack of shirt when he tucked the ends beneath his waistcoat. "We've already risked far too much tonight."

"Yes, I know." That quiet reminder of all she'd been through before with Samuel hung in the shadows between them.

"Damnation…" Facing her, he ran his hand through his hair and left it in a rakish mess. One she found her own fingers itching to comb through and set right. "Do you want me to stay?"

"No."

"Are you certain?" he asked somberly, calling that out for the lie it was.

Her shoulders sagged. "No."

With a grimace, he snatched up his soiled shirt and tossed it into the fireplace. The linen caught fire and flared brightly before dying away, leaving the room in the same quiet shadows as before.

He asked into the fire, "Are you regretting tonight?"

"No." *Never.* She'd been weak and succumbed to her desire for him, despite how risky it was for her reputation. And her heart. But she certainly didn't regret it.

"Good. Neither am I." He reached for the bottle of whiskey sitting on the mantel. "But you're upset. So what's wrong?" When she hesitated to answer, he reminded her gently, "No more secrets, remember?"

Not quite. There was still one huge secret that lingered between them. She rushed out the question on an unsteady breath before she could turn coward— "Who was she?"

He absently swished the whiskey to judge how much was left. "Who was who?"

"The woman who hurt you so badly by hiding her true self."

The bottle stopped just before it reached his lips. For a long moment, he didn't move. Then he admitted quietly, "That's not what I expected you to ask."

Confusion panged inside her chest. After all, that secret was what had driven everything between them for the last few days. "What did you expect?"

"If I planned on proposing." The bottle continued to his mouth, and he helped himself to a healthy swallow.

"No," she whispered, unable to find her voice. "That isn't what I want to know."

Because she already knew the answer. *He wouldn't.* That was the God's truth. If she wasn't good enough in society's eyes for the youngest son of a viscount, then she'd never be good enough to marry an earl. They both knew it. Making love changed that not at all.

"Someone hurt you, and deeply." Her words came softly, barely louder than a breath, but she couldn't stop them. "You practically said so when you asked me how many people I'd hurt by hiding my past. You would only have thought to ask that if you had been hurt that way yourself." She pressed on, ignoring the swift stab of jealousy. "Who was the woman who broke your heart?"

"No woman has ever hurt me in that way." He forced a grin that didn't ease the tension radiating from him or loosen his tight hold around the bottle's neck. "I'm a blackguard, remember? We blackguards don't have hearts."

She carefully kept her expression from registering the unwitting sting of that comment. "But surely, someone must have—"

"His Lordship, Rupert Alexander Redmond Sinclair, the Right *Honorable*"—the word emerged as a derogatory sneer—"Earl of St James, Viscount Haddon, Baron Stiles…" Then he lifted the bottle in a mocking toast. "*My father.*"

She gaped at him, stunned.

"The old earl wasn't at all what he appeared to be." He took a drink and set the bottle aside. "To the world, he portrayed a proper and pious façade. But underneath, he was Satan himself."

"What do you mean?"

He turned sideways to her and fussed with his jacket to finish dressing. The move was intentional, she knew, because now she couldn't clearly see his face and any emotions that might have strayed beyond his control. "Gambling, drinking, prostitutes…"

"All peers do that."

"Do most peers tie prostitutes to the bed so they can't escape, then alternate between reading the Bible to them and beating them with a riding crop in an attempt to drive out their sins?" She felt the blood drain from her face, but he continued, not yet bringing himself to glance her way. "And if they didn't repent, if he was convinced that they couldn't be cured of their evil, he raped them. A punishment he believed fitting for their sins."

Olivia couldn't speak past the knot in her throat, too shocked to make a sound.

"Those were the prostitutes he liked." Alec held up the jacket and shook it, as if he could shake off his father's deeds as easily as he brushed off the evening's lint. "Others he simply abused, doing such things to them…" His voice faded off. When he finally continued, he kept his gaze riveted on the jacket. "There were children, too—girls so young that they hadn't yet started their courses, starving boys from the streets desperate enough to do anything."

She pressed her hand to her belly. She was going to be sick!

"And in his own home, he'd forced himself on the maids. He got at least one of them with child before she could flee." Finally, he shot her a glance over his shoulder. "You met my half brother at the ball when he spilled punch on you."

"Captain Reed," she guessed in a whisper. The two men looked alike, but she never would have thought... *Good God.*

"And he did all that while sitting in the church box every Sunday, donating to the poorhouse, and preaching morality and responsibility at every turn. He was an expert at pretense and hiding the evils he committed. I swore that I would *never* be like him." He slipped on the jacket and yanked the sleeves into place at his wrists. "Yet some of that expertise rubbed off on me anyway."

Icy fingers curled up her spine. "What do you mean?"

"When he died, I had to continue to hide what he'd done or risk that the title would be taken away, our fortune and family reputation with it. That the Sinclair ladies would be ostracized from society, Beth never able to marry..." His voice lowered to a harsh mutter. "The bastard continues to threaten us even now, even from beyond the grave."

"What you did was understandable," she whispered. She, of all people, would never judge him for that. "You had to protect your family."

"I was also protecting my own pride." With a sober expression, he quietly confessed, "My father beat me for years, and I told no one."

"Alec..." Anguish for him radiated through her.

"Most fathers chastise their sons, some berate and yell," he muttered half to himself as he turned back toward the mirror to fuss again with the cravat. "Mine beat me until I was covered with welts and bruises, until I couldn't sit or stand from the pain." His voice grew impossibly quieter. "Always, I blamed myself. I thought that if I'd been a better son, the beatings would have been unnecessary. But I was never good enough for that self-righteous bastard, no matter how hard I tried. So one day, I simply stopped trying." He smoothed down the front of his waistcoat. "What I learned was that the beatings were just as unpredictable and severe no matter what I did. But at least then I was actually doing the things the earl accused me of." The corner of his mouth twisted into a pained smile. "I had my pride even then."

Pride. He owned it in spades, more than any other man she'd ever met, and even while half-dressed and confessing the greatest humiliation of his life.

"Now the bastard is rotting in his grave where he belongs." He straightened his shoulders and turned away from the mirror, yanking his lapels into place. "And if there's a hell, then I pray he's burning."

The darkness that gripped his face made her gasp. He must have heard the soft sound, because he forced a self-deprecating grin and reached for the whiskey.

"Don't pity me, Olivia. The prostitutes had it worse." He brought the bottle to his lips. "At least I never had to listen to him recite the Bible."

He hid the pain behind that facetious comment by gulping down what little remained in the bottle.

Olivia couldn't bear it a moment longer. She scrambled out of bed and into her dressing robe. She barely had time to cinch the belt into place around her waist before she reached him, before her arms wrapped around him.

He softened in her embrace, and her heart wept for him as he buried his face in her hair.

"When I left England, I didn't yet know what else he'd been doing, who else he'd been hurting," he confessed. "I thought it was only me, that it was all my fault every time he took a strap to me."

She nuzzled her face against his neck to provide whatever physical solace she could. "That is *never* a child's fault."

"How is a boy to know any differently when he knows nothing else?"

"But surely, your mother—"

He placed a pained kiss to her lips to silence her and squeezed his eyes shut. "Mother never knew. She still doesn't."

Olivia pulled back just far enough to search his face. "Why didn't you tell them?"

"Pride," he admitted quietly with a small shrug, "shame, fear… My mother loved me, and I feared that if I told her about the beatings, I would have to tell her why I'd deserved them. I was terrified she'd agree with the earl that I was wicked and a disappointment as a son, and I didn't want to lose her love, too."

"How could your mother not have known?" Her heart broke for the little boy he'd been, for all the terror and pain he'd suffered during what should have been the happiest years of his life. And at the hands of the man who should have loved and protected him. "If you were being beaten that severely—"

"Because Bivvens helped me hide it and never told a soul. Because she had her own troubles to deal with. Because the earl never beat me where the marks would show." He wrapped both arms around her and whispered into her ear, "You didn't see the scars on the backs of my legs tonight, and I was inside you. If *you* were that close and didn't see them… As I said, I was very good at hiding it."

When a sob escaped her, he placed a kiss to her hair to comfort her.

"That was why I left England. I wasn't willing to endure it any longer." He paused. "I knew that if he raised a hand to me again, I would have killed him."

She gazed at him through tear-blurred eyes, yet she could clearly see the raw pain and barely controlled anger that seethed inside him even now after all these years.

"I was eighteen, finished at Eton, and expected to return home to Pelham Park. But I couldn't bring myself to do it. So I called in every favor I could to purchase an army commission. I didn't tell anyone where I'd gone until I set foot in Portugal, not even the Sinclair ladies. I made certain they couldn't stop me." He lowered his voice and muttered, "I was in northern Spain when word reached me that the earl had died. By the time I arrived in England, I'd missed his funeral." Harshness edged his voice. "I thank God every day that I didn't have to sit in the church and pretend to mourn when I was happy he was dead and couldn't hurt anyone again."

"But he is," she whispered. "He's still hurting you."

He stepped out of her arms. Lowering his face so she couldn't make eye contact, he tugged again at all his clothing to bring it fully into place. Despite that, he still looked like a man who had just scandalously made love. And one who was relentlessly haunted.

"He's dead and buried where he belongs. But you—" Finally, he lifted his gaze and looked at her, and the grief that darkened his face took her breath away. "I couldn't bear to know that you might also be hurting people by hiding behind a façade. Or if you were hurting yourself."

His earlier words returned to her… "You said you wanted to save me. That's what you meant."

He gave a hard nod. "Yes."

"Then we have a problem." She cupped his face between her hands. "Because you can't save me until you save yourself."

He laughed darkly at the notion. "I don't need to be saved."

More than you realize. "Alec, you have to tell your mother."

"What good will that do?"

"It will let you start forgiving. *Truly* forgiving. Starting with yourself."

He didn't move for a long while, and when he finally did, he let loose a harsh breath and sagged his shoulders. "Beth said nearly the exact same thing tonight."

"Well then. Proof that you have very wise women in your life." She rose onto tiptoes to kiss him before he could contradict her. And before he could remind her that she wasn't a true part of his life.

She melted into him as the kiss intensified, and when he reached down to untie her belt, she knew he'd gotten dressed for no good reason. But this time when they made love, she wanted to heal him, to tell him with her body how much she loved—

A loud crash shattered the silence around them.

She jumped back with a cry of surprise. The sound of smashing furniture and breaking glass reverberated through the school.

Olivia's heart stopped with fear. "The girls!"

She raced to fling open the door and charged into the dark hallway. Sounds of fighting, scuffling, and muffled shouts echoed through the halls and stairs. But the noise didn't come from the dormitories on the floor below where the girls were all tucked up asleep for the night. It came from—

"Henry!"

She ran toward his room just as the door flew open and smashed against the wall. Two large men pushed her brother out of the room. One painfully clamped his arm behind his back to keep him from struggling while the other held his shoulders and shoved him forward.

"Let go of him!" She ran toward them.

"Olivia, no!" Henry yelled before one of the men punched him in the face. The blow reeled him backward and left him stunned enough for one man to drag him down the stairs and out of the house.

The second man turned on Olivia. He grabbed her by the shoulders and shoved her backward. She slammed into the wall so hard that her teeth jarred and the air tore from her lungs. He forced her arms up over her head with one hand and pinned her helplessly beneath him.

In desperation, Olivia shoved her knee up between his legs. But she missed her target and struck his thigh.

"Bitch!" He hit her with the back of his hand.

She cried out in pain as the force of the blow smacked her head against the wall.

With a ferocious growl, Alec grabbed the intruder's shoulder and spun him around. His fist plowed into the man's chin, and the punch sent the attacker staggering backward.

The man recovered, then launched himself at Alec and lowered his shoulder as he plowed forward.

A grunt tore from Alec as the man's shoulder slammed into his gut, but his hands attacked. He grabbed the intruder's wrist and bent it back until it snapped. The man screamed in pain. Alec punched him in the jaw, then stepped forward to shove him hard with his left hand.

The attacker stumbled backward and tripped down the stairs. He cried out in surprise and pain as he somersaulted onto the landing below. He staggered to his feet and tucked his broken wrist beneath his opposite arm, then ran the rest of the way downstairs and out the front door.

Olivia's knees gave out beneath her as she gasped for breath, and she crumpled to the floor. The pain pounding in her head was blinding, and she lay still, unable to move. All her strength focused on nothing more than forcing herself to breathe.

Immediately, Alec was at her side, gathering her into his arms. "Are you all right?"

"They...took...Henry," she choked out between harsh gasps for breath.

"I'll go after him and find—"

"No!" She shook her head, and the pounding pain slammed into the back of her skull like lightning strikes. "The girls—count the girls!"

"Olivia!" Mrs. Adams raced up the stairs in her dressing robe and bare feet. "Dear God, what happened—"

Then she saw Alec and froze in her steps, her eyes wide.

Olivia placed her hand on Alec's chest to signify that he was a friend and not one of the kidnappers.

"Intruders," Olivia explained frantically as darkness pressed in around her. The floor rose and fell beneath her, and dark spots formed before her eyes as she forced out, "Count the girls…make certain…all here…"

Nodding, Mrs. Adams raced back down the stairs toward the dormitories on the floor below.

Olivia's hand clenched at his waistcoat. She *had* to make him understand. "If they've taken any of the girls…" Her throat tightened, and she choked. A hot tear rolled down her cheek.

"They didn't take…" But his voice came garbled and distant, as if he were speaking underwater. "I promise…"

The world spun around her, and she couldn't catch hold to stop it. She closed her eyes to stop the sickening dizziness that swelled inside her. She felt herself falling away… falling…

The last thing her mind registered before the darkness overtook her was Alec frantically calling her name.

Twenty-Two

ALEC GAZED SOLEMNLY AT REED AND CLAYTON FROM behind Olivia's small desk in her office. "Nothing?"

Clayton shook his head. "There's no trace of Henry Everett."

With a curse, Alec sat back in the chair. Around him, the school was finally quiet. The girls had settled down just after dawn, believing the story that Mrs. Adams had spun about a stray dog who'd slipped into the school and caused havoc as they'd attempted to chase him out.

Thankfully, none of them had seen Alec.

Olivia was still upstairs in her room and hopefully still sleeping. They'd sent for a doctor who'd assured them that she would be fine and simply needed a long rest. But Alec was ready to kill the bastard who'd struck her.

"My men are asking around the docks to see what can be turned up." Clayton added solemnly, "But I don't expect to learn anything. The men who took him are most likely half-way to the Channel by now."

Exactly what Alec thought himself. The two men who broke into the school had been hired from the docks—or from the tavern next to the docks, more likely, given their stench of stale ale and rotten fish. They could have taken

Henry Everett anywhere, collected their money upon his delivery, then sailed away on the first ship. Even Clayton's network of spies and Reed's guards wouldn't be able to find them.

"I did discover the connection between Everett and Lady Rowland, however," Reed interjected. "The lady employs a very chatty kitchen maid."

Alec shook his head. There was no hope in finding Henry Everett through the baroness. "Even if Sydney Rowland is caught up in this, she won't—"

"How, exactly, is Lady Rowland involved with my brother?"

All three men glanced toward the door. Alec's heart skipped.

Olivia.

She stood in the doorway, and her eyes traveled warily between Alec, Clayton, and Reed. Like any other morning, she was dressed in a fresh day dress, her hair neatly but simply pinned into a chignon. But her beautiful face was pale and drawn, with dark circles beneath her eyes, and her cheek was marred by an ugly bruise. Alec thought he could see her hands shaking before she deftly folded them out of sight behind her back.

He rose and went to her. He took her elbow to escort her into the room and gave it a reassuring squeeze when what he wanted to do was pull her into his arms and hold her close.

"Miss Everett, this is Captain Nathaniel Reed and Major Clayton Elliott, old friends of mine from my army days," Alec introduced quietly, providing no more information about the two men than that. She needed to know nothing more, except… "You can trust them with your life."

She gave no acknowledgment of that. Instead, she pressed Reed by bluntly asking, "What connection does the baroness have to Henry?"

Reed looked questioningly at Clayton, who nodded his consent to bring Olivia into their confidence, and said, "Your brother has been frequenting gambling hells and accumulating huge debts, including at Barton's on the same nights when Lady Rowland was present. They've been seen talking privately several times during the past fortnight." He paused. "You didn't know?"

"No," she whispered.

Alec waited for her to say more, bracing himself for the argument about her brother's innocence that had always come at this point in their previous conversations.

This time, though, she didn't defend him.

"They were introduced by Sir George Pittens," Reed explained. "The baroness took pity on your brother and offered to pay his gambling debts."

She frowned, confused. "Why would she do that?"

Alec exchanged a grim look with Clayton, who answered, "Most likely because she wanted him to be indebted to her and the men she's working with so he'd be compelled to do their bidding."

Alec felt her stiffen. This time, a squeeze to her elbow wasn't enough to comfort her, so he rested his hand on the small of her back, not giving a damn what Reed and Clayton suspected about the two of them.

"He said he did it for the money, but I didn't believe him," she whispered hoarsely as all the pieces of what her brother had been doing finally fell into place for her. "He said it was for the school, that we had spent too much money on it… that I had. He never mentioned gambling debts." She slipped away from Alec and absently reached for a little wooden box sitting on her desk. Her fingers trembled as they traced over the delicate carvings of flowers that decorated its lid. "All the while, it was his fault. He put our lives in jeopardy, risked the school…hurt people."

"He was determined to become part of the Royal Society," Alec explained quietly. "He had to lead the lifestyle its fellows expected from him, which cost a great deal of money and included time spent at clubs where he would have been expected to drink and gamble as much as the men around him. He couldn't sustain that without going into debt."

She trembled from her brother's betrayal, but her spine remained ramrod straight. "And when the baroness offered to pay his debts, it was in exchange for working calculations for the Admiralty Club, to determine the weakest structural spots…where explosives could cause the most damage." Not a question. Her hand dropped away from the box, and she pulled in an anguished breath. "He said he didn't know what the plans were to be used for, that he suspected the club wanted to check the architect's work."

"He was most likely telling the truth about that," Clayton confirmed. "Scepter wouldn't have told him their endgame in case he was caught and questioned. He was simply a pawn they controlled through his debts."

She nodded, but Alec could see her hesitancy to accept that truth about her brother. "I want to speak to the baroness."

"No." Alec refused to relent on this. It was too dangerous, and the men couldn't risk showing Scepter their hand. "We have to pretend that we know nothing about Lady Rowland's involvement."

"But we will keep looking for Henry, yes?"

We. The word warmed Alec's chest. They were still in this together, and that thought brought him more pleasure than he wanted to admit. "Of course."

"I've positioned men to watch the baroness in case anyone else attempts to contact her," Clayton assured her.

"And I plan on finding out more about what her household staff knows," Reed added. "We'll let you know what we discover."

"Thank you." She released her breath in a small sigh and blinked rapidly to clear her watery eyes.

With small bows to Olivia and nods to Alec, Reed and Clayton quietly excused themselves and left.

Alec closed the door. Then he gently pulled Olivia into the circle of his arms.

He closed his eyes against the warm, unfamiliar sensation sweeping through him. Although he couldn't put a name to it, he knew everything in his life had irrevocably changed last night. Because of her.

He touched her chin and gently turned her head so he could examine the black-and-blue mark on her cheek. If he ever found the man who did this to her, he would kill him. "How are you feeling?"

"I'm fine." When he challenged that blatant lie with a lift of his brow, she surrendered her false bravado and amended, "I have a terrible headache, but otherwise, I'm all right. Truly."

He lowered his head and kissed her lips. He couldn't keep himself from shaking. Dear God, what would he have done if she'd been seriously injured?

She sighed beneath his kiss and accepted his solace. Then she shifted back, breaking the kiss but not leaving the circle of his arms.

She bit her lip with worry. "How are Mrs. Adams and the girls?"

"Most likely still all in their beds." He released her and stepped back, reluctantly putting distance between them before he made a fool of himself by crushing her to him. "I consulted with Mrs. Adams and Miss Smith, and we decided it was best just to tell the girls that a stray dog had gotten inside the house. All the noise was from chasing it out."

A dubious frown wrinkled her brow. "And what excuse did *you* give for being here?"

"I was returning the reticule you'd accidentally left at the musicale and arrived at the school just in time to help with the intruders."

"But I didn't take a reticule."

"My mistake," he answered, deadpan.

Her shoulders slumped with fatigue and worry.

He caressed the side of her face with his knuckles. "We need to talk about last night."

She nodded. "Henry didn't go willingly. That means those men weren't the ones who—"

"I don't mean your brother."

Dread darkened her face, and he stiffened. They had a lot left between them to hammer out—two people couldn't reveal their ghosts to each other as they'd done and not have issues left to exorcise before they could move forward. But he certainly hadn't expected *that* look from her.

"I can't," she whispered, barely louder than a breath. She stepped away to put just enough room between them that he couldn't reach for her. "I can't think about anything else until Henry is safe."

"We made love last night," he murmured.

She wrung her hands and began to pace. "*Especially* that."

"Olivia—"

"I'm not ready, Alec." The pleading look she sent him nearly undid him. "I can't even think straight right now. Please…later."

He nodded his agreement despite the cold apprehension that rose inside him. He couldn't shake the feeling that she was slipping away even though they stood less than six feet apart.

Yet he would grant her this reprieve. For now.

A knock rapped at the door, interrupting them. Olivia turned toward it with a look of relief. "Yes?"

The door opened slowly, and Mrs. Adams poked her head cautiously inside. "Miss Everett, there's someone at the door asking for you."

Olivia dragged in a deep, shaking breath, and in that fleeting moment, he saw something in her that he'd never seen before—helplessness. She was overwhelmed.

Her voice trembled. "Please tell whoever it is…that we're not accepting visitors today."

Mrs. Adams's mouth tightened with worry, and she flicked a glance at Alec, as if hoping he would overrule that order. "He said it was about Mr. Everett."

Olivia's face paled, and she reached for the back of a chair to steady herself.

"Who is it?" Alec asked quietly.

"A boy, my lord, who claims he has a message for Miss Everett."

"Please show him in." When Mrs. Adams left, he covered Olivia's hand with his on the chair back and laced his fingers through hers. "Your brother will be all right. I promise you."

She nodded and looked away in a weak attempt to hide her worry. But by doing so, she also turned her bruised cheek fully into view and gave him an unwitting reminder of all that was at stake.

He would protect her with his life.

A skinny boy walked into the room and halted midstep when he saw Alec. He wasn't more than nine or ten, dressed in rags and covered in black soot. A chimney sweep. The perfect messenger boy for Scepter because no one would have paid any attention if they saw him walking through the streets of Westminster with the other sweeps and deliverymen.

Then the boy shrugged and stepped forward. From his swagger and dirty appearance, he'd lived a hard life on the streets and wouldn't be intimidated by someone like Alec, even at ten years old. It was a harsh life that would only get harder once he grew too big to work the chimneys and lost even that terrible position, which at least provided some measure of protection against starving in the streets.

The boy snarled defiantly, "You Olivia, then?"

"Miss Everett," Alec sternly corrected the boy's insolence.

"Don't know no *Miss Everett*," the boy responded cheekily. "Was told t' give me message t' an *O-liv-i-a*." He dragged out each syllable of her name. His eyes, far too old for his true age, pinned on her. "You her?"

"I am." Her hand went to Alec's arm for support—and to keep him from tossing the boy out right then. "What message do you have for me?"

"Yer t' take these 'ere papers an' work 'em." He reached up his filthy coat sleeve, withdrew a rolled sheaf of papers, and held them out toward her.

"Work them?" She hesitated before accepting them.

"Aye. That's the message—t' work 'em. To…to work…" The boy scrunched his face as he searched his mind for the words he'd been forced to memorize by the man who paid him to deliver the message. With no written message to deliver, there was no way to trace handwriting or watermarks, and a boy like this would have been hungry enough to take any offered money without question. "To work out the best places on 'em t' cause the most damage, then take 'em to the same place i' the city where you went the night you followed your brother. At midnight tonight. Or they'll kill 'im." He gave a proud nod at finishing the message and turned to leave, his work here done. "That's all."

Alec swooped down upon him, grabbed him by the scruff of his collar, and lifted him into the air until only the toes of his hole-filled shoes touched the floor. All skin and bones, the boy barely weighed anything, but he fought like a trapped rat as he flung his small fists and kicked wildly in the air.

"Stop that." Alec dropped the boy onto the desk and leaned over him.

The boy's face turned instantly hard, and he cowered, as if expecting to be hit.

Alec recognized that look. He'd worn it himself too many times to count. "I'm not going to hit you."

He would *never* strike a child. Besides, this boy had been beaten enough times in his young life already that physical violence would only increase the lad's silence. Hadn't Alec learned that same lesson from his own father?

Bribery was the better option. Alec withdrew a coin from his pocket and held it up. Instantly, he had the boy's attention.

"What's your name?" Alec demanded.

The boy looked longingly at the coin. "Don't got one. But the old man in charge o' the sweeps calls me Filth."

Alec didn't let his anger at that register on his face and placed the coin in the boy's hand. Then he withdrew a second one. "Who gave you those papers to deliver to Miss Everett?"

"Don't know." The boy's dirty hand closed tightly around the first coin, and he stared at the second one as if mesmerized by it. Of course he was. It was enough to buy a month's worth of food. "Didn't give no name."

"How did he find you?"

"This mornin', 'fore dawn, me an' Grunt were walkin' back from cleanin' a couple o' chimneys a few streets from 'ere, an' a man 'pproached us. Said he 'ad a job fer me, made me memorize that message fer the lady." His eyes darted from the coin to Alec's face, and his lower lip jutted out defiantly. "*He* paid me *three* coins, 'e did. That's the mark o' a good gentleman."

Alec's lips twitched glumly. Ten years old and the boy was already an expert extortionist. He placed the second coin in the boy's outstretched palm and withdrew a third from his pocket. He hoped he could get all the information he needed before he ran out of coins. "What did he look like?"

"Like you."

Alec was taken aback by that. "Like me?"

"All fancy an' rich, fine clothes wi' shiny boots. Shorter than you, though, an' fatter."

"Did you see his hair and eyes? Anything to distinguish him from other men?"

"Brown 'air, brown eyes. Nothin' special 'bout 'im. No pox marks, no scars."

Alec made to place the coin in the boy's hand but pulled it back, letting the boy grab at empty air. "Are you to meet up with him after you've delivered the message?"

"Aye, sir. Owes me 'nother coin. Said I'd get it after I delivered the message t' Olivia—to the lady, I mean."

"Where?"

"Same spot where 'e found me. Back o' Cairn Lane near the butcher's."

"Good boy." Alec gave him the last coin—and a fourth

for good measure, knowing the man who'd hired the boy wouldn't return to pay him what he'd been promised. Then he lifted him off the desk. A spot of black soot powdered the oak where he'd sat.

The boy gave a sarcastic tug of his forelock in mockery of how he'd seen older workers do to gentlemen, then turned to leave.

Olivia reached for his shoulder and stopped him. She knelt in front of him, as gentle and unthreatening as an angel.

"Before you leave, why don't you go downstairs to the kitchen with Mrs. Adams?" She brushed his hair off his forehead, revealing a white streak across his brow where her fingers brushed the soot away.

Alec stared at her, nearly as mesmerized by her surprising actions as the boy. Heedless of how dirty the lad was and how he was most likely a breeding spot for fleas and lice, she fussed with the collar of his threadbare coat. Not to straighten his appearance—only a hot bath, a tub of soap, and an hour's scrubbing might be able to do that—but to comfort him with the first motherly caresses the boy had most likely had in years. Or ever.

Based on how the boy softened visibly beneath her hands, it was working.

"She made far too much bacon and eggs this morning for breakfast," Olivia divulged, "so there might be some left over for you."

Hunger had the lad nearly drooling, but the lure of the second payment won his loyalty. "No thanks, ma'am. Gotta meet up wi' the man who—"

"He won't be there," Alec told him somberly. "You've done your job. He doesn't need you to report back, and he certainly won't be there to pay you."

The boy suspected that, too, from the way he clenched his jaw.

Olivia interjected, "So why don't you stay and have yourself a good meal for your trouble?"

The boy eyed Olivia warily, then decided she was trustworthy enough and tugged again at his forelock. This time in proper deference. "I'd like that, miss."

She smiled. "Then help yourself to as much as you want to eat, Phillip."

He looked at her as if she'd gone daft. "Me name's *Filth*, ma'am."

Ignoring that, she nodded past his shoulder at the housekeeper, who still lingered at the door. "Mrs. Adams, while Phillip is eating breakfast, would you see if there are any sticky buns left over from the girls' tea yesterday? You can wrap some up for Phillip to take with him."

The housekeeper nodded, although it was clear from the expression on the woman's face that she also wanted to grab the boy by his ears and dunk him repeatedly in a soapy tub. "Yes, Miss Everett. I'll show Mr. Phillip to the kitchen."

The promise of sticky buns got the boy's attention enough to not care that Olivia had given him a proper name. "Thank you, ma'am."

"And if you come back tomorrow, Phillip, there might be work for you outside in the service yard in exchange for a hot dinner." Olivia narrowed her blue eyes as she studied him and tapped her finger against her chin with mock thought-fulness. "Of course, if you're going to work for the Everett School, you'll have to wear the new jacket we'll give you. And boots. That's a requirement of the job, I'm afraid. We mustn't let anyone think we don't take care of our employees, you understand, so you're just going to have to wear new work clothes, whether you like it or not."

The grin that blossomed on the boy's face stretched nearly from ear to ear.

"Go on, then, Phillip, and follow Mrs. Adams. I'll see you again tomorrow."

"This way, Phillip," Mrs. Adams repeated the boy's new name as she pointed down the hall.

He paused in the doorway and turned back in after-thought. "M' friend Grunt's a good worker, miss. Won't cause no problems. You think you might got any work fer 'im too?" He held out the coins on his grubby palm. "I can pay fer 'is work clothes, if 'n that's a trouble."

"It's no trouble at all." Olivia smiled. "Bring Grant with you tomorrow. There's more than enough work."

The boy beamed, transformed. The moment he obediently followed Mrs. Adams from the room, the boy became Phillip. No longer a chimney sweep who would be lucky to live past the age of twenty but now a school employee—although a dubious one—with a real chance at a decent future.

Olivia remained on her knees a moment longer as she watched the boy disappear down the hall. A poignant mixture of hope and sadness shone on her face.

Alec couldn't tear his gaze away from her. He'd never seen a woman so selfless as to invite an abused boy into her home and give him food, clothing, and employment. More, in changing his name, she'd changed his identity and increased his self-worth. The goodness in her stole his breath away.

That she was the same woman who challenged him intellectually, who thrilled him physically—the same hellcat who darted fearlessly down dark alleys, then melted when he held her in his arms—the entirety of her made him tremble.

She looked up at him, and he feared she could read his feelings for her on his face. So he warningly teased, "I think you just started a workhouse for runaway chimney sweeps."

She smiled. "I'm perfectly fine with that."

Then she surprised him again by sitting right down on the floor. She quickly unrolled the sheaf of papers and spread them out across the carpet to examine them. Her smile faded.

"More building plans," she told him, not looking up from the large pages.

"They're planning another attack," he murmured as he came forward and looked over her shoulder. "Just as before."

Her face paled as she swept her hands over the plans to find any distinguishing marks. "But where? Three stories, central staircase, flat-front façade, no windows in the side walls...no architect's notations that I can recognize." She sat back on her heels in defeat. "This could be almost any building in London."

"There's no way to tell who created those plans or when?"

She shook her head. "But I do know why they sent them to me." She raised her glistening eyes from the plans to meet his. "Henry can't do these calculations, not for something as complicated as this. He must have told them that, must have admitted that it was me who did his work and refused to help them, and they—they kidnapped him to force me into working them." She pressed her hand to her mouth and whispered starkly through her fingers, "He's being held hostage because of me."

"You are *not* responsible." Alec dropped to the floor beside her and cupped her face in his hands. With every ounce of resolve he possessed, he willed her to believe him. "This is all Scepter's doing, and you've been swept up into it because you love your brother. You've done nothing wrong."

"It *is* my fault," she argued gravely. "But I can save him." She took on a sudden look of grim determination as she pointed at the plans. "I can work these, deliver them, and free Henry."

"No, you won't," he assured her quietly. "You have too much goodness in you to harm others."

Tears of frustration gathered on her lashes. "But if I don't do as they demand, then Henry will…" Unable to finish the sentence, she clutched the plans to her breast, as if they were as dear to her as a child.

He didn't have the heart to tell her that most likely her brother was already dead. Scepter would treat her no differently from the messenger boy, who was promised a reward he would never receive when he finished the job.

"Then blame me because I won't let you put yourself in danger," he said instead. He gently touched the ugly bruise on her cheek, and his chest tightened with regret. "Again."

He leaned down to kiss her, with more tenderness than he'd ever felt for a woman before, as if trying to pour his soul inside her with that small kiss and somehow make her understand how much he cared about her.

Yet she put her hand on his chest and pulled away.

Sitting back, he expected her to continue to argue with him. Instead, intense emotion lit her eyes, and the hand that rested on his chest curled its fingers into his waistcoat.

"Alec," she whispered. Her voice pulsated with hope and excitement. "I have an idea…"

Twenty-Three

THE HACKNEY STOPPED IN THE DESERTED CITY STREET, and the driver pounded on the roof. "We're here."

Olivia's heart lurched into her throat. It was time for the trap to be sprung.

Unfortunately, she was the bait.

Taking a deep breath, she opened the door and stepped to the ground. She pushed back the hood of her cape to look up at the buildings overhanging the narrow street ahead where the carriage couldn't squeeze through to take her any closer to her destination. It had to stop here. So did any visible protection she had. She didn't dare look around in the darkness for any sign of the men who had followed her, out of fear of who else might be watching her.

Tonight, she had to play her part to perfection.

"Wait here for me," she instructed the jarvey as she held a coin toward him. "I'll pay you twice that to take me home."

"I'll be waitin' right 'ere," he assured her with a tip of his tall hat.

She began to shake as she walked away from the carriage and into the dark alley, following along the same path she'd traveled the night she met Alec. That was the same night her life changed forever. She silently prayed that her life wouldn't *end* here, too.

As she walked through the shadows, Olivia held her breath. Over the low tolling of a church bell striking midnight, she heard the faint echo of her footfalls against the cobblestones and, in the distance, the fading beat of horse hooves and shouts of drunken men. The clank of buoys in the river and an odd ship's bell marked that the Thames flowed nearby—another reminder that she was walking through the most dangerous, darkest part of London.

Fear churned in her stomach, yet she had no choice but to go on in order to save Henry. If there was any hope of capturing the men responsible for the Admiralty Club bombing, it had to be through her. Scepter's men expected her to deliver the calculations, and she knew they'd be waiting.

The sheaf of papers she'd slipped up her sleeve scratched against her arm with every step she took. She'd spent all afternoon working the calculations while Alec and Captain Reed finalized their own plans for tonight, but she'd worked the equations wrong. Instead of noting where the building's structure was weakest, she marked the strongest places. If all went well tonight, these plans would never reach Scepter's hands. But if they did, she wanted to make certain that they couldn't be used to murder innocent people. She might not be able to stop them from placing the bombs, but perhaps she could minimize the damage.

More—if Alec and Captain Reed couldn't find Henry tonight, she knew Scepter would force her brother to look over her work, so she'd placed a warning to him in her calculations. To anyone who wasn't a mathematician, her equations would look real, with algebraic orders using the common letter symbols of N, E, Y, H, and R found in any schoolboy's mathematics primer. But her brother would see her secret message and know she hadn't given up on finding him... H-E-N-R-Y.

The alley was pitch-black. The buildings were too close together even for the scant crescent moon to light her way, and no candlelight glowed from the windows, all of which were shuttered or boarded up. Her stomach roiled so fiercely that her hand darted to her belly to physically press down her growing nausea. Was she doing the right thing? Was she saving Henry's life by doing this, or simply putting both their lives at risk?

Alec and Captain Reed were following her unseen through the shadows. They'd been with her from the moment she'd first stepped out of the school and into the hired hackney. She wanted to take comfort in that but couldn't, not when the city around her was so dark and ominous. Neither was she put at ease by Alec's warnings... *Deliver the papers, draw out the men responsible, and we'll take it from there. Do not leave our sight.* Alec and Captain Reed would swoop in and capture the men, and Olivia would flee back to the waiting hackney and home, where she was supposed to spend a long and worried night under the protection of Home Office guards until it was all over. *That* didn't bring her comfort either.

Yet she walked on, determined.

A movement in the shadows startled her. She froze midstep with a gasp as a lean figure emerged from the darkness.

Another messenger boy, but this one was several years older than Phillip—and far larger. As he drew nearer, a hard scowl emerged on his young face that would have fit a man decades older. Something about the way he held his shoulders and clenched his fists at his sides told her that he'd hurt people before, perhaps even murdered them, and that he wouldn't hesitate to hurt her.

He pointed down the dark alley. "This way."

"Where are we going?"

"This way!"

He grabbed her arm and shoved her forward.

She staggered along beside him. When they reached a building halfway down the alley, he pushed open a small wooden door. The loud creak of rusty hinges echoed like a scream, and she shuddered. Solid darkness greeted her beyond the doorframe.

"Inside," he ordered.

Absolutely not! Fear swept over her like a burning fire, and she dug her heels into the hard-packed dirt and refused to budge. "I'm supposed to deliver these papers in exchange for my brother." She pulled them from her sleeve and held them up. "So tell the man who wants them that I'm here and to come out to receive them. And to bring my brother with him." She held the pages back to keep them away from his grasp and lifted her chin in challenge. "No Henry, no pages."

The boy glared at her. "He's waiting inside for you." He jerked a thumb toward the door. "Go on."

"No." She took another glance into the darkness, and another shiver raced along her spine. "Send him outside to me."

"Inside," he repeated in a snarling growl.

"Then I'm leaving." With her heart hammering against her ribs, she turned around. Dear Lord, this wasn't at all the plan that Alec and Captain Reed wanted to carry out! But even though she hadn't drawn out Scepter's man, they were watching from the shadows and would know which door the lad had brought her to, which door they could charge through and—

The young man grabbed her arm and yanked her backward. He pulled her inside the dark building and slammed the door shut after them.

Before she could scream, he shoved her in the back and propelled her forward. "Go on, bitch!"

She stumbled. Her heel snagged her hem, forced her off-balance, and plunged her forward. She sprawled onto the dirty floor on her hands and knees, yet she still gripped the plans in her fist.

A flash of light lit the room. She blinked rapidly to adjust her eyes as a lantern blazed to life.

She lay less than six inches from a pair of highly polished boots.

"Ah, Miss Everett," a man's refined voice called down to her. "How very glad I am to see you again."

She flinched, fearing a kick in the face, and steeled herself for the blow. Instead, a hand appeared in front of her.

She glanced up the extended arm, to see the face beyond—"You?" she whispered, stunned.

Sir George Pittens smiled icily. "Who else were you expecting?"

"My brother." She sat back and glanced frantically into

the room's shadowed corners where the lantern light didn't reach, but she couldn't find Henry anywhere. "Where is he?"

"How the devil should I know?" he answered with a frowning scowl. "You're my only problem to deal with tonight."

Deal with… A chill tickled down her spine.

"I don't understand," she said calmly and forced her breath to remain steady despite the rising urge to scream. "I was told to deliver the calculations to save my brother. I've brought them." Growing anger offset her fear. "So where is he?"

"I don't know anything about your brother or what you were told." He reached beneath his jacket and withdrew a long dagger. "My instructions are to silence you."

He grabbed for her.

A scream tore from her throat. She smacked his hand away and scrambled backward across the floor until her back hit the legs of the young man who'd pulled her into this hell. She cast a desperate glance at the door even as her hand slipped beneath her skirt for the knife sheath strapped to her calf. *Alec, where are you?*

The lad grinned toothlessly, grabbed her arm, and yanked her to her feet.

As she rose, she propelled herself toward him. She raised the knife to her waist and let her weight carry the blade forward, just as Alec had taught her in the alley. It sliced into the lad's hip with a sickening resistance as the sharp blade pierced his trousers and the flesh beneath.

He howled in pain and threw her aside. Blood blossomed

bright red at his thigh, and he stared down at himself as if he couldn't fathom what had happened.

Olivia ran for the door.

A hand closed around her neck and shoved her forward against the wall. She slammed so hard into the bricks that the air exploded from her lungs, and black spots flashed before her eyes.

Sir George pressed up against her from behind. She struggled as he tried to hold her still, and with every breath, she thanked God that he wasn't good enough with a blade to strike at a writhing target as she kicked at him and threw hard elbows into his paunchy gut.

She screamed again, a bloodcurdling sound that tore free from deep inside her. If he was going to kill her, she'd fight until her last breath—

With a shatter of wood and glass, the door broke open as Alec hurled himself into the room. Captain Reed followed a second later, ripping open the shutter and smashing through the window.

Alec grabbed Sir George and flung him away from her, then leapt onto the man and tackled him to the floor. His fists landed with dull thuds against Pittens's jaw. The dagger's blade flashed as it arched toward Alec's shoulder. But he rolled away, and the blade missed its mark, striking against the stone floor with a spark. Alec kicked the knife out of Sir George's hand, and it tumbled across the floor and out of reach.

Alec pounced, every inch the deadly panther Olivia had always seen in him. His left arm pinned Sir George's above his head. Then he struck his fist into the man's face over and over until Sir George crumpled into a helpless heap.

Alec climbed to his feet and stood over the beaten man with clenched fists, his head bowed and his chest heaving hard from exertion. Sir George wisely remained on the floor. If he moved, Olivia feared Alec would kill him.

"Alec!" She ran forward and threw herself into his arms, to save his soul as much as Sir George's life.

He embraced her and buried his face in her hair.

Sobbing openly with relief, she swayed as the fear of the last few moments finally overcame her, and her knees buckled beneath her. Alec caught her as she slid toward the floor, scooped her into his arms, and gently lowered her to the ground. His strong arms never loosened their hold around her.

The young man hobbled from the room, dripping a trail of blood across the floor.

Reed started after him. Alec stopped him with a raised hand.

"Let him go," Alec ordered quietly in response to the questioning glance Reed threw at him. "Scepter hired him for brute muscle. He won't know anything about their plans." His eyes narrowed furiously on Sir George as he writhed in pain on the floor. "We've got the man behind the bombing."

"No, you don't," Sir George protested even as Reed pulled his arms behind his back to pin him to the floor. "I don't know anything about that."

Olivia's heart tore. If Sir George wasn't part of the assassination attempt, then he didn't have access to Henry. *Dear God*…where on earth was her brother?

Reed pressed his knee into Sir George's spine, digging it hard into the man's back. Then he ordered in such a calm, even tone that Olivia shuddered, "Explain."

"Go to hell!"

Reed glanced at Alec. "He's not willing to talk. That's a shame." His face was stoic. "Guess we'll have to hurt him, then."

Alec shrugged impassively. "I don't mind. Do you?"

"Not at all. May I go first?"

"Be my guest."

Sir George's eyes widened at the strange exchange between the two half brothers, who possessed the same low timbre of voice and deadly expressions.

Olivia grabbed for Alec's waistcoat to keep him close. They were threatening to torture Sir George if he didn't cooperate. She knew they would never stoop so low, that it was all an act.

But Sir George didn't, and he shook with fear.

Reed pulled a knife from his sleeve. The blade flashed in the lamplight as he brought it toward Sir George's face—

"Don't hurt me!" he begged quickly. "I'll tell you everything I know!"

The knife stilled at the man's cheek as Reed ordered, "Go on."

"I was blackmailed," Sir George choked out. "A street urchin showed up at my door this morning, told me I had to kill Olivia Everett, here at midnight. If I didn't, my life would be ruined, my reputation destroyed in scandal."

"Who sent the message?"

"Who do you think?" Sir George gave a strangled laugh. "Scepter."

"Who in Scepter?"

"If I knew that, do you think I'd be here?" he snapped.

"Why does Scepter want Miss Everett dead?" Alec interrupted calmly, still holding Olivia in his arms. But beneath her hands, she felt his muscles tighten with anger.

"Don't know, don't care." Spittle and blood trickled from the corner of Sir George's mouth. "It was her life or mine. I chose mine."

Olivia buried her face in Alec's shoulder and shuddered at how close she'd come to dying tonight.

Reed pressed, "What is Scepter planning next?"

When Sir George didn't answer, Reed again threatened Sir George, this time with a hard grind of his knee into the man's back.

The movement was threatening enough to start him writhing on the floor in an attempt to cower away. "I don't know! All I could drag out of the boy was that a woman had paid him to deliver that message."

Olivia looked up in surprise just in time to see the same knowing expression darken both Alec's and Reed's faces. A woman... *Baroness Rowland*.

"The building plans," Reed demanded. "What were you told to do with them?"

"Nothing! That's all I was told—be here at midnight and kill Olivia Everett. No one mentioned any plans."

Fresh fear seized Olivia. If they didn't want the plans, then why did they ask for them? And where on earth was Henry?

"What did they use to blackmail you?" Reed asked.

"I took money from the War Department," Sir George confessed. "Moved it through various accounts so no one could trace where it went or that it ended up in my own bank." He breathed more easily as Reed's knee moved away from his lower back in small reprieve for that bit of honesty. "Scepter threatened to expose me. I'd lose my seat in Parliament, my fortune, my reputation… I'd be imprisoned or transported." His eyes darted to Olivia, and she felt hatred in that glance. "If I didn't kill her, my own life would be ruined."

"It *is* ruined," Reed commented dryly and tied Sir George's hands behind his back. He yanked harder than necessary to cinch the short length of rope. "You'll rot in Newgate for this."

"No, I won't." Sir George laughed bitterly with a sputter of blood spraying from his split lip. A ghastly, mad smile stretched across his face. "I'll never go to Newgate. Not now."

Alec rose to his feet and lifted Olivia to hers. "Take him to Clayton," he ordered Reed. "His men will get the truth from him." When he looked down into Olivia's face, his affection and concern took her breath away. "We're leaving."

He took her elbow to steady her and led her out of the building, leaving Sir George in Captain Reed's capable hands.

As soon as they'd stepped into the cold darkness of the London night, he placed his hand to the small of her back and leaned over to speak into her ear.

"I'm escorting you home, safe and sound." He brushed his lips across her temple. "And then I'm tucking you into bed myself."

Despite how wonderful that sounded, sadness over-shadowed her heart. He would only be hers for tonight, and only for a short while until Reed handed Sir George over to Major Elliott. Then Alec would have to leave her to track down Henry. After all, Sir George must have known *some-thing* about her brother that could lead them forward in their mission, someone who possessed the power to—

Shock flashed through her as a terrible idea struck her. She whispered as she turned toward him, "Alec, the plans…"

He absently searched the shadows around them, not yet trusting that they were safely free of Scepter's trap. "What about them?"

"Sir George didn't want them. He didn't care that I'd worked the calculations and brought them with me."

"Because he only wanted to kill you," he reminded her grimly.

"Then why wouldn't they have tried to do that at the school? Why force me out into the City like this?" The truth slithered icily down her spine. "Unless they wanted me away from the school. Unless…unless they didn't find everything they wanted last night when they took Henry and needed to sneak back inside to get it."

"What's there that they would want? You said that the charred paper was the only copy of the Admiralty Club's plans. There was nothing left at the school they would need to destroy to cover their tracks."

Including Henry. She fought down her grief and tried to think, but her whirling mind couldn't seize on anything.

She gave a groan of frustration. "I don't know. I can't think of any—" The realization pierced her. "Waterloo!"

His brows knitted together. "Pardon?"

"The work Henry was doing for the Royal Society, his article on architectural tensions and compressions—I told you about it, the first night when you came to my room as the masked man, remember?"

"I remember. And?"

"When I was checking his equations, I came across a page of new calculations." She drew a deep breath to settle her roiling stomach, but it did little to soothe the dread that gnawed at her. "It was little more than data sets for a series of parabolas. But there was a word written across the bottom— *Waterloo*. At the time, I thought he'd taken notes for a second article on gun targeting and had gotten them mixed up with his other papers, that he was working out calculations for making artillery more precise, but…but he wasn't. He wasn't working parabolas. He was working *arches*." Her fingers twisted in his lapels so tightly that their tips turned white. "Oh God, Alec—Waterloo Bridge!"

He immediately took her shoulders. "Tell me."

"I think Henry was calculating weaknesses in the new bridge." Her heart pounded, and the rush of blood in her ears was deafening. "With those calculations, a minimal amount of explosives could bring down an entire span." Horror at the idea clenched her chest so hard that she could barely breathe. "The prince regent is scheduled to be at the opening ceremony tomorrow, along with half of Parliament and all the city officials. They've already moved the royal barge to the dock at Westminster to take him downriver." She dragged in a jerking breath. "Scepter wants to assassinate the prince regent."

Alec shook his head. "Guards will search the bridge before he arrives. If Scepter has planted explosives, they'll be found. Scepter knows that. They'd never attempt a plan that could be stopped so easily."

"Unless Scepter really has infiltrated all levels of the government and the military, as you claimed," she whispered in a hoarse rasp. "Unless the men who are supposed to be searching for explosives are the same ones setting them."

"Christ," he muttered, stunned.

"They knew Henry felt guilty about the Admiralty Club bombing and would never hand over his calculations for the bridge. They wanted me away from the school so they could return tonight when I wasn't there, so they could force Henry to hand over his calculations, and then—" She choked. When they didn't need him anymore... "They'll kill him." And along with her brother— "Oh, God, Alec, *the girls!*"

He grabbed her hand and ran, pulling her along behind him. They raced down the alley to the waiting hackney.

"Westminster," he shouted up to the driver as they hurried into the compartment. "Now!"

Twenty-Four

THE HIRED CARRIAGE STOPPED IN FRONT OF THE school, and Olivia dashed to the ground. She stopped on the footpath and stared up at the building. It was just as quiet and dark as when she'd left, all the shutters closed and the doors locked up tight against the night. Nothing moved, and nothing broke the stillness except for the horses behind her shaking their harness and Alec following her out of the carriage.

Was she wrong? Had she let fear and paranoia guide her to—

A blast tore through the building's basement.

Olivia screamed as the cellar windows shattered, throwing glass and wooden shutters high into the air. Alec grabbed her and pulled her to the ground to protect her with his body. The explosion shook the earth, and the horses bolted, the jarvey unable to control them as they scrambled down the street in terror. Flames leapt from the basement and licked up the sides of the building as if they were stretching up from the fires of hell.

"The girls!" Olivia pushed herself out of Alec's arms and climbed to her feet. She raced up the front steps and into the burning building.

Immediately, darkness engulfed her. Black clouds of

smoke billowed up from the basement so thickly that she couldn't see through them, and skin-prickling heat followed after the smoke. But Olivia didn't turn back. She made her way through the building, blinded by the thickening smoke and feeling her way along foot by foot. Above the noise of the growing flames around her, she could hear the girls screaming for help from their dormitories.

She found the stairs and started up.

Another explosion blasted from below. The force of it threw Olivia against the wall, and she cried out as she grabbed for the banister to keep from falling. The black smoke filled her lungs, each breath a choking and burning gasp. She coughed painfully and covered her mouth with her arm, but she didn't stop. Around her, the building grew ominously lighter as flames began to eat their way through the lower floors. With panic swelling inside her, she staggered up the stairs.

She reached the dormitories at the top of the town house and heard the girls screaming inside.

Olivia coughed violently as she shoved open the door. Then she sank to her knees and into the small layer of good air still lingering right above the floor.

Inside, the terrified girls huddled together in the corner. Justine Smith and Mrs. Adams were with them, doing their best to calm them and keep them together. They both urged everyone toward the door, but the girls refused to move. They were too frightened to flee.

"Go!" Olivia yelled in a raspy shout. Her voice was already hoarse from the coughing and smoke, her hands and dress blackened from the thick smoke and soot filling the school as the fire spread and consumed it. Flames roared around them, and the heat burned her skin. "*Get out*—now!"

Justine Smith grabbed the first girl by the hand and pulled her toward the door. More terrified by Olivia's shouts than of the fire, the girls joined hands and ran from the room. Their screams only grew louder as they moved toward the stairs. Mrs. Adams came last. Her face was completely white even in the dark smoke.

Olivia counted them as they fled, then did the same with the girls in the room across the hall as Mrs. Adams followed her lead and opened the door to order them to safety.

One short. *Oh, God*, one child was missing!

Her heart knew—

"Cora!" Olivia frantically dropped to her knees to search under all the beds even as the dormitory filled with smoke and the room grew unbearably hot. "Cora, where are you?"

"Olivia!" Alec hurried into the room in his search for her. He coughed into his jacket sleeve as he visibly struggled for breath. "We have to leave, right now."

"Cora's missing!" Olivia shook her head as she ran past him and across the hall to search the other dormitory room. Around them, the house creaked and groaned as the flames devoured it. "I can't leave her!"

He grabbed her arm. "Get yourself out. I'll find her."

Overhead, the roof caved in with a sickening bang and destroyed the bedrooms on the floor above.

"Olivia, go now!" he shouted and led her toward the stairs. "I'll find her. I promise."

Nodding and coughing uncontrollably, she stumbled down into the darkness of the smoke and ash billowing up as if it were coming from the mouth of hell. She groped her way by feel, her eyes stinging and blinded from the smoke.

She froze and jerked up her head when she heard... *crying.*

The sound came so softly that it was nearly lost beneath the growls and snarls of the fire. Then it came again, louder this time, and Olivia followed it down the first-floor hall. She opened each classroom door and called out desperately between coughs. Unable to breathe, she fell to her knees and gasped at the last remaining good air just above the floor. The crying grew louder. She reached the last room and flung open the door.

Her brother sat tied to a chair in the middle of the classroom.

"Henry!" She ran to him and tore off the gag that silenced him. "What did they do to—"

"Get out of here!" he yelled at her, angry and fearful as the ceiling above them now began to crack and creak. The fire had eaten into the supporting joists, and the integrity of the building was failing around them. They only had a few minutes before the entire building collapsed.

"Not without you and Cora." She knelt at his feet and tore loose the ropes with her fingernails, then clawed at the ties binding his wrists. In the deepening darkness, she noticed the bruises on his face and drops of blood staining his torn shirt. He'd been beaten. Badly.

"Dear God...who did this to you?"

"I don't know." He coughed hard. "Men I'd never seen before."

When the last rope gave way, he climbed stiffly to his feet, only to collapse to the floor, overcome by smoke and his wounds. She grabbed him into her arms, and he shuddered against her as he gasped deeply for air.

Her chest screamed in pain, both from the smoke and for her brother, and she knew the awful answer even before she asked, "Did you give them the calculations for Waterloo Bridge?"

"I had no choice." Guilt radiated from him. "They said they would kill you if I didn't."

Her shoulders sagged. They'd both been played for fools.

"Go, Olivia," he ordered between coughs. "Get out of the school. I'll make my way down after you."

She refused to leave him behind. "Where's Cora?" She pulled him to his feet and staggered with him toward the wall. "We have to find her."

A soft cry came from the hall.

"Go!" Henry ordered and slumped against the wall, ordering her on. "Save her!"

Olivia crawled into the hall, following the sound. It came from behind the old rear door where a rickety set of wooden steps led down into the basement. They'd once been the servants' stairs before the old house was converted into the school. But they were far too narrow, dark, and dangerous to use and had been closed off for years. Yet if Cora had felt trapped, with no other way to escape—

She threw open the door. "Cora!"

Olivia saw the little figure half a flight down from her, huddled against the wall.

"Miss!" The girl sobbed in shuddering pain and pointed toward her leg. "It hurts…"

Through the darkness, Olivia could just see her right leg. It lay twisted beneath her at an unnatural angle. *Broken.*

"I fell," Cora forced out in gasping, pain-filled breaths. "I tried to go down. I tripped…"

Now she was trapped. On her broken leg, she couldn't crawl up or down.

"I'm coming!" Olivia moved gingerly down the old stairs. Each board creaked angrily beneath her, and she held her breath at the possibility that the old structure might give way at any second. "Just stay there. Don't try to move."

Olivia reached the girl, grabbed her into her arms, and pressed her tightly against her, careful not to hurt her leg any more than she had to. Cora's slender arms wrapped around Olivia's neck. Slowly, she rose to her feet to carry the girl with her. She glanced down the stairwell. A bright light grew from below as the flames at the bottom of the stairwell licked their way upward. There was no going down.

She turned to climb back up the stairs when a great groan rose up from the house. With a terrifying shudder, the structure shifted around them. The entire set of stairs shook and cried out like a dying animal, the wooden anchor in the basement devoured by the flames that now leapt higher up the narrow stairwell toward them. Without warning, the stairs broke loose from their supports. They dropped with a hard thud and smacked against the wall, coming to rest at a dangerous, leaning angle.

Olivia screamed as she held frantically with one hand to the banister to keep from plunging into the flames below. Her other arm wrapped like a steel band around Cora.

"Olivia!" Henry leaned into the stairwell on his stomach and reached down for her. "Put Cora down and take my hand."

"No! I won't leave her—"

"The stairs won't support both of you. Give me your hand! I'll rescue you first, then save her."

Knowing she had no choice, Olivia set the wailing child down onto the precariously leaning stairs and reached up to take her brother's hand. With a groan of exertion, he pulled her up the steep incline and into the hall. She sprawled across the soot-blackened floor.

"Stay here," he ordered. Then he slipped down into the disintegrating stairwell.

"Henry!" Olivia screamed and grabbed for him, but he had disappeared into the darkness.

Seconds later, he thrust the small girl up toward her. "Take her!"

The steps groaned and creaked angrily, threatening at any moment to give way completely and tumble him down into the flames.

Olivia reached for Cora—

"I've got her!" Large male hands reached past Olivia as Clayton Elliott scooped the frightened girl into his arms.

"Take her out of here, please!" Olivia choked out.

He nodded, and Cora wrapped her arms around his neck. He ran with the little girl down the hallway as fast he could in the suffocating smoke, toward the main stairs and the only way of escape.

As Henry tried to lift himself out of the stairwell and back into the hallway, the stairs groaned and shifted beneath him. They crumbled away into the flames below, bringing the doorway down with them. It collapsed, and the fallen timbers pinned him across his legs. He was trapped.

"Go!" he yelled at her between gasps of pain. "Leave!"

"I am not leaving you." She dropped to the floor at his side and pushed frantically at the beams, but they were too heavy to lift. She couldn't free him, while around them, the fires grew closer and the smoke thicker.

"Olivia, I'm so sorry for what I did," he told her through a coughing fit as the smoke pressed in upon them. "Please forgive me before I die."

"Stop talking like that! You are *not* dying. I'm not leaving you here." She pulled in futile frustration at his legs but couldn't move him. Not an inch. "I will get you out. I *will*—"

"It happened without me realizing, and once I was swept up into it—" He broke off as the building shifted around them again and prepared to collapse in upon itself at any moment. Then he rushed out the confession. "It wasn't the school. It was me—I was gambling, running up debts and bills… I couldn't pay them. Lady Rowland bought them and demanded repayment. She threatened to have me placed into debtors' prison!"

"I know." Despite her stinging tears and growing terror, she soothed him. "It doesn't matt—"

"When I was approached to do the calculations for the

Admiralty Club, I couldn't pass up the money. But I had no idea what those plans would be used for. When I found out—that's why I disappeared for those two days. I was hiding, afraid I'd be arrested. Then they wanted the plans for Waterloo Bridge, and I couldn't refuse or—" Guilt filled his voice. "Now you know the truth. Forgive me."

Stunned, Olivia stared at him, unable to fathom all that he was telling her. Yet compassion rose inside her, and she whispered, "I forgive you."

"Olivia!" Alec emerged from the black smoke.

She turned toward his approaching figure in the darkness and grabbed at her brother's shoulders, refusing to let go of him. "Help him! Please—don't let him die!"

Alec bent down to lift the heavy beam from Henry's legs. With Olivia pulling at his arms, Henry scrambled forward until he was free, then collapsed onto the floor. He panted hard to breathe in the smoke-filled air, only to collapse in fierce coughs.

"Can you walk?" Alec demanded.

Henry shook his head.

Alec yanked him to his feet and tossed him over his shoulder like a sack to carry him to safety.

"Come on!" Alec's free hand grabbed hold around her wrist and pulled her with him down the hall toward the front stairs.

Her legs stumbled to keep up with his long strides as they hurried through the blinding smoke and heat.

Clayton Elliott waited for them at the bottom of the stairs, risking his own life for a return trip into the burning building to help them. He took Henry from Alec and carried him outside.

Around them, the building groaned and growled as the fire devoured it. The ceiling above them gave way, and it fell in a shower of sparks and cinders. One of the beams broke free from the floor above and dropped toward them.

"Look out!" Alec shoved her away.

But he wasn't fast enough himself. The end of the board caught him across the shoulder and sliced down his arm with a sickening rip of clothes and skin.

"Alec!" she screamed.

He fell to his knees beneath the force of the blow. Olivia rushed to his side, to slip her arm under his shoulder and lever him to his feet. With a painful curse, he gritted his teeth as he leaned against her and staggered through the door and into the cool night air.

As her feet touched the footpath, Olivia released Alec and collapsed to her knees. She gulped in great mouthfuls of air between fierce coughs to clear the suffocating smoke from her lungs. Through stinging, blurry eyes, she saw a crowd in the street and a few men attempting to start a bucket brigade, not to save the school but to keep the fire from spreading to the other houses. Shouts and alarm bells rang through the night, bringing even more people into the growing confusion.

But she also saw Henry being whisked away through the crowd by Clayton Elliott, Mrs. Adams clutching Cora in her arms, Justine Smith huddling all the girls together on the other side of the street…and Alec, who dropped to the ground beside her to gather her into his arms.

She stared over his shoulder at the building that had been her home and her life, that had been her only future. With a great groan, the walls and floors collapsed in upon themselves in a giant inferno of flames and sparks that shot up into the night sky like uncontrolled fireworks.

Her arms tightened around his neck, and she buried her face in his shoulder, no longer able to keep back the flood of tears as a desolate cry of anguish and loss tore from her. *Gone…all gone…*

Twenty-Five

ALEC HANDED NATE REED A GLASS OF COGNAC AND leaned back casually against the large reading table in the library at Harlow House. He'd rather have had this meeting with his half brother back in his own study at St James House, but considering that the Everett School girls were temporarily encamped there, he much preferred to be here in the relative calm of the dower house.

It was a little too early in the afternoon to be drinking, but given all they'd been through in the past few days, a stiff drink seemed appropriate. It was also a first step in the reconciliation he hoped for with his brother. The two of them might never be friends, but Alec now knew he could trust Reed with his life.

Outside, cold rain beaded down the windows in thick rivulets. Last night's drizzle had turned into a near downpour, and the rain would extinguish whatever embers still glowed at the school. When the weather broke, Alec planned to ride to the site and search through the debris. He hoped against hope to find any evidence to link the destruction to Scepter, but in his heart, he expected to find nothing.

After all, Clayton Elliott had already been to the school before dawn. He'd had work to do. Not only had he combed through the site as best he could given the still glowing embers, but he'd placed a dead body among the debris—a man who'd died in another fire the day before, his corpse so burned as to be unrecognizable. A man the same size as Henry Everett.

When the body was found at dawn, everyone thought it was Everett, even though the man himself was halfway to the Continent by then. He'd been exiled, given a new identity, and told he could never return to England. Nor would he want to, given that Scepter would kill him the moment they discovered he'd survived.

Olivia would never see him again, but at least her brother would be alive.

Reed took a healthy swallow of the brandy, then glanced around the library without comment despite a disdainful look for all the obvious benefits of rank and wealth on display. As a bastard son, Reed had been cheated out of those benefits, the same ones the Sinclairs had always taken for granted.

Guilt gnawed at Alec's gut. The feeling had only grown over the past few weeks that they'd been working together. Before, Alec had been happy to live his life ignoring Reed, whom he'd seen as only another reminder of their father's secret life. That was no longer an option.

Now that Reed was in their lives, the Sinclairs would have to find a way to make amends. Somehow.

"How is Miss Everett faring?" Reed waved away Alec's invitation to sit in the leather chair before the fire.

"As well as can be expected."

Olivia was upstairs in one of the guestrooms, still sleeping off her fatigue of the last two nights. He'd brought her to Harlow House immediately after the fire, ordered a hot bath for her, and managed to avoid most of the Sinclair ladies' questions. Then he'd tucked her into bed himself so she could rest, recover from the night's ordeal, and grieve for both the loss of the school and for her brother's exile.

"Does she know yet about her brother?" Reed asked quietly.

Alec rubbed at his bandaged arm as it rested in its sling. "I told her last night."

With a slow nod of understanding, Reed swirled the liquor in his glass. "Clayton will make certain he's hidden away where no one can find him."

"He'll also make certain Sir George swings."

"No," Reed corrected somberly. "The man was right last night when he said he wouldn't go to Newgate." He looked up from the cognac. "He's dead."

Alec's heart skipped. "When?"

"Dawn. He grabbed a knife from a guard and killed himself rather than face scandal. Or Scepter."

Alec took a healthy swallow of cognac and let the liquid burn down his throat. *Christ.*

"So the next question," Reed said quietly, "is where does that leave our mission?"

Our mission. For the first time, Alec's chest warmed at the idea of the two of them working together. "With the assassination plot against the prime minister solved and the attack on Waterloo Bridge thwarted." He tapped his finger against the crystal tumbler in emphasis. "We're only one or two people away now from finding Scepter's leaders."

"And Lady Rowland to guide us to them."

Alec carefully kept his face inscrutable. Sydney Rowland involved with traitors… He still couldn't believe it.

"Clayton confirmed what Everett confessed last night to his sister," Reed informed him. "He'd built up huge debts attempting to ingratiate himself with the Royal Society. Last month, Lady Rowland quietly bought up those debts, then demanded immediate repayment. She threatened to send him to debtors' prison if he defaulted."

That was also very much unlike the baroness. But then, Alec thought he knew Sir George Pittens, too. Apparently, Scepter was turning all kinds of people into murderers and traitors.

"When Everett was presented with an opportunity to make money by working on the plans for the club, he jumped at the chance as his only way to stay out of gaol. But in the end, Scepter's payment wasn't quite enough to bring him out of debt. Conveniently, they offered more money for another set of calculations. This time for Waterloo Bridge. And this time, they threatened to kill both him and his sister if he refused."

Alec shook his head and voiced his doubts. "I've known the baroness for years. She's not the sort of woman to be involved with revolutionaries."

"Yet she is." Reed swallowed the last of his drink. "She put those girls in danger last night and nearly killed the little one." He stared into his glass. "With that broken leg, she'll be lucky if she's not in pain for the rest of her life. I won't let Lady Rowland get away with that."

The anger that edged his half brother's voice over little Cora didn't surprise Alec. But the fact that the two of them were finding more and more in common certainly did. Oh, they would never be as close as true brothers, would never spend holidays together or visit each other's homes for social calls.

Yet for the first time, Alec considered the possibility that they might somehow be able to come to terms with their father's ghost.

Reed set his empty glass down with a small thud of determination. "I'm going after the baroness. She's my part of the mission now."

Alec gestured toward his bandaged arm. "I won't be of much help."

"I've got Clayton to call on if I need him." Reed grinned at him. "Besides, you've got Miss Everett to look after."

Alec tossed back the last of his cognac. He wasn't nearly so certain of that himself.

"Alexander, are you able to—" Isabel Sinclair choked off in midsentence as she strode into the library and found the two men together.

Her startled eyes landed on Reed, and her face paled as if she were seeing a ghost. Exactly that, Alec supposed. She was seeing Rupert Sinclair in Reed's hazel eyes and curly chestnut hair, the sharp cut of his jaw, and the muscular breadth of his shoulders.

"My apologies for interrupting," she forced out in breathless surprise. "I didn't realize we had company."

"Mother." Alec quickly shoved himself away from the reading table and took her arm to lead her forward.

Reed and his mother had never met, so introductions were in order, yet both of them certainly knew of the other. Thick tension instantly swirled around them and added a solemn apprehension to the moment.

"May I introduce Captain Reed of His Majesty's Horse Guards?" Alec reassuringly squeezed her elbow. "Captain Reed, my mother, Isabel Sinclair, Countess of St James."

Reed politely bowed with the finely honed honor and decorum of an officer. "A pleasure, my lady." Although from the icy tone of his voice and the stiff bend of his body, the meeting was anything but pleasurable.

"For me as well, Captain," she said softly, but Alec heard a hint of earnestness that surprised him. He would have thought the last person she'd ever want to meet was the walking, talking embodiment of her husband's debauchery.

Awkward silence stretched between them, with the countess not knowing what else to say and Reed refusing to say anything, yet neither of them had stormed out of the room. Alec took hope in that. Perhaps the two parts of Rupert Sinclair's life might come to acceptable terms of peace after all.

Then his mother pulled back her shoulders, lifted her chin, and admitted what they were all thinking. "I suppose there's no point in pretending we don't know the truth about each other, is there?"

Reed's mouth pulled down. "No, ma'am. There's not."

She nodded slowly, accepting that at least they were all

standing on common ground now. "I've always wondered… how long have you known about us?"

"Since I was fifteen, ma'am."

She caught her breath. "So young…" Her slender shoulders drooped beneath the weight of the past that pressed down upon all of them. "So much longer than I supposed."

Reed said nothing but tightened his jaw, which unwittingly made him resemble their father even more. What Alec didn't know was whether the man was resisting the urge to ask how long the Sinclairs had known about him or if he was biting down the temptation to tell the lot of them to go to hell. He certainly had every right.

Wringing her hands, Isabel took a hesitant step toward Reed. Alec let her go, watching her curiously. His mother was never awkward or uncertain. Always she was confident, like a force of nature. But this meeting with Reed had visibly shaken her to her core. "Your mother…is she well?"

Reed's eyes narrowed as they studied her, and he asked quietly, yet not at all rudely, "Do you really care?"

She gave a jerking nod as if to convince herself as much as him. "I do."

Reed considered her for a moment, then relaxed his spine just a fraction and answered carefully, "My mother is well, your ladyship."

The iciness of his overly formal answer forced a self-conscious smile from Isabel and an attempt to dissolve the growing tension between them. "A mother always worries about another mother's—"

"She is well," Reed repeated, the finality in his voice

boldly stating that he no longer wished to discuss his mother. "Thank you for asking."

And please do not mention her again. The words lingered between them as clearly as if he'd actually spoken them.

Alec cleared his throat. "Mother, perhaps we should let the captain—"

She ignored him and persisted, "I'm certain she's very proud of you. During the wars, the *Times* was filled with stories of your bravery, especially at Toulouse. I know that Lady Agnes took a special interest in following all your deeds."

Reed stiffened. His eyes darted over the countess's head to Alec, not in an appeal for help, Alec understood, but in warning. Isabel Sinclair was treading where she didn't belong.

"Mother," Alec said, more firmly this time. She wanted to establish peace between Reed and the Sinclairs, but pushing forward like this would only anger the man and most likely cause him to turn his back on all of them. "Captain Reed is needed at the Horse Guards."

"Of course. My apologies for keeping you." Yet she gave him a pleading look for understanding. "There have been so many wrongs committed over the years, so many reasons not to trust or forgive...but I hope the future might be different."

Reed's mouth tightened. Clearly, his patience with this impromptu family gathering had reached its limit. "Thank you, my lady." But his voice held no hint of gratitude. "I'll see myself out."

Reed nodded to Alec, then bowed again to Isabel as he excused himself to leave. As he stepped past her toward the door, she impetuously reached for his arm and stopped him.

He stared coldly down at her hand, as if considering whether to shove it away.

"If you or your mother ever need anything," she assured him, "you can come to us for help. Please know that. Despite everything, you have friends in the Sinclair family."

Reed stiffened, and Alec knew that his brother was fighting to control his anger and nearly fifteen years of hatred. Alec knew exactly how he felt, because he'd experienced the exact same emotions himself when he'd learned about his father's secret life—fury, betrayal…most of all frustration at not being able to change the past.

With hard-won control, Reed slowly shifted his arm away from her. "Thank you for the offer, ma'am." His voice was cold and distant but painfully polite. "I don't believe that will be necessary."

He walked from the room without looking back.

When he'd vanished into the hall, Isabel sank slowly into a nearby chair.

"Are you all right, Mother?" Alec leaned against the reading table to give her space, but his chest squeezed brutally with concern as he fought back the urge to go to her side. She'd paled to a ghostly hue, and her hands clenched the chair arms so tightly that her fingertips had turned white.

She nodded jerkily, her eyes fixed on the door as if she expected Reed to return.

Alec could assure her that wasn't going to happen. Ever. "Perhaps I should call for Aunt Agnes to—"

"No." She pressed her hand against her chest, not yet lifting her eyes to look at him, as if afraid of the anger and accusation she would see in him. "Captain Reed's mother was a maid at Pelham Park. She was young and beautiful, and your father was...drawn to her."

Alec stiffened. What a polite way to say that his father had raped the woman. Even now, his mother did her best to protect her family from the evils the old earl had committed. "I know."

"Not everything." Her voice choked as she continued, "She left in the middle of the night without notice. Even then, I assumed... But at the time, I had no way of finding her and making whatever amends I could, as if anything could ever have made up for what St James had done to her."

He said nothing. He'd already suspected all this.

"When your father died, I was finally able to hire investigators to find her. They told me she'd left Pelham to elope with a groom from the neighboring estate, been widowed, and then gotten employment with the Earl of Buckley after her husband's death. So I went to visit her. The moment I met her, I knew that story was a lie."

She raised her tear-glistened eyes to meet his.

"She'd fled Pelham after he'd attacked her, only to learn that she was with child. So she created the story of an elopement and dead husband, then changed her name to appeal upon the kindness of family. They took her in until her baby was born and she could secure a position. She raised him on her own. She never gave him up to the foundling hospital." Her voice dropped to a hoarse, pain-filled whisper. "I knew there was nothing I could do to give back to her all that had been stolen, but I could help her son. I could give *him* a better life."

Alec's heart slammed against his breastbone so hard that the thud jarred through him. He *knew*... "The money you withdrew from the accounts after Father died," he rasped out. "That's what you mean."

She nodded and whispered, so softly he could barely hear her, "His mother used it to buy an officer's commission for him in the dragoons."

He stared at his mother as a wave of remorse consumed him. He'd blamed her for squandering those funds on gowns and frivolous purchases made in a rush of newfound freedom after his father's death, in a wave of grief—or relief that the old bastard could never hurt them again. For months, Alec had barely spoken to her because of it, and all the while, she'd been doing everything she could to save those lives his father had destroyed.

"You never told me," he mumbled.

"Because I didn't want you to know." Shame filled her voice. "It was enough that you were already dealing with the knowledge of what your father had done. You didn't deserve to also have to come to terms with his illegitimate son, not then."

He glanced down at his empty glass. Sweet Lucifer, he needed another drink. He pushed himself away from the table to refill his glass.

"But it's time now," she countered with resolve. "It's time for all of us to come to terms with the past." She paused and pulled in a deep, trembling breath. "And we will recognize the captain."

He stopped, surprised. "Are you certain you want to do that?"

To recognize Nate Reed as a son of St James… The repercussions would be immense for the entire family.

It was one thing to have an illegitimate half brother, yet something completely different for that brother to be recognized. Alec would become an even greater object of gossip, potentially lose power in Parliament and Whitehall. Beth's standing among the unmarried ladies of the *ton* would be threatened, along with Aunt Agnes's already fragile hold on respectability. The consequences could be even worse for his mother; no matter that half the men in the *ton* had fathered bastards, Isabel Sinclair could very well become a social pariah if society blamed her for her husband's infidelity.

She knew that, too, yet she nodded resolutely. "We owe it to Captain Reed and to his mother."

Alec exhaled a rough breath. Reparations for his father's evils would be made. Even from the grave, Rupert Sinclair was still hurting people, still finding a way to destroy lives. And his family was still forced to suffer the repercussions.

Although now, this step toward absolution came as a welcomed relief.

"Why did you keep this secret for so long?" he pressed gently. "Why didn't you tell me when he first arrived in London?"

"So many years had passed by then. What good could have come from revealing it?" Her voice grew softer. "No one else deserved to be hurt because of the past."

He murmured, half to himself, "Olivia said almost the exact same thing."

A faint smile teased at his mother's lips. "She's a smart girl."

"Downright brilliant." Especially about what mattered most. What mattered was love and trust, forgiveness and charity, and nothing was as simple as it appeared on the surface. Illusion, all of it. What was important was the heart beneath. Olivia had taught him that.

"I don't believe I've ever seen you like this over a woman, Alexander." She tilted her head to study him. "I'd wager you were in love."

He paused with a denial poised on his tongue from rakish habit. Then he lowered his shoulders. "Yes." He slumped against the reading table and pressed his eyes closed. There was no point in denying the obvious. "I am."

"Well, then," she asked softly and with motherly happiness coloring her voice, "what do you plan on doing about it?"

He shook his head. What choice did he have? "Marriage is out of the question." Since he was a boy, he'd been raised to put the title and the earldom above all else, including his own happiness. Now, for the first time in his life, what he wanted as a man conflicted with what was best for the title. He wanted nothing more than to say to hell with it and choose what *he* wanted for once. Yet he was still obligated to his family, to their happiness and future, and so still obligated to the earldom. "I owe it to the title to find the daughter of a peer to—"

"You owe nothing more to this title."

His eyes flew open at her answer and at the harsh resolve with which she'd uttered it.

"Everything this family has now is because of you.

I haven't always agreed with the activities you've been involved in or the people you've spent time with—"

He rolled his eyes. Some things never changed.

"But my dear boy," she said softly, her voice trembling, "you deserve to be happy."

He shoved away from the table and began to pace. He simply couldn't remain still, not with the way the world was tilting beneath his feet and everything he thought to be true was turning upside down.

"I'm an earl, and she's a schoolmistress. We're as opposite as can be." He stopped in front of the window and watched the raindrops drizzle down the glass. Not daring to look at his mother, he quietly confessed his fear— "She might not want to marry me."

His mother rose and went to his side. Her soft hand on his shoulder brought his attention away from the rain and to her. "She loves you. I see it on her face every time she looks at you. She follows her heart, and it's led her to you." She added meaningfully, "Where is your heart leading *you*, Alexander?"

Marriage to Olivia…could he truly have that? His pulse spiked with hope at a future with the only woman who made him happy. The only woman he wanted to spend every morning and night with, every day for the rest of his life.

But reality crashed back over him. "It's not only about me. It might make life harder for you and Beth. Already she's the subject of gossip for having a bastard half brother. If her legitimate brother marries outside the *ton*, she might be cut completely, and you and Agnes right along with her."

"Do not worry about us. Elizabeth is going to marry Mr.

Mullins, so there's no need to worry that she won't find a proper husband. Agnes and her eccentricities have become endeared to society, in their own way, and the gossips won't be bothered by me, an old dowager." When he began to contradict her, she cut him off. "Besides, the lot of us could dance down Pall Mall in our unmentionables and society still wouldn't dare snub the most powerful and wealthiest earl in England or his family."

Alec wasn't convinced. He shook his head. "If we marry, there will be gossip and scandal."

His mother cupped his face in her hands just as she used to do when he was a boy. "When have you ever cared about gossip and scandal? You've always lived your life the way you wanted. This is no different."

He lifted a brow. "You hated the way I lived my life."

"Yes, I did," she admitted with a long-suffering sigh. "But I cannot find fault in the honesty of it or in relegating that old life to the past." She leveled a hard look on him. "Especially if it means you'll finally have the wife and children you should have had years ago."

Alec gave a choked laugh. Isabel Sinclair was always true to form.

"And quite frankly, being with someone like Miss Everett might just be good for you. She's not the daughter of a peer, but she'll give your marriage respectability."

His lips twitched. If she only knew the truth! The real Olivia who lurked beneath that painfully proper façade was a wild creature of her own, who possessed the daring to venture down dark alleys at night and into his arms...

But *he* knew the truth about her. That was all that mattered.

"Do I have your blessing then, Mother?"

She beamed. "Of course. And you also have this." She removed one of her rings and placed it in his palm. It was a delicate sliver of tiny pearls and aquamarines the same blue as Olivia's eyes. "This belonged to your grandmother. I think she would be thrilled to have Miss Everett wear it."

Unable to say anything past the knot clenching his throat, he closed his hand around the ring and kissed her cheek. For the first time, he allowed himself to believe that he and his family might finally find happiness.

But there was one more stretch of hellfire that had yet to be endured before they could put the past fully behind them.

"There's someone else who deserves to know the entire truth from the past," he said solemnly, gesturing for her to return to her chair. She needed to be seated for what he had to tell her.

Worry darkened her face as she sank onto the chair, but thankfully, she didn't interrupt.

"About my childhood." He knelt beside her and took her hand. "And Father."

Twenty-Six

THE ROYAL COACH WOUND ITS WAY THROUGH Westminster toward Whitehall and the Thames. Around it, all the pomp and grandeur of the monarchy was in full view. Despite the ongoing drizzle, the Horse Guards stood out boldly in their red uniforms on their black horses, gold gilded carriages followed after in the long parade, and other dignitaries walked the puddled parade route from Carlton House to the Thames, where the regent and his party would transfer to the royal barge. But the unexpected cold and damp had succeeded in keeping home most of the spectators who would normally have crowded the route to watch the royal procession roll by.

A shout went up, and a captain of the Guards galloped past the line of carriages to the front of the parade. He reined his horse to a stop with a quick word to the master of ceremonies leading the procession. Behind him, the parade slowed to a stop, as it had done several times already and would undoubtedly do several more before reaching the Thames.

The footman expectedly flung open the door of the royal coach, and the guards allowed a man to climb inside. Dressed in silks and furs as formally as the retainers around them, he removed his black velvet hat and gave a reverential nod to the surprised prince regent on the seat across from him.

"Your Royal Highness." Another nod, this time with as close to a bow as the seated confines of the carriage allowed. "My deepest apologies for the interruption."

The regent's bloated face pinched with indignation. "Who the devil—"

"Major Clayton Elliott, Home Office undersecretary and formerly of the Coldstream Guards." Then Clayton added quickly to soothe the royal temper, "Who served proudly in your honor and in defense of the Crown and England. In truth, our field marshal at Waterloo only won the battle because of our field marshal in St James's Palace."

Clayton was enough of a diplomat to manage to spew that nonsense without his true disdain showing, and the flattery helped to smooth the regent's ruffled feathers. Barely.

"What is the meaning of this?" the regent demanded. "How *dare* you interrupt—"

"Your Highness, I'm here on official Home Office business." He reached beneath his velvet robe and withdrew a sealed message. "For you, sir. From Lord Sidmouth."

The regent snatched it from his hand, broke the seal, and impatiently scanned the message. His ruddy face paled.

"Our plan is in motion." Clayton signaled through the window at Reed, who nodded and raised his hand to order the parade to move onward. "The bridge was inspected before dawn, and all explosives have been removed. But we need to delay your arrival until the men who planned to detonate them have been arrested. I'll remain here in the carriage with you as your personal bodyguard."

The regent's eyes darted between Clayton and the Home Secretary's message. Stunned, his flabby jowls flapped as his mouth worked like a fish's.

"Your carriage is going to be attacked by a mob of protestors when we reach the corner of the park. It's all a ruse, orchestrated to make the crowds think that your visit to Waterloo Bridge has been delayed due to unrest rather than any kind of problem at the bridge." Clayton leaned forward to stress the importance of what he was explaining. "You must remain inside the carriage with me, and you will not be hurt. I pledge my life on it." He nodded toward the note, which now shook in the regent's trembling hands. "So does Lord Sidmouth. You must trust us, Your Highness."

Clayton kept his own face carefully impassive even as what little blood remained in the regent's receded and left a ghostly pallor in its place.

"Riots happen all the time these days, Your Highness. No one will doubt that a mob struck out at you on your way to open the bridge. And you must not tell a word to anyone about me or what I've told you today. Do you understand?"

Stunned, the regent nodded. Surely, he was wishing that he was making his way to the bottom of a bottle of fine cognac at that moment.

God knew Clayton was.

The regent finally found his composure and straightened his spine as much as his bloated, gout-ridden body allowed. "What can I do to thank you?"

Clayton leaned back against the gold brocade squabs, appreciating a few last moments of relaxation before all hell broke loose. "The grateful thanks of Crown and country are enough."

The regent began to smile. "Well, if that is—"

Clayton stretched out his long legs to make himself at home and grinned. "But I've always wanted to be a general."

Twenty-Seven

OLIVIA GAZED OUT THE WINDOW OF THE ST JAMES carriage at what was left of the school and her home. Charred beams and blackened chunks of wood filled the basement kitchens and storage rooms, with only the stone walls still standing to show where the building had once been, like a distorted brick skeleton. So much damage…and nothing left that she recognized.

She'd arrived in hell.

The tiger opened the door and reached his hand inside to help her down.

Olivia hesitated. Facing the loss of everything she'd held dear was almost too much to bear, and she smothered the urge to order the coachman to drive on, to take her…*where*? She no longer had a home, no longer had a brother to help create a new one.

The tiger frowned. "Miss?"

She pulled in a deep breath and slid her hand into his to step to the ash-covered ground.

Alec had already been gone from Harlow House when she'd finally given up on the idea of gaining any more rest and come out of her room that afternoon. His leaving had struck her like a blow. The intimacies, friendship, and support they'd shared during the past few weeks was over, its end announced with the finality of his absence.

He'd left a short note asking her to meet him here. Although he'd given no reason, she knew why—he wanted to tie up loose ends. His mission was over, and she didn't need a better metaphor than this burned shell to signal that whatever had sparked between them had ended right along with his mission. Scepter had been stopped from assassinating the prime minister and the prince regent, and her brother was at that very moment being whisked away to the Continent while his grave was being dug for the unknown body that would fill it. The same unknown body that she was expected to publicly put to rest and mourn as if he truly were Henry. How long would she have to put fresh flowers on that grave? She supposed that was yet another loose end that Alec would explain away, right before he said his final goodbyes.

She'd always known what they'd shared could never be permanent. But knowing that didn't lessen the pain. What surprised her was that she could still feel anything after the destruction of last night.

"Miss, would you like us to wait here for you?"

She glanced up at the gray sky with its layer of clouds that pressed down upon the city like a suffocating lid. More cold rain threatened to fall before the afternoon was over. "Please," she whispered and couldn't stop herself from shivering. "I don't expect to be long."

The tiger nodded and took his position by the carriage. With no choice, she wrapped the cloak she'd borrowed from

Elizabeth tighter around herself and stepped slowly forward toward the destruction.

"Olivia," Alec's deep voice called out from behind the charred remains of the town house and sent a shiver of longing curling down her spine. "I'm in the service yard."

Cursing herself for letting her emotions get the best of her, she blinked hard to clear the hot tears from her eyes and started carefully down what had once been a sliver of a side yard between the town house and the next row of terrace houses. Thank God the gap had served as a firebreak and kept the flames from destroying the next house. But now the gravel underfoot was covered with a slimy layer of ash and rainwater that was punctuated every few feet by large, charred chunks of wood. Beside her, the once-solid wall ended only two feet above her head and allowed glimpses through shattered windows of the black pit below. She kept her gaze focused on the surviving rear garden wall and the saddled horse tied there.

She emerged into the service yard and stopped.

Alec stood near the short stone steps that had once given access to the back of the town house but now led nowhere. Despite the bleak surroundings, he looked every inch an aristocrat, even with a sling wrapped around his arm. In his gray greatcoat and waistcoat, black trousers and boots, he was just as colorless as the day around him, yet his presence seemed to glow with an inner strength and resilience that could never fade into the gloom.

She loved him. He'd made her feel happy and protected, and she would have given anything to have a real future with him, a home and family. She didn't care about his name or title, his wealth or influence—it was the man she loved. She loved *him*.

But her feelings were pointless. He'd asked her here to say goodbye.

Somehow, she willed her heart to keep beating and her lungs to keep breathing as he came toward her across the debris-strewn yard.

His boots crunched on the gravel as he stopped in front of her. "How are you feeling?"

"I've rested."

At that dodge, he lifted her chin and looked into her watery eyes. There was no hiding that she'd been crying. "The truth, Olivia."

His gentle concern nearly undid her. At least the understanding still existed between them that they could always tell each other the truth. She prayed she could find comfort in that.

"The truth…is that everything I'd dedicated my life to is gone, along with my brother." While she might have nothing material left now, she still possessed her pride and squared her shoulders. "But I'm alive, and so is everyone I care about. That's all that matters."

His face remained carefully impassive. "Not quite all."

She knew what he meant. Another loose end to tie up… "Ah, yes, the girls." She forced a grateful smile and conceded past the knot in her throat, "It was very kind of you to take them into St James House."

"It was nothing. The girls whose families live in London

were taken home this morning, and the house has enough rooms to accommodate the rest until decisions can be made about the school."

Looking at the fire's remains, she nodded, although he was wrong. There were no decisions to make. The school was finished.

He continued, "Mrs. Adams and Miss Smith have decided to carry on with lessons there, to keep the girls occupied. Apparently, my library has become a geography classroom." She didn't have to look at him to know he was frowning. "There's a liquor tantalus there in the shape of a globe."

Despite the tears threatening at her lashes, Olivia gave a small laugh. The Earl of St James had turned into a schoolgirls' savior. To upheave his own life like this, just to help a group of girls… She never would have believed that of him only a few short weeks ago. Proof, she supposed, that people could change.

But not enough to save her heart, and his kindness only made her futilely love him more.

"They're driving Bivvens and the staff mad with their giggles and energy." He added with a grimace, "I don't think the Greek urn in the hall is going to survive."

"My apologies." She took a deep breath and wrapped her arms across her chest. She was as cold as the colorless day around them. "I'll send word to all their parents today to let them know that the school is closed and to ask them to come for the girls as soon as possible. But the…"

But the scholarship girls. She couldn't admit her fears about them without sobbing and making an emotional cake of herself in front of him. They had no families, no money, no place to go except back into the streets where she'd found them. The school might only have been a building, but it had also been a place of refuge for so many of them. Just as it had been with her. How could she ever keep them safe now?

"They can stay at St James House as long as necessary," he offered gently. "Until another building can be found for your school."

She shook her head, unable to answer. There was no money for another building, not even to rent a small one in an even less fashionable area than here, and without Henry's help, she'd never be able to run it.

"Don't worry," Alec assured her, misreading her silence. "The house is more than big enough to accommodate all of them, and the excitement is good for Bivvens. The old man's as stodgy as King George and could use a little disruption to spice up his life." He paused, suddenly thoughtful. "I'm beginning to think that a little disruption is good for the lot of us. In fact, I'm counting on it."

Warning prickled across her skin. "What do you mean?"

"I spoke to my mother this morning."

Olivia caught her breath. "About…your father?"

"Among other things." He glanced up at the gray sky as if to gauge how soon the next round of rain would come. Olivia read it for what it was—an excuse not to look at her. "She was devastated to learn the truth and angry that I'd kept it from her all these years, that I didn't tell her when it first happened so she could have stopped it. But it was good she hadn't known. God only knows what the old earl would have done to her if she'd interfered."

"Alec…" His name was barely more than a breath.

He grimaced at a low-hanging cloud. "We'll both be fine."

The finality of that told her not to press for more, that he wouldn't share with her the rest of his conversation with his mother. Olivia understood and didn't fault him for it. His private life was no longer any of her concern. His anguish had finally been relegated to the past. Exactly as it should have been.

She could find happiness for him in that, at least, even if her heart was breaking. "I'm glad to hear—"

"We also decided to support the Everett School."

She squeaked out, "*Pardon?*"

"Mother thinks it would be a marvelous opportunity for me to become involved with a respectable organization." His mouth turned slightly downward, the unrepentant rake in him distressed at the idea of propriety. "I also want St James House returned to my private residence again as soon as possible." Then he added in a murmur, "I have new plans for the place."

Of course he did. He would want to return to the life she'd interrupted. She didn't know whether to sing for joy that her school would now be able to survive or to wail in pain that she'd lost him.

She had no idea what her future would bring, but at least she'd have her school. Somehow, she'd make that be enough. "Thank you."

"Don't thank me yet," he warned with mock sternness. "This deal hinges on the survival of that Greek urn."

"Then I'd best get your signed agreement now," she teased despite the heaviness crushing her chest.

He sent her a lazy smile, only for it to fade as he promised, "You have my word." He reached inside his coat. "I also have this for you. I found it here in the rear yard when I was looking through the debris."

He pulled out a limp and dirty bag of rags—Cora's doll. Its little dress was singed from the embers, but otherwise, it appeared safe and sound.

Olivia's throat tightened as she took the doll. "She must have thrown it out one of the windows to save it from the fire." Her trembling fingers pulled the mussed hair into place. "She's going to be so happy to have this back."

"How is she? Have you seen her today?"

She gave a jerking nod. Cora was at Harlow House in the guest room beside hers. "Her leg was set by the surgeon, and Dr. Brandon gave her some powders—and candy, which I think did more to help the pain than all the powders. Lady Agnes hasn't left her side." Olivia hugged the doll to her chest, then somehow coaxed a smile from her frown. "I think your aunt wants to adopt her."

His expression tightened. "I can't let that happen."

Her smile faded. "Of course not."

Not the spinster aunt of an earl, not some urchin who had been found on the street. While Olivia might be able to give a home to boys like Phillip and Grant, Alec had to preserve his family's reputation. An orphan from the streets would never be acceptable in the eyes of the gossips, who might even say that the child was his by-blow. But the truth of society life didn't prevent the piercing reminder of how far apart their two lives were.

Her eyes dropped to the doll. "I was only exaggerating when—"

"Because I plan on adopting her myself."

Olivia's gaze flew up to his, and her mouth fell open, speechless.

"That is," he murmured and brushed his knuckles across her cheek, "I plan on you and I adopting her. Visiting the lawyers will be the first thing we do after we're wed." He sent her his best rakish grin. "Well, perhaps the *second* thing."

She couldn't breathe. "Y-you want to…marry me?"

"Very much." He fished into his coat pocket and removed a small box. He opened it, removed the object inside, and dropped the box to the muddy ground. "I would lower onto one knee to properly propose, but I don't think I'd be able to stand up again by myself." He nodded toward his injured arm, then took her left hand in his and slipped the delicate ring onto her finger. "I hope you'll forgive me for not kneeling." He lifted her hand to his lips and placed a tender kiss to the ring. "I plan on having a lot more forgiveness in my life from now on."

She blinked hard to clear the gathering tears from her eyes, her foolish heart not yet knowing if they should be tears of joy or anguish. "But we can't marry. You're an earl, and I'm…" Her voice grew impossibly softer. "I'm no one."

"Don't *ever* say that." He cupped her face in his good hand and narrowed his eyes sternly. "You are the woman I love, Olivia Everett. You—the prim and proper schoolmistress and bluestocking mathematician with her chalk dust–covered fingers and her schoolroom scoldings. And yes, with your carving knife."

Her chest stung at his teasing, and she swatted his hand away from her face as she stepped back. "Don't make fun."

"I've never been more serious in my life." When she grimaced dubiously, he dared to risk another swat by reaching to rub his thumb over her bottom lip until the grimace disappeared. "Because I love every bit of you, including that other side of you, the one nobody else sees…the daring woman who holds a world of passion inside her, who made me realize how unforgiving and harsh my life had become and how empty." His voice cracked with emotion. "You've changed all that. You've changed *me*."

A tear broke free and slipped down her cheek. He wiped it away with his thumb, and in that gentle caress, she felt all the love he held for her.

"Marriage to me won't be easy," he warned. "There'll be gossip, cuts right to our faces, and all manner of viciousness aimed at us because a schoolmistress dared to make a lord fall in love with her. You'll have to walk through the flames with me to come out the other side and have the life we both deserve." He placed his forehead against hers to emphasize the struggle to come. Then he promised, his mouth so close to hers that each word trembled across her lips, "But we'll raise our future together, just as you'll raise your school anew from this."

Happiness filled her veins. *This* was why he'd asked to meet her here of all places, to prove that their future could rise from the ashes of their pasts. At his gesture of determination and strength, one so filled with love, she was convinced that she could rise—more, she could fly!

"Do you love me, Olivia?"

Too overcome to find her voice, she choked out, "Yes... so very much."

"Then marry me." He slipped his good arm around her waist and tugged her to him. "I'm strong enough to survive the trials to come as long as we're together." His eyes glinted with challenge. "Are you?"

"Are you certain you love me?" She held her breath. Everything hinged on his answer...

"Absolutely." He claimed her mouth in a kiss that sent a heated promise cascading through her of all the days and nights they would share, the home and family that would be theirs.

She sighed beneath his kiss. "Then I can survive anything."

Author's Note

On January 28, 1817, the prince regent's carriage was attacked on his return from the State Opening of Parliament. The carriage was mobbed and nearly overturned, its glass window shattered. It was never conclusively determined if the mob was comprised of reformists who had been furious over Parliament's inaction to implement changes to grant universal suffrage, antimonarchy revolutionaries who were seizing on an opportunistic moment, or frustrated Londoners who were near starvation from the skyrocketing price of food and falling wages; it was also never conclusively determined if it was a rock or bullet that broke the window. What is certain, however, is that the incident caused enough fear in Westminster that legislators implemented some of the most repressive laws against civil liberties in the Georgian period. Tensions eventually came to a head on August 16, 1819, in Manchester at an event that would come to be known as the Peterloo Massacre.

I'd so very much wanted to use the actual date and purpose for the attack on the regent. After all, even today, the cellars of the Palace of Westminster are searched before the opening of Parliament in a largely (but not completely) ceremonial nod to the Gunpowder Plot, and the royal regalia and imperial state crown are sent in advance to great fanfare. (Did you know that the Palace takes an MP prisoner during the State Opening to guarantee the safe return of the monarch from Parliament? You cannot make this stuff up!) But January isn't at all a good time for garden teas, so I had to change the date. After much searching for an event at which the prince regent could easily have been blown up, I discovered the opening of Waterloo Bridge. Perfect!

On June 18, 1817, a new bridge over the Thames was opened in a ceremony that commemorated the second anniversary of the Battle of Waterloo, thus giving the bridge its name. The ceremony was presided over by the prince regent, who arrived via the royal barge to large crowds and much fanfare, and he officially opened the bridge by crossing it, accompanied by the Duke of Wellington and the Duke of York. Still the longest bridge in London at 2,456 feet, it was originally constructed from granite in a series of nine 120-feet wide...*arches.*

Keep reading for a look
at the next book in the
Lords of the Armory series from
USA Today bestselling author
Anna Harrington

A REMARKABLE ROGUE

Available July 2022

from Sourcebooks Casablanca

One

Captain Nate Reed lifted the glass of cognac to his lips as he watched her from across the crowded club.

Her hand played delicately with a gold locket dangling around her neck as she placed her bet at the faro table. Dressed in the shimmering green satin of a low-cut gown and emerald jewels, whose bright color and cost announced to anyone who saw her that she was happily widowed, Sydney Rowland was certainly striking. Undeniably regal. Graceful. Beautiful.

And most likely a traitor.

Nate took a slow sip of brandy and narrowed his eyes on her. After two days of watching every move she made around London and trailing her from one soiree to another, he was still no closer to solving the mystery of her connection to Scepter's assassination attempt on the prime minister and prince regent, except that he knew for certain she was involved. What he didn't know was how deeply. Was the baroness one of the masterminds behind the group, or was she merely another pawn in their game?

Tonight, he planned on finding out.

Slowly, he made his way across the room toward her.

Barton's was filled with elegantly dressed ladies in furs and jewels, foppish men adorned just as ostentatiously, and the lot of them drinking far more than they could tolerate, smoking cigars, and flirting shamelessly. A few of them surrendered to the lure of the high-priced prostitutes lurking in the club and retired upstairs for an hour's worth of private amusement. Both gentlemen and ladies enjoyed themselves with all the pleasures offered by the club. It was one of the few places in London that welcomed women through its doors and at its gambling tables, where the uniformed attendants brought glasses of liquor to the ladies as well as the men, and where it was accepted that no one inside need fear for their reputation.

Barton's belonged to the underbelly of London society. It was an exclusive club whose name everyone in the *ton* knew but which no one would ever dare admit to having entered.

Nate was only here himself because of Sinclair. Thanks to his half brother, Alexander Sinclair, Earl of St James, all Nate had to do to gain admittance was dress the part of a society dandy. With the help of the earl's valet, he now wore exquisite evening clothes of black superfine and blue brocade, finished off with a diamond cravat pin which surely cost more than his captain's commission. No more soldier. Tonight, he wore the borrowed uniform of a gentleman.

When he'd given St James's name to the doorman, the man let him enter the club without a second glance. It had been that easy.

Getting close to Lady Rowland, however, was proving much harder.

Normally, she moved in exclusive social circles he couldn't infiltrate, and so for the past few days he'd been forced to note from a distance every place she went and every person she spoke with. As a cavalry officer, he was used to reconnaissance, but he preferred rushing into the fray for a quick and decisive ending. His patience had worn thin from waiting. It was time to attack the enemy head on, no matter that the enemy was draped in soft satin.

Nate approached the faro table, sat down on the chair next to the baroness, and tossed a coin to the dealer. He silently played out two hands, lost both, and slowly finished his cognac as he bided his time.

If Sarah could have seen him tonight, oh how she would have laughed! He was doing his best to fit in with a crowd of people who would never have given him the time of day, yet they'd all expected him to kill—and be killed, if necessary—fighting the French. Tonight, he was among them in an attempt to get closer to one of their own beautiful widows.

Well, perhaps his late wife wouldn't have laughed at *that*.

Sarah had always been a jealous woman although she'd never had any worries in that regard. He'd never betrayed her through the long stretches of separation forced upon them by the war. Not once. Not during the two years of their marriage, and not a day since it ended.

He pulled in a deep breath. He could never make right what happened to her and for not being there when she needed him. But at last he had the opportunity to provide the best future possible for both their mothers with the reward money he'd earn for stopping Scepter.

The woman sitting next to him held the key.

Nate slid a slow, sideways glance in her direction. "Would you like another drink, my lady?"

Her bright green eyes blinked as she acknowledged him for the first time. "Pardon?"

"I asked if you'd like a drink." He signaled to the attendant. "I'm ordering one for myself, and in this crush, it might be a while before you can get another."

She hesitated, then conceded to his generosity. "Yes, thank you."

He held up a second finger and gestured at the baroness. The attendant nodded, then hurried behind the bar to pour their drinks.

Taking the opportunity to start a conversation, Nate murmured, "So you like to gamble."

She returned her emerald gaze to the dealer and corrected, "I like to win."

"So do I."

A quick tension emanated from her as her fingers toyed with the gold locket dangling from a simple chain around her elegant neck, oddly mixed with a necklace of expensive emeralds. "Then I fear faro is not your game." Her eyes remained focused on the cards. "Perhaps you'd find more enjoyment playing at something else."

Had he not just spent the past hour watching her outright dismiss every attempt by a roomful of men to proposition her, Nate might have thought she was inviting flirtation. But he knew better. What she wanted was for him to leave. "My game is here."

"How unfortunate, then," she commented dryly. "I don't believe you'll end up winning tonight."

"Then I suppose I'll just have to find satisfaction elsewhere."

She froze, and her fingers stilled on her locket. Nate could see that she couldn't tell whether he was propositioning her or rebuffing her. Truthfully, he didn't know himself, although getting her attention was all that mattered, and he'd certainly done that.

Her red lips pursed with irritation. She tossed in a coin for the next hand and ignored him.

"This is my first time at Barton's." He'd force the conversation onto her whether she liked it or not. "Do you often spend evenings here?"

She lifted her chin, and a stray tendril of sable hair tickled against the nape of her neck. "Occasionally."

"Then perhaps you can tell me—"

"No." With a tired sigh, she turned on her chair to face him and unwittingly gave him a full-on view of her low-cut neckline. "I am sorry, sir, but—"

"Captain Nate Reed," he interrupted with a forced introduction.

She caught her breath. "I am sorry, Captain," she began again, her words a well-practiced recitation, "but I am not interested in accompanying you upstairs this evening, nor returning with you to your home, nor even enjoying your company for a few minutes in one of the alcoves along the back hall. So if you don't mind—"

"Good."

She blinked at his unexpected refusal and repeated as if she hadn't heard correctly, "Good?"

"I'm a soldier, my lady, not a rake. I have no intention of inviting you upstairs tonight nor to my home on any night." He turned back to the dealer to signal for cards. "As for a few minutes alone in an alcove, I would never ask a lady to share her pleasures in such a demeaning place." He slid her a sideways glance. "And be assured that the enjoyment would be for much longer than a few minutes."

Her red lips parted delicately, stunned speechless.

He punctuated his refusal by tossing a coin to the attendant as the man set two drinks on the table in front of them. But even as Nate silently reached for his cognac, he could still feel her curious gaze on him, as if she didn't know what to make of him.

Good. That meant he'd captured her attention, and he'd done so by purposefully behaving the exact opposite of every other man in the place who'd approached her.

Fighting Napoleon had taught him the value of taking an opponent by surprise. Tonight, he'd use that to his advantage, even if down deep he was truly no better than the other cads. Even now his cock tingled at the tempting thought of taking her to any place where they could be alone. Including into a cramped alcove.

He would never act on that temptation. He'd never once betrayed Sarah, and he had no intention of doing so tonight, especially with Sydney Rowland, a woman he couldn't trust as far as he could spit. But he was still a man, for God's sake, and he still felt the pull of a beautiful woman.

It had been a long time since he'd been in a woman's bed, that was all. Three years, two months, three weeks…

"My apologies, Captain Reed," she offered quietly. "I didn't mean to offend."

He tossed in a coin for the next round of cards—and another for her, to keep her in the game and in the chair beside him. He wasn't finished with her yet.

"No offense taken."

"Usually, when a man sits next to me, he's not interested in playing cards. His intentions usually lie elsewhere." She grimaced as she dryly added, "In lying elsewhere."

Despite himself, he grinned at her clever turn of phrase. She was sharp. "I'm only interested in conversation, I assure you." He handed her the second glass of cognac. "Now, shall we begin again?"

She hesitated, then took a deep breath. "All right." She accepted the drink. "It's a pleasure to meet you, Captain Reed."

He inclined his head slightly. "Baroness Rowland."

"No."

His brow inched up at that. "No? Am I mistaken that—"

"I'm not addressed as baroness but as lady," she corrected self-consciously, her voice low so she wouldn't embarrass him. "Lady Rowland. I am not a peeress *suo jure.*"

"A woman as regal and self-possessed as you? You should be." He boldly met her gaze. "Or perhaps the men of the aristocracy don't wish to be bested." He lifted his glass to her in a toast and purposely misstated, "Baroness."

Her lips smiled with a surprising touch of shyness at the rim of her glass. "Captain."

There. Introductions made, conversation begun. He let out the breath he'd been holding. That hadn't been so difficult…so why was his gut clenched in a knot?

Sydney Rowland was nothing more than a mission asset, after all, just another link in the chain he had to sever before Scepter could kill again. Tonight was simply questions and answers in a polite conversation…or in an interrogation session if she failed to cooperate willingly.

"You've never been here before?" she asked. Now that she knew he wasn't interested in ravishing her, she visibly relaxed into the conversation. Still turned toward him, she draped her arm along the back of her chair and smiled faintly. Her presence was as soft as her lilting voice against the boisterous club around them. "I thought everyone had been to Barton's."

With her full attention on him, she was even more beautiful now than only a few moments ago. Nate realized like a punch why Scepter had chosen her as their liaison for mathematician Henry Everett. A besotted schoolmaster who desperately wanted to be included into society's ranks would never have stood a chance against the baroness's beauty and charms.

But she'd have no such effect on him, no matter that he wondered if her lips tasted like brandy.

He cleared his throat. "A friend recommended this place. Perhaps you know him." He watched her over the rim of his glass as he raised it toward his mouth. "Henry Everett."

Her eyes flashed wide, startled. Yet within a heartbeat she'd skillfully recovered.

She cleared her throat and turned back toward the table. "I've met his sister Olivia on a few occasions. She's a wonderful woman, very dedicated to reform." She expertly maneuvered the conversation away from Henry Everett. "We're both interested in children's charities and so had a natural connection. I'm certain I've met her brother, but only in passing."

If she wasn't working for Scepter, Nate mused, then her talents were being greatly wasted. The Home Office could use someone like her, *if* she didn't turn them all double agents first.

Her hand returned to the locket at her neck. "They run a school in Westminster, I believe."

"They used to."

"Oh?" This time, she'd been prepared for his peculiar correction, and there was no widening of eyes, no catching of breath. Nothing except a heartbeat's hesitation. But he noticed.

Of course, he noticed. How could any living, breathing man not notice every move this woman made, no matter how small?

"Haven't you heard?" He forced himself not to stare at her red lips. "It burned down a few days ago."

Her hand began to tremble. "Burned down?"

"Henry Everett died in the fire."

The glass slipped from her fingers.

He darted out his hand and caught it but not before the brandy splashed onto her skirt. He set the drink down, but her outstretched fingers remained empty in the air as she stared at him. A stricken expression blanched her face.

Slowly, she lowered her hand and brushed futilely with shaking fingers at the liquor as it seeped into her gown. All of her trembled as harshly as her hands, and she didn't lift her gaze from the stain. "I-I didn't know," she stammered out. "I hadn't heard…"

From her stunned reaction, she was telling the truth. For once.

Nate narrowed his eyes on her. Was there more between Henry Everett and Sydney Rowland than he knew? Henry Everett had denied they were lovers when Clayton questioned him after the fire, yet her shock at hearing the news of his death was not the reaction of a passing acquaintance.

Nate knew grief—and guilt—and both flashed across her pale face.

"I'm…so very sorry to hear that." Her voice emerged so softly from her lips that it was almost lost beneath the noise of the club. "I'll have to…send my condolences and…"

Unable to finish, she pressed the back of her hand against her mouth.

Regret pierced him. She was truly distraught by the news. Not even a Covent Garden actress could pretend such distress. But she could never learn the truth—that Henry Everett was alive and on his way to exile in exchange for information about Scepter and that the Home Office faked his death and left another charred body in the school's ruins to take his place. The well-orchestrated ruse meant a few days of grief for the baroness, but the lives of countless others would be saved.

Still, Nate knew the shattering pain of losing a lover, and

if she truly hadn't known about Everett until that moment...
Christ.

"I'm sorry," he murmured sincerely, low enough that no one around them could overhear. "To lose someone you loved that way—"

Her head snapped up, and her glistening eyes flared in the lamplight.

"You are mistaken, Captain. Mr. Everett was nothing more to me than a passing acquaintance. I am grieving for his sister, that is all." She paused, and her hands rested lightly against the table to steady herself as she took a deep breath and began to rise from her chair. "If you'll excuse me, I must see to my dress."

"Stay." He put his hand over her wrist and stopped her, forcing her to remain unless she wanted to cause a scene and draw the attention of everyone in the room.

Stiffly, she eased down onto her seat. "Release me this—"

"Only an acquaintance?"

"Yes."

"Then why did you give him money?" He forced a pleasant smile for anyone who might have been watching them. He wanted to appear to be nothing more than another in the long line of men determined to persuade her to visit his bed tonight.

Everyone would believe it, too, from the way she glared at him. "I did no such thing."

"A great deal of money, in fact. You bought up his gambling debts. Twelve hundred pounds in all."

She stared down at her hand which now trembled beneath

his not with anger but fear. Years of watching soldiers march into battle had taught him the difference. But who was she afraid of—him...or Scepter?

"Let go of me, or I'll scream."

"No, you won't," he coolly dismissed her weak threat. "Everett brought attention to himself, and look how that ended. You're far too smart to do the same."

The tops of her breasts rose and fell rapidly over her low neckline as her breath came shallow and quick. She looked up at him in a heated mixture of fear and fury that left no doubt she'd scratch his eyes out and run if given half a chance.

"You bought up his debts, then asked for immediate repayment even though you knew he couldn't pay. Not a poor schoolmaster." When Nate was convinced she wouldn't flee or cause a scene—or attack him—he slowly released her wrist and leaned back in his chair. His eyes pinned her. "Why?"

She pulled her hand out of his reach, then rubbed at her wrist as if his touch had scalded her. "Who told you that?"

"I have my sources." He had no intention of telling her that those sources came from within her own household, or that she should pay her groom a larger salary in order to ensure his loyalty. "You're wealthy already. Why bother with a few hundred pounds from an indebted mathematician?"

Her stormy eyes gleamed as she tried to see through the carefully controlled expression he wore like a mask. "You're not one of the messengers, then?"

"What messengers?"

She started to reply, then snapped her mouth shut. Whatever she was about to say vanished.

Nate turned cold. She knew far more than he and Sinclair suspected.

Without warning, she shot to her feet and stepped away from the table before he could stop her.

Damnation. His gaze darted to the mountain-sized men standing at the sides of the room who provided security for the club. He'd be tossed into the street on his arse if he made a grab for her now, and all the ground he'd gained tonight would be lost.

"You're not leaving this club," he warned as he rose to his feet, as if he were truly a gentleman instead of the soldier set on arresting her.

She sniffed haughtily. "You spilt brandy on my dress."

He'd done no such thing, although he strongly suspected *she* would have tossed her drink directly into his face if she didn't have to brush past him to reach it.

"I have no intention of leaving before I'm ready," she informed him coldly, then snatched up her reticule from the table. "But even you, Captain, must be enough of a gentleman not to prevent a lady from visiting the retiring room to clean up a spill."

He bit back a curse. She'd cornered him. By standing, she'd shown the front of her dress to the crowd. Anyone watching would think it peculiar if she remained at the table instead of attending to the stain, and she would draw the type of curiosity neither of them wanted.

He had no choice but to let her go.

For now.

"Very well," he conceded. She may think she'd won, but

the battle had just begun. "When you return, we'll continue our conversation."

"Right where we left off?" Her brow rose in mocking challenge. "With you accusing me of extorting money from Henry Everett?"

Oh, this woman was a handful! If she and Everett had truly been lovers, Nate suspected, she would have devoured the scrawny schoolmaster in a single gulp.

"If you'll excuse me, captain."

She slid past him as she stepped away from the crowded table. The side of her breast brushed against his arm and shot heat straight down to his groin.

He sucked in a mouthful of air through clenched teeth.

With a sashay of her hips, she slipped her way through the crowded club, not toward the retiring room in the rear but straight toward its front doors. By the time she reached the steps, she was running.

Nate blew out a frustrated curse. *Stubborn woman.* Why did she have to make this so damned difficult?

About the Author

Anna Harrington is an award-winning author of Regency romance. She writes spicy historicals with alpha heroes and independent heroines, layers of emotion, and lots of sizzle. Anna was nominated for a RITA award in 2017 for her title *How I Married a Marquess*, and her debut, *Dukes Are Forever*, won the 2016 Maggie Award for Best Historical Romance. A lover of all things chocolate and coffee, when she's not hard at work writing her next book, Anna loves to travel, go ballroom dancing, or tend her roses. She is a terrible cook who hopes to one day use her oven for something other than shoe storage.

Also by Anna Harrington